IN THE
CENTER
OF THE
NIGHT

Jayne Blankenship

IN THE
CENTER
OF THE
NIGHT

Journey Through
A Bereavement

G. P. Putnam's Sons   New York

The text of this book is set in Electra.

The author gratefully acknowledges the following sources for their permission to reprint previously published materials:

American Folklore Society for Navaho chant from "Navaho Legends" in *Memoirs of the American Folklore Society* by Washington Matthews, copyright © 1978 by American Folklore Society.

CBS Songs for lyrics from "Carnival" by Bob Merrill, copyright © 1961 by Robbins Music Corporation, assigned to CBS Catalogue Partnership. All rights controlled and administered by CBS Robbins Catalog, Inc. All rights reserved. International copyright secured.

Indiana University Press for "The Story of Baucis and Philemon" from *Ovid: Metamorphoses*, translated by Rolfe Humphries, copyright 1955, copyright renewed 1983.

Little, Brown and Co. for poetry from *The Complete Poems of Emily Dickinson*, copyright 1929 by Martha Dickinson Bianchi, copyright renewed © 1957 by Mary L. Hampson.

Random House, Inc., for lines from "As I Walked Out One Evening" from *W. H. Auden: Collected Poems*, edited by Edward Mendelson, copyright © 1940, copyright renewed 1968 by W. H. Auden.

G. Schirmer, Inc., for lines from *The Medium* by Gian-Carlo Menotti, copyright © 1948 by G. Schirmer, Inc.

Special thanks for a grant from the Rocky Mountain Women's Institute.

LIBRARY OF CONGRESS CATALOGING IN PUBLICATION DATA

Blankenship, Jayne.
In the center of the night.

1. Blankenship, Jayne.   2. Widows—United States—
Biography.   3. Kantor, Harvey.   4. Leukemia—Patients—
United States—Biography.   5. Bereavement—Psychological
aspects.   I. Title.
HQ1058.5.U5B53   1984   306.8'8   84-8356

ISBN 0-399-12995-2

AUTHOR'S NOTE

In the interest of protecting the privacy of individuals whose real identities are not central to the true story told here, certain names and other descriptive details have been altered in several instances.

for Harvey

The glacier knocks in the cupboard,
The desert sighs in the bed,
And the crack in the teacup opens
A lane to the land of the dead.

—W. H. AUDEN

The

FIRST YEAR

The Glacier Knocks
in the Cupboard

Spring

There is no one to talk to.

I went by myself to Maclay Gardens this morning, slipping in onto the grounds under a heavy long chain with a sign hanging from its center: PARK CLOSED APRIL THROUGH DECEMBER. I knew what I wanted to find but I didn't know how to get there. I took a deep breath and picked a direction at random.

Dense planting hid me from the street. Lawns I remembered as winter-manicured were now grown high with summer grass. Bushes which had been draped with flowers were all an even green. I strayed off the brick walk onto a narrow arm of grass. Walls of shrubs and trees on either side led me deeper into the garden. Birds called; then it was silent. Birds again. The trail dead-ended into a glade of ferns with an empty iron loveseat on the far side. I paused for a moment, then turned and backtracked along the path of grass my feet had bent, veering left at the first intersection. A clearing opened and there it was—the ivy-covered archway where we were married. The reflecting pool. The lake.

I sat down carefully under the arch, legs crossed, back straight, and gazed down the quiet long pool, feeling the vista belonged uniquely to me. I prepared myself for the memory, deliberately, as one might wipe a razor blade with white linen, might feel for an artery's bulge.

Dew and early sunlight through my veil. Lifting the long skirt to step from dry red brick to damp morning grass. Silken slippers trimmed with satin. The slow simple walk. "Greensleeves." Coral azaleas over-flowing like foam. Friends arrayed around the arch. Four parents. The sun behind us glowing through the full-length veil to make it

seem itself a source of light. Chalice of wine, sun-warmed. Sala-
mander at our feet, crawling up onto Harvey's polished shoe. Harvey
drawing me to himself.

I gagged over onto the grass, arms limp at my sides, face pressed
directly into the ground. Slow heaving groans rolled through me. I
yielded to them, hoping the earth would break and take me in,
would push brown grit between my teeth and tongue, would stuff
my throat and close my ears against the thoughts. Hoping the grass
would close over the back of my head so that no one would ever
know that I was there. . . .

I don't know how long I lay folded up like that, sobbing, but
finally I opened one eye a slit and saw blades of grass looming close
and knew that I was still an ugly hump above the ground. The lower
half of my face was covered with clear mucus and pine needles. I
had no handkerchief. Pulling myself partway up, I tugged my shirt-
tail from my pants, unbuttoned it enough to reach my face, and
wiped away the tears and slime. Then I leaned there on my elbow,
spent. I looked up at the old pines lining the reflecting pond and
thought how the park's desertion was like my own, inside. It made
me think of a world after mankind, after war. This garden would be
much the same as it was today—long pool filled with rainwater—
but the trees, released from time, would be turned by then to stone.
My spirit would be there too, drawn back again, alone. Oddly, I
could imagine myself dancing—not crying—dancing alone in the
air, with stone trees all around. Without getting up, I milked cold
droplets from the shaded ivy strands and bathed my swollen face.
And then although my torso slumped, I sat cross-legged once again.

On the way back, I heard a scraping sound ahead and came
around a bend to see a large turtle dragging its heavy shell down the
middle of the brick walk. I followed it for a while, walking so slowly
that I noticed something I might otherwise have missed—a shadow
on a leaf. Back and in, beside my right shoulder, was a large, vivid
spider—black with chartreuse, royal blue, and orange—in a huge
and perfect web.

I am not looking forward to Mother's party Saturday. I feel too weak, still, to talk to strangers. Doesn't she remember this need to hide? Didn't she feel it when Daddy died? Why is she insisting? It's not that she's cajoling me out of my shell—there is anger in her voice. I don't want to go, especially since she said, "Be sure that Jordan isn't here!" No kids at a garden party? Not even her only grandchild? Is it that she doesn't want to be thought old enough to be a grandmother? Or does she truly disapprove of our young child?

He's sitting at the deep end now, dangling his feet in the water. We're at the neighborhood swimming club. He has jumped off the high diving board several times this afternoon—gutsy for a three-year-old. When he climbs the ladder, I slip into the pool and wait for him, nervous. But he has no fear at all—jumps in with gusto and goes under to touch bottom in water way over his head. He bobs up naturally, but cannot swim, so I have to be there to help him to the side.

It's like being home on school vacation here in Tallahassee. The town was just as strange then, though Daddy was still alive. But the things we're doing are from an earlier, familiar time: swimming, iced tea, novels (though it is still quite hard to read), not working. Writing letters—my stationery is spread out across the round white metal table in front of me. It's just that everything has changed.

Dear Lynn and Joseph:

Harvey died in February after four and a half years of battling leukemia. He didn't want people to know—we had so much hope for more time. I am unstrung, skidding. Where are you and what is happening in your lives?

I must write his old professor, too. I wish I could say what is really in my heart:

Dear, dear man:

How much we love you and how fervently, desperately, I wish it could have been you instead. You're in your seventies; Harvey was only 31. You have no children to raise, no wife to mourn. If you had died, he might have had your job at N.Y.U. End of our year-to-year contract worries at Rhode Island, return to the scene of our young married happiness, restoration of the natural order. Oh, why couldn't it have been you?

Mother's party was tonight. I survived it by retreating to the kitchen at regular intervals. A compromise was reached on Jordan. I hired a sitter to be here, and after he said his hellos—cute in navy blue jacket and new white shorts—she took him out in front to ride his big wheel up and down the street.

I am relieved that Mother has found as kind a man as Foster, but I feel uneasy. When I look at him I cannot tell what he is feeling. Will I ever be able to read a soul in a face again? I wish that he were the third or fourth man she had dated, instead of the first. Their infatuation is obvious—he keeps rubbing his fingers along the inside of her arms—yet something is amiss. She's just not happy enough.

The wedding today didn't feel like any wedding I've ever been to. It was strangely low-keyed. It's the only "second marriage" I've ever witnessed, so maybe it's just the nature of the event, but I didn't feel sad, or jealous for Daddy, or thrilled or anything. Mother was slender and elegant. She wore a simple, graceful dress, pale oyster, featureless except for its flowing line. The starkness set off her delicate cheekbones and clear blue eyes. She looked elegant—but not radiant. She and Foster both acted surprisingly matter-of-fact and relaxed there in the unfamiliar church, as if the ritual were not a sacrament at all, loaded with peril, but something one did every day. I'd have expected her to be nervous and agitated—especially since Jordan was whiny—or animated and glowing. But she was coolly perfect. The whole thing was mildly pleasant, that's all. I don't know. Maybe it's just me.

I dreamed last night of Harvey's eyes.

He has been pronounced dead but at the funeral home slowly pulls himself up on the table to a sitting position, head hung low. Then he drags himself back into his teaching duties, despite the fact that his body, especially the eyeballs, has begun to decompose.

The first dream I had which acknowledged his death was like that. It was more than a month ago. After weeks of dreams in which a living, healthy Harvey came to hold and comfort me—relief from that day's grief-ache—there came a dream in which his eyes weren't right. They had turned a grayish yellow, and this told me he would die.

The four of us—Mother, Foster, Jordan and I—drove down to Wakulla Springs this afternoon to ride the glass-bottomed boats. I took my camera. The light was luminous, even deep beneath the green water. Snakes hung from the swamp-bank trees, and Jordan's shirt stood out red in a way red never manages in New England. The body of a 200-year-old crocodile was displayed in a glass case outside the restaurant. Some redneck had shot him while he was sunning on a sand bar.

At dinner, Foster ordered wine from Orvieto. The name made my throat stretch taut. He had no way of knowing that it was special to Harvey and me, no way of knowing how we drove down from the Italian Alps toward the village, struck by the natural fortress its bluffs make. I had to force myself to swallow. It was the weekend we got back from that trip that Harvey first started to feel bad. Cancer doesn't happen overnight. It had to have been growing as we traveled, but why weren't there signs—fatigue, uneasiness? The whole trip was lighthearted, buoyant. It doesn't seem possible that something hidden could have been so drastically wrong.

It's true, though, that our first hour of disharmony did happen on that trip. We were walking through Chartres Cathedral. Slowly, in and out of shadows, Harvey grew sullen and uncommunicative, and then, abruptly, strode outside. I was offended that he wouldn't share what was bothering him, and waited before following. When I strolled out to where we'd left the car, it was gone. Stunned, I waited, then walked back into the church and sat down. An hour passed. I went outside. Still no car. I walked back to the cathedral's south door. The round rose window on the north framed the statue of Jesus like a great blue halo. Someone in the group ahead of me said, "This is where the knights entered." I followed them through the door and sat back down. Harvey had the passports, everything. The darkness helped. When I went outside again, I could see the car was back. Harvey was leaning against the rear, studying a map. When I approached, he took me in his arms and held me tight against his chest. Lips beside his ear, I whispered, "What happened?" And he whispered back, "I don't know. I don't know."

When the four of us got back to the house, we found a dove dead near the walk, where Mother had put out mole poison. I could see her distress, the ache of her responsibility for its pain. But I wasn't seeing true. She reached into the garage for a shovel, scooped up the dead bird and turned on me, "It's not this dead flesh I mourn. It's the one that remains, that will never remate, that will always be alone." It took a moment for me to realize that she was grieving not for the birds, nor even for me, but strangely, since she is newly married, for herself.

It is very early. Jordan is still sleeping. I don't know when I have actually been up before his needs pulled me from the bed. I am exhausted. Yesterday Mother and I had words about setting out the garbage. As she left for Perry with Foster to see about the move (they'll be back tonight), she told me to be sure to get up early and put out the garbage cans. I said that I'd be glad to set them out before I go to bed, but she countered, "Oh no. I can smell raw garbage in them (implying I put it there), and if I can, the dogs can, and they'll get into them and strew trash all around."

This made me angry, realizing she just wants to punish me by making me get up early again—she has turned the TV on loud at seven every morning since we got here. As evenly as I could, I replied, "Mother, there is no unwrapped garbage in them, and even if there were, the cans have snap-tight lids. I'll be glad to see that the garbage is disposed of even if I have to take it to the dump myself, but I'm not going to get up early to do it since the only reason we're not going to Perry with you is that I need a full night's sleep. I told you that' already." By then her voice was fierce, threatening:

"It's time for something to be said. . . . I haven't asked you to do *any*thing."

"Oh, but you *have*, about four hundred tiny veiled demands. . . ."

"Oh no, I haven't," she interrupted, "not this time. . . ." (meaning because I'm grieving?) and then she walked abruptly out the door.

To her back I called out, "Don't worry about your garbage, but I'm not going to set an alarm and wreck my sleep either."

I checked last night, and all the neighbors put their garbage out the night before, some just in plastic bags, so marauding dogs must not be a genuine local problem. I set out the cans, but I worried about them all night, even in my dreams:

A delivery man has placed two black rubber bags full of 400 pounds of dismembered human flesh in those garbage cans. Harvey's body is in one, and three other young men, Vietnam casualties, in the other. I cannot comprehend it because Harvey has already been buried. I keep trying to understand, at the same time worrying that dogs will get to the bags and tear them open. And then Harvey himself comes back, ill but alive. The funeral has been a trick so he can have other women with him in the hospital, but now he has come back to me. I am jubilant, but hurt, too.

There are lots of people around—Harvey's distant relatives, strangers, one man in a black wet-suit. Everything has a Jewish aura, with me as an outsider. Then Harvey blends into Bruce, who is also dying, and who begs me, as his sister, to make him a dogwood freezer to be buried in, to preserve him. "It will only take you five days to build," he says. I don't know how to do it—saws and hammers, men's expertise—and am afraid I'll fail but know I have no choice but to try.

Then a horrible ominous train roars straight through the house, and we all flatten against the walls, which are like tunnel walls, and clutch our candles, most of which are blown out as it rushes by with its charnel house load. It is like trains to Auschwitz, except it is a "garbage train" and carries already-dead bodies.

I try to compose myself and walk out onto the porch. It's a second-story porch like ours off the kitchen in Stonington. Looking to the left, I see a long, long series of porches like that, and I hear an old woman weeping and wailing softly, "Swing Low, Sweet Chariot." I lean out to see. Far down, rocking in a wicker rocking chair, holding her stomach, is my father's mother. I feel an overwhelming pity for her and step back inside to hide my tears, afraid people will see me and think that I am crying for myself.

Rabbi Friedman sang that song—"Swing Low"—to Jordan the other night because it had his name—"Jordan"—in it. But when I sang it to him again in the car on the way home, he demanded I stop. Could he possibly understand it's about death?

My father's mother's grief . . . it's grieving I failed to do three years ago because of Jordan's birth. Within hours of the phone call about Daddy's death in open-heart surgery I was in labor. It was all too much: my first death and first childbirth all in the same twenty-four hours. I spent his funeral in the hospital in Rhode Island instead of here. I need to find his grave before we leave. So much has happened since he died, so much I want for him to know. He knew we faced the cancer, but Harvey wasn't really sick then— Myleran, sturdy old friend of a drug, was still holding him well. We never anticipated real trouble, never prepared for it: "Someday perhaps, twenty years from now." Daddy supported that. One day he called long distance to tell me about a man he'd just met who'd had leukemia for ten whole years. Three is what we got—three good years past diagnosis. And this last obscene one.

The downward spiral started summer before last, when Harvey's own father died. I was coming back from the little market across the viaduct, down the steps onto Elm Street when I heard him calling, "Jayne . . . !" "Jayne . . . !" I saw him at the top of Sal Tinker's Hill, mutely shaking his head. He came toward me down the steep

street, eyes locked into mine. "My father died. My father died. Can
you believe it? A heart attack." When we got back from the funeral
in Kansas City, he fell into a depression. I'd never seen him like
that. In the seven years we'd been together he had never shut me
out. If there were problems—religion, parents against our marry-
ing, no money, graduate school exams, testy colleagues, broken
bones, baby's colic, even the cancer—he was always cheerful, always able to reassure and make me laugh and feel safe. But with his
father's death he changed—started walking with a slump, sleeping
with his back toward me. I tried to comfort him, remembering how
I felt when Daddy died, but he turned away. Dismayed, I waited.

The spell broke in October. We went to San Francisco for him to
deliver a paper, and he was himself again—generous, affectionate,
full of puns and historical trivia. I remember him leaning back in
his chair, laughing, a sprig of parsley dangling from his hand.

Somebody stole my antique ruby ring from our hotel room that
trip, the ring Mother and Daddy gave me for high school gradua-
tion. Five rubies in a row. It had been the wedding ring of the first
white woman to travel into the territory that was to become Illinois.
I had visions of her changing babies' diapers beside a stream in the
forest, covered wagon nearby. Now that ring is just a thing. No one
will ever know its story.

But still the trip was good. Harvey was vigorous when we got back
to Stonington, and he dove into his teaching and the project he was
conducting for the Rhode Island Historical Society. Everything was
fine until Thanksgiving. Thanksgiving before last. To think that
Daddy doesn't know a bit of this . . .

> Harvey pulling off the highway on the drive back from picking up
> Mary and Stephen at the airport, complaining of dizziness. Calling
> me into the bathroom next morning.
> "Hey, Jayne, look at this"—the inner white of his left eye blistered
> with blood, as if a vessel had burst.
> "My God, Harvey, call Fogle."
> "Oh, it's no big deal." Starting to shave, sending me downstairs.
> Bacon in the frying pan when Mary comes down, a look on her face I
> have never seen in all our years as sisters.

"Come upstairs," she whispers, eyes wide open, "now!" Harvey unconscious, half on the bed. Stephen and I pull him to the floor. I grab the phone, dial Dr. Fogle at home—busy, busy—ambulance, hospital, get help. Stephen's hand on Harvey's pulse—then mouth against his mouth. I drop the phone. Ear to chest. Nothing. Oh God. I pound him with my fist. Furious energy. Astride his chest, leaning into his heart, releasing, leaning. Live. Live. Live. Live. Long minutes, then a rattled breath (Stephen's eyes meet mine), another. Still unconscious, but breathing. Where *is* the ambulance? Thirty-five minutes. Volunteer mislaid key. At last—onto stretcher. Halfway downstairs, convulsions. Panic, confusion. Still no Fogle.

In the ambulance I try to ram my comb between his clenched teeth, but only cut his gums. Yell to the driver for oxygen. He calls back, "We should pick up Dr. Austin—he's closer." Philip running out from his office, coatless, climbing in the back.

"I'm Dr. Austin." Haste, sirens, frustration. No oxygen. Philip helpless too, unprepared. Seizures—earthquakes of the brain. Fogle waiting at the emergency room. Injections of Valium. More. Harvey starting to rave—wild guttural growlings. They tie him down, wheel him to X-ray. I try to hold his head steady while he fights. Repeat the pictures. Repeat again. Fear for his blood—all those X-rays. Nothing. Waiting through the night. Animal noises echoing through Intensive Care. I sit at his head, desperately cool, whispering Lamaze breathing into his ear, hoping that some level of his subconscious will hear those exercises from Jordan's birth and fall calm. Now and then he pauses, seems to hear, and falls into a simple coma's rest. Then more seizures, more raging.

He comes to mid-morning, asks for me. His eyes roll separately. "Where am I?"

"In Westerly Hospital. You've had convulsions."

"I dreamed I died." And then he sleeps.

To know that dream. . . . Every hour again, the slurred question "Where am I?" Short-term memory gone. A day of it, two. Then long drawled sentences, strewn with adjectives—eighteenth-century descriptions of his health, a paper cup, presidential antics—startlingly eloquent, out of character. Doctors cautious, uneasy. Blood counts tremendous, leukemia out of control. Myleran has given out. But a new drug takes hold.

Recovery is gradual. Muscles hang from his bones as if the convulsions have been a kind of electrocution, but his speech grows normal and his spirits soar, and that is all that matters to me. Warm, caring Westerly Hospital—nurses, in-jokes, flirting. Visitors, cautious at first because they know he's been near death, but quickly reassured by his easy, reliable humor. For them, for all except my family (who leave after the weekend), his sister in Kansas City, the Logans and our friend Sonia in New York, the seizures are his only problem, albeit a scary one. No one knows about the blood.

Three weeks later he is home. More seizures—in the kitchen (Jordan saw), once in bed, again there, once beside the bathtub. The agony of leaving him to call for help. Before each time, a funny little cough, warning enough to drop his center of gravity and avoid a fall. Every time I have to force a plastic breathing device down his throat until Philip can get there. Afterward, he sleeps, deeply. Epilepsy— the very thing, along with leukemia, he's always feared.

Back into the hospital. This time in New London. Unpleasant. Testy nurses, not like Westerly. Neurological exams and many drugs—Dilantin, Phenobarbitol, on top of the cancer medications. Then New York for specialists. An important neurologist, who blames the blood, and our original hematologist, who says the seizures are separate. For the leukemia, he recommends an experimental program in Buffalo—where injections of live tuberculosis are being used to stimulate attacks by the immune system.

The trips to Buffalo are hard. We can cover the weekends for others, but cannot pretend to ourselves. A hospital for cancer only. The man beside us in the waiting room has only half a face. But still a great hope. Despite fevers from the shots, and swollen oozing arms, Harvey is "responding well." The doctor there foresees a journal article from his progress.

In August, Westerly Hospital again. Another change of drugs. Another recovery. But something in our perception of what is going on begins to change. When his mother comes to Stonington, he tells her the truth—leukemia. Things are too serious to put it off longer. She pulls out the border of violets which surrounds our whole backyard, calling them weeds. And yet the context still is hope—we are planning on a record.

We run out of money. By September, Harvey has to fly to Buffalo alone. On Yom Kippur he goes to services there. Someone calls him to the Torah; he feels the cough coming, flees, and seizes on the sidewalk, alone. When I meet him at the airport, he is ashen, walking slowly once again. Once more, as after his father's death, he withdraws into himself. I suffer, wanting him close, but I have no effect on him.

His illness organizes our life. He can no longer drive. I drive for him. Between hospital bouts, he teaches and laughs and lies to others. In the hospital he laughs the same way, teaches in another, lies in yet another—to himself, to me. The nurses compete to get him on their floors, hang WELCOME BACK, DR. KANTOR signs, joke about "the treatment for sleep."

This last Thanksgiving we return to Kansas City. In front of his mother and sister he treats me lovingly, which angers me because when we are alone, he is harsh. He falls ill there—flu-like symptoms. Fever, aches, but now his gums are bleeding, his knees are aching. We leave early to get him back to Westerly Hospital. It doesn't work. Missing connections in Chicago, we are snowbound at O'Hare, marooned with thousands of other travelers. The pain is now intense, especially in his knees—he can no longer walk. No one will help me find a wheelchair. Midnight, a crying two-year-old, and Harvey twisting on the floor in agony. A beleaguered airlines clerk threatens to have me arrested for badgering him.

By the time he makes it to a bed in Westerly Hospital the following afternoon, Harvey is crazed, barking at me "Go away, leave me alone. I don't need you. I don't need anybody." He has never spoken to me like that. I go home alone, destroyed.

But in the morning he calls, full of tenderness. "Where are you?" And is himself again. That day they tell the two of us Blast Crisis has come. The disease has entered its final phase. He strokes my cheek, kisses my fingers. As much as we know about leukemia, as much as I have read about terminal illness in general, as clearly as we both can recite that, realistically, no remissions occur after this point, neither of us accepts it. We are young. We are in love.

I want to find Daddy's grave and tell him all of this. I want him to know about the three remaining months—more victories, futile hopes, the death itself—but I cannot deal with them now. The feelings are too deep and incoherent for higher parts of my brain to translate. As it is, I wonder how I will make it through the long day ahead, alone with Jordan.

Mother is back, angry this time because I won't go to the neighbors' for drinks with them. For her, our relationship seems only to mean "face" with her acquaintances—"My daughter is here. Therefore, I must be likable." On a real level, she seems to hate me so pointedly that I couldn't possibly bring her any happiness. It is hard to understand. I had hoped that this marriage would soften her, would let good feelings flow through her to us as they did when Daddy was alive. In coming here, I had set my heart on change, on comfort, on having someone to talk to about losing Harvey. I wanted to throw myself into her care for a week, to cry in her arms. But she is even harsher than before. Widowhood seems to have made her permanently bitter. Will this happen to me as well?

Tomorrow we go home, so this afternoon was my last chance to see where Daddy is buried. When Jordan went down for his nap, I risked asking Mother to look after him. Usually she says no, but maybe because Foster was there, she agreed, and I left for the cemetery knowing I had to find the grave myself, no matter how long it took. I parked the car, prepared to hunt all afternoon. As I walked and looked, I remembered gazing out the window from my hospital bed on the day of Daddy's burial—tiny unnamed baby asleep beside me in a plastic crib. The grief that they had missed each other so narrowly. The snow began there on the Connecticut–Rhode Island border at the same time as the Memorial Service here in Florida, and I watched it fall the entire afternoon—a private vigil—until the tree outside was blanketed and everything was dark.

I wandered barefoot in the cemetery for about forty-five minutes, squinting into the low sun because all the markers faced east. There were many graves of young people. Ours is not so special a fate. Two little boys, seven and nine, with the same death date—drowning? fire? automobile? I thought about what should be inscribed on Harvey's stone and saw a plain, strong marker I liked:

JAMES EDWARDS

ARCHITECT

1909–1968

Simple block letters. Too grandiose, though, to say "historian" on the grave of someone as young as Harvey, even though his book will be out soon. Besides, there was so much to him—it seems wrong to leave anything out by mentioning just one aspect.

Then I found it. Sitting down in the May grass beside my father's grave, I looked down the long shadow at my bare toes. I had showered and put on white jeans and my favorite green smock and felt like my own self—no shoes, no masks—for the first time in a long while.

Suddenly, something stung me on the bottom, and I leaped to the top of the gravestone. It was warm from the sun, and I felt at home there. I could imagine Daddy sitting beside me, in shirt and work pants—I could even smell his sweat—chuckling at how I had jumped from his pinch. Everything casual and natural, finally right. I wept again, freely, as I had in Maclay Gardens—for him, for Harvey, for myself. I imagined telling him about Harvey's death:

> 7:00 bolting upright in bed
> 7:10 one ring
> "Mrs. Kantor . . . This is Cassie on B-1 . . ."

I cannot write the words. I can't write what it was like to see him lying there. I can't write about any of that day.

> Flying into Kansas City the next morning with Harvey's body in the hold, like luggage. The city glassy beyond recognition. An ice storm there the night before. Each twig glazed, sparkling in the winter sunlight. The cemetery itself magnified, transparent, as if the universe had altered to set the day apart. Icicles, glancing prisms, disorientation. Air cold as trumpets against my eyes. Pale wood—soft, unfinished, curving. Moving . . . lowering. Horror unrolling itself.
>
> Afterward, at Sharlene's, she and Harriet—mother and sister bereft—busy their hands, setting out food. Mother arrives, taking me in her arms for a moment, and a long strange sound comes up out of my chest—subhuman moan—frightening everyone in the room.

I told Daddy about that black tent of a night a week after the death, when even local friends withdrew, saying, "You have to get used to being alone." By the time I finished, it was getting dark. I felt better, having shared what I needed to. It was hard to leave, hard to face returning to the bright, nagging household ("Where have you been?" "You're so morbid." "Get the phone, will you please?" "This boy won't eat his peas."), and I walked back to the car very slowly.

Stonington. When I unlocked the door, the house was dark and cold and dead silent. It smelled damp. The door would open only halfway because of the pile of letters and junk mail which had collected underneath the slot. Upstairs, the kitchen and living room were just the same as when we left. Ever since I came home from the hospital the morning Harvey died there has been an indescribable but quite palpable difference to these rooms, like when you get a new pair of glasses and can't tell if the floor is six inches closer or the walls off square or what. That morning there had been a red balloon tied to the back of one of the kitchen chairs. I sat down and stared dumbly at where it had hung. That was Harvey's breath caught inside.

I tucked Jordan in and wandered around the house. It was late but I didn't want to go to bed. Everywhere I glanced, I saw Harvey's handwriting—in the note tucked into *Fathers and Sons* beside our bed: "The Colonial cities were the beachheads of imperial mercantile designs"—in our checkbook, in the two words "Third World" printed tiny inside his soft brown tobacco pouch. How long had those words been there? Why had I never seen them? I ran my thumb over the leather. I could leave our bags by the door, I thought, and take the first plane out to anywhere tomorrow morning.

Putting off going to bed, I realize, has now become a habit. It's partly because the sheets are cold. It's like not wanting to jump into a cold swimming pool; I know I have to do it, but I dawdle, pacing along the edge. Once there, my own side eventually warms. I am still afraid, though, to reach out to Harvey's. Every night it's the same. I put on his pajamas, turn down the covers, crawl in, turn out the light, and sink into my pillow. I let its dark softness hide me, pull my knees up close, and then I cry myself to sleep. If it brought comfort, I would suck my thumb, as Jordan does. Anything to ease the despair.

My sleep is deep, deeper than it's been for years (Why should that be? Merely because I am sleeping alone? Because there are no more seizures to dread? Because Death has come and gone?), but the dreams are a torment. In one not long ago Harvey's spirit hovered above me as in intercourse, but it was threatening, malevolent, as if he longed to harm me. And last night I dreamed I left Jordan with friends for an hour. Returning, I saw from a distance one of them carrying his unconscious body to a car. Blood was on his head. No one could hear me screaming to wait as I ran after him.

It is raining. I am sitting in the living room windowseat watching rivulets run down the pane. The day we came back to Stonington after Harvey's burial I lay curled here, face in, for a very long time while friends sewed burlap curtains to hide me. At least now I'm sitting up.

Jordan is bent over the kitchen table, his knees on a chair, head pillowed on the hard cassette recorder. After lunch he begged to hear the tape again—the one they made in January, three weeks before Harvey died. He insisted on a pink popsicle, too, because he'd had one that night. I can see him through the door, cheek against the source of his daddy's voice, sucking a popsicle, trying to make the love come back.

    J: What doing? What doing, Daddy?
    H: Putting the dishes away. What are you doing?
    J: I'm a lion and you are a tiger (growls), R-r-rrrrr. . . .
    H: A lion with wet underpants, it looks like! Did you pee in your pants or spill something?
    J: I . . . I spilled some pee!
    H: (laughs) Not bad.
    J: Carry me up . . . can't come up.
    H: OK, Jordan, it's January 29, 1975.
    J: When I be a baby.

H: No, you're not a baby now. You're what you are now. How old are you now?

J: I'm a boy.

H: You're a boy?

J: Yeah.

H: Are you sure?

J: Yeah.

H: How do you know you're a boy?

J: Because I *am* a boy.

H: Because you are, that's a good reason. Why don't you talk about what you did today, and if you had any fun, and who you saw, and who you were with and everything, OK? No, leave that alone.

J: I gotta talk at the people.

H: No, it's better just to leave the microphone right here. Did you help your dad today?

J: Yep.

H: What did you do?

J: . . . should take these off. So I can . . . better.

H: What did you do with your dad?

J: I been working with him. With you. What's this part?

H: That's the volume. It makes it louder or softer. Did you see your cat today?

J: GreenEyes?

H: Yeah, GreenEyes! Where'd you get that cat?

J: I got that anywhere. What's this?

H: A microphone. Where are you now?

J: Right here!

H: You're up on the counter.

J: You're teasing me. . . .

H: No, I was just telling the tape recorder where you were. *I* know where you were, but *it* doesn't know, does it?

J: I won't fall down.

H: Hey, Jordan, what are you eating?

J: Popsicle.

H: What color is it?

J: Pink.

H: Are you getting it all over your clothes?

J: (laughing) Noooooooo.

H: Why not?

J: Because I have 'em off!

H: Right. You don't have any clothes on, do you? Eric Sevareid interview. Do you often go without clothes?

J: Yeah.

H: So tell me, did you go to the library today?

J: I go to the library.

H: You did? Who did you go with?

J: With Christy, and it was closed.

H: It was closed? What do you like to do best at the library?

J: I like to read . . . that monkey hurt himself on the fire alarm. He got in the ambulance and get at the hospital.

H: Is that right? The monkey got hurt?

J: Yeah. He did.

H: I'll be darned. I hope he's better?

J: He's not better now.

H: Oh, he's not?

J: No, that's his bad work. So the piking mans . . .

H: The what?

J: The piking mans. I said the piking mans.

H: Oh.

J: Their jobs. And that was his job. Is this on? The people?

H: The people are on. Where's your mom?

J: She went.

H: Where'd she go?

J: She went somewhere. Where, Daddy?

H: She went to sing. You knew that, didn't you?

J: She went to sing? Where we listen? At the Ertsop?

H: You mean the Art Center? Yeah! OK, well, say goodnight.

J: How come?

H: We're going to turn it off. Goodnight.

J: No, I got to talk at it.

H: Say goodnight.

J: I want to talk about Nibble. The little squirrel. Nibble, Nibble, Nibble.

H: OK, you can talk just a little bit more. I've got an idea. Sing that song you sang for me today.

J: (singing) "When the cat come back, all . . . around his neck. Oh give me a check . . . play man. And every stuff." How's that?

H: Oh, that's a good little song. I like it. Do you know any other songs?

J: (singing) "Oh, you better not shout, you better not cry . . ."

H: (singing softly) "You better not pout, I'm telling you why." Why?

J: Because.

H: Because why?

J: (shouting) Because I like you!

H: OK, kid, it's getting late. We've got to put out the trash. It's time for bed. We'll talk some other night, OK?

I have little appetite anymore, but find myself eating compulsively, or rather drinking, especially before I leave the house. I'm not actually hungry, but I'm afraid I will be, afraid I won't be able to stand that little extra discomfort for even an hour if I am caught away from food. Repeatedly I open the refrigerator but then can't find anything appetizing. The food is there, but it never appeals. I find myself drinking milk, again and again, to fill the emptiness.

I tried to eat some raisin bran just now before I came upstairs, but it hurts to chew. I have a canker sore under my tongue, which makes me think of the enormous mouth ulcers Harvey had last fall from the drug Cytosar (he called it "the Czar")—or was it Vincristine ("the Count")—and how he couldn't talk. How did he eat? Why can't I remember? Why didn't they feed him intravenously? One day the sores fell off, a couple of hours apart. They were the size of quarters—gray and ugly. That was the day he started peeing blood. Emptying the urinal, I found it and told the nurse but not him. The next day he kicked the thing over, full, and blood spread all over the room and he was frightened and yelled at me for not telling him, and he was right. I was ashamed. But he was carrying so much anxiety that week, having learned he'd entered Blast Crisis, I just couldn't. He recovered though, after Fogle said no one expected he'd ever leave the hospital again. They were all waiting for cerebral hemorrhage because of the dropped platelets. The nurses shook their heads as we left—broad, broad smiles. It didn't surprise me. Our love was there, and his beautiful determination.

Those miraculous recoveries built false hopes, prevented me from recognizing the genuine onset of his dying. Oh, God, if only I could have seen it coming. If only I had spent that last night with him. I had stayed over before, in fear, but when it really counted, I was blind. I failed him.

I am trying to get back out into the world again, but it is very hard. Even when I wear sunglasses and pull my hair over my cheeks so less of me can be seen, I still feel dangerously exposed. I went back to chorus rehearsals for the first time tonight, but found I couldn't sing. I spent the whole evening fighting back tears, fumbling in my purse for Kleenex. I am grateful to these people—the purity of their voices at the Memorial Service stunned. The loud straight tone, coming suddenly from the balcony behind us, carved away the muscle of our resistance, laying bare the clean white bone of grief. But it is hard to be in public, even with them.

I am deeply troubled that I still cannot envision Harvey's face. Have I perhaps put our life together into a soft cocoon because it is too intense to deal with now? Or have I lost it utterly—will it just get worse? Some days there are tiny windows into it, for a second or two. But in general I have lost my memory. I can't even recall where Jordan and I slept in Kansas City when we went for his burial. It must have been at Harriet's, not Sharlene's, but there's no bed there for Jordan. Did they borrow a crib? I just can't remember. It's blocked. I do remember waking in the night, panicky, short of breath, stagefright waves in my stomach continuous for more than an hour. The light came from the right of the foot of the bed. Couch in Sharlene's den? I remember too, my compulsion to take a bath while the Havra Kadisha people were preparing his body for burial. I wanted to be bathing him myself, holding him, caring for him. An urgency to soothe, to share, to absorb the pain of it. Or was it guilt? Was it because something in my head said, "If he had only felt more loved, he would have wanted to live, could have beaten the cancer"? Was I washing away my failure to keep him alive? Maybe it was just a means of postponing the finality of his burial. I kept everyone waiting, black limousine running, while I washed.

More and more I notice myself doing things that he would have done even when they are things I'd never do myself. Tennis (if only he could see me learning to play tennis), buying matzoh and gefilte fish, saying Kaddish (the Judaism was his, not mine. Why can't I shake this?), renewing his magazine subscriptions, using his shaving cream, wearing his pajamas and robe at night and his jeans in the day, saying things twice the way he did. Why am I doing this? Is it that I love him so much I want to *be* him? God! Maybe that's why I can't see his face. Because I am turning into him! I am really scared.

It startles me to look at pages I have written, even just grocery lists. I am constantly misspelling words. Freudian slips, substitutions, repeated syllables, phonic spellings everywhere. They shock me, show I'm more undone than even I would judge. And the others—my friends—they infuriate me. Everyone seems to find me perfectly normal and capable. They don't even notice when I forget, mid-sentence, what it was I meant to say.

My inner life is a shambles. Thinking muddled. Loss of structure, of will. Entire psyche rotates, still, around Harvey—only his human force is not here to balance mine. Incessant depletion— strength sucked into a black hole. Directionless floundering. My work is disrupted too—a smaller, but genuine problem. The women's exhibit I put together, focus of eight months' concentration, ended for me with the opening the week before he died, momentum lost once it was framed and hung. The show has moved on now and is creating a stir in the Ætna Building in Hartford, the first place it has visited that is not accustomed to fine-art photography. Half the audience there is outraged by simple nudity (why do they seize on those few images?), and the others are threatened because the same figures aren't centerfold material. Hard to believe. Only a few have responded to the simple humanity in the photographs—women's portrayals of birth, work, friends, aging. I should feel good that it has generated corporate controversy—definitely a plus for the movement—but I am too fragile to feel anything but hurt that they don't admire it as they did in New London or Kingston. I am too tired to defend my efforts, and not really interested anymore.

Grant money for morning child care ended when the show opened, too. The financial aspect is meaningless because Jordan needs me now, not a sitter, but full-time mothering is devastating for me. I cannot complete a single thought. Constant interruptions. Wait. Endure. I hate this feeling. No purpose. Even the disease gave a framework—afternoons and evenings at the hospital, doctors' office visits, trips for immunotherapy, secrecy, driving Harvey to work, drugs, transfusions, seizures, Philip, friendships with nurses, and a constant girding for the unspeakable distant event. Now all I do is "babysit," and I'm incapable even of doing that well. I couldn't be teaching this semester if I had to. I cannot think or organize or care. My arms and legs are leaden. Every simple gesture saps me—getting out of bed, pouring milk on cereal, folding a towel, listening to Jordan, turning the steering wheel, writing a check. Nothing can be accomplished automatically anymore. How many years will this last? Forever? I have no enthusiasm for photographs—my own or others'—for teaching, for anything I know.

I wonder if it would be any different to go through this in a community where I had lived for a long time, where my own genuine deep friends—Sonia, Claire—were close by, and family, and family friends, and former teachers and ministers. Could it make a difference? Could anything soothe a hurt like this?

I am furious! Someone stole our red and purple geometric towels from the laundromat. I left them tossing in a dryer separate from the whites while I went to the hardware store and the market. Then I came home and unloaded the groceries. When I went back to the laundromat, the dryer door was standing open—just one purple washcloth left inside.

I could hardly restrain myself until I got home. I lugged the baskets in together, the full one nested inside the empty, half threw them into the office—clean clothes spilling out onto the rug—and slammed the door behind me. I leaned against it, clenching my teeth and fists and starting to growl. Then I lunged forward onto the stairs up to the kitchen and pounded them as hard and fast as I could with both fists. I kicked out backward, too, like a horse, against the door, not caring if I broke it down.

Those towels were special, damn it! We bought them for our crazy red bathroom in New York, for our first apartment. We always had red and purple anemones in there to match, under the silly framed picture of Mayor Lindsay. Damn! Damn! Damn! Haven't we been victimized enough? My husband died, World! Doesn't that earn us some kind of exemption?

Oh well, it's over now. I bruised the bone in my heel. Can't put any pressure on it. The limp makes me laugh. Sort of.

Today is the 18th of May—the three-month anniversary of Harvey's death. I am obsessed with the fact that I used the last of his shaving cream today. Nine and a half years of red-and-white-striped Barbasol cans—over. That can seemed to keep him closer in time—like the shiva candle, which I kept burning for weeks. As long as it held foam, as long as the candle burned, it couldn't have been very long since he was here. Why did it have to run out on the 18th? The 18th of March and April were hard too. Will this day of the month ever resume a normal face?

A special dream last night, like the early ones.

I am having dinner with friends but interrupt the meal because there's a documentary on TV about how my class at the Ecole Française made films. I am wild with hope to see Harvey, because he was in the last one. The color TV seems to enchant me. I enter into the program physically, like going through the looking glass. Harvey and I find each other in a gleaming snow-covered landscape, a limitless Sahara of snow. No cold, no coats, no trees or features on the drifts. Only the yellow clarity of love. A warm, clinging, wordless embrace—on and on—without a future, without a past. The feel of

*his neck and back and face and hair in my hands brings a peace
beyond anything I have known.*

And then I woke up. I was lying on my stomach. The deception
slipped away, and the nausea of truth flattened me onto the sheet.
To wake up was to be told he had died all over again.

I took a piece of beef out of the refrigerator tonight and set it on
the counter. Jordan looked at it and asked, "Is Daddy's body like that
now?"

Harvey's life insurance money came today. I stood in the hall
with the unopened envelope in my hand. The world would have
me be grateful. Do they call a piece of paper a fair trade? A piece of
paper for Harvey's warm flesh and smile and compassion and intel-
ligence? Do they call this compensation for his fear and suffering?
For suffocating alone at night, drowning in the fluid of his own
lungs? For not getting to watch his son grow up? For losing every
star and snowflake, leaf and friend on this planet? I tore the end off
the envelope and pulled out the check: $20,000. I felt like spitting
on it. It could have been twenty million and I would have felt the
same. It's as if they consider our not having to worry now about
finances some sort of consolation.

I went back into our room, put the check on my dresser, and
knelt down to finish sorting through the third drawer of Harvey's
bureau—I've been doing one drawer each month. The Social Security doesn't make me angry like this, except that no one let us
know about it before he died. He must have worried about what
would happen to Jordan and me. The doctors had to have known,
the lawyer. Why didn't anyone tell us? I suppose they thought we
knew already. The monthly payments are adequate really, not
much less than all three of us used to live on after doctor bills. But
the insurance money makes me sick.

I couldn't make any more decisions, so I took the one box of
things I thought might mean something to Jordan when he is 10 or

12—his father's crepe-soled shoes and favorite tie, his denim jacket, trench coat, Norwegian sweater, wallet—down to the basement and carried the carton of things for the chorus thrift shop out and put them in the back of the car, leaving the rest for another day. Then I pulled a sweater over Jordan's head, put him in his car seat and drove to Westerly and dropped them off.

Now I am home again. The need to cry is acute. Oh, the tears come and my face contorts, but I can't let go or sob. And I need to, I crave the release. It started out all right at the very first, but Jordan got so upset, repeatedly, when he saw me weeping that I developed a kind of inhibition. One day he even threw his blanket over my head. The orgasmic dreams I experienced the first two months are apparently gone now, too. I am a taut coil of grief-tension.

This morning it was raining again, and the grief was pressing out on my skull so hard I was afraid the bone might crack. A sound too violent for others to withstand was going to bellow up out of me. Desperate for privacy, I tried to get a sitter. I called six or eight people, straining to be casual, "I know it sounds silly, but I need to take a walk." No one was free. I began to get frantic. It was hard to get my breath. It felt like I was trapped under water, pinned against something by a crushing current. No, not right—the pressure was *in* me, not outside. Something inside me that used to go to Harvey now had nowhere to go. It built and built and I was afraid that I would fly apart.

Finally I drove Jordan over to some friends—people I've known only a few months—and begged them to watch him for a while. I must have looked deranged. They seemed surprised but said, "Of course, go ahead. Why don't you go to Napatree?" I drove through Westerly too fast, propelled by the yearning to let out of me the ugly sound I felt still building. But when I parked my car and ran, stumbling, up over the dunes to where I couldn't be seen, it wouldn't come. The gray waves were roaring in, ready to cover anything, but nothing came. I couldn't believe it. I just stood there feeling blank.

Disappointed, I headed slowly out toward the point. From time to time, I bent and picked up a translucent pebble. After a while, as I walked, I decided I should keep no more than three—a kind of exercise. So I kept searching and discarding, searching and discarding, for as long as it took to walk out to the point and halfway back, probably an hour—until I had the three most beautiful stones on that long stretch of beach. Then I walked up to where the waves end and stood there. The wind was not as cold as I had thought. I picked one of the stones out of my palm and forced myself to throw it far out into the ocean. "See?" I yelled at the wind, "I can do it. I can play your filthy game." And then I took the second one, "Here! Take it! I can stand it!" and threw it too, defiantly.

But then there was just one left. It was exquisitely hard to let go of that last one. I paced back and forth for a while, clutching for alternatives. Then I went back to the spot in the sand where I had started and simply stood there. The sky was gray, the sea was gray, the beach was gray. I pulled my arm up and did it. As my body came around on the follow-through, doubled over with loss, there appeared at my feet, instantaneously, three extraordinary yellow starfish.

Somewhere deep inside the pain, something shifted. Full of awe, I picked them up—fragile, perfect—and stood with my back to the ocean, absorbing what had happened. With them in front of me, in my hands, I slowly started the long walk back. On the way, I stopped and sat in the damp sand by some big old dock posts. I set the starfish down beside me and leaned sideways against the biggest post and felt the tear-restrainer loosen a little. The wood was cold and smooth against my cheek. It was sunk deep into the earth. It used to hold a pier. I hugged that old post, then, with both my arms. I hugged it and it held me up, and the real crying finally came.

Summer

After supper Jordan and I walked down to the Little League field to watch the big kids play. He had on his Red Sox cap, and as we passed around the library park, he ran ahead and swatted the big trunks of the chestnut trees with his pink plastic bat.

When the game was over, he pulled me out on the grassy outfield to throw him wiffle balls. After maybe the second pitch, a young girl, about eight years old, covered with freckles, came up to me and said almost tauntingly, "I know you. We used to be friends." I'd never seen her before. Then somebody tapped me from behind. It was another little girl, saying, "Her name is Rosie, Rosie Furtado."

Furtado . . . Furtado was the name of the young woman in the hospital room next to Harvey's, Linda Furtado. She died a few days before he did. She had suffered awfully: both breasts, a leg cut away. She was only about twenty. She had raged openly, cursing the cancer, shrieking, beating the wall. The nurses avoided her. I never saw any children visiting. I only remember the sign on the re-frigerator in the hall: "Do not take any of Linda Furtado's soda." I certainly didn't know these girls at all.

The first one hung on me aggressively, all her weight on my left shoulder. The second one asked, "Where's your husband?"

I told her, "He died."

"What of?"

"Cancer."

"My sister-in-law too."

The first girl chimed in, "Linda got married on *my* birthday, March 30th."

I gasped; that is *our* anniversary too! What is going on? Am I related through death to these people?

I am irritated with my gynecologist. A year ago I called his attention to a lump on the underarm side of my right breast, and he made me feel like a hypochondriac. Today, lump unchanged, he said, "It has to come out." Then he had the nerve to ask, familiarly, "How's Harvey?"

"I don't really know," I said, half-laughing, bitter. "He died in February."

After a brief expression of shock he sent me on to a surgeon, who also says operate. Strangely, I'm not worried about malignancy—feel certain all of this is unnecessary. What I'm actually worried about is my throat: it hurts more than any sore throat I've ever had. It is this pain, this one, that makes me ask if I could have cancer. So I went also to Philip. Three doctors in one day.

I sat on the examining table as he took my blood pressure. He stood close to me as he always does, my arm under his, warm. More than anything in the world, I wanted to lay my head on his shoulder and rest for a moment. I didn't want to speak or embrace or have anything more demanding than that pass between us. I had thought of telling him about the Furtado thing, but feared he wouldn't understand, would only think I am crazier than he already does, and anyway, I didn't have the strength. I just needed to touch someone. I wish that he could have seen how desperately I needed to be held. So many differences between us—his suits, control, and quiet British wit—my jeans, emotional incontinence, chaotic life and house. What is it that makes me feel connected to him? That he was one of Harvey's doctors and therefore held magical powers to stave off death, to keep my love alive? Harvey said he slept well in the hospital only when he knew Philip was in the building. And back home in Stonington, between hospital stays, when we returned from evenings out, we'd drive by his house to see if the lights were on, to see if he was there and we were safe for yet another night. Or is it our own friendship? Confidences exchanged, his pains and problems, as well as mine. Shared decisions—whether Harvey should be moved to New York or Buffalo when the going got rough or be kept in Westerly. Going to the hospital together that night and hearing Harvey preempt our votes, announcing his own irrevocable decision to stay near home.

Perhaps it's because of our talking that same night, Harvey and I, lying together yet again in a hospital bed, warming each other. Dr. Fogle had said to him, "Your chances are terrible." To me, the hour before, "It's a matter of days. Maybe two weeks." Teeth chattering, I went in to him and he reached out to touch my face. The contest had changed. No more counting on undiscovered cures. Death's hot breath. After the months of withdrawal and bitterness, of refusing to look at me, or speak, or hold me when I clutched him sobbing, "Please come back to me, please, please . . . ," suddenly he reached out and stroked my face, and everything was right again. We were together as we had always been. Odd in the terror of that night to be so full of joy. We talked long, tenderly, finding each other again. It was then, among the simple and serious things that passed between us, that he said, "I know that you and Philip will be together after I die. Not forever, but for a while. It makes me glad to think of you together. He will take care of you; I know it." The weight of that ordination, even after he recovered and came home. How long will I wait for its fulfillment? Philip has no way of knowing Harvey said, or wanted, this thing. And Harvey had no way of knowing Philip and Karen would grow so close that she'd move in with him.

Deep down, I guess the truest reason for my attachment is that there is something bonding in his having been with me the morning of Harvey's death; something sacred in his having been the only one to have sensed its coming, even though he failed to make it clear to me; and something permanently intimate in his having driven me to the hospital after the phone call. The most vulnerable and private hour of my life, the most crucial—he shared.

Today he agreed with the gynecologist and surgeon: I should have surgery when we get back from the lake. He said the throat looks like strep.

I still wish I could have just leaned against him. I know it would have helped.

I'm sitting in bed facing the pillows with the blankets pulled up over my head like a tent. I can't sleep. About an hour ago I was staying up late, watching TV, doing beginning yoga. Jordan awoke just after midnight, insisting he needed to go outside and ride his tricycle. The normal mother in me wanted to send him back upstairs with a "That's ridiculous," but something inside me rose up quietly and said, "Why not?" So we went out into the night, and he cycled up and down Temple Street in his pj's. The air was exceptional, warm yet sea-fresh. The sidewalk was exactly as warm as my bare feet. I looked down. There on my right, at my feet, was *my name*—Jayne—written in long grass, in Harvey's handwriting! Grasses, arranged into script, the word about a foot long—exactly as he always wrote it. I pulled Jordan inside, heart pounding, and locked the doors.

After that I couldn't get to sleep. Dawn came, finally, very pink, and as soon as it was light, I crept downstairs and out the side door, which doesn't creak, and down the garden stairs to the sidewalk. The grasses were still there, though they had blown about five feet toward the corner. If you stretched your objectivity a little, you could still see my name. Was it only imagination that made it so legible last night, or had the wind now defaced what had indeed been perfectly clear?

Right before dinner Harriet called. She was in labor all last night in Kansas City—gave birth to a girl today at dawn: Robin Leigh. Harvey is an uncle. It all happened at the same time. I am very uneasy. This is not the kind of thing one can talk about to others.

I had a terrible telephone argument with Mother about going up to Minnesota. I had called her to make sure it was still OK for us to use the cabin. At first she said "fine," which I had counted on; we always go as soon as school is out in June. But then she called back because she found out friends had planned to use it at that time. I guess they thought that Jordan and I wouldn't be going without

Harvey. When they heard we wanted to come, they offered to stay elsewhere, arranged it in fact, and called her back; but Mother wouldn't hear of it. She insisted they go ahead—a friend's vacation, she did not hesitate to admit, more important to her than our recuperation. I begged, literally, but she wouldn't relent. Bruce and Mary are having equal difficulty with her. I can't understand why she is acting so especially heartless right now. A month married, supported by Foster's love, her bitterness at losing Daddy should be waning, shouldn't it? I *need* to go to the Island. It's the only haven I can think of, the only home. We can't go later because nursery school begins.

Well, Mother softened, although "softened" is hardly an appropriate word for a voice as angry and critical as the one which finally relented on letting us use the cabin next week. It is incomprehensible to me that she'd have chosen this particular year to say "No, you may not go." I haven't missed a summer there for twenty years straight. And now, of all times, when my self-esteem and hold on dignity are so fragile, to make me grovel. It just doesn't make sense. I called her three different times and was refused. But I badgered and entreated, forcing events to line up, forcing a mother to act the way my shaky perception says mothers ought to, and on the fourth call, she said "Yes."

We'll leave the morning after the concert.

At final rehearsal this afternoon I was shattered to see the director wearing a shirt of Harvey's—one I had sent to the chorus thrift shop: faded red and blue stripes. He is so physical when conducting— vibrant, muscular, dynamic. And my husband . . . I have often hugged Harvey in that shirt and know the warmth and substance of his body through the fabric. I dropped to the riser and sobbed for a few seconds.

Tonight we did *Belshazzar's Feast*—a very angry piece, suitable for me. The performance was thrilling—the orchestra decibels

beyond imagination; and on the ringing of the last chord I was so
moved that I felt my life justified in the velocity of its living sound.
Felt that if I died right then, it would be acceptable.

Cass Lake. I came out of the cabin this morning into a light wind
and weak sunshine. A narrow line of foam angled out from the dock
along the drop-off. It is a hundred feet deep there where the Mississippi swings in near the shore. So far there are just a couple of
other docks in. The rest are stacked in neat bleached piles in the
sand, receding off to my right and left like so many bonfires waiting
for a torch. At the marina they said there are only six other people
on the whole island, and no other children, so it looks like I will be
baby-sitting pretty much full time.

When I was unpacking, I noticed a snapshot of our family, lying
loose on Mother's desk. It is probably one of the last pictures of our
bona fide nuclear family—I am in the center, protected and surrounded, close to Daddy—childish needs, yet I think this is one of
my first "grown-up" appearance pictures. Mother looks especially
lovely, radiant even. I gave her that skirt. Daddy is in an uncharac-
teristically undomineering position in this group, and Bruce actually looks happy. Mary shows up bigger than she is in real life.
Mother has her glasses in her lap, and Daddy's health starts to look
weak. I now wear those light blue socks he has on, to keep my feet
warm in bed. Bruce is most obscured—as ever the least public
member of the family. I like all the hands in this picture. Mary,
obedient, mirrors Mother's position exactly. Bruce, Mary and
Mother wear neutral clothes. Daddy and I are in strong colors.

I guess these people cared about me, but they would have had to
care for anyone who was born into that picture. In those days if I
tried to explain something I had been thinking about, they'd say
"What's that?" or answer in tangents that showed they didn't really
understand. My school friends were the same. I was made to feel
that if they ever really figured out who I was, they wouldn't love me
anymore. There were a few—teachers, mainly—who understood,
but they were distant. Harvey was the only person I had ever met
who convinced me I was lovable for who I really am. I'd share a

fledgling thought and he'd take it up, elaborate, and bounce it back to me in a way that proved his comprehension. And hug me. Every day. He completed me, and I loved him in an unpremeditated way. I remember him puzzling, when we were still in school, why I didn't push for marriage, why I didn't seem to want anything specific in return. I just wanted to be near him. What more was there?

I hate mealtime—there is no one to talk to. I race through my food and Jordan dawdles, and I try to hurry him in order to get the meal and dishes behind me. We have been eating alone together for four months now, and it still has no sense of routine or normalcy. I keep waiting for the other grownup.

I am very frustrated this week. I wake up every two hours at night—get up, go to the bathroom or get a drink, open and close windows. Ovulation. What a futile feeling. Last night I tried to come by myself in the moonlit living room. I lay on the floor in front of the empty fireplace and started to dream of Harvey, but as soon as the image of him entered my mind, the pain coiled up. It's too soon. Tears—press them, him, back down. Too soon for me to think about our lovemaking. How will I ever be able to accept someone else into me without longing for Harvey? Maybe the best thing now would be to sleep with as many men as I could find in order to diffuse my total equation of sexual feelings with him. Then someday I might be able to love another man for himself, free and clear.

The yearning to be held is so fierce.

The Island is beginning to help. This morning I remarked how small something was, and Jordan said, "Is it small as a mouse's tail?"

After breakfast we walked west along the shore to look at the other cabins. At the campground, he knelt in amazement and said, "Those dragonflies are just like helicopters!" When we got to the end of the sidewalk, he climbed to the top of a six-foot stack of dock-timbers and practiced great leaps off into the sand.

"Watch this, Mommy!"

"That's terrific! Daddy would love to see you doing that."

"The clouds are high, Mommy, look." He pointed up and jumped again, his arms outstretched. I looked up at the clouds, higher than they are in Stonington, smoother, blue sky behind.

"Harvey," I whispered, head held back. Then louder, "Harvey!" Then I was yelling, making a fiction for Jordan, yelling to the high white clouds. Jordan joined in, "Daddy! Daddy, look!" and it didn't feel like a fiction anymore. We were a whole chorus of "Harvey"s and "Daddy"s, shrieking merrily, scarily, loudly, sadly.

I need to be careful about this. Something in me is not accepting the rational conclusion that Harvey's personality has been extinguished. I actually wanted to believe he could hear us. It is stupid to try to make sense of his death. I know that, but I have been indulging myself with whys. Why did this happen? What caused the cancer? Was it because there was leukemia in his family? The doctors insist it's not inherited, but there it is, on both sides. Was it because there was something else wrong with his blood? When he was ten, there were massive, spontaneous bruises—"ideopathic thrombotic pupera." They removed his spleen, which they'd have done for leukemia, too. What about mononucleosis? He had it the year after I did—we were just starting to date; I drove him home to Kansas City from the University. Could he have possibly caught it from me, a full year later? And could the mono itself have triggered the leukemia four years farther down the line? They both affect the blood. I read somewhere that the virus which causes mono can live in your body for months after you're well. That I might have been the cause is horrible to contemplate.

I am afraid of the approaching breast surgery, the loneliness of it. Never in my life have I been without someone—parent or Harvey—who sort of owed it to me to be there at a time like this. I want to be able to stand it, but feel sorry for myself, driving alone to the hospital with my little bag, unloved. Am upset for Jordan as well. Will he fear that I, too, will disappear forever into Westerly Hospital? Should I lie about where I'll be for those three days? I wish it didn't have to come just now. I don't want to go in there again, and I'm afraid of losing consciousness.

Optimism. My grieving last night was so utter that I feel I have finally touched the bottom of it. I will never be that soul-wracked again. Unconsciously I must have set up the whole thing. Music. I know I can't take anything with more emotional range than Bach's Two-Part Inventions, and what did I put on the stereo? "Romeo and Juliet," "Love Story," Bachrach songs. I fought the pathos for a while—leaned against the sofa and tried to read. But finally I buckled to the floor, limp, resistance gone. My face fell into the carpet. There was wool in my mouth as I cried—long heaving moans pushed each other out of me, like cattle unpenned. It was an ugly surrendering, but now things will improve, I'm certain.

Deep fatigue still comes about a half day in every three, and then all seems lost. I can't lift my arms or legs or move about much. I lie on the couch for whole hours at a time. But I am feeling a real buoyancy occasionally and marvel at the long-ago memory of the sensation. I didn't realize it had been so many years since I have felt it. So, the old lightning-stripped trunk is putting out new shoots. I am maimed, but I am still alive and have faith that one day my life will yield something of meaning. If only I can bear these slow waiting years—Harvey's illness, widowhood—my apprenticeship as a person.

Jordan panicked when he learned that today was my birthday, cried and clung to me. It took me many minutes before I connected—flash—it was three days after Harvey's birthday that he died. I pried him away from my legs, knelt down, and took his tear-streaked face in both hands.

"Are you afraid that I'm going to die?"

He kept his eyes squeezed shut but nodded several times very fast.

"Oh, Punky," I sighed, drawing him to me. "I'm not going to die. Birthdays don't have anything to do with dying."

"But Daddy . . . ," he sobbed.

"I know, Daddy died after his birthday, but that just happened. He'd been sick for a long time. It doesn't usually happen that way. I'm not sick. I'm fine. I'm not going to go away. I'll be here to take care of you."

He pulled back and looked at me for a second and that was it. I couldn't believe it was so easy. Off he went to play in the sand, reassured. Nevertheless, I no longer felt like celebrating, not that I'd planned to, and the day has gone by otherwise unmarked.

Now it's evening, and he is in bed, and I am asking myself what it is I want from life. Work—fulfilling, purposeful. Time off for physical things, nature, exercise, unprofessional thought and study. Health. Jordan's happiness, but not to have him make so many demands on me. Hard to admit it, but I want him peripheral, not central. Passionate love again, with friendship and true intimacy, but not requiring a lot of time or routine. I wouldn't marry. When I die to be reunited with Harvey. That's about it.

June 30, 1975. My thirtieth birthday . . . me, defined by what I want.

It's 2 A.M. and I am not tired.

I can feel a little health coming back into my body, suppleness, youth, the flush of regular exercise. Yoga and tennis. Even though there's no one to hit with here, I carry a minnow bucket full of balls down to the court in the morning and practice serving. There is something remarkably helpful about tennis. Hitting, running—it satisfies the need for both fight and flight. And sweating is magic.

I have adjusted to celibacy somewhat. To come by myself makes me feel lonelier than not to come at all. It accentuates Harvey's absence. And even if I try not to think of him, I still feel diminished, reduced, that I must touch myself; that what was once a communion is now only a silent search for relief. So I refrain. The orgasmic dreams are back, though, and I have figured out that they occur with ovulation and menstruation. Clearly, my erotic cycles are hormonal. That is a little humiliating. Thankfully, though, I am now in a calmer, less driven state.

It is good to have neighbors nearby again. The Hendersons arrived a few days ago. Bob just had his last cobalt treatment on a tumor inside one of his vertebrae. He is sick, but his face is beautiful, tanned and wreathed with smile lines. He is kind to Jordan—a substitute for the grandchildren he will not live to see? Yesterday he carved him a toy boat and attached it to a line on a cane pole, part of the "keep-the-kid-off-the-dock campaign." Then he painted a pun for "Jordan" on it—"Chore Dun"—in dark green letters. I photographed the two of them, while they were carving together beneath the pine trees. Bob's fingernails were white, I noticed, white like Harvey's, white with death. As I backed up for one shot, a knife of his, stuck in a tree, entered the frame, slicing visually into his spine where the cancer is. For myself, surreptitiously, I snapped the shutter again—a secret image that admits my pain.

I want to talk with him, with Martha too, but Jordan is always there interrupting. As we walked back out toward the lake yesterday, Martha stood very close to me, our shoulders almost touching, but Jordan tugged at me to get home to try his boat, and we just looked at each other with full eyes.

It's been raining for two days. Yesterday was not too bad. As the wind came up, before the storm, Jordan stood on the mound along the beach that the ice makes when it breaks up in May, his hands spread out in front of him, and yelled, "Be quiet, lake!" I took a picture of him like that, from behind and to the side—hair blown back in all directions, firm round belly sticking out, the horizon of the far shoreline coming out of his eyes like a spear. It looked as if he were standing on a fresh grave. Later, I hauled in wet logs from the woodpile, edgy about spiders, and made a fire in the fireplace. He lay in front of it for a while watching the flames and drinking "warm hot chocolate, Mommy" from his blue plastic bottle, and I took more pictures of him. Before supper we went for a walk down to the other end of the beach, just to get out of the cabin. The orange adult rain-jacket I dug out of the metal locker was full-length on him, and he looked like some strange sideways gremlin as he trotted ahead, rain whipping the garish cloth.

This afternoon was awful, though—gruesome, involuted. I'd read him all the simple-minded children's books that I could find, and when I started "Sleeping Beauty," he wouldn't let me finish.

"Don't tell me that. Don't read me that," he said when the princess pricked her finger. He forced the book closed: "Take that away." Then he wouldn't take a nap. I needed him to, I wanted to rest myself, but he just wouldn't stay in bed. Finally, as I was getting ready to put him down for the night, the rain let up a little, and the setting sun came out, and we saw, over the lake, a double rainbow! He ran out first, then just as fast came racing back into the kitchen and grabbed a saucepan from the bottom cupboard for a hat and ran back out with it on his head like Johnny Appleseed. He held it by the handle to keep it on and looked up into the southeast sky, amazed.

"Did Superman paint that?" he asked.

I looked at him standing barefoot on the wet sand, one pajama leg rolled up, one hanging down, raindrops plunking on the pan, and thought, "His first rainbow. Mine too, in a way."

I am sitting at Mother's desk paying bills. Here is one from Cyto Medical Laboratory for my Pap smear, when the doctor told me to have breast surgery. Their logo is CML—the acronym for Harvey's disease: chronic myelogenous leukemia. I am getting used to the idea of the hospital business when we get back to Stonington. Stella will be home from her year in London, and I feel certain she will help, and Philip. I still hope to find someone to tell me I don't have to do it, though. When we get back next week, I will go up to Boston for another opinion.

A little before lunch I phoned the drugstore in town to see if the film I left there on Friday was ready. They told me the negatives were back, but they weren't any good so there weren't any prints, and asked if they should just throw them out. Groaning inside because I knew it meant camera trouble, I told them, "No, I'd better come and have a look."

I suited Jordan up in a life jacket and pulled the little boat around to the end of the dock, then got in and pointed it toward the mainland. It's three miles by water to the town dock. Jordan sat in the front and held on to the rope like a bronco's rein. The lake was fairly rough and he bounced on the cushion as the bow beat against the waves. We landed at the big dock, ordered a tank of gas, and headed into town. There's only one drugstore—the town is even smaller than Stonington—and it has general goods as well. Jordan looked at beaded Indian belts and wooden leave-a-note boxes and I asked for my negatives.

I was not prepared for what I saw when I pulled the first strip out and held it up to the drugstore window. My heart stopped. Superimposed on every frame, overlapping his son's young face, was Harvey's, ghostlike. I tried to act natural, but my hands were shaking. I pulled some money out of my purse and we left. I knew I didn't dare look at the film again until we were safely home and Jordan was down for his nap. My hands still shook as I started the motor and steered the boat out of the marina. As soon as we were past the piled stone breakwaters, I gunned the throttle, and we crossed the lake with the engine wide open.

When Jordan was in bed, I sat down on the sofa, my back to the sunlight, with the unopened picture envelope on my lap. Then I took out one of the strips, very carefully, and studied it. The pictures of Harvey, I realized, were ones I had made last fall when we went to Kilravock Inn for a weekend to recuperate after a trip to Buffalo. Somehow that roll of exposed film had not been completely rewound, had never been developed, and had found its way into my supply of fresh film ten months later. That is eerie enough. But the compositions are even stranger.

In one image their mouths, identical in size and shape, brush in a soft kiss. In another, Harvey's hand, holding a small leaf, reaches down into Jordan's chest. In yet another Jordan's arms cradle his father's shadowed head—dark, decapitated, with what looks like blood (a little tree?) running from his mouth. It is remarkable the ways, totally by accident, the images fit together. They are too much to behold.

Tomorrow, early, we head home.

Stonington once more.

How wide our bed is without Harvey beside me. At the lake there were only twin beds. . . . As certainly as I know I'll have bad dreams tonight, as certainly as I know it will turn gray in the morning, as certainly as I know Jordan will wake me too soon and too late—this is how certain I am that he'll return. I can't even put away his glasses. They're still in the bathroom beside the sink.

Jordan already feels how awful it is not to have a daddy—not just the loss, but its social implications. Today the tough kid down the street "shot" at me with his rifle from behind a bush, yelling to Jordan, his eyes narrow, "I'm gonna kill your mother and then you won't have a mother *or* a daddy."

At five o'clock we went down to the point for a swim. Most of the kids were going home for supper, so it was peaceful. Stella and Laura were there. Laura and Jordan had dog-paddling races, and Stella and I sat in the sand and talked about her year in London and about Harvey's death. I bit back tears.

She looked at me and shook her head. "Forgive me for saying so, Jayne, but it's been six months since Harvey died. How much longer is this down-in-the-mouth stuff going to go on? I think you need a good swift kick in the butt!"

I looked at her in astonishment, my first thought, How can she not have known an attachment that would bring this long a grief?

All I could say was, "If only someone would tell me 'It'll just last another year,' then I could stand it."

"Another year!" she interjected.

"But I can't *see* an end to it. I'm afraid I'll feel this way for the rest of my life."

Jordan has started nursery school. His separation anxiety has been acute lately, so I decided to wean him away from me gradually. I stayed with him the whole time Monday, left for fifteen minutes Tuesday, thirty Wednesday, an hour yesterday. It seems to have worked. Today he is on his own. My stomach folded over itself as I watched him scamper away down the back drive there this morning, lunch box flying. A grief that Harvey couldn't see him. He sat in on three different nursery schools last fall to help choose. How many fathers do that? He'd have been proud today—would have had a lump in his throat, too. I hate it that we can't share this—can't look in each other's eyes and see the milestone there and take an hour off before work to commemorate it over coffee somewhere.

I am on the train back from mammography in Boston. The seat beside me is empty, and a rainy day has rarely looked so good. I found Mass. General with no difficulty and waited in a small interior examining room, cold in a paper gown, for a long time. Finally, a doctor came in, followed by three young men, medical students, I think. With no preliminaries, he said, "Take off the gown." I did as he said, pulling it down from my shoulders, and sat there uncomfortably, on the edge of the table, bare from the waist up, being stared at by four men. Then he said, "Lie down." I did, and he palpated the breast and pointed to it for the others to do likewise, which they did. No one spoke. Then the students left, one of them throwing me a sympathetic glance over his shoulder, and the doctor sat down beside me on the table. I held the gown to my chest.

"If you were *my* wife," he said, "I'd have you in here tomorrow.

But go on down to Radiology, and we'll see what they have to say."

What they said was, "Fibrocystic lump: surgery not indicated"! I was so proud of myself—elated, really. I felt fifteen feet tall as I soared down the street, licking the rain from my face, laughing out loud. I called a woman photographer I hardly know in Cambridge and met her for lunch at the Blue Parrot, just to have someone to celebrate with.

A justification of intuition and restoration of self-confidence. Aha to you, knife-happy three at home! The big-timers say nix on tricks.

Today, with no forethought whatsoever, on the way home from dropping Jordan at nursery school, I stopped at Freddy's Boat Yard and bought an overturned old wooden runabout and an equally battered eighteen-horse motor. I saw the hand-lettered FOR SALE sign from the street, pulled in, and bought it, just like that. The evenings are very long and empty now that August is here. After dinner there is sunlight still, the harbor is glassy calm, and the hours stretch out vacantly until Jordan goes to bed. I don't feel like working in the yard. The boat should be a perfect solution.

We worked all weekend, scraping barnacles, sanding, painting. The boat is now brick red and gleaming white, with a bright aqua bottom.

On our first ride we drove really slowly out of the backwater harbor, watching for rocks, out into the main harbor. There we were, right among the yachts and racing sailboats. We went out beyond the breakwater for a while, but the swells made rolls of fear inside me, so we came back into the harbor. The tide was high when we came back, and the steering wheel barely passed under the railroad bridge—maybe two inches to spare. We had to lie down on the floor of the boat to get back through.

Unbelievable. I met someone. I met a man who has been through some of what I have. His wife has cancer and is in a mental hospital. He is raising a seven-year-old son by himself. His name is Spencer and he is a poet. He brushed mosquitoes from my arms, liked my long peach dress, gazed at me so intently that I had to look away. It was at the Arts Center. When I pointed him out to Stella (we had gone to the crafts fair together), her chin dropped. "Jayne, Jayne," she said, "he looks just like Harvey!"

Why did she say that? I don't think he looks like Harvey.

A woman from the Arts Center invited me to observe a writing workshop there on Thursday night. I about flipped when I found out Spencer would be leading it. I saw him from the car, tall and slim with soft dark hair and a denim jacket, walking toward the old frame church building with a woman potter I know, and felt left out. Once inside, I felt quite shy. He hardly seemed to notice me, said a simple "hello" to me like everybody else when I sat down. I wanted him to remember who I was, so when there was a round-table exercise—analogies for the color red—and it was my turn, I said, "Red as my husband's blood." The two women across the table from me sucked in their breath—I wondered if they knew who I was, or maybe knew Harvey—but Spencer showed no emotion or recognition in either his face or voice.

At the break, however, he came up to me and asked quite bluntly, "May I see you home tonight?"

"So you do remember me, after all!"

He sort of choked. "I've had your name on a slip of paper on top of my desk all week."

Then he ignored me again for the second half of the class. As we drove along Route 1 toward Stonington afterward, two cars, four headlights in the night, I asked myself what I thought I was doing taking a strange man home. He followed me up the stairs into the kitchen and said, "Do you have this whole house?"

"Yes?"

"Only two of you live here?"

"Yes. It's really quite small. Is that so odd?"

"Do you own it?"

"Yes, this is where we live."

"I don't think I know anyone who lives in a whole house."

I waved him to a seat at the kitchen table, paid the sitter, whose eyes were very large, and poured him a beer.

"You can help yourself to the refrigerator," I said, "but I'm not fixing anything. I'm not cooking for men anymore." I couldn't believe I said that. I didn't even know I thought it.

He took a bunch of grapes. We bantered for a few more minutes, but very soon were sharing intimate stuff.

I must have played with a piece of chalk from the kitchen blackboard for two or three hours while he told me about his marriage—he's been separated for five years. Finally, he asked for a drink of water, and we both got up at once and stepped over to the sink. I took down a glass and handed it to him. When he finished drinking, he just stood there with his back to the sink, both hands on the counter. We were both silent. I still had the piece of chalk in my hand. Awkwardly and cautiously, deliberately and not, I touched him with it, touched his hand. He swung around and trapped my hand on top of his with his other hand, then lifted it up, chalk and all, and kissed it, held it to his cheek and looked at me. My insides turned over on themselves—contortions in my uterus like I have never felt before.

It's far too soon for a genuine relationship—how can I give him anything when I'm still married inside? But someone to hold me— at last, someone to hold and comfort me, a place for gratification and understanding. I am swept with confusion—pleasure, guilt—it has been only six months since Harvey died.

We talked till dawn. As he was leaving, he whispered, "I don't want to pressure you."

"Pressure me?"

"Sexually, I mean."

"Oh . . . I don't feel pressured."

"Good. I'll call you later." He kissed me and went down the stairs. The elderly neighbor lady saw him go. She was standing on her porch. I didn't think anyone around here got up that early. She stared and stared. I am definitely not ready for a public couple-number. Stonington is Harvey's place. Seeing Spencer at his house in Providence or anywhere else seems acceptable enough, but I feel disrespectful in our house.

I wonder what it will be like to sleep with him.

A small brocade-covered book came from Spencer in the mail today—Japanese, lovely. He must have sent it the instant he got home.

Spencer's son Jonathan was invited away for an overnight last night, so he called and asked me to stay at his house in Providence. I had to talk to people up there at the Extension Division anyway, about my teaching assignments, so I got a sitter here and packed the canvas satchel I usually take on picnics and drove up 95. It was very awkward going to the strange house at the appointed time, 4:00 P.M., ringing the bell. Ringing it again. There wasn't any answer. I wanted to get back in my car and turn around and drive straight home, but instead I sat down on the wooden porch steps and waited. The sun was hot. I had on my jeans skirt and a new, gathered T-shirt and sandals. I wanted to take my sandals off but was afraid the landlady would come out and wonder about me. After about twenty minutes, Spencer's light blue VW bug buzzed into the driveway.

"Had to take a friend somewhere," he said, unfolding himself from the little car. "Come on up. I've been cleaning in your honor."

He had indeed been cleaning. The upstairs apartment was torn apart, like moving day. The cluttered rooms ran into one another. We had to go through the living room, which had a wonderful bed with curving wooden sides like a sleigh, and dining room, which he uses as a study, to get to his bedroom and then through that to get to Jonathan's room, where he was currently working. Sheets were heaped on the floor, and books and toys were piled on the bare-mattressed bed. The bookcases, which ran along the outside wall under the windows, had been wiped clean, and he was putting things back, one at a time, in order according to size. It looked as though it would take him days to get it done. I waited while he worked awhile at this, and then I waited while he cleared out and scrubbed the refrigerator. He had defrosted it in anticipation of my visit. Finally, I couldn't take it anymore. He was bent over, his back to me, wiping out the crisper drawers. I draped myself over him, arms around his neck.

"Spencer, I came up here to see you, not your house. Don't you think we could go out and get some supper or something?"

He put his free hand on my forearm.

"I just wanted it to be nice for you. The bathroom's done, at least."

"I know, but it feels like you're avoiding me."

"OK, let's go get some food."

In the car he told me about his favorite professor in Oregon, the one who recognized his ability, who was his mentor. I had thought we were going to a restaurant, but he pulled into the parking lot of a big grocery warehouse. Inside, we wandered up and down the aisles, but all he bought was a large plastic bag of peaches, which he presented to me, ceremoniously, outside the store: "In honor of your dress the other night."

It was really hot and sticky back in the apartment, and after a couple of hours we went for a walk. We walked around and around the block, barefoot. How to begin to describe him—exuberant, kinetic, turbulent, idealistic in the extreme. His sensitivity and perceptiveness take my breath away. He seems the most moral, giving person I have ever encountered. He has been too selfless in the past—probably masochistically so. But now he is quite determined to assert his own needs. He's a very physical guy—grew up on a farm, the oldest of five brothers and sisters, played football—and is a very gifted teacher, I gather. He won't let me see his writing yet, so I can't evaluate his work, but the man's mind excites me, and his tenderness and breadth comfort and nurture me. He is 34 going on 17, though he blames his current boyishness on being in love with me. Expansive, expressive, self-made intellectual. Informal, physically affectionate. I am full of good feelings. I am quite certain that whether or not our "affair" endures, our friendship is going to last all our lives. I will be able to count on his care, his advice and help with Jordan, his humor to entertain, his arms if I need to be held!

We're going to have some sexual problems though, at least for a little while.

"You know the other morning when I said I didn't want to pressure you?" he whispered, as we lay beside each other in the bed that looked like a sleigh.

"Yes."

"Well, it was really me who didn't want to feel pressured. I could see this coming."

He was afraid to let go. And me—I felt a strong passion for him until we were actually making love. Then it disappeared. Being close to a man's body felt like being with Harvey. I needed for him to keep talking. Without his voice to anchor me, I couldn't hold on to reality. Afterward, I didn't sleep at all—was too stirred up and nervous.

I am eager to meet his son because there's no way he's not going to be intense and perceptive and kind. I am not interested in mothering another child—I can't even give Jordan what he deserves—or in being part of another family, but doing things together—camping, traveling—sounds wonderful. I have an urge to do just that, to take our boys and set out for an unspecified place for an unspecified time. Get out of this town. Write and photograph and eat, camp out, play with and teach the children, and learn. Rural England, Morocco, Nepal, Japan, New Zealand, Greece, Kenya, Yucatan. Stretch and grow, meet people, escape old patterns. Explore and delight. Yes, it's a good idea! Take my camera and journal, tennis racquet and jeans, Jordan's night-night and a suitcase full of film. Yes. Yes. I'm actually dreaming. I'm projecting into the future. Have feared to do this for five whole years because of the cancer. It feels terrific.

To remember—the uterine contortions I experienced, standing beside Spencer the first night here in the kitchen. The frightening force of my desire for him. This has not recurred. In fact, my feelings have diminished rapidly over the last week. That bothers me. Am I only forcefully passionate about an unknown, growing merely fondly aroused by the familiar? Or am I less impressed by him the better I know him? He seems so very young, not really manly. It's healthy, I think, to have some doubts rather than to fall prey to blind infatuation. But I would hate to lose someone by undervaluing him, as Mother seems to be doing with Foster.

She is now talking about divorcing him. It's not even three months since they were married. There have been some misunderstandings—financial, she says—but I suspect that on the deepest level, it is because he did not automatically turn into Daddy when she married him. I can see how easy it is for a widow whose marriage has been a good one to fall into another too quickly, expecting the institution itself to supply the love and security she has known. I wish I had the energy tonight to call her and offer support, to talk her through this disappointment, to urge her to move here near us, but I haven't. I am exhausted.

Spencer spent his second night this week here last night. I can never really get to sleep when we are together, and the day that follows is inevitably hard. If only I could take a nap, could catch my spirit's breath. But Jordan is here, and his needs must be met. He just brought me a "surprise": a Band-Aid for the cut I just got on my finger. That finger will be all healed by the time Spencer gets back from the bus trip he's planning to take through the South. He's bringing his son to spend the night tomorrow, before he leaves. He is so good with kids—Jordan squeals with delighted terror when he gives him airplane rides in the big basket, falls asleep this week holding the pink elephant pillow he brought. It makes me feel inadequate. How will Jonathan and I relate?

Well, everyone got along just fine. After dinner I put the children to bed and Spencer took a two-hour walk in the moonlight. When he got back, he said he had just done the best writing of his entire life. I was very pleased to have contributed to that. But his notebook is a problem for me at other times. It is omnipresent. He claims it isn't writing. "Writing is the anguish at my desk." But still I feel excluded and bored when he stops to write for ten minutes in the middle of a conversation. I have no desire to be "the artist's woman." I don't want to serve and I don't want to be served. Can't there be a time for both of us to work and a time for both just to be together?

The sex is better than at first, but it certainly makes me grateful that Harvey was always so lusty. It is late that I come to appreciate his reliable body. God. How could I apply such a word? If ever a body betrayed. . . . I shock myself. What I meant was: he was never impotent, never, even when he was ill. I took his desire for granted—placed it, like a child, with life's other inalienable rights: food, shelter, fresh air, a family's concern. Now all of them seem fragile and endangered.

I phoned Mary long distance last night and told her about Spencer. Her reaction was "Oh, no! Why couldn't it have been in a year or two." It made me feel bad that my own sister was more concerned about propriety than about my happiness. I asked her at least not to say anything to anyone yet, especially Mother. What am I doing? She's right. She's wrong.

Last night Jordan and I sat together on the moonlit seawall behind the lighthouse. I felt Harvey very close. It was a completely calm night, and I sang to Jordan,

> *"Who has seen the wind?*
> *Neither I nor you:*
> *But when the leaves hang trembling,*
> *The wind is passing through."*

A soft but insistent breeze caressed us.

"Spirit is like wind," I explained. "You feel but cannot see it."

Jordan got sad, said, "I want my night-night."

Later, when Spencer called from the bus station, I told him about it, and he said he had been "with us." *No.* If it was anyone, it was

Harvey. Sometimes I think he is sent to me by Harvey. It is dangerous to confuse the two of them, I know, but inescapable—they do look alike. There, I've admitted it. Olive skin, square chin, dark hair, soft eyes. I've said it. Good night.

New York. For a long time I've found upper Park Avenue to be the most desolate part of the city. The street is too wide, the scale inhuman. This morning, driving into Manhattan, it clicked—why. I see two beautiful young people, having just walked out of a hematologist's office, standing there in the fall rain, sobbing and clinging to each other.

Jordan and I are helping Sonia housesit the sprawling Riverside Drive apartment of friends. She has arranged a regular midday baby-sitter so the two of us can do city things alone together on her lunch hour—restaurants, museums. Today we revisited our favorite Matisses at the Modern, then went next door to the Museum of American Folk Art. A perfect setting for Sonia—all those quilts and elegant primitive objects precisely displayed. Her own collection of Iowa quilts is growing.

Right now she has taken Jordan down to ride his tricycle in Riverside Park. She "aunties" him morning and evening—listens to him, helps with decisions and discipline. I am relaxing into her support. We stay up late at night talking, giggling even, about books and friends, food and jobs and men. Fourteen years now we have been friends, since we studied at the United Nations together. I wonder if we'll ever get to live in the same town again.

The city exudes Harvey and our life together here—those three happy years. Where is he? In front of the New York Public Library today, at noon, in the intersection just north of the building, I thought I glimpsed him ahead of me in the crosswalk. Unquestioningly, I shouldered past the others. But then he turned, a stranger.

Two weeks now, and Spencer hasn't called. Jordan and I have been very busy, but still, this long silence is devastating. I guess I have given the man more of myself than I realized. More than wanted to. I want some of me back—psychological self-reliance. I have potential for that; I know I can learn it. Spencer is only a prop holding up the house of my self until it is rebuilt. Then the prop can be withdrawn.

We had a good afternoon today wandering around the Museum of Natural History. Claire came up on the train from Pennsylvania and brought Elizabeth Jane along, so the children had a little reunion. It is captivating to see them together: different sexes and dispositions but exactly the same age, and they always remember each other even though months pass when they're not in touch. Claire was full of anecdotes about people she encounters with Michael in the business world. She can make anything entertaining, but this time she had me guffawing about how ridiculous people can be when they fall in love with someone inappropriate.

It was a lift to be with her, although she still seems to expect more of me than I am strong enough to muster (like when she came in March loaded with groceries and flats for the garden—yes, I should have been strong enough to care for those plants, to get them into the ground; yes, it would have been good for me, nurturing new life, but I simply did not have the energy. I was doing well to get food on the table and brush my teeth at that point). I showed her the clothes that I bought Monday and she was appalled at what I'd spent. It's easy enough for her. She's tall and beautiful—long black hair, Cherokee cheekbones. A gunny sack would look striking on her. I hear defensiveness in my tone; she must be right. She certainly was about the tennis. What would I do if she hadn't dragged me out that same trip, short of breath and protesting, to learn?

Finally, word from Spencer. Finally, he came. He stepped out of the elevator into the apartment alcove wearing a rakish Panama straw hat and holding out in front of him a bottle of peach brandy.

"For you," he said. "I've had it in my suitcase for two weeks."

"In your suitcase! You're lucky it didn't break."

"I know," he said, touching my nose with a forefinger, "but sentimental acts are charmed."

When Sonia came back and saw him sitting there at the big open window overlooking the Hudson, reading, she recoiled with fear. Thought it was Harvey. Thought she was seeing a ghost.

Lying with him is now wonderful in many ways—warm, sexual, comforting. But when he sleeps, his face looks strange to me. Something is missing, something I can't name. In a deep place, a place Harvey reached, I am not satisfied. Spencer seems so pleased when I come, as if an orgasm—as if 400 of them—could release the yearning in me. It is never complete enough. I want to keep going, fading, melting, dissolving. I want to fall—freed—into the ancient darkness Harvey and I traveled.

Home again. I took Jordan with me down to the study tonight to try to work on tomorrow night's lecture. The windows were black and shiny, so I pulled down the shades, then dropped into the swivel chair at Harvey's massive desk. Jordan took a stack of books from the bottom shelf of one of the bookcases and lay down on the orange sunburst rug Harvey's parents gave us, his chin in one hand, turning pages with the other. I started to read, but he was chanting to himself:

> In the Center of the Night
> The Indian crawled outside.
> He ate a hamburger. It was soft and sweet.
> His feather was scratchy, fucky and neat.

I swung around in the chair, slowly, so as not to distract him. He was studying a Persian miniature in an old Metropolitan Museum of Art bulletin.

He snapped and buckled his earring.
He snapped and buckled his shirt.
So they both married each other
And lived happily together.
The Lady saw a ba-a-d horse
It was the Lone Ranger
She flied away.

Turning his head from the angel in the picture up to me, "How can she fly, Mommy?" Then not waiting for an answer,

When the woman flied outside,
Out of her bed nice and sweet,
She ate a good apple that didn't even have seeds.
Do you know what happened after the apple?
She did something silly:
She went upstairs and made her bed
And went all the way to the playground.

I couldn't believe it! He's never done anything like this before. I looked at him wide-eyed: this was the quiet Pisces child I'd dreamed of in my pregnant months. "In the Center of the Night"—what an image! Harvey should *be here.* Not for my sake, not for Jordan's—for his son. He's missing this.

When Jordan finished his "poem," he reached under my chair, deep into the dark kneehole of the desk, and pulled something out. It was a wishbone, the "lucky" wishbone I gave Harvey a long time ago, which he was always too scared to test. He took it to the hospital with him every time. Jordan wanted me to wish with him. We braced our thumbs on the bone, looked at each other, and pulled. The thing snapped in three! The center flew up toward the ceiling and landed on the rug, a miniature of its former self, and we were left holding equal pieces.

Fall

The air is cool. I am sitting on our narrow screened-in kitchen porch, with the plants, which must soon come in. GreenEyes is sitting on my lap. I wish she could come in when the house plants do, but already she is making me sneeze. Jordan is at the neighbors'. I will see him from up here, from underneath this potted palm where I am hiding, when he comes back. Why couldn't nursery school last four hours as I thought it would, instead of three? It changes my whole view of each day from one in which there is time for work to one which only fragments my efforts further.

The fall semester has begun. Last night I showed my class how to read photo albums for what they reveal of family dynamics—body language, predilections of the photographer—then gave them the option of using their own as source material for next week's writing piece. Seems like a reasonably good group—better than average belligerence.

I am beginning to get used to daily life without Harvey and actively avoid thinking of him, which I know increases the neurotic detours in my grieving. There are sudden strokes of pain, though, which put me back on the track. Today at the Ledyard Fair, amid the general confusion—loud country music, whining children, etc.—someone sat down at an organ and played very slowly the opening bars of "Greensleeves," our wedding song. I gasped, realizing I hadn't thought of him for an hour, maybe two. I turned around in a circle, trying to find where the sound was coming from. I couldn't locate it. Just then I saw my shadow in the dust—both

hands holding my head in distress—and was startled. Hadn't realized I was standing like that in public, unaware.

I can't deal with Jordan. He presses me past my limits and I yell at
him every day. The last two weeks have been especially bad. He's
gotten accident-prone, both small injuries and the knocking-over-
juice variety. This morning there was thirty minutes of screeching
because he wanted *only* to wear his filthy dungarees and shirt (full of
dust and manure from yesterday's fair), and I said he couldn't go to
nursery school except in clean clothes. Then he got all dressed, and
I gave him his orange juice, which he spat out over his fresh clothes
and the floor. I've mopped that floor *three* times in the last fifteen
hours because of him. Then the car wouldn't start and I had a lot of
trouble finding one to borrow. When we got to nursery school he
whined and complained that he had a boring lunch. I couldn't get
an appointment for the car for another full week and have to drive to
Providence to teach again on Wednesday.

Incredible, the things my students chose to share from family
photo albums: foster homes and arguments with mates and things
they wished they'd told a mother before she died. An energy is
coming back at me, but now what do I do? Should I work to
channel it, or will that inhibit it? Should I maybe prepare very little
and just trust my abilities to improvise? That scares me, because I've
always worked from outlines, but perhaps it's what is called for.

Slightly, all right, *rather* drunk, after a lovely impromptu dinner
at friends' here in the borough. I'm loosening up. Am encouraged
by the knowledge that I'm learning to recover. No matter what
happens to me now, that's a strength. I resented Mother's saying,
the day after Harvey died, "You'll be stronger for all this," as if any
amount of personal growth could justify what he had to go through.
I still resent it. But today, seven months after the death, hundreds of

months after the endurance of fear—and still in it—I do feel the
growth, the competence, the loping skill, the survival instinct, and
know it is not red in tooth and claw but great in beauty and awe. I
am sperm. I am life. I am thrust and hurt. I am forward. I am
shrink. I am go and wait and then I am grow again. I yearn for
Spencer—to prove, to show off, to display my life, my energy,
Harvey in me, spirit of my spirit, firing itself into the future, courage to pierce the void—I am that.

I am Harvey freed. I am Harvey silly—the Harvey he couldn't let
himself be I will be. I will let go, will love, will participate for him,
will thrill reincarnate. Will be him in miniature, in huge. The wine
releases. The desire rises. The convergence beautifies. (The child
moans in sleep.) Purity of camaraderie. Simplicity of flow, of automatic writing, of Spencer's notebooks, I know you. The relief of
pee. The pleasure of come. The homage of want.

Dark deep power, oh love. Harvey beyond. Harvey here. I mem-
orized your every cell, your well body, your shriveled body—were
they both yourself? I'll always know their touch. Two in one. Three
in one. One from two. Jordan ours. Jordan yours. Jordan his. Not
Jordan mine. And now it comes. This moment release the waterfall. Wash me.

Some kind of victory! The house is a mess—dishes piled up,
fourteen projects on the kitchen table and every desk, toys, film,
clean laundry, teapot, purse, keys, lecture notes, dirty laundry.
During our marriage, I always felt uncomfortable if the house got
messy. Something in me said, "You are bad because of this." But
today I actually like it. There is life around me. Hello, self, relax,
you're all right. I *can* live out who I really am!

Spencer brought Jonathan down on Friday night, and they are
still here. It is Sunday afternoon and I am at an organ recital at
Christ Episcopal Church. The music hasn't begun yet. Spencer
wouldn't watch Jordan and Jonathan because he wanted to write, so
I had to get a sitter even though he's there. It felt so good to get away

from them; my back ached from the tension as I drove over. I need the solitude of this concert to go into my heart, to get back in touch with myself. I avoided friends at the door, went to another part of the church. But now, damn, someone else I barely know has moved to sit by me.

The program. There is much to wait through until the Bach "Prelude and Fugue in E Minor." Is that "O God Our Help in Ages Past"? The Sweelinck has started—"Mein Junges Leben hat ein End." My youth has had an end? My young one's life has an end? Buxtehude now: "Prelude and Fugue in A Minor." Rolls off, runs like white caps on waves. I see a teenaged girl from chorus across the aisle. Her mother died in a car accident last month. How did I get through my first 26 years unaware of grief, even the grief of others? Do you have to suffer personally before compassion comes? In what other areas am I deficient? Air over, strict fugue chops out, drives steady. I love this. (Though the organ bothers me: the physical distance between certain pipes must be very great.) "Organist and Kantor," the program says. "Nicolas Kirche, Leipzig, East Germany. Late 17th Century." Kantor, Harvey A., 31, timeless, escaped from me like smoke.

Now Bach. The third pew from the left rear—my God, I'm sitting where my family always sat at First Presbyterian. Daddy passing walnut collection plates with the other elders, walking in step with clinking silver trays of tiny communion goblets. Loss. Loss. Harvey. Now I understand better the feelings of your youth, the grief of a Temple move. My love, my love. To hold you, rock my grief, my love to you. Tears. If only the nose wouldn't run. If only these people weren't here.

Harriet and Mike have come from Kansas City. Jordan was amazed by his five-month-old cousin—looked at me and exclaimed, "She can't even say 'juice and cookies'!"

For all their good intentions, so far I feel Harriet and Mike are here only because we're her brother's son and widow, not because

we're who we are. Tonight we watched "The Ascent of Man" together on television. Bronowski featured the stone heads on Easter
Island. I was thunderstruck: they looked exactly like Harvey's head,
dead—enormous, mute, eyes sightless but gazing with an un-
thinkable knowledge toward the heavens. The music, too, was in-
comparable—Allegri's unpublished "Miserere." I lay on the
window-seat sofa trembling, transported, shaking from the effort to
conceal what was happening inside me. Harriet and Mike chatted,
mundane and normal. Jordan nagged, "Mommy, fix this truck."

I am frustrated and irritated not to be able to call Spencer. The
phone registers busy, as it did all last week while Harriet and Mike
were here. When I see him he says it's out of order, but the phone
company denies it. If he wants to take it off the hook, why doesn't
he just admit it?

I sometimes have to remind myself that my life has externals.
That's why I like to make entries on my calendar: because really it
seems that all there is to me is the churning cauldron inside. I am
almost exclusively preoccupied with my inner turmoil. Some of this
is beneficial—scales fall from my eyes daily. And some is inescapable—a necessary part of grieving. But some, I fear, is excessive, is
unproductive, is emotional masturbation. I wish I knew when to
give in, relax, let the waves rush over me, and when to fight them.
    I miss Mother. I know it is a hard time for her too. I have tried to
call her almost hourly for the last two days, but there is no answer.
Mother widowed, Mother divorced, Mother decayed. Where is
she?

October 7. Daddy's birthday. He'd have been 62. I drove to
Kingston this afternoon to show Jordan the yew tree Harvey and I
planted on the URI campus after his death—yew for remembrance.
    "Grandpa John knew all the names of all the trees," I told him,
"even the Latin names."
    He knelt down beside the little tree.

"You put that there?"

"Yes. We did."

"You and Daddy?"

"Yes, and you were here, too. We have a picture of you taken on that day. I'll show it to you when we get home."

Jordan and that little tree are both three-year-olds, I thought, surprised at how much, untended, the tree had grown. I wished I had something else to set in the ground, something else to give to the future for my father.

Then we went upstairs in the history building to look at Harvey's office. The chairman had told me the department is going to turn it into a graduate reading room as a memorial. We walked down the hall and tried the knob but the door was locked. I hadn't thought to bring his keys. I tried the knob again. It wouldn't budge. Senselessly, I shook it. Then I stepped back, took Jordan's hand and walked back down the hall.

I finally reached Mother this evening. She had gone to New Orleans for a couple of days, to get away. She said she had her answer ready, though, if "snoopy people" wanted to know why the quick divorce.

"I'll just say, 'It didn't work out,'" she said. "And if they ask for more, I'll say again, 'It didn't work out.' And if they press me further, I will say, 'IT DIDN'T WORK OUT!'"

I know just how she will say it, too, with her lips stretched back in a mock smile, and her lovely white teeth clenched.

Jordan to the TV at the end of "Mr. Rogers": "Stop! I need you, everybody!" He appealed to them not to end, not to go away. I felt for him, for his little magical mind. After lunch today he sounded out: "Butter, buh, B." It's the first time he's done that! He said, "I thought about it while I was sleeping."

My own sleep is less clearly instructive, murky in fact. Last night I dreamed that Daddy was back with us:

He is alive again after one and a half years in the grave. I want desperately to know how his body has started up again, want to know for Harvey, for myself, but can't talk to him about it. Finally I ask Mother. She says, "His mind never died. His body just hibernated, and there's no need for oxygen, water, food, if the body is not functioning." He seems his customary unperturbed self; everything is normal to him. Mother even complains, "Now he has too much, you-know-what" (sexual desire). How can she complain? Just to have him back is such a miracle. I am worried, fearful that the stress of coming back to life, of having died at all, will be too much for him. I want him to have a psychiatrist for help, but can't bring up the subject. There is so much I want to say and share. Want to take him for a ride in our little wooden boat. He doesn't know I have a boat, doesn't even know I have a son—has missed so much while dead.

Then the others say, "We only found he was alive because his mother hired a black man with a Y-shaped divining stick. He felt his vibrations underground." African natives begin to reenact the scene. They bring him before the Queen, a beautiful witch-doctor woman with one bare breast. Her breast makes all the white people nervous; they whisper as they plan the performance. Daddy is across from her—his belly swollen as if pregnant or distended with "grave gas." He is female for a few moments. Then I am prostrate on the steps to the altar. I lie flat—begging? praying? Someone intrudes, picks me up. I hide my face.

I had forgotten that, as a boy in Kentucky, Daddy used to dowse. He could locate water underground with a forked willow branch, so people would know where to dig their wells.

How to go about this? Frightening thing. Deeply disturbing. Claire called from Pennsylvania tonight to tell me she had gone to see a medium about Harvey. A medium. I didn't know that anyone I knew even knew a medium. This is what the woman said:

Harvey had very large plans and things weren't right. He chose to leave life in order to start over and do it bigger. He chose to go it alone. He had several good reasons to take this death on himself. He appeared happy, but was not satisfied with his life. Often despondent. He has had a very long rest and is often near. Jayne, yes, for the spirit holds no grudge. He doesn't feel badly about their life together. This was a foolish woman. They are well and happy, Jayne and Jordan. Harvey will appear to her.

Well and happy! Did Claire think this would help? All I feel is more distressed—condemned, afraid. Can there possibly be any truth in it?

Sleep-starved, two nights short again, and again I want to die. I can't bear it that Jordan no longer naps. Last night, after my weekly overnight in Providence, I needed to sleep—cravingly, head-achingly needed to sleep—and he kept waking me up, calling out, afraid, four different times, until finally I couldn't go back to sleep at all. Please, please stop. Someone, can't someone take over for a little while? I am afraid I will kill myself. Why can't I find a regular, reliable baby-sitter? Jordan is so anxious when I leave that I feel guilty going at all, yet what I need is to leave more, stay away longer. If only I could cry.

A lot of this has to be premenstrual tension. Why can't I just step back and say, "Go to it, hormones, I can outlast you"? I want my period to come just as I want the tears to come, just as I want the come to come. Why is the orgasm so feeble? I don't think my orgasms are "orgasmic" at all anymore—not as they were, not even as my music is.

Yesterday morning in Providence I got up, already exhausted, expecting Spencer back from dropping Jonathan at school. An hour passed, slowly, teaching me he wasn't coming, had already gone on to Boston. Depression. Then slow self-will and a big effort toward independence on its way to success. Then he appeared, and it shook me. I was vulnerable again the second his foot hit the stairs.

Jordan asks every day in one way or another if he can have a new daddy. Today for the second time he asked if Spencer could be his daddy. I always say, "I don't know. I don't think so." I wish I could give Spencer to him and run.

Damn! I wanted to read Emily Dickinson on the garden step for two minutes while Jordan went to the bathroom before we left to play in the park, but he screamed something inside the house, sounding terrified. I ran up the stairs, three at a time. When I got to the landing I realized he was shrieking, "Don't don't don't you read that!" Damn it! I worked hard to built up an alert, receptive peacefulness—worked all day toward it, won it, then he ripped it from me. Now I haven't the strength to go to the post office, or the library, or to play football with him in the park.

Still no period. I am very irritable again, and deeply tired.

This afternoon I left Jordan in the care of a young sitter, the girl who lives downstairs next door, while I went to the library to work. Evidently Jordan got the plant-misting bottle out from under the sink and was spraying it in his mouth the way he often does—it's just pure water—and the sitter panicked that it was weed-killer or something and called her mother and the mother panicked too and the two of them rushed him to the hospital. They wouldn't believe him when he told them over and over, "It's only water. It's real plain water. Mommy lets me do it." It took double doses of Ipecac before the doctors could get him to retch. And then on top of everything else, they lost his night-night! We'll have to drive over there tonight to hunt for it. I'm angry at their refusal to trust him, at their overreaction—what they put him through. I feel guilty too; I hadn't left a number. Why, the only time I've ever failed to, did they need to reach me?

I've had a terrible dream, set here in my bed and on the dark stairs, as if it were really happening. Harvey came—was visited upon me—came for revenge.

Horror. I know he is on the stairs, but can't see him. I wrench myself from bed, staggering, trying to awaken. A vague dark shape is at the top of the stairs, crouched demonlike. I try to lean across it/him to switch on the light, but he grabs my legs. I start to fall down the stairs—must clutch something to keep my balance but all I can reach is his head. I'm afraid to touch him (cold?) but must. He is tangible, sort of, and warm, very warm. Goblinlike. He's a physical being but definitely not from the world of the living. I fear for my life, my sanity. I struggle to awaken, even as another part of me says, "No, face him." Then we are both crouched in the dark on the floor by the bed, facing off for a deadly struggle. I can never decipher his shape. His eyes glow red. He threatens me, terribly, undefinably, with obliteration, sharp suffering.

I awakened in real terror—like the episodic panic I felt those times right after he died. I am still afraid to go back to sleep. Know he is waiting for me there. Claire's medium said he would appear to me. I feel that what has happened has really happened, not in rational physical life, but somewhere. It was not a figment of my imagination.

I dressed carefully this morning, against the demon dream and against a queasiness in my stomach: dark red jacket with black pin-stripes over my rust turtleneck, and the rusty-red beret with shiny black beads scattered over it which I bought in New York. I kissed Jordan good-bye. When I walked down the hill to Stella's house for our backroads day-trip to Amherst, she exclaimed: "Boy, you really have to get up early to compete with Jayne!" I was too distracted to appreciate the compliment.

We headed north. "Look at that tree," she said, slowing the van. "It's red. Plain, primary RED!" The brilliance seemed fake to me. Last fall, when Harvey and I drove that same road together, our jaws dropped at the colors. Today I couldn't respond. After about an hour we stopped at a roadside greasy spoon. The sight of gooey doughnuts under a plastic dome and the smell of coffee made me want to throw up. I sipped a cup of tea, keeping one hand spread flat on the Formica counter, its coolness a brace against the growing nausea.

By the time we got to Amherst I was feeling better. We waited in the living room of Emily Dickinson's house with a little group to be led through by an English professor from the college. I looked at the piano and thought about Emily playing it alone at night while the others slept—weird full melodies which neighbors could hear when the wind was right. Startled by the guide's arrival, I stood up too quickly and felt sick again. What if I am pregnant?

We saw the kitchen, then climbed the stairs. I couldn't make myself listen to what the guide was saying. Then we got to Dickinson's own small room, where she wrote. Each footstep echoed on the bare wood floor. There was something holy about the space, as if we shouldn't be speaking out loud in there, should have removed our shoes. The professor opened a closet door and lifted out a delicate white cotton dress on a padded hanger. Someone asked my own question, "Is that really Emily's?"

"Yes," he said, stepping toward me, "it is," and held it up against my body. I shrank back, horrified at the intimacy of the act. "Your height and coloring are like hers," he went on. I cast a wide-eyed glance at Stella, and when the group moved on across the hall, we slipped downstairs and out into the air and sunshine. The trees were heavy with yellow-green pears. I touched their roundness and imagined Emily, lost in imagination. ("Wild nights! Wild nights! Were I with thee Wild Nights should be Our luxury!") From under the tree I looked up at her second-story window.

The professor-guide caught up with us.

"Would you ladies like to join me for a drink?"

I reached for Stella's arm, but she had already said, "Sure, why not?" We went to a dark-paneled English-feeling inn and ate onion soup. My nausea was gone.

"I sense your interest in Emily is somewhat deeper than curiosity," he said, looking at us conspiratorially. "Am I right?"

"I suppose so," I said. "Stella is a writer, and I'm giving a lecture this week." The two of them talked after that, and I tried not to think of Harvey. ("Renunciation is a piercing Virtue, The letting go a presence—for an Expectation.")

After supper, Stella and I sought out the grave. The cemetery would have been dark but there were bright artificial streetlights. I had forgotten Dickinson's epitaph—self-composed, scrawled on a scrap of paper by her bed as she lapsed into coma. "Called Back." That's all. The stone said simply: EMILY DICKINSON CALLED BACK.

10:30 A.M. More nausea. What is my body doing? I have felt consistent cramping ever since the Amherst trip. My period is now eight days overdue. My breasts seem enlarged—new lumps on the left one, which were never there before. Am I full of cysts? Full of tumors? Full of child? Can it be morning sickness? Please, not a pregnancy. . . . Please, not a hormonal screw-up either. I couldn't have another child. . . .

The Center cannot hold. Everything's breaking down. Wherever I turn, the physical world is collapsing:

    The car won't start
    The stereo blew
    The dishwasher motor burned out
    The oven is stone cold
    The septic tank is backed up
    My bike won't roll frontward or backward
    Every felt pen I reach for is dry
    The closet door came off its roller
    And *nine* light bulbs have popped in the last week alone.

Endure, hang on, ride it out. The worst is the light bulbs. Every time I flip a switch, another one explodes. I had the electrician out to check the voltage in the house but he couldn't find anything wrong. Said, "Oh, bulbs tend to wear out about the same time. Maybe they were all put in at once." But that would require them all to have burned the same number of hours! This will pass, I know. I just need to hold on. It doesn't threaten me as much as the demon nightmare. But what if it is connected to it? Wait. Breathe. Do not resist.

I'm home after speaking on a photography panel at the University of Bridgeport. The exhibit I organized, "Women Look at Women," just opened there. It's uncomfortable to be doing public things, things that don't acknowledge my inner turmoil. Feels hypocritical, especially when the theme that guided me in designing the show was women's private realities.

Three women in the front row heckled me when I used the phrase "the feminine." "Don't use that word!" shouted one. "'Feminine' means lacy cuffs and panty hose!"

"Look," I said. "Give me a synonym for 'that which applies to women,' and I'll use it," but they just stomped out of the auditorium. "'Female,'" I said to the rest, "we'll use 'female.'"

There I stood, glibly fielding questions, no hint of my ongoing battle with grief or current fears of an unwanted pregnancy—women's private realities if ever there were any.

November 6, Thursday. Positive pregnancy test. Fighting back tears at Birthright. Basement laboratory, subterranean, windowless. Green Naugahyde chairs. The woman's kindness: "You will need counseling—a second loss following so closely. . . ." She did not try to persuade me to keep the child. Behind her in the sworls of knotty-pine paneling I saw a fetus face.

I called Spencer from a pay phone on the street. All he could say was, "Faint," and again, "Faint." Then, "Call me at four o'clock."

I drove back down 95 to Connecticut in a different state. With child. I couldn't get my bearings, recognize exits. Grief for the child. Please don't let it be a daughter. I couldn't bear to lose a daughter. Unnatural twisted act. I could have stood it if I hadn't already borne a child, nursed and caressed him. Murder. Get a hold of yourself.

I am pregnant.

When? How? "Birth control fails us," the woman said, "because the methods are imperfect, not because we are irresponsible." Nevertheless, the consequences fall on us. Anguish. What soldiers feel when ordered to kill. To save ourselves we do it. Brutalizing ourselves.

There were moments of obscure pleasure today, all day, elation even. Conception. Spencer—our union manifest. I fear he may want me to have this child, may read my choosing an abortion as rejection of him.

Four o'clock came. I thought he'd be home alone, free to talk. He had set the time. But when he answered, it was like talking to a stranger. Monosyllables, distance. I asked if he could come to Stonington, to hold me. I need help. I need him here beside me now. I feel alone and sad and frightened. He refused. Said, "Maybe in a few days." A few days? This can't be happening. He is rejecting me. Now, when I need him most. It can't be.

Surely he'll come.

I just called the Wayfarer Inn—thought seeing a film would get my mind off Spencer. They told me *Ninotchka* with Greta Garbo is playing. That was the film Claire and I saw in 1971 the afternoon we confided our mutual suspicions we were pregnant. We had the same due date, too.

Abortion. It's not because I don't want a new child. I am filled with longing for a baby, remembering the times of rapture with Jordan and Harvey.

It's not because I'm single.

It's not even because it would insult Harvey's memory for me to have been sleeping with someone else.

It is simply because a second child would kill me. Would leave Jordan a total orphan. In this weakened state, I cannot properly mother even him, much less an infant too. Adding even the smallest extra burden—watching a friend's child for an afternoon—pushes me near suicide.

It is impossible. I would be destroyed.

Another day. Grading student exams, I find I have been writing "Spencer" for "Spenser," the English poet.

He has not yet called or come. If I were hit by a car, he'd come to see me either after I recovered or after I died.

The phone rang at 2:30 A.M. It was Spencer. How can he do that—wake me in the middle of the night, knowing how sick I've been? He talked only of himself. He said he and Jonathan would come today at 2:15 P.M. No show. The table has been set for five hours. I am giving up.

This is the fourth week of nausea. It's wearing, depressing. I wish they could move up the operation date. I understand now, the loss of will in people who are terminally ill. How can I be angry that Harvey gave up? I feel like giving up myself, and I know this discomfort will end soon. The physical discomfort. But I too feel little hope emotionally—am severely depressed and alone. The phrase "What difference does it make?" keeps running through my mind. It seems clear that the relationship with Spencer can't be counted on even on the most minimal level of friendship. He is unable to get outside himself. I still feel I could love him, if only I could see his mind operating on some subject matter other than itself. The main thing though, is me, not him. My inconsistency looms—to have begged the universe to spare one human life and now, myself to take another. I feel I am forfeiting my natural right to life by it. Feel that now, far more than before, I must show a reason for taking the space I take, breathing the air I breathe. Must prove myself. Must compensate for the baby's death. But how?

Claire met me in New Haven for lunch, she took the train up from Pennsylvania and I drove down from Stonington. I needed her support about terminating the pregnancy. Everything she said, everything, was helpful, and just the fact of her making the trip meant a great deal. We talked a lot about Spencer (she was compassionate but strong in advising me not to see him again) and some about the medium she went to. The scary message seems less condemning now. We lingered over tea and then I drove her back to the station. I was touched by her seriousness—she didn't make a single wise-crack—and as she ran for the train, long dark hair flying, there was a lump in my throat from affection for her.

Driving home toward Stonington, I got hung up behind a giant propeller. It was braced at an angle on a wide, wide truck—more than two lanes wide. For what was that designed? Impatient to be going so slowly because of my lecture tonight, I looked up into the rearview mirror. The setting sun behind me was a smoky orange disc. When I got home, I fixed a quick supper for Jordan and was back on the highway in less than half an hour, driving east again to give the Emily Dickinson lecture in Westerly. At virtually the same spot in my window, up there to my right, was another smoky orange disc—this time the full moon rising. They were exactly alike.

Later, when I got home again, I looked up at the sky and thought how Dickinson's spirit is as available to me in the starlight as Harvey's. Once you die, it cannot matter when you lived. I reached up and felt as if her two hands were warmly grasping mine, her energy running into me, her understanding calming me for what I am about to do.

November 14, Friday. Abortion day. Sabbath candles, which lost their meaning when Harvey died, burn on the kitchen table. Other-wise, the house is entirely dark. Jordan is coughing through a fever upstairs. I have never been this alone. Friends helped, at a distance—Stella drove me to and from New Haven and Sonia came from New York to stay with Jordan for the afternoon—but no one touched me. No one put a hand on my shoulder, much less a hug, a caress. Harvey, Harvey . . . I need you.

It was the reverse of Mass. General: they told me to strip from the waist down, to keep my blouse on. I didn't want to keep it on, didn't want it always to remind me of what was about to happen, but I did as I was told. Again I had to sit there half undressed, and wait. My teeth were chattering when the doctor finally came in and said, "Scoot forward on the table." My heart was pounding but I lay back on the paper and looked up at the ceiling. I spread my legs. The air was cold. I heard the snap of rubber gloves and felt the speculum inserted. A silver pointed instrument flashed off to the left. My hands were cold. The nurse put a blanket over my chest and arms. I clutched my hands under my chin and panted to relax. Injections stabbed and instruments clanked as they were thrown into trays. A whining, whirring steel machine was turned on. The pain was piercing, severe, not drawn-out like labor. The machine sucked noisily, unevenly. And then an intense yellow-white light appeared—something I knew as light, and could see, even though I wasn't seeing it in the normal sense. It was the kind of seeing eyes do when turned toward the sun with lids closed—black sunlight—but my eyes were open. I had seen it before, in a dream where Daddy and I were hit by a train: the mightiness of impact, which I knew brought death, had that same intense light. Could it have happened just as the tiny child in me was destroyed by the suction machine?

They went away for a while and then came back and repeated the machine-work. It cramped me just as badly. When they were done, I tried to sit up, but the nurse told me to lie back down, I looked "too white for her." Again I was alone. I heard a woman moaning in the next room and wanted to cry for both of us, but held it in. The ceiling had frosted plastic panels with fluorescent lights behind them and dark dividers. I was dizzy and for a time it seemed that I was facing a wall with clouded windows. Finally they came back and the doctor offered me her hand to help me sit up. I clutched it with gratitude, despite her Prussian remark: "This is what you get for having intercourse." The papers beneath me were soaked with blood. I put on one of the thick cotton pads they gave me, fumbled legs into pants and arms into coat, and somehow made it through the waiting room, avoiding the eyes of other women. The rain slapped cold in my face when I opened the door, and it was hard to keep my breath as I walked carefully to Stella's van. I had to strain to get up into the seat, and then I slumped against the door, bleeding like a hot garden hose (I still am; it frightens me). When we got home I crept into the clean sheets Sonia had put on the bed before she left and slept in deep exhaustion.

I dream of a doll's house filled with tiny living people unaware that they are being watched—naked women on the right, clothed men on the left. It is erotic to see them. I need to come, try to find some privacy in my dressing room (I am an actress), but there is always someone at the door. I grow frantic, looking for an umbrella, a pole, anything to slide between my legs. Finally I come somehow.

The orgasm woke me—a terrible twisting pain, as if my wounded uterus were being wrung out. Jordan was asleep, so I could cry. I wept for about an hour and a half. Wept not just for the baby but for my abandonment and that of the thousands of other women who have lain, bleeding and cramped like me, some dying, shoved out of mind by men they depended on. I've never felt the bitter sisterhood more strongly. The moonlight is cold, accusing. Spencer is probably out walking in it, his nose in his notebook, his hand on his cock.

Please, Harvey, come to me. Come to me, come to me, come to me, come to me, come to me, come to me. Have compassion: come to me.

I keep listening for Spencer's Volkswagen, keep hoping he'll change his mind, drive down.

There's the town clock again. I have heard it ring every hour this last week—1:00 to 2:00, 3:00 to 4:00—A.M., P.M., whenever. The slowest week—four centuries long. The nausea passed at once with the embryo, though. A reprieve, as if my body had been fighting invasion by Spencer's cells, and now could rest.

Jordan's coughing worries me. He begged for his bottle again tonight, and it was very hard to refuse him. I hate this weaning. And then when I finally gave in, I felt bad about that too. A rotten mother, incapable of either standing firm or giving in with love. And having just murdered my second child. "Self-esteem" a term applied to others. At last we were close, Jordan and I, and I rocked him back to sleep. I must learn to forgive myself. I am trying.

Will blow out the candles now, and hope for sleep.

Winter

The temperature outside has dropped. Sleet is clotting around the windows, but it's not actually snowing. Jordan's fever is still high. We both slept most of the day.

Jordan just awoke. This is his fourth day of 102 degrees and coughing. I comforted him, made him some apple juice, and rocked him back to sleep. I kept on rocking him even after he was asleep, pushing his hair back up off his forehead. Precious, cherished. I felt strong and giving all morning, truly motherly instead of motherly-by-default. My responsibility is great, yet today I feel stronger, strong enough, even, to raise him by myself.

"Power resides in the moment of transition from an old to a new state." I looked in the mirror tonight and felt myself beautiful for the first time in months. A resurgence of energy. I am through this. I have endured. Alone. I made it alone. I should be grateful to Spencer for belittling me, for failing me, because now I fear less. Something brought me through. I am thankful to the forces of regeneration, whatever they are. A dream helped.

In my dream there is an earthquake, a terrible disaster, maybe the whole world is cracking. Then an immense blue balloon holding 30,000 people rises slowly into the air. It tells me that what will make me happy again is a brown Baldwin grand piano. I find one in a ruined factory, open to the sky. I sit alone in the rubble, and play it—lovingly—and it is true, I am happy.

A cold moon, nearly full again. The whole sky is pale blue with it, gleaming, as light tonight as if the ground were covered with snow. Jordan's fever is down (although my own is now 102 degrees), so I could take him out, and we walked over to the news office for the Sunday *Times*. The air hurt my lungs, but it cleansed us both, and the moon clouds seemed to sing. Tomorrow I will take the stereo to be repaired.

It's Monday now. An icy rain again. I had chills all night, and my fever is up to 103 degrees—terrific headache and pains in my pelvis and hips. I thought I was getting Jordan's cough bug, but am afraid now it's some complication from the abortion.

I resisted calling Spencer, although it seems phony, game-playing. I still have a grasp on that thread of self-reliance which carried me through the weekend. It's weaker, shorter, but still there. I haven't lost it entirely. Come on, Jayne—400 more pushes and the baby will be out.

Fever still high, I drove myself to New Haven. The doctor's "sounding" started me bleeding again. She put me on Ampicillin and said that I can't go to Providence to teach tomorrow—have to stay in bed. Our boat is a foot under water from all this rain. I am too sick to stand in cold water and bail, so I screwed up my courage (my courage seems to screw *me* up) and called Spencer and asked him to come get the exam tonight and deliver it to my class. He said no, but he will come down tomorrow and try to save the boat.

I feel uplifted just knowing he's coming and hate myself for the malleability. Will he look me in the eye, will he touch me, hold me? Or will he be full of weird recriminations and projections? I hope he'll stay for supper, for the night even. All I want is an hour alone with him—an hour to make peace, to connect with each other again—at least to test it.

They came! Spencer and Jonathan really came! Spencer was distant, withdrawn, stood at the door to my bedroom and said, "I am only here to bail the boat," but at least he was here. When he came back from the dock, I pleaded with him, patting the bed.

"Please, come sit here."

"No, I can't do that."

"Please, I need you. I need you to touch me. Can't you just give me a backrub?"

"All right. But that's all. Roll over."

The backrub was harsh, painful. Finally I said, "Stop. That's not helping."

He sat back on the end of the bed, looked away. I leaned forward and put my head on his knee. He allowed it, but did not touch me. "It's all right that you didn't come," I said, "that you weren't with me through this. Who would want to be with someone through a thing like this?"

"You only called me because you wanted to torture me this way, didn't you?"

"What?"

"I don't want to be forgiven," he said. "I'm despicable. It would be better for you if we ended the whole thing."

I put my arms around him. His cheek was warm against mine, his hair sweet. "Look," I said, pointing out the window. "The clouds have pulled back. The moon is full. I'll watch the kids if you want to go for a walk?"

He shook his head.

I sat back on the fold of blankets and tried another tack. "What are you and Jonathan doing for Thanksgiving?"

Silence.

"Jordan and I are going to Long Island."

A self-conscious smile peeked through his sullen pose. "So are we."

"You are!? Could we ride down with you?"

But he wouldn't say yes and he wouldn't say no.

When they left, he refused to shake my hand good-bye. I made a scene, cajoling him, insisting, but he left me waiting there in my nightgown with my arm stretched out—in front of the children.

Why is all this necessary? If I'm willing to let bygones be bygones, why can't he?

Spencer has sent me a cold letter in which he both misspells my name and presents me with a little gift—a small white tennis appliqué. I can't decide which is the basic gesture—the thoughtfulness or the punch in the face.

I am suddenly furious, remembering he told me that his novel has a chapter about a bunch of high school boys who plotted to "punish" the girl they were sleeping with by perforating all their condoms so she'd get pregnant and never know how or by whom. Appalling. He says this really happened in his Catholic high school. The girl did conceive, dropped out of school and out of their lives. What hell there must have been for her after that! A child can drown you even if you have a loving husband. Did Spencer do this to me, too? Did he sabotage our contraception through some deep hatred toward women?

This morning, in light sleep, I was able to see Harvey's face clearly. We were lying in bed here together, wrapped in each other's arms and legs—close, loving—no reference to death. I knew it was only a fantasy even as I was dreaming it but was swept all the same with gratitude for sight of him. I can't now remember the look of him in the dream, only the feelings I had while gazing into his face.

I'm in a wave of appreciating him, missing him, overlooking the ugly months of pain and withdrawal. Remembering his laugh and the way he'd swoop into a room and grab me and whirl and laugh. We were exactly the right size for each other.

Tonight I am alive and wish I had some work of meaning in which to pour my strange energy. It's nearly midnight. Harvey feels very close. Our bedroom mirror knocked many times before the zoning meeting this evening—an inexplicable banging against the wall. I went in his behalf because he cared about protecting the borough. Then when I got home and turned on the TV, Jacob Bronowski was stepping into the mud again at Auschwitz—a rerun of the "Ascent of Man" episode we had watched and wept through together, lying on the sofa. I came upstairs and took out the necklace he gave me when "Women Look at Women" opened—copper and silver set with agates, rounded sections linked into a kind of cross. Made by an Israeli. The note tied to it said, "You have done a terrific job. I admire you. I need you. And I love you." That was nine days before he died. Why didn't I recognize it for the good-bye it was?

I'd give my life simply to talk to him, to hold him for five minutes.

Thanksgiving was blank. Jordan and I took the train to Long Island. Manny played catch with Jordan, bought him a real baseball bat, Nora asked me about dating. It was a bit like old times, drawn up around their table, but not really. The meals Harvey and I shared with them were before Jordan was born, so I had no reference for them both to be there. It felt marked-off, strange and empty.

"Set me as a seal upon thy heart, Love is as strong as death." I read this quote this afternoon in Viktor Frankl's book *Man's Search for Meaning*. He used it describing a vision of his young wife's face, as he stumbled through the puddles with other Auschwitz prisoners on a pre-dawn trek to their worksite. Then this evening at class in Providence, several of my students chose to read, in hushed voices, the ethical wills they had written for their families, and the last woman's paper ended, "Set me as a seal upon thy heart, Love is as strong as death." I walked to my car thinking, "I know what the verse is supposed to mean, and each of those settings took it out of the realm of platitude, but I just don't see how it can be true. Thinking about Harvey is not the same as having him here."

I didn't go to Spencer's house; I drove straight on home, and when I got back to Stonington, I checked in with the sitter and then walked over to the Eatons' party. I accepted a glass of wine and was about to take a sip when I heard a man behind me remark, "You know that saying: 'Set me as a seal upon thy heart, Love is as strong as death.'" I froze, the glass at my lips. Scarcely breathing, I set down the full goblet, lifted my coat from the stack in the front hall, and stumbled back out through the front door.

I am cooking potato pancakes. Big deal. Chanukah is nothing without Harvey. Even last year, scrunched into the little room on Pediatrics, we had a holiday. Every night all week the glow of candles transformed that modern cubicle into somewhere older and more comforting. Harvey sang really soft, so Jordan's voice would stand out, "Boruch atoh adonoi." The nurses peeked in, afraid we were going to set the place on fire. The room was decorated like a clubhouse—posters, mobiles, cartoons. Funny I should remember with fondness the cell in which things turned, irrevocably, for the worse. But I do.

For Christmas, we'll go to Bruce and Virginia's in Ann Arbor. Mother will meet us there, and Mary and Stephen. I am having trouble making a Christmas list. It's because no one is important to me compared to the ones who are gone. I feel no holiday spirit, no excitement. "What difference does it make?" That phrase goes through my mind a dozen times a day.

After the 25th we'll go on to Kansas City to pick a marker for Harvey's grave. Then we'll stay with Mark in Santa Fe for the week it takes for the stone to be carved and return to Kansas City for the unveiling. It won't be on the exact anniversary of death, so we will still have the real repetitions to face when we get back to Stonington, but it's the closest I can come with teaching.

I dreamed of my brother last night, on the eve of this trip to see him. A dream, terrible as the Old Testament God is a Terrible God:

I am with Bruce and a friend of his on a rocky, barbed-wire shoreline. We are out on a jetty. I look back behind us and see water through the forest as well. The shades of gray and green in both sky and woods are more lovely, more unusual than I have ever seen—forebodingly serene. I want to swim. There is a calm area, designated by ropes and buoys as protected. I am glad. I dive in with abandon, but hit rocks just beneath the surface. Stunned and scraped, I pull myself out, feeling betrayed.

We watch the sky. In the distance small fluffs of very black clouds are moving too fast. I point it out as danger—we should try to get to safety—but there is no time. A huge black cloud covers us in darkness, and the city skyline across the water suddenly glows end-of-the-world Hiroshima orange—buildings too hot for flames. The flames are yet to come. I cringe in anticipation of the shock-wave. Are we under attack from outer space? The water becomes a mile and a half of city streets. I scream involuntarily, "Harvey, Harvey!" I know he's not there, I know he's dead, but still he's the key. Death is certain for all of us in a matter of seconds or minutes. I don't cry out for him to save me but merely so we can hold each other. Separation seems worse than the inevitable burning to death. Bruce is a few blocks away. His friend tries to hold me, but his embrace merely hampers.

Then I know the only hope is Bruce's camera, left out there on the rocks—to get to it, to leave in it a record of the apocalypse for some future archaeologist (Don't I know the camera too will melt?). I climb out over the rocks, toward the flames, to get to it, try to figure out how it works. I get one picture only—of the ordinary street before me, no flames, nothing—and then it is too late. A great hopelessness comes over me, and I wake up.

Suddenly Jordan was with me, crawling into bed. I pulled him in under the covers and projected my fear onto him, worrying that he should ever cry out "Mommy!" in that same complete need and I not be there.

Driving from the airport into Ann Arbor today with Bruce and Virginia, I remarked, "Did I see a red bow on that dog?"

"What dog?"

"Back there, on that porch." I twisted around and pointed out the rear window of the car, but we were already in the next block.

"It was an Irish setter with a big red bow around its neck. Sitting up on the porchrail, that brick part."

No one had seen it. But two blocks later, we all saw an Irish setter wearing a red bow, sitting on a bungalow porchrail.

"Now there's a dog with a red bow," Jordan said.

I was shocked, but nobody else seemed surprised, so I kept quiet. The whole day has been like that. Tonight Mary and Stephen and I played tennis at a club which had blue courts—blue, like something out of *2001*. The snow has to be a factor—we haven't had any in Connecticut, and here everything is deeply white. It's like a dream. These seem like dream people—mother, siblings, three red chairs. I can't get *here*. It must be the snow, absorbing my sounds.

We opened presents in the living room. Mother sat so straight in her chair that her back never touched it, but she didn't criticize. Just sat there with her ankles crossed, making little lists and smiling, speaking only when she was spoken to. When it got dark, everyone but her went for a walk. There was no traffic at all so we walked down the middle of the snow-packed streets. The tire-tracks were icy and Jordan ran ahead to slide. He'd throw himself forward and skid on the stomach of his snowsuit like a stone thrown across a frozen lake, then get up and do it again. Nobody said much of anything.

Tonight we all went out for pizza at a local college dive. The place was deserted except for us, and we sat around two metal tables pushed together, with several empty places. When we got up to leave, Barbra Streisand was singing "The Way We Were" on the juke box. Virginia held the big glass door open for me—the others were paying the bill—then put an arm around my shoulder and burst into tears.

"That song," she said. "What you must feel . . ."

I nodded, unable to speak, grateful for her understanding. None of my own relatives seems to care or even to notice. No one mentions Harvey. We act a charade of togetherness.

Back at the house, the two of us sat up late, talking. She told me about her first marriage, and I shared my nervousness about returning to Kansas City tomorrow to deal with Harvey's mother, relive his burial. When I went in to brush my teeth, I saw my face was covered with hives.

Kansas City. Sharlene went with me to the monument company. They had nothing beautiful, individual, simple. They pressured me instead to buy something large and shiny-slick. I refused. As we were leaving, I saw it—a piece of white Vermont granite cast aside in a stone heap behind the parking lot. Soft and glowing—perfect. The salesman couldn't understand why I would want it, it was so plain. And when I said I only wanted it to read "Harvey Alan Kantor 1944–1975," Sharlene walked out of the shop without me. She was offended that I wouldn't have it say "Beloved Son of Sharlene." I feel very good about the choice, though, and am relieved to have it behind me.

Santa Fe. I can feel the world's swirl more here—feel that my hair, my arms, ought to be whipped out to my side from the momentum as I try to keep my balance. I just went out into the yard. There are thin strips of snow on the ground, and the night air is so clear that the stars don't flicker—they gong, gleam, constant full organ chords of light.

Spencer has faded. And Harvey, the good Harvey, has flooded back in where he belongs. I know his toes, his flat old instep. What do Spencer's feet look like? Do I care? What a tenuous bond is having slept with someone, even twenty times.

I bought myself a ring today—wide gold free-form band with a pale opal, made by a woman goldsmith here. I like everything about it. I am nearly ready to remove my wedding ring, and this will give me something of my own to replace it with.

Mark is chopping wood. I can see him through the kitchen window. Simple masculine things have grown exotic to me. Not the things themselves—I can chop wood, I think—but the way men do them. Shoulders, heft. Jordan is watching him, too.

I wish that Harvey were here. He'd have especially liked Bandelier yesterday—an urban Indian society. Jordan and I climbed up to the cliff caves, and I photographed out from inside them, the openings framed like eyes of a skull seen from the brain.

Today we drove up into the mountains in Mark's red pick-up and he showed us an amazing vast caldera—Valle Grande—a sunken plain atop a mountain where the earth has bubbled and then collapsed back. We pulled off onto the shoulder and got out of the truck. My jaw dropped at the unbroken expanse of snow—an endless moon of white. I ran swooping down into it, arms outstretched, as if at any second I would lift off into flight. It was like running down the broad hill in Assisi, in front of St. Francis' Cathedral. I couldn't help it then either, the site was too stunning, perched on cliff's edge like that. I ran there too with arms outstretched. Only Harvey was at the base to meet me, to greet and hug and twirl with the thrill of it. But then that stupid monk wouldn't let me in, said I'd been "disrespectful."

I trudged back up to the ledge where Mark and Jordan were waiting and had to shield my eyes against the sun glinting off the snow. I turned around before we left and looked out across the caldera one more time. It reminded me of something else too, but I couldn't think what. My trail was the only line for miles.

Kansas City again. The unveiling was today. People stood in two lines along the grave, facing in. Jordan was beside me, holding my hand through his little mittens. As the canvas was drawn off, he squirmed away, dropping to his knees in front of the marker. People choked. The rabbi read on. Jordan traced the carved letters of his daddy's name with a woolen-mittened finger over and over. Red and white puppet mittens. He scooped up some winter mud from the base and patted it on the white stone. When it was over, we stayed for a while by ourselves. I quit trying to comprehend. I just sat down in the January mud and laid my cheek on the cold sweet stone and cried.

As we left, Jordan pulled out the pebbles he had brought from Stonington beach—from home—and set them carefully on the marker.

Spencer met us at the airport. I was surprised and a little suspicious. He took us back to his apartment and put the boys to bed. It was already late. I sat on the sofa in his study, numb. Then he came and sat beside me, putting his hand on my arm. Too drained to protest, to inquire of motives or discuss the trip, I simply let myself cry. For two hours he sat beside me, rubbing my arm, knowing there was no room in the sorrow for him, permitting it. We slept apart—me on the sofa—and in the morning Jordan and I drove home.

A sour cast of light—brown, blue—came over my left shoulder as I awoke this morning—the exact light that hung in the room when the phone call came the morning Harvey died. I fought with the horror—pushed it down. This is the first time in eleven months our room has looked like this.

Stonington is oppressive. The limited horizon traps my eyes. There is no depth of field. A forced myopia. About noon there was a call that due to a communications foul-up at the university, I have no job for this semester. What will I do without the focus teaching gave my week, without my nice Wednesday, have-to-prepare-for, intellectual-effort, encounter-with-other-people, get-out-of-town focus? I am disorganized, floundering.

So I told the Arts Center I'd chair their concert committee after all. It's the wrong thing for me—volunteerism, fragmentation of energy, avoiding the point. But at least I'll be with people.

I made a big angel food cake for Stella's birthday this afternoon, just like the one I made for Harvey almost a year ago. It was a sunny, snowy day like this one, too. Did I make it again for him?

Jordan was on me like glue all day—never more than three feet away. Up the stairs when I went up, down to the office when I went down. He even tried to follow me into the bathroom. I am worried about him. He washes his hands compulsively; they are red and chapped. He must feel he's dirty inside somewhere—guilt because his daddy died? I've gone over it with him many times, explaining that Harvey loved him and would never have left him on purpose, that a little child can't make anyone die; but it must not be sinking in. Or else I myself am the cause of his symptoms. I am sick and he's too little to pull his sense of well-being away from my own.

We looked around for GreenEyes on the walk back this afternoon. Where is she? Three nights now we've been back and no sign of her. What if she has permanently given up? Even if she wasn't really our cat, her little cries to come in for a while in the evening . . .

A horrible day—huge contrary emotions—my self not mine to control. Early blues (every morning now, the light stays ugly), but I got over them, took Jordan to school, came home and thrust myself into a productive morning in the office. Then did some housework, anticipating the noon visit of a young man to interview for baby-sitting. He called, canceling, and my motivation withered. Retreated to the heavy warm water of the bathtub. Pulled myself out to go get Jordan. Tried to write letters while he napped, but grew weary with depression. Lay down myself, slept fitfully. Awoke with palpitations, acute spiritual distress. Felt I was whirling in the air, glowing red, laughing insane with pain. World about to disintegrate. Undone. Wild-eyed. Called Stella—had to see someone. She was writing, couldn't come. Started counting minutes till Christy due. Then she called, she couldn't baby-sit either. So I sorted dirty laundry. Keep your hands busy, Jayne, or all will be lost. Jordan woke. We went to the laundromat. Rational control now. Went to the hardware store for change. Discovered grocery money missing from my purse—$100.00! Baby-sitters? Left at bank? Toyota? Paranoia—freak-out. Can't control my own pocketbook. Mean to Jordan—yelling. Came home to hunt. Phone rang. The dean calling to say I have my URI course back—I'll be teaching in Westerly, start classes tomorrow. Suddenly very happy. Structure, order, ego. Doing fine. On top of things. Then started to run too fast. Went back to laundromat—folded clothes like a fast-motion movie, figuring how to find another sitter, fix dinner, plan class all in next hour. Managed. Then Arts Center board meeting. Overstimulating: film on New Haven arts group. Nervous to get home (late for young sitter and zoning calls), but had to wait for chairperson. She didn't have the stuff anyway. Raced home. Still speedy, speedy. Picked up toys. Must relax. But how? Yoga, I ought to do yoga. Lay on the big rug, began deep breathing, slow positions. Jordan woke, calling, "I need extra loving." I gave up and went to him, declaring the day a loss.

The young fellow from Connecticut College, who was supposed to come yesterday, arrived this afternoon. I have been trying to find Jordan a regular male baby-sitter. Except for kind Bill next door, he lives in a world of women—baby-sitters, teachers, my friends. But this young man does not seem right. He had a glass of water in his hand all afternoon, never set it down. Played with Jordan one-handed. And I was embarrassed by his vegetarianism, not his eating habits themselves, which I admire, but his insinuations.

"Can Jordan, at least, eat meat while you are here?" I asked.

"No, I'm afraid not. You see, I don't *touch* meat."

I felt accused. I am going to hire him for a while, but it will mean extra work. I can no longer say "just give him a hamburger" as I head out the door.

One of my new students explained in class last night how presenting her father with his first grandchild was one of the major thrills of her life. My throat cramped shut—partly in envy, but mainly in shared grief. Her father, a fisherman, was lost at sea the same week Daddy died.

Sunday, February 1: Death month.

Icicles are falling off the roof, their hold loosened by the sun, clomping, startling me. Melting—a hint of spring far off—will I be able to stand it when it comes? The second spring since Harvey's death.

The right side of my body seems missing to me, blackened, charred. Harvey slept on my right. I incorporated him so completely that with his death my own body image is altered.

I am nauseated from unspent grief, exhaustion.

I had my first meeting with Dr. Dale Kramer, the child psychiatrist, in New Haven today. It was right after lunch and the sun was shining, but his waiting room was dark—no natural light. Just one shaded lamp. A tenor was singing "Song of Norway" on the stereo. Two tense parents came out, and then it was my turn. His office felt sterile—Marimekko panels, obligatory plants. Can kids be comfortable here? He is young, clean-shaven, open-faced—will he know enough of grief? He claimed he's treated two dozen children who had either lost a parent or were themselves dying. His voice was soft and studied. He had good body language—legs apart—and wore a sweater vest and made some sensible remarks: observe Jordan's night wakings, try to get at his dreams. And he'll include me in the first couple of sessions because of separation problems. It seems all right for starters. I am more committed than before I went but still not sold.

Spencer called, asking me to Providence for Valentine's Day. The shift unnerves me—he's no longer holding me off, is actually pursuing my company. When I pointed this out, he said, "Your

common sense is finally overcoming my neurosis." I'd have to see
it . . .

Jordan didn't wake up last night or remember any dreams, but I
had another big one.

*There is an icy whirlwind in my room, silvery clear, blasting freezing
air as it spins, taking my breath away. Terror. It is Harvey's spirit.
Slowly the terror turns to manageable fear. I get more accustomed to
the whirlwind. It comes and goes, and I discover I have the ability—
through sheer will power—to cause it/him to appear.*

*Then I am in a hospital where the doctors and nurses are forcing
injections and drugs on me because they judge I'm going insane
under the stress of this discovery. I cause the whirlwind to come for
them, so they know it's true. I start to tell them I am trying to get
used to it, not destroy it, but then I realize they want to kill me, to
lobotomize, not to help. I mustn't let them drug me. Must save my
reason. Must escape, prove the truth to others.*

*I flee through a window, pursued by police. It is night, they're only a
block behind me—I can see the squad car's light flashing blue on the
houses and bushes. I run, very scared. Must get out of their jurisdic-
tion. How to hide? How to hurry? Roller skates? A scooter? Kids are
on the darkened sidewalk playing before bed. Everything is ominous.*

Valentine's Day, early. I don't want to see Spencer. He doesn't
belong in this week—the anniversary of Harvey's death. He didn't
know him, and he doesn't really have time for me or my grief. I feel
justified in keeping him away from this special pain; his presence
would profane it.

Last Valentine's. Harvey didn't give me one. I had found him an
antique—lace and cupids and a heart a foot high: "You are my one
true love." But he had withdrawn again. I knew the symbolism: not
sending one meant not loving. Bitter, familiar situation. Carry on.
But then that night, sitting at his desk, he grabbed my waist, pulled
me to him, and buried his head in my belly in apology, saying he
had looked and there was nothing anywhere that could convey the

magnitude of what he needed to say. I was taken off guard—so big an exception to the rule of his hurting me. Not like his yelling, "You can use this office as much as I do when you earn as much as I do and not before!" Not like his taunting me with the names of women he fantasized about. Not like his pulling away from me in bed.

I still don't know which to believe. Will I—will we—ever feel again the unquestioning confidence in each other that we knew before he was ill? How strange and blissful that instinctive love was. I want that love, want him to feel the power of my loving him. Please, Harvey, please feel my love. Me, yes—you had a whole campaign to punish me. But you . . . I can't imagine him grieving for me.

The princess glass. Thin crystal tumbler with a gold band. In New York, when I was worn out from teaching, he used to bring me Alka-Seltzer on the rocks with a twist, in that glass. What ever happened to it? Did it break? When? How can I not know? He used to care about me. He loved me once.

And Europe the summer before diagnosis. The Italian Alps. We drove up and up in our little car, lost in heavy fog. An inn, closed for the season, took us in. Floppy golden retriever. Vita Bath bubbles, warm tiles and towels—our first hot bath in ten days. Forgrantedly beautiful lovemaking, the simple sleep of children. In the morning, a whole sunlit landscape from our balcony. Pines, valleys, miles of beauty where there had been nothing but fog. Disbelief. Laughter—we saw our breath in the clear morning cold. Birdsong.

The left sleeve of my nightgown is cold—soaked from crying. Jordan just came up and found me weeping. I told him I was missing Daddy. He hid under the covers, then behind the door, then went downstairs and reappeared with a cup of orange juice to cheer me up. Sweet small person. I am grateful he is mine.

February 15, 12:45 A.M. Full moon. Harvey's 32nd birthday.
I still have not slept on his side of the bed—or even touched it

except in changing linens. I have tried to cradle his head between my hands on the pillow, but the bed itself is taboo. Holy? Or deadly?

I miss my young husband. Missouri. New York. His warmth, his joking, the zany unpredictability of his remarks, the total predictability of his support. Always there for me. I can't have lost him. A year—now, a year. A year since the angel-food cake with the surprises in it. A year since I refused to call him from the table to the phone for Claire and Michael's birthday call because the pain in his knees was so great.

Harvey didn't sleep this night a year ago. I feel his malaise next to me now. He paced, wild with a vague panic, driven out of bed by some last-ditch energy. A final trying to live—an animal, cornered by the butcher, stricken, but trying to escape—before the pain threw him down altogether. This was the night he commenced to die, the night that death hooked into him, started to draw him away.

Did this happen to him against his will? Or did he somehow desire it? Why is this the crucial question for me? Either answer is unbearable: the injustice if his life was extracted forcibly; the rejection if he chose to leave. Meaningless.

I am hot with grief. It bubbles out of me like lava, glowing flamingo orange, brighter than the sunlight on Stella's amaryllis this afternoon. Floating, driven up into the air by the hurt—I am even with the second-story windows. Teeth bared, squeezing blood out of themselves, hurt beyond sublimation. It's here—ordeal of mortality. Penalty of loving. Hurt Hurt Hurt Hurt Hurt.

February 16.

I walked down to the point this afternoon. Everything was steely gray. The water was lower than I've ever seen it—a low, low spring tide on the full moon. The harbor was transformed—breakwaters, Watch Hill, Sandy Point, Fisher's Island—everything standing taller than normal. I sat out on the rocks, aware that last year this time I was struggling to dress him, wrestling gray corduroy Levis over his knees, under his hips, racing the acceleration of pain, trying to get him to the hospital.

Looking west over the low water, I sang to comfort myself— "Who Has Seen the Wind?"—as I did for Jordan last summer:

> *"Who has seen the wind?*
> *Neither you nor I:*
> *But when the trees bow down their heads,*
> *The wind is passing by."*

And again something came over me. The clouds parted for a minute and the orange fireball of the setting sun burned right into me, as if in response to my need. Then as quickly as it appeared, it was gone and everything was gray again. I sat for a while longer, then got up and picked my way back over the boulders to the beach.

February 17.

Green daffodil sprouts are up three quarters of an inch. The unfailing fertility of the earth. Thank you. Caught here between Harvey's birthday and death day, it is good to see that the plants have hope. Self-confidence in the right to live.

Scott Joplin piano rags are on the stereo, and I am waiting for Jordan to come from school. *New York Times Book Review* and Bertrand Russell biography on the table before me. I have to stop at the Arts Center on my way to URI tonight. Last year this was the day I went there from the hospital to ask them about a Memorial Service, not knowing, consciously, Harvey would die soon; certainly not that it would be the next morning. . . .

7:00 sharply awake
7:10 one ring

Confront it. Face the memory. Hold his cold foot through the sheet again. Push his body to the morgue again.

Hospital
Call Philip   Get sitter   Get dressed
Kansas City   Must call Mike

Tell Harriet   Tell Sharlene
Earth shoes
Can't see
Call Mother
Died   Stand by
Philip parka
Ride in rain
Jawbone cracking
Un-sat-is-fac-to-ry
Gather
Go in

Corpse of Harvey
Even, straight
One eye open
Blank   Stunned
Not like sleeping
Yellow glaze   One eye gaze
Frozen distant
Lips black blisters
Tongue fixed, foreign
Rocking sideways foot to foot
Anguish Morphine never given
Forehead cold   Stun of touching
Hair, hair's the same
Stroke stroke
Stroke and stroke
Nurse in shadow
Bring up chair
Sit, stare
Fogle comes
"Get ahold"

Conference room
Dry harsh rigid curbed
Autopsy don't want, wrong, no
Must have
No
Must
Sharlene accuse
Rabbi permit

Alone collect   Whirl up Release

Back in room
Deserted   Utter
Harvey where
Body there
Open window
Where is roommate
Waiting spooked
Gray Gray morning

Alone together
Sit again
Soul-scalped   Gaunt
Plain awkward bitter blank

Nurse, want help wash
Yes hold and comfort
Do you know rigor mortis, sphincter let go
Hesitate, no he would not like

Time to go
Help lift to stretcher
Insist push him myself
Sheeted face
Nurse closes doors
Hold his cold foot
in my left hand
Push aluminum stretcher bar
with my right

Pass Pediatrics
Nurses, allies
All now know
no pain allowed
Faces blank
Blank as mine
Push to morgue
Butcher opens
Rubber apron to floor
Blood
Hold on to bar, refuse

Wait for doctor
"Stay with him, please
Not alone . . ."
Brown paper bag his things

As I wrote the above, sitting in this chair, I began to cry and then my body started moving to the piano rags. As I sobbed I kept moving, thinking hard of the new daffodils and the life force in us both. I made myself get up and dance, keep dancing, live, live, go on. I held my right arm straight up and leaned my crying face against it, stretched out my left, and moved through the living room in time to the music. I saw the sun gleaming in on the starfish on the window sill and danced harder and sobbed harder. The deepest pain was just about to show its face when the carpool car pulled up.

February 18.

Leading up to a big sickness, a tense day. Mostly there were problems about the piano for Sunday's concert—no money to rent a good one, and the Boston Musica Viva refusing to play the old grand at the Center—and everyone coming down on me, the innocent volunteer. By 4:00 P.M. my teeth were chattering from worry about the piano, poor ticket sales, and mostly from fighting for three weeks to deny the grief its full anniversary expression. At 7:00 P.M. to Stella, and Warren's for dinner. One and a half tall glasses of sangria on an empty stomach and then a huge plate of chili. I felt stoned—was acting outrageous, singing with Laura and Margaret— very wild and goofy, lots of old songs. Then I started singing alone from *The Medium*:

> "The sun has fallen and it lies in blood.
> The moon is weaving bandages of gold.
> O Black Swan, where o where has my lover gone?"

and cracked at that phrase into heavy sobbing. Then I got terribly dizzy, and felt as if I was going to pass out. I fought it hard, scared,

I've never been unconscious. Laura rubbed my back. I started vomiting, then gagged and gagged. I couldn't move—thought I was dying. Tried to tell them to get Philip, call Claire and Michael for Jordan, but it was hard to talk. I couldn't see. It was worse than anything physical I've ever been through other than just after giving birth—same as that haze and pain, and my womb twisted tight through this too, held in sharp contraction.

I lay flat for I don't know how long. Then Mack and Laura carried me, under my arms, down to the basement bedroom for some cool air. I was proud of the disconnected feet moving beneath me, unfelt. Laura praised my efforts. Stella stayed close by, too. Fear kept me conscious somehow, even when I couldn't focus, couldn't see.

The two of them stayed in the room with me for two or three hours. At midnight Polly brought down tea. I can't remember what they talked about. Only remember the beauty of opening my eyes and knowing, though the room still spun, that I wasn't going to die, was going to pull through. Stella sat on my bed the whole time, smoking, which made it harder to overcome the nausea. Laura lay on the other bed. Finally at 1:00 A.M. they started trying to get me up, and by 2:00 A.M. I was home. Stella walked up the hill with me, too fast, paces ahead. I can't believe I made it and then had the presence to write a check for the sitter. He said Jordan had had a lot of trouble going to sleep, had been very worried about me. I must have looked pretty awful because he said as he left, "Take care of yourself." There were big scummed places on my glasses—I could hardly see.

Bed. Spin. Sleep despite my efforts. And Harvey came to me. I haven't dreamed of him for a long time—a month at least—maybe since the abortion. He held me and it was all right. I dreamed all night. By morning he was both him and not-him, Spencer and whoever, vague loved-person. Lovemaking in a flooded garden I wanted to bail so the little plants wouldn't drown.

Harvey came to me. At my rope's end, the final strand of sanity about to give, he comes to me; and for the duration of a dream's embrace, *all this* is not, and I rest.

The
SECOND YEAR
The Desert Sighs
in the Bed

Winter Again

Earlier today: Jordan downstairs crying, "I am not not not not happy" and "I want my Momma to be happy." Me upstairs in bed, trying desperately to recoup from last night's blown gaskets and from my broken sleep—he woke me five times. Fury just builds in me when I am jolted up again and again like that. I can't seem to control it. I lay there aware of his desolation and my own and saw how plausible infanticide-suicide would be. I know certainly that if he develops leukemia I will poison us both. Finally, somehow, I was able to let go a little, and cried. It was so grim—his crying downstairs and my crying upstairs—the distance between us, my inability to help either of us. Actually, once I cried a little I felt better and was able to go comfort him, to make up.

I got him dressed and then dressed myself and then we stepped out into the side yard to see what the day was like. The sun was faint and I hugged my flannel-shirted shoulders. I turned to go back in and make some soup but the door wouldn't open. I had locked us out. I didn't want to ask for help again, especially after last night, but couldn't think what else to do, so I took Jordan down the hill to Stella and Warren's—shivering—to borrow a crowbar. The doors to Warren's garage were open. He was squatting beside one of his antique English motorcycles, working. I felt bad to have to bother him and hesitated before I stepped through the door into the half-light. He looked up, then stood up quickly and grabbed me in a big fierce bear hug. No one had said anything. It must have been compassion left unexpressed the night before. It took me so much by surprise that I couldn't return it or even properly receive it. He is usually so tense and undemonstrative, I didn't know what to do, how to thank him.

"Can I get on the vroom-vroom?" Jordan asked.

Warren lifted him up and I explained our plight and then he got the crowbar and we all walked back up the hill. He pried up a window and I crawled through and came around and unlocked the door. I thanked him and then he went back down the hill.

Stella called after lunch and said we could use her grand piano for the concert tomorrow. I have to call the movers before they close.

Climbing the steps at the Arts Center for the Musica Viva performance this afternoon, I saw tiny white flowers pointing up at me on tender stems—the year's first. They had taken advantage of a melted place the size of a saucer between two snow drifts on the south side of the stone steps. Then I realized "Today is Sunday, February 22. Harvey's Memorial Service was in this building a year ago today, Sunday, February 23." Maybe this will all be over soon.

I finally bought a new mattress pad. It's sitting here on the table, wrapped in plastic. Jordan remarked on the small yellow stains on our bed last week and I was embarrassed. Bleach doesn't budge them, so I bought the new pad, which has been on my list for a year, but I don't want to put it on the bed. Those stains are testimonies—of love, of pain. Tears and semen—the juices of our youth. Wild perspiration and drops of menstrual blood and milk from my overfull breasts. Blood from Harvey's gums and the black-staining saliva of chemotherapy. They are more than testimonies—they are actual remnants of his person, they are his molecules.

His plaid shirt, too—the one he loved. Tonight Jordan asked me to make it a painting smock. It seemed too final and mutilating to cut off those sleeves, too rude. What if he came back? Unutterably rude to have nothing left for him to wear. Jordan saw me moving slowly and went upstairs. When he came down he said, "I looked in the closet for another shirt of Daddy's for you to hug, but they were all gone."

I replaced the mattress pad and cut off the shirt sleeves. I guess external observers wouldn't know that I'm still dealing with symbolic matters—heavy stuff—on a daily basis. I'm tired inside. I've fought my way through this month, hour by hour. Only one day left and then it's March. I hope I'm not disappointed to learn I have to fight my way through March as well.

Much still to do—his books, the Reading Room at URI, our letters in the basement, the other clothes, the top dresser drawer, then answer condolence letters, clean out desk drawers, find that tape at the Historical Society. But today, this week, I can't.

Jordan fell asleep on the way to New Haven for his first visit to Dr. Kramer, the child psychiatrist. It's a real ordeal driving down there. We were about fifteen minutes early, so I sat in the parking lot for that long without waking him, trying both to catch forty winks myself and not to fall too hard asleep to waken for the appointment.

Jordan had to pee the minute we got in and as we left. I was nervous during the evaluation, but Jordan really seemed to like it there. He didn't want to leave, wants to go back. I took some of his drawings to give Kramer (showed him the figures with no bodies), and Jordan built with blocks, drew, and played with a fire truck. They spoke of rainbows.

"I saw one yesterday at Cass Lake," he said.

"Last summer, you mean," I interjected.

"Yeah! I had a pan on my head."

"Why did you have a pan on your head?" Kramer asked.

"To keep the rain away. There was two rainbows!"

"I saw a round one once," Kramer said. He held his thumbs and forefingers together to make a circle. "Tell me, Jordan, how many grandmothers do you have?"

"Two."

"And how many grandfathers?"

Jordan—quiet, helpless, "None."

At the end Kramer's eyes and mine connected warmly, and I realized how I've been avoiding real eye contact, especially with men, watching instead their mouths as they speak.

"K." I am now spelling "Kantor" to Jordan as I write—he's learning to print. We went to Macy's lunch counter after the session. I was worn out and a little depressed. Jordan had a chocolate soda, which he relished—"A"—but then threw a tantrum when I wouldn't buy him a football jacket he saw. "N." So we had to leave. He was hysterical. He calmed down once we got into the car. "T." I can't drive out of New Haven without reliving the drive home after the abortion, without feeling again the hot blood gushing out between my legs. Shaken from the death. Culpable. "O." We've been listening to records since we got back; I sat still for the first time in a month. We had a tea party and "danced" sitting down on either side of the Jordan-bench. "R." But just now when he went upstairs, my dull ache for Harvey opened itself again. I bent over the table gasping. The grief just grabs me whenever it finds an opening. It needs no trigger, the provocations having been denied their pound of flesh X times in the previous hours or days. Then the tears sensed Jordan on the landing and dried up, as they always do, like an erection going limp.

A nightmare last night about our brown Toyota.

I come out of Spencer's apartment and find my car all dented. Bad guys have taken it and used it as a getaway car and badly banged it up. Worse, I left my purse there (irresponsible) and they've taken charge cards, know my address, have keys to our house. Still worse, they have Mother's address and key, and I have to call her and tell her to change her locks. "I only left the car there for an hour," I say. "You shouldn't have been so naive in a city," she replies.

I have a definite aversion to going to bed again. Too tired to work on lectures or read and scared of the dark, I watch TV, huddled under my old down comforter. I am afraid to move around in my own little house, feel endangered when up and about after Jordan is in bed. I even put off going to the bathroom because of the fear—some vague fear. Is this another facet of grief or is it just a part of learning to live alone? I seem always to cry when I get to bed. And besides, it's cold. So I put it off not only with TV but with picking my face, eating yogurt, fantasizing conversations with Spencer in which I tell him to get lost. The last time I saw him he took me to a late movie I didn't want to see, and then when he recognized people behind us in the line, he stood away from me, didn't introduce me.

I've been putting off getting up, too. I waken early, 6:00 or 7:00 A.M., then don't get up until 8:00 or 8:30. I try to come then—not for sexual release, but for the convincing dream of someone close to me. It is always fleeting, unproductive, dreary. And orgasm is still painful from the abortion. I am lonely—a chronic emptiness.

Sears wanted $90.00 to fix the dishwasher, so I have been doing dishes by hand. Actually, I like it—warm water, simple order. I was placing all the plates together in the draining rack, all the glasses, all the spoons face down when the sudden resolve hit me to phone Spencer and call an end to it. I hadn't been thinking about him. I hadn't been thinking about anything. I was just washing dishes and it struck me that that was what I wanted to do. I ran down the stairs to the office—didn't even dry my hands—dialed the phone and told him it wasn't going to work and I didn't want to see him anymore. It all happened so fast and easily, I couldn't believe it. When I hung up, there were soap bubbles on the dial.

I feel sorry for the children, for Jordan especially, feel guilty to have put him in a position for another loss. But under the circumstances—Spencer's inability/unwillingness to participate fully—I know it's a step in the right direction.

I have had my first "dates"—all of a sudden—four in the last six days! People must have been waiting for the seemly first year to end. I shook with nervousness talking to the first. I wish this fear would run its course and permit me to relate to men as individuals—the same as I do with women. I miss those early encounters with

Spencer. I was never nervous with him. It is pointless to long for Harvey, unproductive, and I will not indulge in it. Not tonight. I have to laugh at the sudden plethora of males sniffing around. I figure this will last three or four months, and then I'll be left to my lonely devices once again.

Spencer called this morning and said he was coming by tonight after his class. I told him not to come but he came anyway, walked in just as Jordan and I were sitting down for chicken soup in the kitchen. I'd been afraid all day that he would show up, and it was just as bad as I had feared. It's been five weeks since I've actually seen him, and I felt nervous, heartsick, uncertain, resentful—on the verge of tears.

"The soup is great. You're great. I can change. We'll make it work." That's the kind of stuff he said, I have to give him credit, right in front of Jordan.

"There are things you have that I could never find in any other woman."

"Yes, just like there are things Judith has that you could never find in any other woman—which is why you don't ever actually divorce her."

He didn't rise to the bait, just got up out of his chair, came around behind mine, took my head in both hands, bent it back and kissed me on the forehead. I held myself tight. It is too dangerously soon to see him. I could fall back into his arms again all too easily. Twice more, he reached out and stroked my hair. He seemed cheerful and together—perverse that he was never that way before.

At seven o'clock I told him, "You have to leave, now. I'm being picked up at seven-thirty."

"I see," he said. I think he was surprised. He turned for a moment at the top of the stairs as if he were going to say something, and then he left.

I should have gone on upstairs to get ready, but I was shaking, so I just played softly with Jordan on the floor for half an hour building

Legos. When my date came, there I was, still in blue jeans. He had to wait downstairs with Jordan and the sitter while I threw something on. I didn't even take a bath.

It makes me angry that Spencer came here, subjected me to the tension of this encounter. I feel a powerful rush of desire for him now, and it nauseates me. He's not good for me. He's totally untogether. I don't want him. I don't. He's Pandora's Box. I want him out of my head. Go Go Go.

I went to a poetry reading tonight full of confidence, hoping to meet a man friends had spoken of. When I introduced myself, he put out his arm to draw toward him his new wife. So it goes.

A little disappointed, a little reckless, I drove then with my lights off (the moon is almost full) to a friend's thirtieth birthday party. The moonlight restored me a bit, but all the Stonington people left early, and I felt alone, alien. I watched people laughing and smoking cigarettes and couldn't seem to join their conversations.

Then I came home and snuggled with Jordan asleep in his moonstream room. I lay beside him on the red spread and saw how the moon singled out the empty rocker. Then I realized Jordan smelled funny. It's been a few days, a week? that he's smelled different. Suddenly I remembered how I could tell by Harvey's smell a day or two before he was going to get sick—each time. A shudder jerked my shoulders and I got up and went into my own room.

Now I am tired, and hoarse from overworking the Bach at chorus. Tonight's lesson: you never find something when you're looking for it. I had schemed: rolled my hair, dressed with care. A clean house, even. Now my lovely curled clean hair smells like a noisy party—smoke and peanuts. And I am still alone.

Yesterday was a special, warm day. Full sun. Purple and yellow crocuses in the yard. It made me angry, like a tease. A month ago it turned nice and then reverted to winter after I had opened myself to

spring. I won't be so easy this time. I refused to let it warm me.
Ignored it, wore my coat. I hate to see my skin growing thick like
this, but how else can I survive?

Singing Bach's B-minor Mass is good for me. The long licks, like
prolonged tennis rallies, are enormously satisfying. You can't let
down: the pressure is unrelenting and there is little recovery time.
But the feedback is swift and sweet when you make it through each
stretch. I have been going to the extra children's rehearsal Mondays
after school, trying to learn this piece—not just the notes, but what
it means. I sing the "Et Resurrexit" with a certainty I could only
have feigned in earlier years. It is important to me to believe in our
eventual reunion. Must I give up this hope before the grief will let
go of my spirit's throat?

It is still warm out. I think of Harvey's body thawing now, smell-
ing, but not really rotting. I wish they hadn't embalmed him—they
said they had to, we couldn't cross state lines without it. It bothered
me in the winter to think of him frozen, ice-hard, like a piece of
beef you take from the freezer with frost on it—so hard it would
break a knife blade. Not just lifeless or cold, but thoroughly un-
fleshlike, unyielding, impenetrable. A boulder—*not* him.

A rush of pain?—gratitude?—what? Going through medical bills
for income tax (I have to get it done early because Jordan and I will
be in France visiting the Bronsteins), I came across all the credits for
blood donations people gave, even after Harvey died. They gave
more than he used, so the hospital extended us credit toward other
things and charged us less. Tears. Dickinson writes of the staple into
the heart that grief is. Oh when will the hurting stop?

Today is Purim, the holiday that celebrates Queen Esther's having saved the Jews from Haman's genocidal scheme. Will I talk to
Jordan about it? Will I tell him that the Jews, spared, were then

permitted to slaughter Persians in retribution? I used the last of the matzoh meal to coat pork chops tonight—incongruous, expressing both my loss and my new freedom. I haven't made a matzoh ball since Harvey died, and may never again, after six years of every Friday night.

I saw Kramer by myself today. He said that Jordan deliberately keeps Harvey's death alive (the fireman games, for example) and that he must stop it, must be helped to stop it by working through the "neurotic conflict." He said Jordan must give up his daddy, must let go. Says he feels guilt for the death, since that is the only framework in which it is explicable. I don't know. Much of what he said sounded awfully pat—the fire-truck hose/daddy phallus equation, the necessary anger, the guilt. Must recovering from grief exclude still loving, needing, remembering someone? I want him to be happy, but I don't want him to lose Harvey any more than he has already.

This morning he told me a dream:

"*A monster was tying up Oscar, but not Rabbit and me. Then he went downstairs and out to 'Miksouki' (Missouri?), where all the monsters and witches live far far away.*"

"*All the pretend scary things?*"

"*Yes, and Santa and bad goblins and 'Lukies.'*"

"*What are Lukies?*" *I asked, thinking leukemia.*

"*Big, big, BIG bad monsters. And the witch in Snow White lives there.*"

Tomorrow he'll be four years old.

For his birthday Jordan asked me to make a rice dish with salami and peas and shrimp—a favorite of Harvey's too. He had four kids over, balloons and cake, the works. Afterward, I was lying in the bathtub, stretched out, looking at my feet propped up at the end, and a memory of Harvey, of us together—a good one—flooded over me. I was soaking like that in New York, and Harvey walked into the bathroom reading me something out loud from a magazine. He glanced down and stopped mid-sentence. Then he tossed the magazine over his shoulder and climbed in on top of me, clothes and all. Laughing, kissing, rolling crowded in the deep warm water, his jeans and shirt plastered to both of us.

It would be so easy to open the long veins on my arms.

Our passports arrived in the mail today. Jordan's picture looks scrubbed and innocent, and my face shows nothing of the exhaustion I feel inside. The dates on mine are peculiar, though. The line marked "Issue date—Date de déliverance" is March 11—Jordan's birthday. Jordan: issue of my body and my deliverance as well? The "Expiration date—Date d'expiration" is March 10—Daddy's death day. I notice correspondences like this far more than I did before Harvey died. In fact, I never used to notice them at all. Did they not occur, or was I simply oblivious? Or do they still not exist in any objective way, claiming meaning only through the lens of my private need?

In any event, we're ready to go. Paris. I wonder how Jordan will react to everyone's speaking French. I feel happy as a parent, but unexcited on my own behalf.

At Sunday's rehearsal I looked past the conductor and saw a figure sitting in the shadows of the last pew, alone. It looked just like Harvey. I jumped inside, nearly bolted from the risers to run to him. Then I remembered seeing a man back there somewhere as I came in. Still, it seemed to me to *be* Harvey, and I thought if he were visiting me, this would be the ideal time—when I am singing and am most fully myself, most full, period. Bach.

The "Crucifixus" bored into me at tonight's concert. "Passus et sepultus est"—the notes descended at the same pace as Harvey's casket was lowered into the ground. It was hard to shift to the sudden, certain brilliance of "Et Resurrexit" a few bars later. The whole concert wrung me out. It has been a great privilege learning this Mass—I am enlarged by it, and cosmic-scale events seem possible under its influence.

Tonight—March 29—eve of our seventh wedding anniversary and the trip to France. I had to move the brown cardboard box that holds my wedding dress to get to the big suitcase in the storage bin under the eaves at the top of the stairs, and I held it in my hands for a moment. Then I sat down on my sewing bench and lifted the top off. Creamy satin, re-embroidered lace. I reached over and turned on the light. The gown had been folded into a box too small for it—it was crushed, like a white flower dried between the pages of a heavy book. I wiped my hands on Harvey's bathrobe and lifted the dress up by its shoulders. An index card slid to the floor: "I no longer have room for this. Mother." She sent it to me right after Harvey died. I slipped the card into the oval wastebasket which catches broken threads and held the gown against my waist. The row of covered buttons ran up my chest—the pliant spine of a young girl's dreams, I thought. I turned the dress over on my lap and let my fingers play up and down the buttons—tiny mushrooms, babies' bottoms. I looked back into the box. The veil was wadded in the bottom. I wanted to put it on and be transformed into the person I was that day, but it was too wrinkled. That's what I wanted to do the day of the Memorial Service, too—wear my wedding dress. I wish it were a custom to do that.

Tomorrow we leave for a month in France. Maybe something there will help me to understand.

Spring

The plane was hot and cramped and dry—eight hours of awfulness during which neither of us slept. It was great to get out of there into Orly Airport and see the Bronsteins' friendly faces waiting for us. Joshua was only a baby when we last saw them, and now he's six. Adam wasn't even thought about. The boys and I piled into the back seat of the Renault and Danielle and Marcus sat in front—everyone talking a mile a minute about something different, the children squabbling about who gets a window, Marcus describing physics at Orsay, Danielle her research schedule at the Bibliothèque Nationale.

"I want my night-night," Jordan said.

We went first to the Bronsteins', then drove here to the apartment we're to "sit" and now Jordan is singing to himself in his bed in the next room and I am sipping from a mug of herbal tea. The apartment is simply furnished but very chic—also rather far from the center of the city.

It is incredibly warm tonight—probably 70 degrees—the first real day of spring. The sidewalk cafés just opened this evening, and people are sitting out, everyone feeling the specialness of the new season. A sliver of moon is bright in the sky over hazy lights. I look forward to the coming month, to this change of place and pace. I intend to think freshly and am glad we came.

Neither Jordan nor I slept again last night—jet lag, culture shock. We stayed inside this morning until we got hungry. Then we sort of tiptoed out into the neighborhood and successfully acquired a carton of milk and some coffee, a baguette and some blood oranges, which I had never seen before—they have dark red veins and outlines. We brought them back and squeezed sweet, fresh orange juice, ate, and then went out again and I bought a Carte Orange bus pass and a map and figured out how to get us back to the Bronsteins' via public transportation.

It was a long ride in, maybe forty-five minutes, but people who boarded the bus talked to us and smiled—they liked Jordan's jeans jacket with the spangles and rainbows and candy-bar-wrapper emblems. I couldn't understand all of what they said, but their smiles made us feel welcome.

We got off at the Église Américaine, where Jordan will go to nursery school with Adam for the next three weeks, and walked in away from the Seine toward Passage Jean Nicot. The street was empty. It felt good to have gotten there on our own, and the afternoon sun was warm, and those people had been so friendly.

We held hands as we walked and sang "Side by Side." Then Jordan broke away from me and bent over the water-filled gutter.

"Mommy, look! A fish!"

"What?!" I bent over the murky water.

"I saw it! I saw it swim by. It went that way." He pointed behind us. I walked with him back down along the gutter and looked, but I didn't see anything.

"I saw it," he repeated certainly. "It was a goldfish."

"I believe you. I do," I said, and wanted to.

A horrible midnight thing. Jordan fell out of his bed and started screaming. I ran to his room, held him, talked to him, but he wouldn't wake up, wouldn't open his eyes. Just kept shrieking, "Don't leave me with a baby-sitter! Don't leave me with a baby-sitter!" and wouldn't open his eyes. He was waking the neighbors, I knew, but I couldn't reach him, couldn't get him to quiet down. I shook him, but it just went on and on—a total freak-out. "Don't leave me with a baby-sitter! Don't leave me with a baby-sitter!" I got frantic, then angry, then more frantic still. I couldn't wake him up.

There was a big knife in the kitchen. Maybe both of us. . . . Finally it ended, I don't know how. The hysteria ran its course and ended and he fell asleep. Exhausted, defeated, I slept too. We both slept till noon.

Jordan was in tears when I picked him up from nursery school. His teacher had forced him to do a "painting for his daddy" along with the other children. She hadn't listened when he tried to tell her.

I don't know where to start on this. I wanted to go to a chamber concert last night, but I was exhausted. The prospect, however, of dealing with Jordan and the Bronstein kids all evening seemed more exhausting still. So since Danielle offered to keep Jordan there, I go off in the rain and darkness to find the church of St. Médard. I get on what I think is the right bus, but it doesn't follow the route indicated in my guidebook—construction detours or something. Confused, I get off. The rain is cold. It is a deserted section of town. I ask directions of the only passerby I encounter. "Cette voie, je crois." I walk about four blocks in the direction he points. No church. "I'm lost," I think. I see a bar—cross the street, go in, and ask again. They don't know. Cold rain again, alone. "Walk fast, act like you know where you're going. Don't look at your map. Watch the alleys. Don't shiver." A few blocks later I ask again, a man with his arms full of newspapers, and follow his directions. Nothing. "Why do people give directions if they don't really know?" Unexpectedly a plaza opens up—the warmth of people: St. Médard, the concert. I squeeze happily through the door between men in overcoats. Candles, warm breath, crowded, happy talk. I find a single seat on the right near the front.

The music is mesmerizing—the finest ensemble playing I've ever heard. Chamber Orchestra of Bernard Thomas. How can they play so softly and clearly at the same time? The breath of the people around me catches, holds itself. I feel transported—my mind lifted or lowered somewhere it doesn't recognize. The universality of music. International. Interplanetary . . . I start to cough, can't stop. I slip out of my seat and into the nearest doorway—a paneled sacristy. Robes hang on hooks and there is a list of coming marriages. A place to prepare the spirit. A closet with a foul-smelling hole in the floor makes a toilet.

After the concert I cannot get a cab. Men step ahead of me and claim the few there are. I am afraid of the Métro so late at night. I walk over a block to a bus stop. I wait in the rain a long time. Some men come by and look at me and say something I cannot understand and laugh. I walk away briskly—up a block to another stop—and wait again, nervous. Twenty minutes. A strange man comes to wait beside me, with two shopping bags. Suddenly I see that he is rubbing himself against the wet stone building. Frightened, I run to the middle of the street—run two blocks, three—my feet echoing. Where is the bus? Forty minutes now. Where am I? No taxis, no cars, rain-dark city. Midnight. Lost, lost, too frightened to think, panting. Then a car, an off-duty cab. I wave it down. Two men in front. One speaks broken English.

"Oh please take me home."

"Of course, get in."

Relief. "Eleven, Passage Jean Nicot."

Banter between them in French. One is Algerian, one Moroccan. More talk. Confusion.

"What does your husband do?"

"My husband?"

"You are married, are you not?"

"Yes. My husband is . . . a teacher."

"Come with us to a party."

"No, I must go home."

"No, come with us. We'll take you home in the morning. We can have a good time."

"No, I mustn't, please take me home."

They are driving faster and faster, not slowing for intersections. My hand clutches the door. Stay cool. Pretend not afraid. Faster, careening, crazy turns, disorientation, which way is home? Panic—

finally an intersection with other cars. I must get away. I jump out, they try to stop me. Moroccan opens his door, reaches for me. I dash to an island in the center of the street where a man in a raincoat stands under the street lights, a bus stop.

"Aidez-moi, s'il vous plaît! Les hommes . . ." I point. "Aidez-moi!"

The taxi men stand outside their cab watching me, arms folded. The man with the raincoat tries to understand. I am in a panic, can't think, can't even read the bus number signs.

"Numéro 6? Église Américaine?" I beg.

Finally, the man takes my arm, walks me across the intersection—many streets come together there—to another bus stop where a woman stands. The taxi men jeer and wait. A bus comes. Number 6. I get on, still afraid. They know my address—they are following the bus. What will I do when I have to get off and walk more dark blocks? I turn and look out the back. They are still following. Now I can't see them. Must get off and run. Here's the Église. I tear off the bus. Run run. Save Jordan. The lock the lock. Danielle, Danielle.

I throw myself on the bean bag chair shaking, unable to open my eyes. Appalled at what has happened. I have been in danger and have panicked. I couldn't plan, couldn't even read the signs. I stammer out what has happened to Danielle. She sits in her nightgown and listens. Then I am so tired I cannot move, too tired to open my eyes. Too tired to wake Jordan and take him back to our apartment. Ready to give up. I sleep on the floor in my clothes.

Today I found out that most buses in the city stop running at 9:30 P.M. If only I had known.

Palm Sunday. It's warm and fresh out—exactly like the day Harvey and I carried new baby Jordan out to the Edwards' land and took off our shirts in the sunlight, basking in parenthood and the heat on our skin for the first time after the cold winter of waiting and Daddy's death.

Tulips are up, thousands of them, but Marcus and Danielle have been bickering. Marcus is "ennuyé" and so am I. We're somewhere southwest of Paris right now, after picnicking in a mediocre section of the Rambouillet woods, not far from where Harvey and I fell asleep beside a stone wall six years ago. I am sitting in a red-striped chair under an awning at a café, waiting to order, thirsty. Across from me is a boring, bothering, something's-not-right, everything's-too-plain château—which the others are touring. I have the cramps.

I am missing missing missing Harvey. Hurt is in the air. I expect to be telling him all my little observations. Everything reminds me of him—the Greek olives in this salade niçoise, the taste of the beer with lunch. This morning I even thought of his farting, how it never smelled.

The fathers are out again. It's Saturday. Weekdays, all I see are pregnant women, walking in the sunshine. The warm wind presses their dresses (graceful milles-fleurs print knits) against rounded bellies. But Saturdays, it's men with kids carried on shoulders, kids with balloons. I walked down St. Germain dodging them, trying not to cry out.

Twenty minutes in the sun here in the Courtyard of the Cluny have restored me, though. I feel like myself today—pain and all. Jordan is off with the Bronsteins, and I am wearing old jeans, a soft white cotton shirt with a new red T-shirt underneath and my green army jacket. I like myself more when I wear this. I am sitting cross-legged on a park bench, gray pigeons cooing beneath me. A nice-looking fellow across the square is sketching all of us.

Death dreams persist.

Bruce is dying—badly. Mother says, "It's certain." We clutch each other in the hospital hallway outside his room. Daddy has been exhumed and brought back to life with a pacemaker-respirator worn

*under his suit. He says it takes tremendous effort—would be too
taxing to endure again. Bruce is also kept going by a device like this.
I see them sitting "normally," side by side—near-corpses kept alive
only by machines.*

Danielle and I went out to dinner last night at a bright noisy
brasserie called Au Pied du Cochon. She said the most astonishing
thing. Broken bread in hand, suddenly fighting back tears, she
blurted out, "You're the most integrated person I have ever known."
I immediately choked on my wine and she had to get up and pound
me on the back. It was just like a *New Yorker* cartoon. How can she
say that, especially after the other night? Doesn't she know the toll
this charade of sanity takes?

I have stopped for lunch in a small second-story restaurant. I
spent a couple of hours this morning sifting through files of old
pictures at a photographic library. I paid for half a dozen or so, put
them in a paper folder under my arm, and walked out. A short fat
man in a black overcoat—he looked like Alfred Hitchcock—followed me through the door. I turned left at the Seine, looked back,
and saw he had turned right. I walked along until I came to a
footbridge to the Right Bank. I was about to cross but then I saw the
sign, PONT DE SOLFERINO, and stopped. Harvey and I used this
bridge every day when we were here. At home there is a snapshot of
me leaning against the railing, coral skirt and Indian moccasins,
squinting. I felt a chill—if I tried to cross, maybe I would meet
Harvey's spirit out there, or that of the girl I was in the photo. I
looked in the direction the man in the overcoat had taken. The river
was sparkling. I hadn't meant to find this bridge. I took a few steps
forward onto it. Nothing happened. I walked to the center. Still
nothing. I looked down over the rail. A boat was pulling an empty
barge over the dark water. Still, nothing happened. The cement felt
strange under my shoes as I crossed the rest of the way. . . .
A man has sat down across from me. Kind looking, elegant. He is

reading a *Herald Tribune*. I want to ask him for his paper when his food comes. . . .

Luck. The man across from me at lunch set aside his paper and I asked to see it. We chatted a bit. He's financial manager for Paris Cartier and after lunch he invited me to see their boutique around the corner. We walked, laughing, close. The shop was closed, though, so we parted, but both of us looked back at the same moment and again we laughed. I feel I could start something if I showed up at that restaurant tomorrow. That would be too bold, though. Maybe day after tomorrow? He's British—I don't know his name. I am curious about businessmen, tend to write them off at once. I didn't even look to see if he wore a wedding band.

I am actually sitting in the same restaurant as yesterday's lunch. The importance of this gesture—its boldness on my courage-spectrum. Who was it who said to me: "You must find your own life—go out and look for it. Life doesn't just happen to a person"? I disagreed. It seems to me that an enormous amount of one's life is decided by happenstance and very little can be governed. But I do admit the necessity of openness to experience and voted for that attitude with my bus ride here, this food I'm having trouble eating. . . .

I had arranged with the Bronsteins' *au pair* to take Jordan home when she picked up Adam, so I had a couple of extra hours after lunch, for shopping. I couldn't seem to bring myself to buy anything, though. There's too much to choose from in Paris and so I choose nothing. I am waiting inside. I have a recurrent feeling of preparation—for what, I don't know. For some enormous task or gift. For death. For insight. For discovering my life's work. Maybe it's just the normal consequence of a life torn down and not yet rebuilt. But I can't deny a feeling of watching for signs. Buying things just doesn't seem to fit.

On the way back to the Bronsteins', I heard someone playing musical scales. Looking up, I saw a young man practicing the saxophone on a fourth-floor roof garden, sunlight glinting from the silver instrument. Then a whirring screech. A woman on the sidewalk across the street was sharpening knives with a spinning-wheel device attached to a bicycle frame. At the end of the block, in an inner courtyard, a gray cat like GreenEyes was sleeping on the warm hood of a car.

My only real days—days when I feel whole—are ones when I have a large block of time to myself. The thoughts which need formulating can't seem to find their way out otherwise. Today I photographed stone eagles at opposite ends of a long official courtyard. Behind each bird was a tree, pruned barren and silhouetted against the sky. One, though, had tiny buds lacing it. I shot them in sequence, bracing myself each time against the wall across the street, trying to hold the alignment of the frames exact. I will print the negatives side by side, so they look like mirror images, the birds facing one another. It will take close observation to catch the buds on the right, to see that something more is being groped for, something about time and renewal.

I have just overheard through the walls of this apartment the most incredible, extreme lovemaking grunts and exclamations—very animal, very natural, very beautiful—and my body swelled as they came. They came together—you could hear it. The rocking bed and the escalating love moans. A full orange moon over Paris tonight.

Our apartment-sitting deal drew to its scheduled close today, but Stella's friend Michel offered us refuge in his place while he's away for the long Easter weekend, so I can put off hotel expenses for a little while longer. I had a start just now, however, returning to his apartment with groceries for Passover and a bunch of red tulips. Just across the street is the Auberge Basque. I have deliberately avoided sentimental spurs from the trip with Harvey, and where do we wind up staying? Directly across the street from the restaurant where we ate most often.

We had a lovely Seder last night, though there was a certain irony that I, the Gentile, was preparing Seder for the Bronsteins. I couldn't find any Haggadahs in the bookstores, so it was just me telling the story of Passover to Jordan, Adam and Joshua. Jordan was very upset about the lamb that had to be killed and the little Egyptian children who died. His lip trembled as he said, "I don't understand why God would have it that way." He's right—it's an awful story to stuff into innocent young minds. Easter, too. Why is religion so violent?

But it was a nice, nice meal. Chicken soup and matzoh and Jordan made the charoses. Roast chicken and salad and an incredible charlotte aux poires from Jean Millet Patisserie. The kids were too cute—all dressed up and overexcited. Jordan had two baths—I promised the second as a bribe to calm him down—and he threw up when everyone left. Big success! I feel happy.

I can't get last night out of my mind.

The day was normal enough. We went to an open-air zoo on the grounds of the Château de Thoiry with some people we met at the playground. It was hot and dusty and crowded in the car—babies, grandmothers, us—but I photographed animals from the window when I could: a lion on its back, limp, near a gaping pit; an ostrich seated immovably in the center of the road, Buddha-like, rows of trees narrowing to a perfect perspective point behind him; a zebra gazing blankly into the car's outside mirror, jowl pressed flat against the window glass.

After lunch we walked up a curving white gravel path near the château with a crowd of other people. A child mistakenly took my hand, thinking I was his mother. I accepted him. We walked together for perhaps a minute before he noticed, was alarmed, and sought his natural mother. It made me ponder the interchangeability of all parents and children. When the wildebeest migrate and calves are separated from cows, a cow bereft will not accept another's orphaned calf. Many species will—certainly humans—but there is magic in the genetic too.

It took us longer to drive back to the city than we had gauged, and by the time we got back to Michel's the children were very fussy from no naps and hungry and everyone was dirty and tired. We trudged up the stairs, and I was dismayed to find the apartment door open and Michel inside. He said we'd have to leave as soon as possible. Something had gone wrong with his woman friend—he didn't say what—and they had returned from the country two days early. She was "upset," he said, and "soaking," and we had to find another place to stay. The bathroom door was closed.

I threw things in our bags. It was Easter weekend: the hotels would all be full. Where could we go? There was a slight sloshing sound from behind the bathroom door. The breakfast dishes were still piled on the counter. I started a sink for them but Michel insisted, "Please, leave them." I got on the phone, called a hotel I'd seen. There weren't any rooms. I dialed another, yet another. On the sixth call we got a room. It was at a hotel called Le Pavillon that I had noticed near the Bronsteins'. I was relieved.

"Oh, you can't stay there," Michel said, "it's too expensive. Give me the phone." I handed him the receiver and he called a place he knew across the city and booked a second reservation. By then Marcus had come, and the two of us hauled all our stuff downstairs and into the Renault again. I was getting very nervous.

By the time we got to the hotel Michel had chosen, I was overwrought, virtually incapacitated—I couldn't think at all. I didn't want to go in. I didn't want to move. I just sat paralyzed there in the car. Marcus waited. Then, after maybe five minutes, I gave up, ceased acting, and began to "float." I saw myself get out of the car and enter the hotel. Suddenly I was seized with an urgent conviction that we should get back to the original hotel, the Pavillon, at all costs immediately. I don't remember ever having felt so certain about a decision. We canceled the room there, turned the car around and drove back, hastily.

I dragged our bags into the small lobby and handed our passports to the young man sitting down behind the counter. He was small, intense, with short black hair and eyes as black as pitch. I looked out the door. It was almost dark. When I glanced back at the clerk, he was staring at me oddly.

"Is everything in order?" I asked.

He didn't answer.

"Avez-vous notre réservation?"

His eyes pierced through me so hard that I involuntarily looked behind me. There were just our bags and Jordan.

Finally he spoke, in English. "Have you relatives here in Paris?"

"No, I'm afraid not."

He looked at me again, long. "Are you quite sure?"

"Really, it would be very unlikely."

"But are you sure?"

"Yes, I'm sure," I said, stretching out my hand for the passports.

Suddenly he blurted out, "I had a special friend named Kantor. She was twenty-five years old. She died five years ago, of that blood disease—leukemia. She taught, how do you say, political science. I just thought . . ." His voice trailed off. I was stunned. A woman who would have been Harvey's age exactly, same last name, similar profession, dying of the same disease?

"No, I'm sorry," I stammered, "we have no relatives. . . ." I picked up as many bags as I could, took Jordan by the hand, and followed a woman who came out of nowhere to a room at the end of the hall. There was dark blue floral print wallpaper everywhere, walls, ceiling. The room was spinning with it—even the beds. I told Jordan, "Stay right here," and went back for the shopping bag. The clerk was gazing out of the window. It was dark now and someone had turned a lamp on in the lobby. His hand was over his mouth. I went back to the room.

I sang to Jordan automatically, tucked him in, sat back on the edge of my own narrow bed. I noticed that the walls ran at funny angles, then realized we'd had no dinner, but Jordan was already fast asleep. I leaned over the sink and splashed cold water on my face. Then I went out into the hall, found the bathroom, used it, and returned. By then it was almost ten o'clock. I was nervous but felt I had to learn more, so I crept out of the room and back down the hall to the lobby. The clerk was still there, writing.

"Excuse me. . . . I'm sorry I ran off like that. My little boy is asleep now. I was . . . I mean, your friend and . . . My husband died of leukemia too."

He looked at me as if I were making it up.

"A year ago, a little more."

He looked down at the pen in his hand, flipping the end of it back and forth in the air.

"The woman you described, she would have been his age."

He looked up at me, a long stare, and then set down his pen. "My name is Salem."

"Salem. I'm Jayne."

"I know," he smiled, and we shook hands. "I'd like to tell you more about my friend."

"Yes, please. I want to know."

"We were . . . classmates at the Sorbonne. We were very close. Her name was Isabelle. We graduated in 1966." That was the year Harvey graduated. "She taught there. Her students loved her."

"Yes," I said, heart pounding. "My husband taught history."

His voice broke: "Elle était très intelligente, très bonne, très aimée par ses étudiants. I am sorry. I cannot speak about her in English. Elle était si *spéciale*." He went on. Everything he said about his friend applied to Harvey: active politically, bright, gentle, Jewish.

"Her family is from Poland or maybe Russia, I think," he said.

"Yes, that's where my husband's family comes from." He didn't seem to hear me.

"There were many, many people—a great number of people—at the memorial service. They were all kinds of people, not just one kind of person. She had been sick for six months." That means they were diagnosed at the same time, too.

"She was just so good, she cared so much . . ." he said.

"It's very strange," I ventured.

"Why? What is strange?"

"That they were so alike."

"She was a special friend," he said, and seemed to drift off into his loss.

"Well, I should get back to my little boy. Perhaps tomorrow . . ."

"Yes, tomorrow," he said. "Bon soir." And I went back to the room and quietly closed the door, undressed in the dark and pulled the covers up around my head, scarcely daring to breathe.

Today I didn't see him at all. It's late now, and he didn't come on duty this evening either. I don't think he came in at all today, but I felt too shy to ask about him.

It seems clear that the disclosure of this whole weird correspondence was connected to my sudden need to get to the hotel. But what can that mean? And what can it mean that Michel came back to Paris early "making" this unfold? These things seem to strike, to flow in, when I get so rattled and tired from trying to control my life that collapse seems imminent. Then, when I finally acquiesce, cease struggling against it, they happen. I'm growing more familiar with them now. The branch of mind has yet to break, and rather miraculous things come to pass. It's interesting to note, too, that many times they happen on the 18th of the month, like this. The starfish, the "Set me as a Seal upon thy Heart" thing. Does my unconscious pull out a certain stop on that day because that's when Harvey died? Are they messages from somewhere else? What am I supposed to do with them?

The air was flat today, a monochromatic gray. It gave the grounds and statuary at Vaux le Vicomte a funereal air, which made me want to take pictures. I photographed the Bronsteins and Jordan and brambles threatening the stony products of civilization. Worked with visual puzzles again—two-frame compositions where major lines continue but the horizon breaks. They will seem to mean one thing but then fall apart, like Escher's designs. Cause and effect is simply not enough.

I finally bought something—a pendant in the shape of a fly. Abstract—flat silver wings with a molded gold body. The attraction it holds for me is compelling. I saw it in the case and knew I had to have it—as if it already were mine, and what was it doing in there? Strange, this is the second time I've bought jewelry. I also bought a cotton nightgown, long and white, with eyelet trim, very Victorian. And I found Jordan—of all things to buy in Paris, France—a New York Mets baseball shirt. Our time here is nearly gone.

The director of the nursery school left word with Jordan's teacher that she wished to speak with me this afternoon. I was nervous that he wasn't getting along well there or something, but she only wanted to let me know that there is another widow among the nursery school mothers and she thought that we might like to meet. I called the woman, Louise, and she invited me to her apartment for a drink. When I got there, it was getting dark. She was putting on her coat before I was halfway through the door.

"Let's go to the bar downstairs," she said.

We took the elevator down. I saw how well-cut both her hair and jacket were. She was my age, American, and I was full of hope for our sharing. I haven't talked before with another young widow.

There was a draft from the door, and we kept our coats on.

"It was a car accident," she said. "I was sitting in the back. André and our friend Robert were in the front. After the impact, I could see his head and knew that he was dead. My back was broken and at first they didn't want to tell me he was dead, but I already knew. After that I had to lie flat for five months."

"How awful. To be trapped in your grief like that."

"Oh, it wasn't all that bad," she said, sipping at her drink. "I never lost my equilibrium. There were some sad feelings, yes, but no pervasive unhappiness. I was determined not to brood, to be cheerful."

"But you must have felt so alone."

"No, I never was alone," she said, talking through manicured fingers, which hovered around her upper lip when she wasn't drinking. "I was always surrounded by relatives. First I was at my in-laws', then my mother came to live with me, and after I got well she stayed to keep house and look after Jonah so I could go back to graduate school."

"Was it hard for you to be away from your son that much?"

"No, he's so dependent. . . . I found he bled my energy when I was home. It's better for us both when I'm busy on my own. I have a live-in helper now who takes him to school and picks him up. And of course, my mother helps."

"Isn't it expensive having live-in help?"

"Oh, I don't have to worry about money. André's company provides a big pension and there was about $200,000 in life insurance. I work because I want to."

"How long were you married?"

"Two years."

"And how long ago did he die?"

"Two years."

"That's not very long ago, is it?"

"Oh, I don't know. . . . What are you getting at?"

"It's just that I've been overwhelmed by what happened to me. Harvey was a part of me, a big part, and I haven't figured out how to live without him yet."

"I never felt that way—a part of my husband. I remember being afraid for a few weeks that I would never be loved like that again, but it wasn't true. I met a fellow from Switzerland nine months after the accident, and he moved here, and we've been together ever since."

"I had a brief affair myself, but it didn't really help."

She was silent.

"Has anything strange happened to you since André died?"

"What do you mean, 'strange'?"

"Oh, you know, supernatural."

"You mean ghosts and things?"

"I don't know. Anything that's just real odd."

"No. Absolutely not. My mother-in-law, though. That's another story. She lost a younger son before André, and she claims the two of them appear to her and stuff. I find her really morbid."

I was quiet.

"I enjoy my life, my job, my man," she said, and signaled for the check. "Anything else you want to know?"

I don't know. I feel as odd and lonely in my grief as before we spoke. I hardly feel that she and I have come through the same experience. Perhaps she just needs to "cover": she spoke almost entirely from behind her hand. When she moved back to Paris she chose to live again on the same block where she and André had lived when they were first married.

Uncanny. I have met a second young widow among the nursery school mothers. It's frustrating because this is our last day in Paris and suddenly I find someone kindred and sympathetic. Her name is Jenny. She's British, with light brown hair and round pink cheeks, a quick smile and hands that reach out to touch. She is also big-ly, beautifully pregnant, and just got married three days ago. She put it off out of loyalty to her first husband, Jack.

They met working in films. They were together for seven years— good friends before they were lovers, like Harvey and me. Unlike us, though, they drew still closer with his illness. Throat cancer. She spoke clearly of their experience, how they had been open with friends. "We made them face it. Made them look at us and admit that Jack was going to die."

He did die—two years ago. "There's a huge difference between the first and second years," she said. "But I still hurt badly, especially when I have a hard day. I miss him and I think, 'If he were here he'd help make things better.' But I need to love. I am in the habit of loving. Jean-Jacques is a different love, not a replacement."

She held out her left hand—she was wearing two wedding bands. "This is Jack's," she said, touching the one on the inside, "and this is Jean-Jacques's. He was hurt when I didn't take the one off at our wedding. I think he thought I would. I warned him though. I tried to hide my grief from him for a long time, but it was so taxing, and finally I couldn't keep it in. I just blurted out, 'I'll never love you as much as I love Jack!' But he was really quiet and patient like he always is and all he said was, 'Jenny, I have the advantage. I have time to work on our relationship.'"

She looked at me. "Having another man doesn't remove the pain."

Then it was time for both of us to go. We hugged each other and said good-bye. I wished her luck with her labor. When I got back to the hotel, a rush of tears burst out. I threw myself on the bed and sobbed for a few minutes. But we had a plane to catch. So I pulled myself up and packed our bags again, protecting the silver-winged fly in the folds of the white nightgown. Then I checked under the beds. At the door I looked back one more time at the swirling dark blue flowers on the walls, the spreads, the curtains. Then I went to pick up Jordan for the plane.

A final note. Jenny's home town in England is *Storrington*.

Stonington again. I knew I didn't want to come home, even before we got to Orly Airport. Earlier in the week it sounded good: "I will go home and start a new life. I will cultivate my garden, will set out blue pansies beneath the row of yellow tulips." But as the plane drew closer to the States, the pressures accrued inside me: term papers to grade, the house to clean, the yard overgrown and full of winter waste, groceries, sitters, thank-you notes for blood and condolences. It's all too much.

I have fled to Claire and Michael's in Bucks County for the weekend—couldn't face the work at home. Besides, Mother was going to be in Philadelphia with a woman friend, and it seemed like a good idea to get off the train and spend a couple of hours with her. She wasn't that happy to see us. We walked around outside the hotel on a plaza with fountains and I tried to tell her about our trip, but she only listened politely—no real interest. She was cold and distant—eager, it seemed, only for us to get back on the train. I am embarrassed to have assumed that she'd be glad we'd come.

I am sitting in a creaking wicker rocker on Claire and Michael's porch now. The house looks west across a broad field toward a soft line of mountains. The sun is setting. Behind me, the door jamb is dripping with tomato juice. Jordan and Elizabeth Jane were picnicking on the top step as I came out. I paused behind the screen and saw Jordan take a stick, dip it in his tomato juice, and paint both sides of the front door. Then he sat back down, put his stick into the cup like a paintbrush, and said solemnly to Elizabeth Jane, "There. Now you are safe from the Angel of Death."

A dream about reunion with Harvey.

We are in New York, trying to find a park on the Upper West Side. The sun is low. Harvey looks great, confident, powerful—is wearing a suit. I am carrying Jordan. Jordan's arms reach for his daddy. Harvey says he'll carry both of us on his back. He is on my right— moves away with Jordan and I call to him shyly, "I learned to play tennis." He laughs, shakes his head—"Shup, you say the craziest things."

Suddenly we are threatened by hoodlums, take refuge in a candy store. They follow us in—it wasn't safe after all. Two men corner Harvey, saying "Let's brush him down." They trap his hands, beat him savagely. I know there are no bones left in his face. A woman is attacking me. I'm on my back, kicking up hard with my feet, holding Jordan close, defending him. Finally they all leave. I turn toward the wall where Harvey was pinned. All that remains is a white cut-out, a silhouette of him, arms trapped above his head. There are bloody scratch marks where his chest and face would be, from the metal brushes. I know it has been a torturous death and am consumed with anguish.

I have been having long periods of trance-like fantasy, which alarms me. In the past whenever I've daydreamed, I've also kept the sensory data flowing enough so that I wasn't suddenly jolted when I "came to." Now I can't tell whether it's been only a minute, or five, or twenty, that I've been "gone."

I feel like an adolescent: "Who am I? What will I be?" I wait, hoping that some patterns will become apparent to me in the chaos of my life. Am in a period of not wanting a whole relationship with any new man. Feel it would be too demanding, that he would only suck energy away from me and give me nothing in return. Maybe that's because of the way things were in the years of Harvey's sickness and all the time with Spencer. I long for physical comfort, but the cost seems too high. I scorn the desperation of last winter when I still had hope for the affair with Spencer on some level. I would have thought that I'd feel pity for the person who endured that, but instead she embarrasses me. And Spencer too embarrasses me— and I take the fact that he does as a sign of immaturity, and *that* embarrasses me.

Grief is "seasoning" my personality. All I want is myself, Jordan (a bit less of him than I have), and futilely, Harvey. Maybe a day will come when I don't even want him.

Mother's Day. On the front page of *The New York Times Book Review* this morning there was a drawing of the gravestone of a young soldier:

MICHAEL E. MULLEN
BORN SEPT. 11, 1944
KILLED FEB. 18, 1970

February 18th: Harvey's death day. The book is about his parents— Iowa farmers who turned against the war in Vietnam. His father: "The slam of a hand hitting a table in rage." His mother: ". . . abrasive, demanding, cocky, maternal, protective and then so suddenly lonely and gutted." "Gutted"—the word made me squeeze my heart hard with my lungs. I got up and called Sharlene.

I was shocked to hear she'd had a coronary while we were in France. She's okay now, and home, but she spent most of the time we were gone in the hospital.

Then I called my own mother. We grappled and tried but nothing real was exchanged. The whole day was bad.

A little better now. Big moon. Setting out the garbage, looking up through the dogwood tree that didn't bloom at all last year, I discovered that the blossoms retain their translucence at night. I'd have thought they'd all look black, silhouetted against the moon, but no, it shines right through them.

Last night I saw the film *Robin and Marian*—about Robin Hood and the brief reunion of lovers presumed dead. Enough beauty to make my teeth chatter. I envy their dying together. Robin's incredible gesture—firing the arrow from his deathbed, Marian at his side, instructing John to "bury us close together where it lands." And then the arrow doesn't come down—soars into infinity, into legend.

On the way home from the group yard sale at Howie's today, Jordan and I passed a streamer-decorated car outside St. Mary's. I explained to him about the honeymoon trip after a wedding. His response, straightfaced: "Do they go in a rocket ship?"

I drove up to the University this afternoon to deliver my grades and stopped off at the Davidsons' in Narragansett afterward. They have a new dog, a German shepherd they rescued. He was to have been destroyed because of fierceness—was kept too long with his mother, a working warehouse guard dog. He lunged at me as I came in the door, teeth bared, snarling. Aware of the danger but not really frightened, I dropped to the floor and lay flat on my back, instinctively submissive, like another dog. Nervous, tentative, he stopped growling, smelled my body. Margot and Lisa came in, upset, apologetic—had thought he was in the backyard—but very interested in what was happening. I sat up slowly, eyes averted, "ignoring" the dog, talking softly to the others. Eventually I got to my feet and walked toward the kitchen. Then I jumped: a cold nose had been thrust into my hand from behind, a friendly muzzle. Margot and Lisa couldn't believe it, said he'd never accepted an outsider before. It made me feel very good. Later I sat on the floor while we chatted and they painted clay beads, and the dog slept with his head in my lap. He stayed near me, our bodies touching, all afternoon.

Summer

Perfection. Star Island. Our first night here. Arrival across a smooth purple lake, turquoise and muted orange dusk—stillness. Soft mosquitoes on my hands. Astonishingly clear water at the cabin. Jordan stripped off his overalls and swam at once. Stephen ran in for towels. Mary doused the spotlight (we rode up with them from Minneapolis), and we all peeled off and dove in—the first swim of the season, the first skinny dip in years. Chill, thrill—the light of half a moon. Freedom, exhilaration, inauguration of the summer. Sitting at the kitchen table after—red checkered oil-cloth, mugs of hot chocolate (we forgot the beer)—was a long step back into our past.

I'm happy to be here. Jordan is thrilled to near hysteria and fell asleep at once. Yes. Thank you. Yes, Lord, Whatever, with a spreading spirit.

We all went fishing this evening. A yellow light on skin—faces, hands—and on Jordan's orange life-preserver. The thrill of bites on his bacon-baited line. Soft late-day wind. Stephen in the bow drinking a Bloody Mary. The sun setting. Mary pulling the motor again and again so the boat could drift over the drop-off where perch gather. Her famous fishing hole. Then tag in the sand. Dashing black silhouettes against a lake of mercury.

Mary and Stephen have gone back to their jobs in Minneapolis. It's just Jordan and me here now, facing the tests of the coming week. There's a terrible dryness on the island—no rain for weeks.

The beach grass is straw-colored and the leaves of the little maples in front of the cabin are limp and curling in. Rangers on the mainland have prohibited all fires.

I spent about an hour this morning filling buckets from the dock and hauling them in to the young trees, but I doubt it can touch their thirst. My arms felt like they were pulling out of the shoulder sockets, so I rummaged around in the boathouse for the old lake pump, hoisted it into the red wagon and pulled it out on the dock to the water's edge. Mother gets a hose to work this way. I made a platform of planks on the sand, lifted it down, and ran an extension cord up to the spotlight plug-in, but couldn't get it going.

Still no luck with the pump. More heavy buckets of water, the dock wavering through the heat beyond the beach. Buds on the wild rose bushes on either side of the front door are brown-tipped, parched. I wonder if they will open at all this year.

Jordan came up with a remark that startled me as I was tucking him in for his nap. He said, "Daddy loved me more than you, didn't he?" I thought he was saying I didn't love him as much as his father did and it hurt my feelings a little. But I was able to reassure him that we both loved him the same and it was *so so* much. Then he started giving examples of big things to compare how much he was loved to:

"Bigger than Paris?"

"Oh yes," I said.

"Bigger than the whole town?"

"Bigger than the ocean and the sky!"

That pleased him and he squirmed with grins, and I pulled the one light sheet up under his chin, and gave him a kiss.

It just occurred to me, though, that maybe he was saying something else—saying that Harvey loved him more than Harvey loved me ("Daddy loved me more than [he loved] you")—which I can see and which scares me less.

Delicious quiet yoga. Mozart piano concertos in the soft light of a waxing moon. A filmy gauze gown which falls away from my clean, lotioned sunburned body. Unusual warm breezes off the lake's night. Listening to my body and feeling the music instead of the other way around. Slow, reverential movements. No striving. The heart's drum—regular, oblivious—rocking me gently, a thing apart. Warm hiss of air shifting in my lungs as torso twists. Complaint of neckbones—small, gritty. The distinct click of a blink. Steady current of sensuality. Relief from unnatural tightness—the daily struggle to hold on and not be swept downstream. The music a friendship of vibrations, massaging the room. Then a cold fresh washcloth on my face, my arms.

Gunshots!

One! Another!

I ran out from the cabin onto the sidewalk, looking toward the campground, the direction of the blasts. Nothing. I walked halfway out on the dock and looked again. Still nothing. Maybe it was firecrackers. Didn't know anyone was down there though. The morning was beautiful and sunny, going to be hot again. I walked back into the cabin and finished the breakfast dishes. A hummingbird came to the feeder just outside above the sink, paused, then darted backward. I looked out the front window again and then went into the back bedroom to shake the sand out of Jordan's sheets and make his bed. Two sharp knocks on the front door made me jump.

A lanky youngish man with a sweaty straw hat and straight hair hanging down over one eye was standing there.

"Well! Hello!" he drawled.

"Yes? Is there something I can do for you?"

"Well, there just might be." (He said it "Mawt.") "Jes' you and your son here?" Jordan had been swinging at a softball tied to the clothesline in front of the cabin.

"Do you need help with something?"

"Well, y'all goin' to town today?"

"We probably will, we need groceries."

"Well, I'm campin' down here aways, and with the weather so hot and all, I sure wouldn't mind it if you brought me back some ice."

I was uneasy, reluctant, but said, "All right. I can get you some ice."

"That's mighty nice." He backed down the steps, without looking, and sauntered out toward the walk.

"Excuse me," I called, "but did you hear gunshots earlier?"

"Yeah . . . ," he kind of leered, "gettin' me some skunks." Then he sounded menacing: "They're gonna come by me, that's what they're gonna get," and left.

I sent Jordan for his life jacket, brought the boat down off the lift, and then did something I never do up here—went back and locked the cabin door. We drove to town, bought food, and were crossing the lake coming back, when I noticed, from way out, someone sitting on our dock. It was that man. He grabbed the end of the boat as we approached, tied it up, stepped down in and picked up a bag of groceries, unasked. I deliberately left an arm free so I could take the groceries at the door and he wouldn't have to follow me inside. At the door, I handed him the ice, we both said thanks, and again he left. Relieved, I put the groceries away and got on my swim suit ready to sit out in the sun and relax. But then I saw him again, out there on our beach, raking. He had evidently gone into our boathouse, helped himself to a rake and now was out there "being useful." I pulled on a workshirt, slammed out the door and approached him across the hot sand.

"Thanks very much, but it's not really necessary for you to do that."

"Jes' thought I'd rake yer beach a little. I kinda like it."

I wanted to grab the rake from him, but was afraid, both of being rude and of him. My bare feet were burning so I hopped back onto the walk and then went back into the cabin to think. The ice, I'm sure, was just an excuse so he could "do me favors" in return and hang around here. He kept raking the beach, shoveling sand, talking to Jordan all afternoon—when all I wanted was to sit on the beach and read and have Jordan take a nap—none of which could happen because he kept "making offers we couldn't refuse." How could I sit there while he worked? It forced me to work too. I didn't want to talk to him, so I wound up working inside the cabin all day, vacuuming, on this gorgeous beach day. Three times I hinted he should leave—said, "Thank you. So long now." But he kept coming back and starting to do something else around the place. The presumption of it! I am really angry. I hope I have a chance to tell him to get out. No, I just wish he'd leave me alone. I'm angry he's camping on our island, angry he's bored, angry he has a gun. Now I have to lock my doors and be aware of windows and avoid nudity and feel exposed. *Drat Drat Drat*. Why come to an island if not for the privacy?

The man is gone. At least we didn't hear from him today. It's baking hot again. I watered the trees this morning and then we went swimming. At noon we dressed ourselves and Jordan exclaimed, "From now on, so not to be messy, I have to eat chocolate ice cream and you have to eat raspberry."

"Why is that?" I asked.

"Chocolate to match my skin and raspberry you!"

I am one big ugly sunburn, but he has tanned dark and fast, like his father.

I am full of erotic feelings for our firm young son, and they worry me a bit. He is so juicy and delicious. I just want to squeeze his thighs and hug hug hug him—hug him too hard, like the urge with kittens and puppies and six-month-old babies. I used to feel this way about him when he was tiny, too. I have to grit my teeth, I want to squeeze him so. I have never thought of myself as even remotely fitting the role of seductive mother, and yet here all of a sudden are these feelings. I remember once remarking to a man friend how erotic babies are, and he was visibly shocked. I thought then, "How out of touch you are." But now I'm suffering a stronger rush of that sweet-melon-young-body lust than I recall before, and at a time when it seems that Jordan is too old to be inspiring it in an appropriate way. Do all parents want their children like this? Or am I a deprived widow turning depraved?

It is still hot and very dry. I set the afternoon for raking dried leaves away from the base of the cabin, and sweeping spiders from the walls—cobwebs and cocoons line the underside of every clapboard. About halfway through the leaves, I overturned an earthworm. Jordan disappeared with it and I continued raking. Then I started sweeping the sticky white cocoons off the screens and planks.

Pretty soon I heard Jordan call. I went to the side of the cabin, where I could see the dock, and there he was, holding up a good-sized fish! He had gotten my old rod out of the boathouse, baited the hook himself and caught a perch from the dock! Four years old! I walked out to him, broom in hand.

"Now if we get lost in the woods, I can get food for us," he said. He was so proud. He kept it in a minnow bucket tied to the dock for several hours—his "pet"—but tonight decided to let it go free, and it flashed out of sight into the moonlit lake.

The unexamined life may not be worth living, but what of the life which yields nothing but self-examination? Work is what is missing—no getting around it—intellectual work. God knows there's enough child-care work, but no work which demonstrates to me my own worth. Teaching doesn't count. When? Ever? Why can't I pull myself together?

There's a small solace in Kramer's remark, "What you've been through the last four years, the losses you've sustained, are enough to knock anyone off her track." Husband, father, dog, father-in-law, grandfather, two friends (one a child I cared for), cat. But I'm sick of waiting for Time to heal. I am lonely for a special man-friend. Is there no one who would hold, listen, intuit, and not make life-altering demands? I resent denying my sexuality—would like to have someone with whom I could collapse on occasion, someone who would understand my need to grow strong alone in daily life.

The moon is big tonight, and there are no tides in the lake. I don't even want to go out there. Hurts too hard, too damn hard. Will dig again into my star charts—am studying constellations in three different books—and wait for the moon to pass.

Fine walk with Jordan last night—the kind of thing idealized into memories of childhood bliss. First I read him *Paddington*, then carried him out on the dock to feel the evening, him in fresh pj's with his blanket to his cheek, me still in tennis shorts. He looked for his fish in the water around the dock but couldn't find him. Then he pointed to the moonstream's light speckles on the lake and said, "Mommy, there are sparks under the water."

"No, it just looks that way."

"Then it must be glowing worms, darting," he declared.

It was too beautiful to go back inside, probably 75 degrees out (it was 95 earlier), so we decided to walk down to the swing. We walked, hummed, whispered, sang, possessed the island. There were no tents at the campground. At the swing I pushed his warm back gently, singing "Rockabye-Baby" as he gazed up at the moon—small round head, innocence, awe and trust—upward tilt. The ropes are tied to a very high branch of an old white pine, so the swing made long sweeping arcs through the night. Halfway home, Jordan asked to be carried. I lifted him up and he clasped his legs around my waist, warm bodies close and love-hugging. He looked back over my shoulder at the southern moon, and I watched the stars in the northern sky. I thought of the countless times I've walked that sidewalk shore in summer moonlight through the years and of how I never projected walking it with my four-year-old child—the two of us in spirit unison like that. Time, eras . . . the stars. Pyramids oriented their deepest chambers to them, to Thuban, then Pole Star.

Walking again, Jordan said, "Look how long I am in the moonshadow." The love comes for our child, pours through me. I enjoy him, no longer resent him, want to be with him. Tonight I felt the benediction that life can be. Despite the curse I carry, my griefbranded soul was washed with blessing.

A bad day today. Ironic, following a night of such closeness. Jordan got us up too early—it was barely light—then whined and crept about all day, insisting sickly, demanding full attention. He wouldn't play by himself for even one minute—was on me like glue, following me to the toilet, out on the dock, into the boathouse, like a bee about to sting. Both of us were tired and crabby. I thought of taking him by the feet like an ax and smashing his head against the refrigerator.

He had wakened me in the middle of a nightmare, which probably contributed to my funk.

Harvey and I are making love—erotic and close and fine, but I am on top and I am very tired of being on top, tired of responsibilities. I want him on top of me, protective for a change. Very suddenly without warning he is about to vomit. I look for a pan, can find nothing, hold out my hands for him to wretch into. (It is like the night before he died, when unannounced he started heaving in the middle of a Demerol-pain-confused conversation—heaving blood at first, then just dry-heaving, repeatedly, helplessly.) What he vomits in the dream frightens me: it is clear pure soup, like won-ton broth with small bits of shrimp and chopped celery—sweet-smelling, not acrid or revolting. No digestion is occurring. He must indeed be in death-danger! I show it to a nurse/doctor who has come in behind me. Events beyond control . . . wild fear. (Jordan wakens me.)

The barometer has been crazy all day. Finally early this evening a storm broke. Big winds and yes, warm rain. Jordan ran out in his T-shirt and jockey shorts, arms extended, yelling. I went out too and we let the sheets of water falling from the sky soak our clothes and faces. I looked at the little trees, bending under the downpour and could have cried with gratitude. When we came in and dried off and sat down to dinner, Jordan wanted to say grace. We thanked God for the rain.

They're back. I just watched Hendersons approach the island through binoculars. Martha—petite and lithe; Bob—hunched, shrunken, posture of suffering, a year's more cancer moving up the spine and into his brain. I saw him only from the back. It could have been Harvey. For the first time I realize how bad Harvey, too, looked—a debilitation I didn't recognize, being with him every step of the decline.

I talked to Bob tonight. He is indeed much changed—skin yellow, hardly any hair, face swollen—almost like he was dead already. It is obvious how much he's been through. As we went in from the porch to the main part of their cabin, he turned too fast and walked smack into the wall. His smile is there, though, and his humor, though the wit is slower. And the familiar hearing aid. But he's on his way away from us. I feel I need to shout but have no right to. I want to say, "Bob, if you die soon, and if there's a way for you to contact Harvey, will you give him a message for me?" Only then I can't think what to say—there aren't words extreme enough for my missing him. I would want him to know how well Jordan is developing and yet also how lame our lives are. Strange that I don't think of sending Daddy a message. He seems omniscient enough to know what we're doing anyway, I guess.

Dramatic heat lightning tonight, and there's a full moon, too. Very odd: light from both the left and right sides of the sky. The lake is totally still. I've never seen it so calm. It's too big a lake to be so calm. I snapped the canvas cover tight over the big boat a moment ago and now can see waterbugs skating on the swelling surface of the lake—it looks like someone snapped a cover tight over the water, too, snaps along the beach. I'm sitting in the cooling sand, leaning against the stern of Daddy's overturned Lone Star. The boat is chained to a tree and hides me from the sidewalk. The long white terrycloth robe I'm wearing glows out in the green black night but can be seen only by the nervous lake and the silent chartreuse lightning, which flashes in and out making clouds appear at the bottom edge of the southern sky—always moving sideways, like

chords smashing visually on a keyboard horizon. The sole sound is
an owl's "who."

Maybe I should change my name. Blankenship. . . . I much
prefer writing Kantor—quick, concise—but who is it? It's my sign—
my visual reference—but not my sound, my name. Blankenship is
my name. Julie and Richard's friend Allison took her own name back
at once when her husband died. The child is still called by the father's
name, though. They say that she has fallen apart in her fourth year of
widowhood, after three years of model coping.

I don't know. I feel a loyalty to Sharlene. Maybe as long as she's
alive, I should stay Kantor. She's lost a husband *and* a son. It seems
the least that I can do.

JAYNE BLANKENSHIP
JORDAN KANTOR

The wind is blowing hard. No rain, but whitecaps on the lake
and a dull consistent roar. It's cold outside and doesn't look like a
very good weekend for Mary and Stephen. They'll be coming in to
their cabin sometime after dark.

Another dream I don't want to write down.

*I am on a dock facing shore. On the hill above is the hospital where
Harvey is. He's had a heart attack and I've been with him all day.
He's been sick a long time. Philip comes out on the dock toward me.
Our right cheeks meet—warmth, relief—we hold there a moment.
He invites me to get a bite of dinner with him. It's ten P.M., though
still light, and neither of us has eaten all day. I am grateful for the
sign he cares for me more than just professionally. At that moment
Harvey appears staggering crazily down the hill (the way he lunged
to the bathroom the night before he died, catheter and all). He
should not be up, but he wants to make sure I don't go out with
Philip. I resent his possessiveness, even in the same moment I am
fearing for his life.*

*Either before or after Harvey comes—before, I think—I have
dropped something in the water and can't reach it. Philip offers to get
it for me. He takes off his suit coat to reach down with one arm. The
dock is extremely rickety out there on the L—big gaps, splintered
boards. He lies down, reaches down, and gets it for me. Then he gets
up and picks up his sport coat. It's all wrinkled—I should have
thought to fold it carefully. I feel guilty and also angry at the glance
implying it was my responsibility. He straightens it out and walks
away.*

The dawn was slow and cold, but now the sun is shining. The
wind, though, the wind still howls—so strong it has blown the
footprints out of the beach, covered the sidewalk with sand and
overturned Mary and Stephen's boat, which they had pulled up on
the beach. There is motion everywhere. Shadows of tree branches
whip the windows, the floors, and there is no escape from the roar.
It's like ringing ears, seems to start within. Rooms inside of rooms.
It's blowing coldly in around the door and window frames.

I've been making verbal errors all weekend. I scramble to cover
them with wit—emphasize them (say "snew" instead of "snow,"
then say "Tonight we have a really big snew"—that kind of thing). I
am not in good shape—nervous, relapsed. It is stressful talking to
anyone, even Mary and Stephen.

Think I'll walk back to Lake Windigo, the lake inside the island—"Wind-crazed," the Chippewa called it. It should be quieter
in the woods, at least, and warmer too. I need to wash my hair, but
the big lake is too cold and violent.

Mary just came in, pulling a scarf from her face, and flopped
down at the kitchen table.

"This doesn't feel like Sunday, or any day, really," she said.

"We ought to rename it. How about 'Noneday'?" I suggested.

Then Stephen stamped in through the door. He had to struggle to
close it after him.

"We're renaming this day," I said, glumly.

"Oh, that's easy!" he said. "Windday!"
I love it. The wind is driving me CRAZY!

They're all arguing down at Mary and Stephen's about whether it's possible to cross the lake and return to Minneapolis today or whether they should call in stranded and stay home from work until the lake is safer. I just walked down there, or rather ploughed my way. I had to lean into the wind, the sand whipping against my ankles. I think it's insane to attempt a crossing. The waves are rolling right over the docks. By the time I got back to our beach, I couldn't see where I had walked. I faced into the wind and it pulled my breath away. Choking, I turned back to it full face and cried, "What is it you want from us?!" Another big gust threw sand in my face. I turned my back and went inside.

Mother is coming tomorrow. There is no rest for me anywhere now.

The lake was rough but negotiable this morning and we took Mary and Stephen over and picked up a tight-lipped, tired-eyed Mother in the same trip.

"The bottom is going to fall out of that sack if you don't hold it on the bottom," she snapped at me as I helped her unload. How, I thought, have I managed to carry groceries successfully by myself all these years?

Inside, she pulled a seven-foot strip of thick plastic from the back hall and laid it from the front door to the kitchen across the green shag rug. "This has a purpose, you know." I wondered to myself what was wrong with the original wooden floor and braided rugs we'd had when Daddy was alive. And the leather chairs and old brown sofa—she replaced them with yellow plastic things you can't lie down or curl up on. As she unloaded boxes, she ordered Jordan to take them to the boathouse, then followed him out and scolded him for putting them in a heap. Finally, she showed me the switch that feeds the spotlight plug. It's only a foot off the floor, behind the

curtains. With scorn, she flipped it on, the lake pump hummed and
water shot out of the black rubber hose.

I could catalogue the arrows Mother has been slinging at me
today—four or five per hour—but I want to forget them, want them
never to have been. Want to dwell on the fact that she gave me
Grandpa's dark green bloodstone ring, which I remember her wearing when I was small.

"I have to tell you that I offered it to your brother first but he
claimed he wouldn't wear it," she said as she handed it to me.
Maybe I should have been offended that she offered it to him first,
but I wasn't. I'm just glad to have it. I wonder why she doesn't want
it anymore.

Before we went to bed she asked me, "Why don't you quit teaching and apply for a job at Kodak? Maybe you could write technical
manuals for a living."

Technical manuals. I tried to explain: "There is something inside
me. Something . . . I don't even know what it is yet. Something I
need to find."

"Well, that's sure not going to put bread on the table."

Jordan and I have stopped in Ann Arbor on the way home to see
Bruce and Virginia and the Lewises. The Lewises told me tonight
that Mother said to them on the day of Harvey's burial, "Does Jayne
need money? Because if she does, I'm not giving her any. If she
were destitute, I might buy shoes for Jordan, but not a dime for a
movie for her."

They waited until now to tell me, but were still visibly shocked at
the hardness she showed at the funeral of her daughter's husband.
Sandy said, "I mean, if ever there were a time you needed a movie,
it was then. How can she call herself a mother?"

At the Detroit Institute of Arts I stood for a long time in front of a
miniature Buddhist temple carved of stone. Muscled warriors,

snakes, and other bulbous forms guarded the doorway. I couldn't see inside. Later, at the zoo, I photographed a peacock approaching a deer, the deer veering away from the bird in fear.

Jordan cried on our way home from the airport—"I don't want to go home. I want to live in Ann Arbor. I want to live at Cass Lake." I pulled off the highway to hold him. "We'll be *sad* at home, Mommy."

Stonington is blanketed by fog. Even the furniture is wet. I have just finished reading the first chapter of Carlos Castaneda's *The Teachings of Don Juan*. The house is dark and I am breathing shallowly, tiptoeing, afraid I will be "jumped." Fear Harvey wasn't "buried right." Guilt at allowing the autopsy. I am afraid of what I may dream tonight. This house does not contain a spot where I can be strong and happy. Cass Lake is where I, too, can be strong and happy. Fear I will fail my child.

We went to a cookout at Paul and Laura's tonight. Jordan was wrestling with Paul, then ran crazily in the dark and hit his head hard on a stump. He screamed hysterically, "I want to go live in the stars."

This is the fourth straight day of fog—you have to cut your way through it if you go outside. I cannot take much more. It's every bit as lethal as the wind was at the lake.

Jordan was good to me today despite, or maybe because of my depression. He brushed his teeth, made his bed without being asked, was cheerful and cooperative all day long. He felt bad that I wasn't having a party (today I turn thirty-one), so he came downstairs to the office where I was sitting at my desk, carrying a bowl of fruit he had arranged himself, with golf tees stuck in every tomato, lemon and lime, for candles!

"This is a fruit cake," he announced, when he had finished singing "Happy Birthday."

After that, Grace, my yoga teacher, called and invited me to dinner with Philip and Karen. She hadn't known it was my birthday. It was a lovely meal and the others were cheery but still I felt lonely. It was hard to hold my body upright in the chair.

Reading to Jordan at bedtime, I got so frustrated with his interruptions that after four warnings I stopped reading "The Ugly Duckling" before we got to the end (the relief of being a beautiful swan— I denied him that ending) and fumed out, hating myself for my impatience. Reading *ought* to be a time for questions, as many as he wants to ask; but I just can't stand it—the breaks in the flow, the impediments to completion. Later, I went back upstairs to check on him, but he wasn't in his room. I looked in my room, and there he was, a little hump under the tan corduroy spread, fast asleep. Why do I run out of love? I pulled him into my lap and held him in my arms, asleep, and then it came—enormous welling love. What determines when it flows? And why does it so often choose the space that falls just after he has gone to sleep, after he could feel its balm? He woke up a bit as I carried him to his room, but then he fell asleep again, holding my hand against his warm small chest.

The fog is gone.

We spent the 4th of July in New York with Sonia and Aaron. Watched the Bicentennial fireworks over the harbor from their rooftop. Jordan was thrilled—couldn't stop talking. Then he was quiet for a bit and said, "I feel sad for the blind men—they can't see the beautiful fireworks. I wish Daddy could see them. He'd hold me on his shoulders and we'd be happy."

Later Sonia and I sat up alone and she asked me, "Where's your anger at Harvey's having abandoned you, leaving you with solitary responsibility for Jordan? You didn't deserve all this extra work."

"I don't know," I said, "I don't feel angry at him. It wasn't his fault. He didn't choose to die. What I get angry at are demands from Jordan. But they're not Jordan's fault, either. It's no one's fault— the universe, maybe."

"It's got to come out someday, don't you think?"

"No, I really don't. Maybe I'm deceiving myself. I mean, I can imagine being mad at someone who committed suicide. Although even that . . . But hate for Harvey? No." I looked at her and shrugged my shoulders. She shook her head and asked me if I wanted another orange juice and soda, then got the seltzer bottle and spritzed one up.

As I fell asleep I realized that this was the week the baby would have been due.

Bad afternoon. I was bribing Jordan with *Peter Pan* to get cooperation. He needed a nap—had fallen asleep in the car on the way home from nursery school—but he wouldn't stay in bed and I was saying "no movie unless," desperately needing a nap myself. He kept creeping out next to my closed door, waiting there unnervingly so I couldn't relax, and going to pee every five minutes, calling out every ten. Finally I went berserk—yelled, pounded on his bed, generally threatened to destroy us both—and then he went right to sleep. I hate being angry, hate it, hate it. Wanted to cry—almost released it by thinking of Harvey holding me, but it didn't work. I realized, truly—maybe for the first time—I'm on my own.

Tonight we went to *Peter Pan*. Jordan was on the edge of his seat the whole time. He was concerned throughout about how Captain Hook lost his hand ("How did it get cut off?"), but was thrilled with the flying. On the way home in the car I was singing "When you wish upon a star . . . your dreams come true," and he responded with startling bitterness.

"They do *not* come true," he said.

I looked over my shoulder to where he was sitting in the back seat leaning his head on the window.

"What?"

"They don't come true, wishes don't."

"What do you mean? Have you made wishes that didn't come true?"

He was silent.

"Some wishes do come true, Jordan. When I was a little girl I wished on a star to love and be loved by a good man, and to have a little boy like you."

"You did?"

"Yes, and they came true. But some kinds of wishes can't come true. To wish for Harvey to come back to life, that wouldn't come true."

"How are you supposed to know?"

"Know what?"

"Which kind of wishes could come true."

Another cookout at Paul and Laura's. Charlie Turner was there, too, give or take a little—he cut off three fingers from his left hand in his lobster pot-hauling machine out near Fisher's Island two days ago. There he was with his stubs hanging out, blood-blackened bits of gauze stuck to the end of each, like postage stamps. He had driven back to Stonington with his boat motor wide open, the loose fingers wrapped in a towel with the bleeding hand. Someone at the dock drove him to Westerly Hospital.

He had also shaved off his beard. It is disconcerting enough having a conversation with someone who is waving a fresh amputation in your face, without having his face, too, look completely strange. The kids were all very wary of him. Jordan walked around the fire with his arms crossed over his chest, the fingers of both hands tucked safely under his armpits, saying, "I don't think it's scary at all." Not much.

Charlie himself seemed quite ebullient. But when the conversation turned away from him, I glanced at his face. It was totally mournful.

I have discovered something: if I turn on all the lights downstairs, put a stack of Mozart and Bach on the stereo, and set out my notebook and reading stuff on a cleared table *before* I take Jordan up to put him to bed, I can bear to come back downstairs again instead of just retreating to my own bed, trapped upstairs by the loneliness of the downstairs. This arranging has to be a definite effort because usually we are coming home into a dark house from being out on the boat or at a picnic or whatever, or else it's light when I take him up and dark by the time the last books are read and the lullabies sung. Another trick is the electric blanket. If I turn it on well before I get to bed, it takes the chill off the sheets. I don't like actually sleeping with heat, so I turn it off when I get in, but by then it's served its purpose psychologically. This might strike others as much ado about nothing. But it is not. It is my survival I am planning.

I took Jordan and a little friend who had a nasty cough to the North Stonington Fair this afternoon. (Why do parents do that, send sick kids out?) The kids were good, though, and I didn't have any trouble keeping them near me. We happened on an event called the "pony pull," in which teams of draft horses strain to move massive stacks of concrete block. There was violence in the horses' eyes, and fear—muscles, sweat, whips, evil-looking handlers.

Then a big man with a fat belly and a full white beard and clean-shaven upper lip walked slowly into the ring. Behind him at a distance of about ten feet: a team of spotless white oxen. They wore a black harness with rows of polished silver medallions, but there were no reins or whips connecting them to the man. They just followed him, like enormous slow puppies. The three of them moved around the ring with the deliberate regality of a coronation procession. Then the oxen backed into position by themselves and someone reached down and connected the grappling hook. They pulled a mighty distance—with little apparent effort and no visible signal from their master—and then they followed him out of the ring again. The crowd went wild.

Jordan has had two nosebleeds already this week. At nursery school today he was hit by a bat. And on Sunday at the beach it was a Frisbee at close range. Shocking amount of blood—it covered his whole bare front body and mine, too, as he clung to me, screaming. Blood so light, bright, bubbling. And now he is coughing. I had a sobering thought while cleaning up after supper tonight. During childbirth, when his heart slowed down and they took him with the forceps, he might well have died. Would I be here today if I had lost my father, him, and then lost Harvey too? Might Harvey not have died, since my need of him would be so great? Or would my depression have killed him sooner? How can I be this egocentric, thinking I had anything to do with his death-timing? No, I couldn't have stood it—empty house, empty womb, aching breasts, no job. Maybe Harvey and I would have killed ourselves together, since he was to die anyway and I had nothing to live for.

I took a black portfolio full of photographs down to Kramer's office this afternoon and showed them to him. There were pictures of Jordan alone, and Harvey, the double exposures from last summer, France, old shots of animals—a lot of different things.

"These are really good," he said, looking up at me in surprise from the floor where they were spread. "But you're taunting yourself with fears of Jordan's death." He tapped on a shot of Jordan in big rubber boots next to a giant steam shovel.

"Taunting myself? I don't think I'd use that word. This stuff is what I see and putting a mat around it takes it out of me."

"Do you write down things like this in your journal, too?"

"Well, dreams, fears, yes—thoughts that seem too negative or embarrassing to tell the people I know."

"Why do you have to save the unhappy thoughts?"

"I'm not trying to save the unhappy thoughts, I'm just saving the *significant* thoughts. I don't think it's so unusual that, at this time in my life, many of those thoughts deal with loss."

"Well, Jordan has to pick up on it, and you, therefore, have to quit recording these fears. You have to be careful not to get angry with him, too, because your anger is read by him as wanting him to die."

"I thought therapists were supposed to be big on 'letting it all hang out.'"

"Well, not in this case."

"Oh."

"Remember now," he said, shaking a finger as he opened the door for me, "no more scary pictures, and don't write down anything unhappy."

I have felt very pressured these last three days—incredible the amount of thoughts I wanted to record that had a dark cast. Damn that Kramer! I feel castrated by that Freudian so-and-so! I'm abiding by the rule—for a trial while longer—but I'm angry.

I overheard some eight- or nine-year-olds beside the tennis court coming back after looking at the fresh grave of a cat in the hedge by the back fence. A boy and his mother, carrying a gray tabby in a clear plastic bag, had buried it there as we started to play. The kids mentioned bleeding from the nose. Then I caught snatches of their conversation about whether the cat still hurt after death, spirits, and so on. As they left, I heard:

Kid #1: (unintelligible)

Kid #2: "I don't know about that. I'm not a Catholic."

Kid #3: "I ain't either."

Kid #1 (the Catholic, I presume): "Well, it doesn't matter. You can be a *Republican* and still be sad!"

Now is that morbid?

I've had a headache all morning, hung over from coughing. Jordan is pretty much well, and has gone back to school, but the thing has me now. It was just bronchitis for a day or two, but now it sounds like it has gone down into my lungs—snapping bubbling sounds at the beginning and end of each breath. I'm determined to be nice to myself, to beat this thing. I took some vitamin C and then sat out on the warm bricks of the patio for an hour. Just sat in the dappled sunlight and sipped an iced tea and read parts of Castaneda. Then I watched the ants for a while. I tried to meditate for five minutes or so, then did some sitting yoga. Still the headache.

Hurricane Belle is coming! TV and radio warnings to evacuate the shoreline started four hours ago. I've never seen a whole town swing into action the way Stonington has. This must be what it was like to prepare for invading armies in earlier centuries (Kurosawa's *Seven Samurai:* "The brigands are coming!") The first thing I did was bring the yard furniture into the living room and the garbage cans into the office. Then I drove down to Freddy's Boat Yard to get the boat out of the water. But it was gone! Everyone was trying to get their boats to dry land and somebody must have just helped themselves to ours to get out to a moored sailboat. I was frustrated but hurried on to the general store—bought yellow rubber knee boots a size too large (all they had left) and a blue slicker and rainpants. Then to the market for canned goods and tape for the windows. I checked the boat yard on my way back to the house, but the boat was still gone. The sky was getting really dark and people were shouting. Our phone was ringing as I came in the house—friends asking if they could stay with us because we're up twenty feet higher than most of the borough. I started the tub and sinks filling so we'd have drinking water, then taped big X's with the masking tape on all our windows to keep them from shattering. The phone kept ringing. A sudden shock of popularity thanks to the elevation of our house. Back to the market: a dozen tins of tuna fish, mandarin oranges. To Freddy's again. This time the boat was there and Freddy helped me haul it up on land and secure it. The harbor, stripped clean of bobbing masts, looked eerie—naked, wrong.

The wind is blowing hard now, harder than it did at Cass Lake, but I wouldn't call it terrifying. It's very strange, though . . . Jordan went right to sleep. I am extremely uneasy physically. Am finding it hard to breathe and can't sit down. It must be the air pressure. The eye of the storm is supposed to pass right over Stonington. People won't come unless there's flooding.

We were spared the brunt of the hurricane—the worst passed to the west. A boat that wasn't chained down got blown over the railroad tracks and was found half a block from where it started and there are a lot of branches down, but that's about all.

I went outside last night when the eye was passing over. It was unbelievably quiet, and clear, too, which I hadn't anticipated. The moon shone down through the quiet center of the storm like a giant yellow eye itself. I stood in the intersection at the top of Sal Tinker's Hill until it began to pass and the winds started again, slowly at first, this time in the opposite direction. Dried leaves whirled around the intersection and my stomach felt queasy so I went back inside and waited out the second half.

Jordan never did wake up; at least he never got scared enough to call out. He did remark this morning, though, "Last night that wind trembled my windows!" It sure did, Jordan. Trembled mine, too.

My cough is much worse—I cannot breathe at all when I lie down—so I finally went to see Philip. Had to laugh at myself as I tried on three different sets of clothes, even ironed a blouse to wear. On the walk over I noticed how many people were peeling masking tape from their windows and how many stores and houses still had large X's taped to them. My hands were cold as I stepped into his office. He listened to my lungs, had me breathe and make noises, then pulled his stethoscope from his ears and said, "I'd say you have 'walking pneumonia.'"

"Is that serious?"

"Not very."

On the way back, at the base of Sal Tinker's Hill, I encountered my middle-aged, hefty, across-the-street neighbor, and we panted up the street together. She is not yet a week a widow. Her husband worked too long on the roof in midday sun and burst his heart. I looked into her face and scarcely recognized her. Either she has changed or else I never really studied who she was before. What is there to say? Mount Everest stands before her.

At the top of the hill she paused, as if I, though twenty years her junior, might offer some advice. I just looked at her and said, "I'm awfully sorry."

Jordan was already down for his nap when I came in, so the sitter and I whispered as I paid her, and she left.

Now Jordan is talking to himself in bed. The "story" he's pretending to read just ended like this:

> *Crawl into those sheets of white.*
> *Good night, good night, good night, good night.*

Fall

Mother called to say that Bob Henderson is failing badly. I want to write, but what to say . . .

Dear Bob:

> I've been informed that your pain is blooming obscenely. I am pacing here, feeling helpless and angry and deeply sad.
> The Koran says, "A soul is never charged with more than it can bear." I can think of a lot of bitter retorts to that. But I know too, that you are a great-hearted man and my life is better because it has been touched by yours.

> Godspeed

My letter arrived too late: Bob died. I talked with Martha long-distance, wanting to hold her. They buried him in the little Cass Lake cemetery. I want to help them but feel inadequate. Especially feel I let Bob down. Why couldn't I have written even one day sooner? Maybe "good-bye" is not that important, but isn't "thank you for being a friend"? I will miss him.

I am bothered, going in to check on Jordan before I go to bed. I've seen him several times sleeping with his right eye half-open, unseeing. Harvey's corpse lay there that way, right eye open. It's like a signal. I hate it.

I am lonely on this warm September night. I'm wheezing, and still cannot lie down without coughing. I can hear the band in the distance at the Portuguese Holy Ghost Society party and can see in my mind the colored lights strung from tree to tree and people dancing. Ordinarily Saturdays don't bother me; I even feel a little superior in my solitude. But tonight I wanted conversation and activity and feel left out, lying here propped up on pillows.

I went to Philip for another chest-listen today.

"When will I be over this thing?" I asked him.

"Probably next spring."

"Right, spring," I said.

"I mean it, spring."

"You're joking."

"No, I'm sorry. It will probably take that long. I want you to go over to the hospital for some inhalation therapy."

"What is that?"

"Oh, it's not bad. They'll just take a machine with an air hose and gently inflate your lungs a few times." I wondered why Harvey never had this done when his asthma was bad.

At the conclusion of the appointment I managed to ask him, "Very seriously, how are you?" He spluttered around, said, "Just fine," and I said, "I feel like we see each other often but never really talk or make contact like we used to." He nervously got up, said, "Yes, well," and ushered me out. I have no idea still, what he thinks of me.

Terrible dream last night.

Harvey is to be poisoned by "the authorities" as a political undesirable, like Socrates. We know in advance that different poisons (chemotherapy?) are to be given at different hours, each designed to torture in a different way. He has made a kind of dye-transfer decal out of an Aries zodiac sign I have given him for insight/strength/luck and has sewn it on his right back pants pocket. (Why Aries? He is Aquarius.) There are a few other souvenirs from his life around us there on the beach where it will take place and all the people who want to watch his death and suffering—like Roman spectators and the Gladiators. I hate them—feel anger, love, grief all at the same time.

The poisons begin to work. His consciousness is fading already, absorbed in pain. Suddenly I realize that it will ease his suffering if he tries to concentrate on the last three fingers of his right hand, send the pain there. I will always be holding that hand, those fingers, clasped together in my own and will drain the pain and poison into my own body. I cannot save his life but can make his dying less painful. I try to make him understand, but there is no acknowledgment. Horrible regret that I hadn't thought of the technique before the poison was given. Awaken.

Harvey's book is a physical reality. I called the man who owns The Other Book Store to inquire about something, and he said, "I certainly am enjoying Harvey's book." Only I didn't catch "Harvey's"—not expecting it as a plausibility. I said, "I beg your pardon?" And he said, *"Prisoners of Progress"* (now that sounded familiar, only I still didn't peg it), "your husband's book." Then it flashed. Harvey and Maury's book was out and someone was reading it and I hadn't even been told it was done! I felt like a husband learning from the grocery man that his own wife was pregnant. He understood how startled I was and offered me his copy, so I drove straight over to their house and picked it up. It was handsome— dust jacket, blurbs, the real thing. *Prisoners of Progress: American Industrial Cities 1850–1920.* The cover is an old browntone photograph of a crowded city street—pedestrians jammed together, loaded pushcarts—with balanced, flashy typography in white and yellow. Pain swept through me. I hurried to the privacy of my car, wanting to get home where I could cry, put it in reverse, and immediately whammed into the car parked behind me. I dealt with its extremely gracious owner, who was coming out of the Customs House, and drove down Main Street with the tears swelling through my whole upper body. A jealousy in Harvey's behalf so fierce. How could he not have had this moment of fulfillment? To see his book. To touch it.

Dedication—"For Cathy and Jayne, who know why. . . ." *Do* we? I don't. I don't even know if Harvey wrote that or wanted it, or if Maury made it up.

Jordan is away—think of it! His first vacation ever, and my first solitary time at home in four and a half years. At breakfast yesterday right before heading to the Hartford airport, Claire said, "Why don't we take Jordan up to New Hampshire with us for a few days?" Both he and I jumped at the idea. I was pleased to see him eager to go: a step away is a step forward. He mainly wanted to see Michael. Poor man-starved little kid. Luckily the laundry was done. I threw some things in Daddy's leather bag, and we were off. Michael missed his flight in, so we had two extra hours to kill with the kids, which was a drag, but I buzzed all the way home, a one-and-a-half-hour drive, knowing how demanding the amount of work I intended to do in the darkroom would be. The house was like a cyclone had just been through. A great deal to do to make order around me before I could begin printing.

I started upstairs, cleaned one room at a time. When I finished, I fell heavily on Jordan's freshly made bed and thought about his absence. Headachy, tense from the stress of four days of entertaining houseguests and general overstimulation, I started dreaming of sitting on the rug with Kramer, talking out my anger, hitting his shoulder—him holding me off—strain, exertion, then a sudden yielding. I awoke with a start remembering the pudding I'd put in the oven. Rice pudding, Daddy's favorite. I pulled it out of the oven, went back upstairs and cried a little on Jordan's bed. Can't think why, really. Everything. The irony of the sexual freedom of an empty house—no child here to protect from passionate scenes— and no one to enjoy it with. What a waste. Oh well, better to work anyway. I need a career more than a man. Dragged myself up. Cleaned the kitchen, then ate the hot pudding. Didn't have to cook a well-balanced supper: no Jordan.

Went downstairs to the office. Looked at the long contract for Harvey's Memorial Scholarship, which the University of Missouri had sent for me to sign. Was tempted not to read it, but it was good that I did—they had said Political Science majors, instead of American History. Compiled a list of addresses for the mailing. Time to leave for chorus came and went; I was just too tired.

Walked slowly to the mailbox in the warm soft night. No traffic. Walked in the middle of the street feeling free, unhurried. No sweater and no sweater needed. Gentle air, comfort. No stars— dark—womblike. Thought about calling Jordan but decided to let sleeping dogs lie.

Then the living room. Ten thousand parts of two thousand toys spread out three inches deep on a nine by thirteen Oriental rug—I sorted them while I listened to Julie Harris be a depressed Mary Todd Lincoln on PBS. Finally turned her off. Missed my broken stereo.

I don't remember going up to bed. Do remember the moment the housework was done; the knowing I had a whole long lovely stretch ahead in the next day to work in the darkroom. Satisfaction.

Hesitated whether to sleep in my bed or Jordan's—chose his— I've wanted to try his hard mattress since the day the bed came—my back always hurts when I get up from mine, plus I'd feel closer to him. Fell asleep before I lay down, but worried in my dreams— printed photographs all night long.

Woke early when I heard the garbage truck. A shame to get up when Jordan is not here to beg breakfast. But more of a shame to waste work time. Did a half-hour of yoga, undisturbed—limbered me up nicely. Then a good breakfast—ham, scrambled eggs.

Then print print print. Fast morning in the darkroom doing sepia-toned animal images from last month's fair—the straining horses. Bleached a rolling eye and framed a team charging toward me, too near, blurred—big looming shapes. Confront what frightens. Portray it. Luxury lunch while prints washed: cold celery, leftover homemade chicken soup, sesame crackers with cream cheese and sweet butter, cold V-8 juice in a crystal goblet. Grass placemat.

Am tired now, though. Supposed to go to a party in Westerly, but

I ache from standing all day and from eye strain—printing is hell. Jordan is gone. Somewhat spooky. I got a lot accomplished but my head and back hurt and all I really want to do is cry.

Halfway through the afternoon I realized that I shouldn't have canceled Jordan's appointment with Kramer. I wanted it for myself—to confront/confess my growing infatuation. Called him back. His voice on the phone like soft brown fur. He said he'd try. Then he called me back. It didn't work out, but he did try to change someone else's appointment for me and I appreciated that. He asked if I could tell him what it was about and I said, "No"—bluntly, period. Angie was here in the room with me—she had stopped in with a fellow photographer's interest to see what I was printing—but even if she hadn't been, I couldn't have talked about it on the phone. I never know if the person on the other end is alone. I hate telephones now, probably because they told me over the phone that Harvey died. Besides, Jordan's always pulling on me while I try to think what to say. Well anyway, I felt bad when I couldn't see him, couldn't get that scariness put behind me.

I felt uncomfortable, guilty almost, showing Angie my work, like it was bragging. She was very supportive, said the grief images gave her chills, especially the double exposures of Harvey and Jordan. I don't know. Her response may have been determined more by knowing us than by the prints qua prints. I wonder what a stranger would think of them.

Jordan is back.

On the way to nursery school this morning, he told me that "last year" he had a bad dream that he was alone in a moving car and had to drive it himself, only he didn't know how. When he pulled on *that* (pointing at the emergency brake) it fell off in his hand. Then he was on the floor pushing in the pedals with his hands (he couldn't reach them with his feet), but they didn't work. Then "something big and white came up."

Heroism day. I actually told Kramer of the attraction he holds for me. First time I've ever dared approach a man that openly. A lot of terror preceded, but look, I did it, I survived.

He sings—even considered a career.

Predictably, he said any involvement with me would jeopardize his relationship with his wife. "That relationship is a good one," he said, "something I want to protect." To my pleasure, he went on. "I'm not at all surprised to hear about your feelings, though."

Famous phrase, I thought. It's what I said to Harvey when he first told me he was in love with me. I meant I felt so loved. He always teased me about it.

"I think much of our previous talk was intellectual 'sizing up' to check out relate-ability," he said, and then he confessed a few "pleasant thoughts" about me as well.

"You're bright, attractive, assertive but not intimidating, open," he said. Platitudes? Does one always politely say such things to someone who has confessed an infatuation?

Then he swiveled in his chair, arms behind his head, and looked out the window. "Another time, another place, it could be different." What is that supposed to mean?

I wanted to take off my boots and curl my legs up under me, make myself smaller. I asked if he minded.

"I can't believe you feel you have to ask," he said. He looked hurt. He may not be intimidated by me, but I certainly am by him. I told him then that I found him judgmental, that I felt he criticized my parenting a lot. He seemed threatened by this, by any criticism of his therapeutic style.

"Tell me, Jayne, do your fantasies of me always have an element of aggression in them?" he asked. They don't, but they're always mixed. Sometimes it's guilt, sometimes frustration.

He leaned toward me earnestly then and begged me not to "turn cynical," not to "lower my standards"—"to wait [bah] for the right person." He warned me away from "narcissistic types"—artists of all kinds—and was firm on no social contact between us, platonic even, while Jordan is in therapy. I couldn't tell if he ruled it out as an eventuality or not. Certainly I would like to be his friend and I would never deliberately jeopardize his relationship with his wife. Can easily see that a friendship could bring many good things that an affair would not. It was only a shred of hope anyway. Mainly I'm glad to have shed the secret.

I still don't know much about him. How many kids does he have, how old, boys or girls? What is his wife's name? What is she good at? Does he like chocolate? Tennis? Skiing? Can he fix things? Does he sleep on his back or his stomach? Will he think about me in bed tonight? Will he tell his wife? It scares me, but I hope he does. Where did he go to school? Brothers, sisters? What religion? Does he have a dog? I feel closer to him, more nearly a friend than before, although undeniably disappointed to discover he's happily married and not at all interested in carrying on with me. And the way he has of dismissing me is still infuriating. He stands up brusquely, a hasty distancing in the quick assumption of a "grownup's" condescension and concern with "greater things." He makes me feel put down, sending me away, and that's what makes me want to hit him. Little waves of anger rippled through me when I got into the car. I wanted to screech out of the drive, but didn't, wanted to spit, to hit him still. I rode home drenched in sweat.

He sings. . . .

October 7, 1976: Daddy's birthday. I wonder what all those dead folks are doin' today?

Down here it was difficult. I had to go over to Westerly Hospital for inhalation therapy—back into its smells and shadows. The place where my husband died. Where he suffered and was alone. Where I mourned for my father. Where childbirth taught my body pain. I parked the car and tried to be cool, adult, not sentimental. As I walked in I noticed down the hall by the morgue several men lifting something into a truck. Out the door. I only glanced, did not break stride, but my heart leaped when I realized they were putting a body into a hearse. Harvey, Harvey. A fleeting glimpse, but their bodies showed care, concern, respect. No one was talking or blasé. I stayed in control, telling myself I had to discharge the place of its mystery. I reported to the proper department and made small talk with the nurse until she had me put the rubber mouthpiece in. The first few forced-air expansions were scary—I was afraid I'd burst or choke—but then I adjusted to letting it happen and after the lungs were pumped up and down with warm salty mist for a while, the nurse turned the machine off, said she'd see me next week, and I left.

Then I did some errands, reasonably happy, kind of soaring about, the ordeal behind me. At the discount drugstore I was writing a check when the saleswoman asked cautiously if I had a relative named Harvey.

"Yes. He's my husband."

"You're Jayne?"

"Yes?"

She looked away modestly. "My name's Darline. I used to be a nurse at the hospital. You don't know me because I was on the night shift—on pediatrics—but I know all about you from Harvey from when he was in that little room. He used to talk about you all the time. And Jordan. Do you remember the day you sneaked Jordan up the back stairs into his room with a bag of oatmeal cookies?"

I nodded. It made me think of Harvey bringing Roo to the circular drive in front of the hospital the day after Jordan was born. He crouched and pointed up at me standing in the window and Rooey saw and barked and wagged her strong black-Labrador tail. I looked back at the nurse. Her eyes were full of tears.

"I want you to know how sad"—she bit her lip—"we all were . . ." She paused again, trying to go on, ". . . all the nurses. Harvey was very very special to us. We couldn't stand losing someone like that. With so many lesser human beings around, complaining . . ." (she wiped away an angry tear) ". . . why *him?*"

The man behind me in line said impatiently, "Do you *mind?*" So I stepped back and let her ring him out. We tried to talk again—I told her how grateful we were for the nursing care he had had—but then there were other customers and it was just too difficult to carry on the conversation so we looked at each other and said good-bye.

Last night on Walt Disney a dog was poisoned. It tugged hard at my grief for Roo, poisoned too. Jordan looked at my screwed-up face as I was about to cry and shrieked angrily, "Don't you *ever* make a face like that again!" Then he kicked my leg really hard. It made me furious to be attacked instead of comforted when I was sad, and I yelled at him through my sobs, "You should help and hug anybody who is sad, not be mean to them!"

The program was over and he went upstairs to brush his teeth and get ready for bed. Then he yelled down, angry, "Now you're going to make me cry," and so five minutes after my tears, he cried too. I think he was mad at me for scolding him, though I'm not sure. Maybe he felt bad, too. Anyway, I held him, and he kissed me on the ear as I tucked him in.

I lay awake till very late afterward, kept up by the neighbor's yapping dogs, and had a major realization. I've been torn for a long time about "which way to live": to compete for "success," establish a career, some sense of mission and individual accomplishment or to "let it be," be passive, allow the life that's in me to show itself when and how it chooses. Quit trying so hard, so that more magic doors can swing quietly open. Accept, wait, receive what happens to me. My realization is that I don't have to choose between these aspects of myself once and for all. I only need to develop a sense of when to let one self dominate and when to let the other. A matter of timing, not of exclusive choice. This recognition brings me a great sense of relief. From now on I will try to determine which side of me needs current expression, and retire from or dive into external activity as seems fit in that season, that week.

I hate myself for not reading Philip better. After having been abruptly ushered out of his office three weeks ago when I tried to open a serious conversation, I went back for this chest-sounding with my defenses up and couldn't readjust fast enough when he questioned me repeatedly about how I was. I felt pressured, skirted the issues. Didn't realize until I left that there were no patients booked after me. He hung around with me in the waiting room, making small talk. Belatedly I recognized he had been ready for a real exchange. I wanted to push him right back into his office and close the door—but the receptionist . . .

Tonight all three of us—Philip, Karen, and I—drove down to New Haven to the Long Wharf Theater. I thought about telling them together about my longings to be held, about Harvey's wish. That seems more honorable than telling just him, but probably destructive, since the whole thing is bound eventually to evaporate by itself. We had a pleasant enough evening, though the play—*Alphabetical Order*—wasn't astonishingly funny. On the drive back, I realized I had been dwelling on similarities between Philip and me—liking sailing and other fast things, hang-gliding dreams, etc.—and was embarrassed. Quickly retreated into a politer stance, more general. Refused his twice-stated offer to drive me home after dessert at their house, saying I wanted to walk in the moonlight myself. I was halfway out the door before I realized he might be wanting to talk to me alone, too! Stupid, stupid. When will all these mixed signals cease?

A group of our friends from college have gotten together and organized a memorial scholarship for Harvey. Here is the letter they're sending out.

October 11, 1976

Dear Friend,

Harvey Kantor, a member of the Class of 1966 and President of the Student Body his sophomore year at the University of Missouri, died of leukemia in February of last year. Several of his friends have set up the framework for a scholarship in his memory, and we are asking for your donation to help make this idea a reality.

Harvey received his Bachelor's and Master's degrees in History from M.U. and went on to earn his Ph.D. from New York University. At the time of his death he was Assistant Professor of American Urban History at the University of Rhode Island and Director of the state's Oral History Project, as well as the author of several scholarly articles and co-author of a book on the American city (all of which may sound a bit heavy to those of you who, like us, especially valued Harvey's irreverent humor). In 1969 he married Jayne Blankenship (M.U. '67), and their son Jordan is now four and a half.

Because of Harvey's commitment to the study of American History, we felt that the Harvey A. Kantor Scholarship should be awarded annually to an undergraduate American History major at the University of Missouri–Columbia. The principal of the memorial fund will be invested by the University, and each year the interest earned will be paid out as the scholarship. In this way the scholarship will be available in perpetuity.

If you would like to join us in this effort, please send your tax-deductible contribution to the University of Missouri in the enclosed envelope. You may also complete and return the enclosed pledge card at the same time.

Gratefully,   The Memorial Fund Committee

I am actively trying to learn how to meditate. Yoga classes have started again at the small Episcopal parish house here in the borough and Grace is helping. She's taken a special interest in two of us, keeping us after class to practice. We sit cross-legged on the blue carpet in a small circle around a burning candle and try to empty ourselves. Meditation is not a forced blankness of mind; rather it's an "allowing." I need to learn to let my thoughts still bleep their neuron paths—straight, simple, quick (like signals on a cardiac monitor)—but not let each one branch out the way it usually does. No lightning filaments, no leaf-veins of association. Just let it pass on through and allow the mind-path to rest until the next one.

During the main part of class we balanced on one leg for a while, a kind of arabesque with our right hands flexed to lean on an imaginary wall—King Dancer Pose. I pretended to lean on the Plexiglas shield around Kramer. The do-not-ask-about-me-do-not-touch. It's hard, seeing him, even for the brief moment of Jordan's entering and leaving his inner office. His gaze holds mine. I read somewhere: "You have to pass 40 to know what not to hope for." Have I learned what not to hope for? I don't think so.

Jordan came in after trying to scrape off the car this morning of the first frost and exclaimed, "That car is burning cold." The frost has dappled the asphalt, so that the street looks like the rump of a gray mare.

We've been working on his Hallowe'en costume this morning—he wants to be a witch. He has found an old black dress in the dress-up basket, and I contributed a mop-head for gray hair. Right now he's working on a pointed hat—construction paper and scissors and phenomenal concentration.

Big event—I bought a new stereo system. Many things to reflect on about the whole experience, but just one pressing enough to interrupt the Gould/Bach Partitas for. Only just now, after I hauled the components home and after Maury helped me connect them (I think he felt guilty for not letting me know the book was out) and after we sat listening to Vivaldi for half an hour—only just now, as I got up to turn the volume down to say our good-nights, did it hit me. Right at eye level on the bookcase, the receiver says, plain as day:

HARMON KARDON

It couldn't possibly be more like

HARVEY KANTOR

And I thought I had done a good job of comparison-shopping—*Consumer Reports*, the works. The connection is so blatant it's amusing—but also a little sad. I am still deeply tied to him. Was I trying to buy him back from the dead?

Why am I crying now? Why is it that on the rare occasions that tears come these days, I can't see just why? Ah . . . now I see. Music . . . where I am most myself. Please, not here. This is not Harvey territory. I had twenty years here before I even knew him. Please, I am trying to find my own separate self. Don't I exist anymore, an entity? Don't I?

Blockbuster. A friend just told me that Kramer's wife has a brain tumor—benign but inoperable. It was like someone ramming a

pointed burning log into my abdomen. Explains many things about
the complicatedness of our dealings, or at least it seems to. His
remark about someday a remote chance for us to come together. His
general uptightness, privacy about his personal life. I drove to
Howard Johnson's after finding out and sat in the car for half an
hour, staring, thoughts tumbling too fast, like raffle tickets in a
barrel. Now I can't recover them. Incredibly many facets. Why he
wouldn't slide fees for us. Why he moved to the country. Why the
house has flat entranceways.

I went inside and hid in the ladies' room. Sat in the stall and wept
for him, for them. Why should I care so much? Again the excess of
empathy, then someone came in, and I had to tighten up. I want to
sob.

The terrible strain of living with a chronic illness and how you
don't even realize you're under it until later. Waves of sympathy for
her; for him, identification. What goes on in his head? How can I
tell him I know? Should I ask for a special appointment? Will he
turn to me as a friend when he knows I know?

Stella's remark about how tight I used to hold my lips, my chin,
always—what about Kramer's stiffness? His brusqueness, his
hurry—always standing up in the waiting room. How long have
they been living with this? I feel like a fool with my confessions and
implied proposition. When I asked him, "Does your wife work?" he
said simply, "No." About baby-sitters and cleaning people, he said,
"We need a lot of help." I couldn't imagine what kind of decadence
required that much help. I could disappear with shame. The implied criticism in my questions. His restraint. Of course he knew I
was bound to find out and then he'd look good. But what could he
do? Cry on my shoulder? She has a brain tumor. God, why didn't
he just say so?

I feel awful having tested him by telling him of my attraction.
Would never never have said anything if I knew he was dealing with
that kind of a heavy problem.

Where did we ever get the expectation that life was going to let us
be happy?

The moon is shining in my window—waxing gibbous—*and* it is raining on the roof. Must be a narrow set of clouds. A huge angry fly has been spinning around the room. I wish it would find a place to light.

Nightmare last night.

A long row of living, crucified dogs. Their eyes—some pleading, some glazed with insanity—sparkle like diamonds. Natives squat among the bushes, waiting with spears. I cannot rescue the dogs, or I, too, will be impaled.

Standing in front of the narrow mirror in the bathroom of the train to New York this morning, trying not to fall over from the jostling, I saw something that frightened me: a dark dent in the middle of my forehead. The faintest black hue, like a soot smudge. I tried to rub it off, then scrubbed it with a wet paper towel and soap, but it wouldn't come off because it was a dent. It's gone now. I don't know how many hours it lasted or what it meant. At Grace's apartment in New York, I tried to sneak a look in her hall mirror, but I didn't have time to tell, so I don't know if it was still there when we went to meet her yoga master Mr. Gupta or not. I was afraid he would see it and consider it a "mark"—of what? No one said anything.

Grace's mirror is framed in a carved wooden design identical to the stone motif Daddy photographed on a column in Greece and which I painted onto needlepoint canvas for Mother to embroider. She worked on it during his open-heart surgery and hasn't been able to pick it up since. Grace's shower curtain and towels are the same light shade of aqua as Mother's too.

Harvey's book has gotten good reviews in *Library Journal*, the Baltimore *Sun* and the Kansas City *Star* and it's going to be an alternate selection for the Library of Urban Affairs Book Club. All the recognition he's getting now—these reviews, the Memorial

Scholarship, the Oral History Association Memorial, the reading room—it's touching, but it makes me angry too. I hate all these people being so goddamned full of praise now instead of when he needed it.

As I ordered groceries on the phone this morning, I found myself sketching Harvey's face at the bottom of the list—his dead face— one eye open. In my dreams this month he's merely gone again— estranged, not dead. Last night he had a birthday and wouldn't let me be with him. The night before, I found out he had asked Laura for a date—after I'd been told he died a year before. I'm still denying; it is ungraspable that his life has ended. This must be what is meant by "living in the past." Not that I think about how it was, but that I don't grant my life today any stature, any reality, spiritually hibernating. This has been creeping in for two or three weeks, but it wasn't until today that I recognized the disease. As we drove home Jordan said, "Your sky isn't blue anymore, it's black as a bat."

My cough is no better. I am exhausted by two o'clock every afternoon and am so sick of that pink vaporizer and its insipid gurgle and warm misty output I could puke. The side of the bed is permanently damp.

Funny. Just yesterday morning I was musing that it had been a week since I'd grieved, knowing it would come again though, wondering when, how long the respite would continue. If only Harvey were here. It's been months probably, since I felt bad enough to say honestly I wished for the most awful moments of the past—his sickness, our estrangement—as better than my suffering now. Months since I would have gone back. But tonight I would have. You need what you love, no matter how much pain is involved. Hu-Kwa tea and brown-edge wafers and "The Well-Tempered Clavier" on our new stereo haven't helped.

The sky was an undifferentiated white all morning, pinkish near the horizons. By afternoon the sun was out, but the constriction in my chest, neck and shoulders from coughing was unbearable. I couldn't draw a free breath. So finally I put on my green tights and did some yoga. Simple beginner's stretches: one leg, the other, Triangle Pose, Downward-facing Dog. Before I stood on my head, I rested for a while in position on my stomach. Then I interlaced my fingers out in front of me and was about to go up into a headstand when I noticed the pattern of the Oriental rug inside the circle of my arms,—light blue against ivory, burgundy against navy—small touches of green and coral. This rug was our engagement present to each other. I lowered my chin back down into the wool, losing the pattern, and examined the tufts, marveling how sunlight transforms things, studying the tiny shadows, the tinier sparklings of individual oily wood threads. Then I stood on my head for a few minutes. Blood to the brain, phlegm to the upper lungs. When I came down into the Pose of a Child, there on the carpet exactly where I had been gazing before I went up—outlined in the last low sunshine—was a mustard seed.

Winter

Things are better. Jordan and I had a really good Thanksgiving day—baked pies together all morning (two pumpkin, a lattice-work mince, fresh apple) and feasted at Marian and Charlie's all afternoon. Jordan played confidently with the other children and everyone was relaxed and completely pleased to be there. Five children played happily together for seven hours with no quarrels.

This has been the first holiday since Harvey's death—since Daddy's, really, nearly five years ago—that has been enough in and of itself, that hasn't made my stomach cramp with the "if-only-he-were-here" of it. Milestone.

Mary is pregnant! A vision of her and Stephen and their newborn, various family and friends, standing in the dappled sunlight back at Windigo. Christening their baby on the island with lake water from the big lake carried in through the woods in a bucket. A wonderful picnic. Me making photographs. Everyone crying and acting silly. A lacy christening outfit—glowing white, fog-haloed white—and the rest of us in plaid flannel shirts and mud-covered boots and love.

I'm worried about the high blood pressure/pregnancy combination though. Mary doesn't have that much reality for me in everyday life—thousands of miles and several years away—yet in my core, both she and Bruce are very significant.

The baby is due in June. My first blood-niece or -nephew!

It "worked"—I found the relief-groove, the moment when the brain idles, quits pulling and straining. I can't breathe and find it at the same time because the breathing requires too much attention, but this afternoon, if I held my breath, it was there. Grace and Leslie and I were meditating after yoga class, sitting cross-legged in our circle of three around the candle. I was visualizing my heart as a rose, opening a fraction more with every beat. Then I noticed this feeling of relief at the top of an inhalation. I lost it when I exhaled, but I inhaled and held the breath five or six more times, and it was there for me, every time.

I went back to the parish house for yoga this afternoon, but no one was there. I sat on the step for a while and looked at the little stone church across the yard. There's a small arch for a bell on the roof, but no bell hangs there. Seemingly hundreds of sparrows flit in and out of the dark green ivy that covers the wall beneath it. There must be dozens of nests there, but you can't see them all. It's as if the birds fly right into the wall and disappear.

After maybe ten minutes I went inside to check the time and then I sat down in a strip of sunlight until I was calm enough for the slow beating of my heart to rock my upper body back and forth. Still no classmates. I figured they weren't coming then, but I already had a sitter, so there was no point in going home. I went over and sat down at the grand piano and fumbled my way through some hymns, sight-reading badly. I played at it for maybe half an hour. Then I came to "Greensleeves," our wedding processional. At first all I could think of was the Christmas version and Jordan dying: "What child is this, who laid to rest . . . ?" Lyrics out of context. I played it through once, missing chords, notes. Then I played just the one-note melody line with a pianissimo tone I didn't know was in either me or that piano. And then suddenly, without thinking, I crashed into the "This, This" chorus. Full chords, sound round, bigger than a continent. Power, the certainty of my rage, my grief for Harvey and for myself. I scarcely looked at the music—it played itself. I was aware of a door opening in my brain, which allowed me to see both treble and bass clefs at once—a whole measure, a whole line at a time. Real pianists must see that way all the time, but not me. Never in my life have I played, seldom even heard anyone play so grandly, or confidently. Then the door closed. I tried to play the piece several more times but was back again to not being able to see enough to register all the notes in each chord. I almost caught it twice more when I quit trying to get the notes right. I tasted it again, then it was gone completely.

When Jordan got home from school yesterday, he went in and got his hammer and brought it out onto the sidewalk where I was unloading groceries and began bashing his Snoopy lunchbox. I was so surprised I didn't stop him, just watched as he splintered turquoise plastic all over the sidewalk. This morning, needless to say, I scheduled a conference with his nursery school teacher, Mrs. T. I told her about it and told her, too, that he hasn't wanted to come to school every day this week. (This morning he took forever getting dressed—five naggings and finally I had to dress him.) She said he's been having trouble at school since he started staying until 3:00 P.M. He's bored, she said. He's been playing fierce death/killing/horror games: Dracula sucking blood out of your neck, then playing dead, guns. She doesn't permit this. Said he probably got the Dracula bit from TV and went into a long harangue about parents who use the TV as a baby-sitter and don't care what their kids watch. The only times Jordan watches network TV are Tuesday when Rose and Brad sit for him while I teach and Saturday morning when he goes upstairs next door to Kitty and Bill's. Those are the only halfway regular times that he gets to be with men, and I wouldn't think of jeopardizing that companionship by pressing the issue. It's true, though, that he's been playing war planes and "Baa Baa Black Sheep"-ing it a lot this week.

A couple of days ago, she went on, he wrecked a little girl's tablework project, so she made him go sit on the "thinking bench" in the other room. (Aha! That's the morning he wanted to come home with a "tummy ache"—I got him at 11:30. Why didn't she tell me about it then?) When she heard him crying, she went in to talk to him. He said he wasn't mad at the kid—he just *had* to do something like that. Another day he tackled a kid from behind. She doesn't like this stuff, and she said, rightly, that he needs to play outside, to wrestle safely, but claims that none of the other children want to go outside and he of course won't play by himself. (I think *she* doesn't want to go out and stand in the cold—so the kids get no recess.)

She said he needs constant stimulation and that we (meaning me) should adapt ourselves to his needs, not expect him to change. Said the last hour is too hard for him—he's bored and "down," should be outdoors playing with a neighborhood friend (I agree, but there's only the tough older boy down the street) or doing special classes somewhere—music or science. So I arranged to pick him up at 1:30 this afternoon, and we went swimming. It was fun because it was so unexpected for him, but it still took an hour and a half out of my darkroom allotment.

She also said, "He's one of the brightest children I've ever seen, and I've taught for twenty years. There's just nothing he tries that he doesn't do well on. A parent doesn't often get a child like that," implying that I wasn't meeting this fortuitous responsibility. I don't know. Jordan strikes me as a normal-bright little kid—no fancier a head than those of his friends. But she said he'll be "harmed" if he's not in the "right school setting" next year.

The last thing she said was how he sticks to her husband on the infrequent days he's home from work and comes downstairs to the nursery room, how he asks him for kisses and hugs, and how he desperately needs loving from a man. He's never given her or the other women teachers whom he knows well any affection at all, but to Mr. T., whom he's seen maybe four or five times in his life, he clings.

I took Jordan into the darkroom with me while I printed today and showed him how the image comes up in the developer. Then I read to him, laughed, hugged. Read the paper a bit, wrapped Chanukah gifts, did yoga and meditated. I am not tired. I was not nervous today. Things rolled along by themselves—unforced, un-planned, really. I got a lot done.

I think it's important on days like today, when I drop into bed at 10:00 P.M. from fatigue, knowing I've gotten absolutely nothing accomplished, to look back over the day and try to salvage from it some self-respect. I was busy from 10 A.M. to 9 P.M. nonstop, but that doesn't account for much. Nothing to show, except that I'm still not in a mental hospital.

The only good thing that happened was that Jordan got to one-up the kid down the street, who is six and smarter and stronger in everything, by showing him how he can ride a two-wheel bike. That accomplishment so swelled his sense of worth that he sailed through all the knocks of the following two hours with smiles and wonderful good grace. But in the afternoon things went downhill.

First we were at the laundromat. After his 500th inane question, I asked him to keep quiet. Furious, he threw one of the empty baskets around and around the machines, pretending it was me, until pre-dictably, he broke a handle off it. I scolded him and gave him a harsh stare, only he was impudent and stared back and wouldn't look away. We locked eyes and finally, I just couldn't help it, I laughed. Does that prove he dominates me? Surely I should be able to outstare my four-year-old son!

When we got home I sat down on the floor, having lugged the last basket of laundry up the second flight. Took off my socks, put my feet up against the wall and marveled that I'd lived through it. Was actually home from the laundromat. A whole day with him—it still depletes me.

Jordan said today, "I think I'll be an artist when I grow up." He was down on the kitchen floor painting a monster. He signed it *Jordan/Jayne*. He puts both our names on everything he draws these days, to signify who it's for and who it's from. I wonder how long this devotion will last. (Or was he naming the monster?) It amazes me how much he both loves and hates me. He worships me as his protector but has learned that parents don't last forever, so he fights me, trying to show himself he can stand alone, doesn't need me, doesn't even like me. So he can lessen his terrible fears of aloneness.

Do I do the same thing—reject him sometimes so I'll think I don't need him so much—so I can tolerate the horror in the idea of his death? I hope not. Face it. Eyeballs searing, look upon it. Grit your teeth, Jayne, until they break off in your mouth, but look upon it. You both will die.

I find myself functioning automatically again, lost in thought, scarcely aware of the taste and texture of the food I eat, not remembering in my bath if I've washed my legs or not. I catch myself whispering, talking to myself out loud. I've never done this before and must remind myself several times a day to stop. The Christmas season has aggravated it. I am worried that I will be slighting someone, that I won't have given them enough or the right gifts. Have never felt this way about the holidays before. Tomorrow night I'm giving a Chanukah party for Jordan, and I don't want to. The effort is too great, and on the day before we leave for Pennsylvania. But tonight I called all those people. It's partly my loyalty to Harvey, to do all I can to expose Jordan to Jewish traditions. But the pressure makes me cross. Tonight he dropped and badly dented one of our silver wedding candlesticks, and I grabbed him by the upper arm and squeezed real hard and snapped, "You don't care, do you? You don't care at all about what's important to me!" This party is no gift if I am nasty.

Things are better. I took Jordan swimming before the party, and in the dressing room at the pool, he pointed out a spider crawling up the white tile wall and quipped, "Look! It has eight legs, four on each side—a moving menorah!"

We're at Claire and Michael's now for early Christmas giving and the Bicentennial re-enactment of a Revolutionary War battle at

New Hope. The fighting happened right here on their land, so we all dressed "Colonial" to watch the maneuvers. It was quite realistic—gunpowder and stomping horses, bloody bandages and fire. At one point a British soldier rode up to Jordan and asked sternly, "Which side are you on?" Jordan, scared, replied, "I . . . I'm from out of town."

Claire's cats are giving me a lot of trouble breathing. Last night after supper I went for a walk in the cold, hoping the asthma would stop. A cat came with me of course, winding herself around my feet, climbing up my coat. A moonless night with bright starlight. I gave the horses some carrots, then climbed the hill beyond the duck pond to the spot where Claire lost her film today, thinking I might find it. I sat down on the cornstalks and pondered the real battle here—Washington and his soldiers camping out the night before, watching Orion just as I was. Maybe even wearing red long underwear as I was. I lay down in the cold cornfield wanting only to breathe, but the cat climbed up onto my chest and lay there like an incubus, rubbing alternate sides of her face against my chin. She was warm and purry, and moderated the extremity of the stars above me, so I let her stay.

I photographed like crazy at Claire and Michael's—logs in the fireplace burned to the shape of horses' heads, flames behind; real horses (Sundance and Timberline, tensely alert in the wind, their gaze riveted toward something I could not see); Claire in her black cape with a distant soldier perched on her shoulder like a small spirit whispering in her ear; Claire again—her hands, the fingers chopped away by a shadow, leaving just the wedding band and little finger. The composition on that one was surprisingly beautiful—a mix of textures and folds.

We exchanged presents just before leaving. Claire gave me a shell pendant with tiny gold drop, a thin cotton lisle undershirt, lace-trimmed, and a brown plaid basket—each something I'd have chosen for myself.

Just a few nights here at home before heading on to Mother's in Tallahassee for Christmas. Tonight we made peanut butter cookies, then lay on the rug near the speakers with the warm cookies and milk to listen to "The Spider's Web" together. I looked at our books, Harvey's and mine, all out of order after friends helped me paint the room eighteen months ago and still not rearranged and could hear him say, "Kantor's Law again: 'Temporary becomes Permanent.'" Ovid's *Metamorphoses* caught my eye, and I took it down while Jordan listened to the radio stories. Out of the corner of my eye I saw him pick a book the same size and shape and turn the pages the way I did, studying the rows of words.

After I put him to bed I came back downstairs and watched two-thirds of Olivier's *Richard III*. I watched too long, wanting the dark mood it brought to break so I wouldn't carry it up the stairs with me. But it didn't, and I recognized the masochism in watching it further, so I switched off the TV and put some apple cider on the stove to warm. As it heated, I read "The Story of Baucis and Philemon" in Ovid, not knowing the legend or its theme, only because it was mentioned in the introduction for its grace and tenderness. Baucis and Philemon were a poor but loving old couple visited by Jupiter and Mercury in disguise. When the gods offered them any wish, they asked to guard the temple and

> "Since we have spent our happy years together,
> May one hour take us both away; let neither
> Outlive the other that I may never see
> The burial of my wife, nor she perform
> That office for me. And the prayer was granted.
> As long as life was given, they watched the temple
> And one day, as they stood before the portals
> Both very old, talking the old days over
> Each saw the other put forth leaves, Philemon
> Watched Baucis changing, Baucis watched Philemon,
> And as the foliage spread, they still had time
> To say 'Farewell, my dear!' and the bark closed over
> Sealing their mouths. And even to this day
> The peasants in that district show the stranger

The two oak trees close together, and the union
Of Oak and Linden in one."

The day Dr. Newman told me Harvey had leukemia—Harvey was in the hospital recovering from the unnecessary appendectomy—I asked Sonia to spend the night. The apartment was totally dark; we could see the lights of Greenwich Village beneath us. I told her Harvey and I were like two trees whose roots had grown round and round each other and that if he died I would take a cleaver and chop the fingers from my left hand because my roots would be severed in the same strokes his were anyway. I wouldn't survive his death.

Mother reminded me yesterday that Rabbi Friedman had cautioned us in our wedding to stand as separate trees with only the leaves touching. I don't remember his saying that. Undoubtedly he did. I didn't hear.

We're in Tallahassee now, at Mother's for Christmas. Her gifts to me yesterday reflected my widowhood, not my personality. Straps and wheels to put on luggage since I have to carry it myself. A strobe light for the glove compartment in case of accident. Two books on money management and personal budgeting, and a ring to wear instead of my wedding band. (Actually, it is a pretty nice ring—a sterling Phoenix.) When I put on the red hat Mary sent, she said, "There! A bright color. You must always wear primary colors to get men to look at you. Otherwise you fade into the wall." Now she has some minor Xerox executive she wants me to meet and had the nerve to say I should "dress up" for him. It's me who's not good enough in her eyes. I can imagine exactly what this guy is like. I said, "Mother, I'm suspicious of men who never wear jeans," but she simply could not comprehend. It's interesting that none of the people who know me best have made any gestures to fix me up. I take that as a compliment to both Harvey and me.

Before we sat down to dinner, everyone lined up in the animal masks Jordan had chosen—Bruce, Virginia, her son Mark, Mother, Jordan: cow, dog, rabbit, cat, pig—and I took a formal family portrait. Then I went to the stereo and put on an album of carols. Mother stormed in from the kitchen, saying, "Take those off. Those belong in church." She wanted only Muzak-y Xmas-rock-bounce: Chet Atkins on the guitar. At the table I mentioned that I'd like to go to a carol service later or any service really and she said, "I don't think there are any on Christmas. Only people who are alone would ever think of going!" How afraid she must still be of the grief within her.

This afternoon she opened up a little. We were in front of the large mirror in her bathroom.

"I can't accept that," she said, pointing disparagingly at her image. "It doesn't look like me. Sometimes I feel like I'm standing six feet behind both my body and that reflection, watching them. I can see them, but it's like they're someone else. I don't know them. I don't know them at all."

Then she spoke of her own mother's dying of heart disease.

"One day near the end I came into her room and she was sitting on the edge of her bed, staring into the mirror across the room, the low mirror on her dresser. She was muttering. She was gaunt by then and what she was saying was, 'They won't recognize me.' She meant her sisters, who were already dead. 'They won't recognize me,' she said."

I am wild to get home. There is no privacy, no individual space permitted in this house, just as there wasn't when I was growing up—no closeness, but no solitude either. Shared rooms, reading interrupted, naps ridiculed.

My head is aching after Mother just woke me. I had asked her *please* not to wake me for phone calls, for *anything* (you have to try to think of all the specific contingencies in advance), and she woke me for a phone call—a friend from graduate school who teaches at Florida State. This despite the DO NOT DISTURB sign I put up, too. There has not been one time in five days that I have retired from the group, whether for a nap, or for yoga, or for a bath (yes, she even barged in while I was in the tub), that she hasn't disturbed me. She is desperate in her loneliness, but I must just as desperately protect my fragile self, and she has won out, worn me out. I'm not in control of my time here—she governs. Head aching. Need rest. Jordan keeps waking me in the night. I am too high strung to sleep in the same room with anyone.

Will I ever calm down?

A final perverse pleasure. On our last morning I saw a cockroach in Mother's sparkling kitchen. Few things in recent memory have delighted me so.

Coming home to Stonington is a relief. The house looks good. It makes me think of the Christmas Harvey came home after Blast Crisis, after they'd said he'd never leave the hospital. Our lovemaking that afternoon—simple, mutual, profound. Strength, power even. He pushed me onto the bed, command and happiness and life in his eyes. Our final joining.

This afternoon I asked Jordan's sitter, Christy, what she was doing tonight (New Year's Eve), and only just now, at 9:00 P.M., did I realize her sweet natural courtesy—how she didn't ask me what *I* would be doing.

I went in to check on Jordan. He was so small I had to look twice—curled in a fold of the blanket. At first I thought he might have gone and crawled into my bed, but no, he was there, our son. I lay down with my nose and mouth buried in his fragrant hair and inhaled him. I guess all mother animals revel in the scent of their offspring, but people just don't talk about it. Sweet warm smell, his own.

I am quiet inside and ready for the new year.

New Year's Day. Jordan and I went ice-skating on a pond in the park behind Westerly Library this morning. It's a Frederick Law

Olmstead park, I think Harvey said, like Central Park—wonderful in every season. I watched myself in Jordan, learning to skate on Storm Lake. Remembered Daddy shoveling a big area clear, beyond the dock, for Bruce and me.

"I wish I could skate all the time, without the ice!" Jordan squealed through his muffler.

"Sometimes I dream about skating," I called back. "It's so free and effortless—like ballet in the air."

"I had a dream that everyone in the world was my age," he said. "Nobody older."

"Ah!"

"Nobody bossing, nobody better." A hockey puck skidded between us, following by two jostling teenagers. "An even better dream," he added, "would be that everyone in the world was three and I was four!"

In Howard Johnson's after an hour with Kramer. Tired, very frustrated—nothing learned, nothing resolved. He still angers me, still draws me.

I told him, "I see two alternatives: absolutely ending all contact and waiting for absence to erase my thoughts of you, or seeing you platonically—getting to know your family, having lunch, slowly letting the thing discharge."

He said, "There's a third: continuing to meet and discuss it, examine it until the magic has gone out of it." This, the obvious suggestion, hadn't occurred to me and I was a little taken aback. But now I realize that I didn't think of it as a solution to the infatuation because I view it as a *cause*. Talking with him, having the undivided attention of an intelligent man, trading thoughts, is what is so seductive.

I sat in a chair wrapped in a comforter for three hours straight when I got home, waiting to feel better, waiting for something to fall into place in my head that would cure these blues. Can console myself that the feelings I once had for Spencer, which also made me miserable, did fade.

A hard day with Jordan too. The minute I walked into nursery school he laid into me—unprovoked anger. Tonight he wanted to play a you're-an-animal game with me as an avenue for his hostility. The names he chose for me:

rat	crab
spider	poison snake
porcupine	butting goat

This was at McDonald's after sectional choir rehearsal, which I had bribed him to sit through with the McDonald's date (couldn't get a sitter). Now that I think of it, he was the one who bribed me, saying, "I'll be quiet if you take me to McDonald's after." After the animal game, he admitted he was angry and had hurt feelings because he was the only one at rehearsal who couldn't read and sing along. That doesn't explain why he was mad when I picked him up though.

I was supposed to go to a movie with Stella tonight, but the sitter canceled, plus I was too tired to drive, strung out from Jordan's unhappiness (he'd just said he goes to school and "waits and waits and waits" for me). Decided not to go, then to go after all—take a quick bath, put on fresh clothes, try to start the day over. He said, "You want to go out because you don't want to be with me, don't you?" I said, "Sometimes that's true but not tonight. Tonight I know I'd only act crabby to you because I'm so tired, and I don't *want* to be crabby at you, so I'll go." But I couldn't get another sitter.

When I tucked him in, I said, "You know how important you are to me. You're the only person I have to love."

"That's not true," he said. "You love Harvey."

"I do love Daddy, but he died. I can't talk to him or hug him."

"Well, I love Daddy because he's funny and tells jokes."

This is the first time he's used the present tense about Harvey with me, though Kramer says that in the privacy of therapy he often does. What I see in him is increasing irritability, fatigue, whining, loneliness-anxiety, and handwashing. He won't play outside, won't

even go outside, without me. Right before he learned to talk in
sentences he acted like this, too. He wants desperately to learn to
read. Maybe this is part of the pressure.

It is snowing wet heavy snow—really fast, like rain. I ought to
print today, but I am tired. In a month it will have been two years.
Seven hundred days and nights. I ought to be getting used to it, but
I'm not. Still I can't let go. I even notice that when it's necessary to
mention it, I always say "Harvey died" or "my husband died," not
"Harvey's *dead*." The verb is somehow less final.

A cup of tea would help to wake me up, but I fear the caffeine.

Today as I silently read the paper, passing over the word "gigantic," Jordan asked aloud, "What does 'gigantic' mean?" It stunned
me. Something else of note, too, though unrelated. In the car on
our way home he stated, "There are three people who don't die:
God, Santa Claus, and Mrs. Santa." This may explain his long-
time desire to be Santa when he grows up.

Who knows? Maybe those two things *are* related.

At chorus rehearsal today the sunlight came in through stained-
glass windows over the harpist's shoulders, back-lighting her fingers.
All the harp strings were translucent as she played the "Interlude"
from Britten's "A Ceremony of Carols." The harp—immense, ivory
and brass, richly carved. I felt my whole being weaving in and out of
those strings in the streaming sunlight.

The reflection of candles in Jordan's brown eyes is like the reflection of candles in Harvey's brown eyes. After supper, as soon as he
went into the living room to work on his block castle, I lay my head
on the table and let five or six fast, nearly automatic sobs ripple
through me, hardly aware I was crying, knowing there was not time

for it before he would come back in—maybe two minutes. Having grieved for such a long time teaches you how to let a small wave of it wash over you quickly without even touching the basic mood of the evening, which in this case was calm and happy, even a little celebratory: Jordan learned to *read today*. When I picked him up at school, he made me sit down and read me a whole, long "See Spot Run" book. I still can't believe it. He knew every single word, even when I pointed to them out of order. Anyway, the pain is like a deep, wide subterranean river that surfaces sometimes only for a second and does not change the landscape at all.

Browsing through the book Harvey gave me during my sophomore year, before we ever started going out together, I find: "Who takes the child by the hand takes the mother by the heart." Perhaps what I feel for Kramer is as simple as that. That was my first thought on the matter months ago. Maybe it will turn out to be the most accurate.

After two months of thinking about it but never getting around to doing it, I finally organized the insurance file regarding the New York car break-in last fall. I called my agent, said I'd bring it by, but before I could leave the house, the insurance company representative from New Haven came to the door—not having talked to the agent or anything. Pure coincidence. Something in me knew he was coming. And what is even odder, he said he thought he had just seen me walking down the street but was too shy to call out. The woman's coat and hat he described are exactly like mine.

I don't know what to make of these things, but they fill me with wonder, and pleasure.

I have been thinking about Kirlian photography, how if you cut away half of a leaf and then photograph it by Kirlian method, the outline, aura, and veins of the part that was cut away, still show up.

Like the magnetic "hole" beside me for three to four days after Harvey died—again and again I felt my arm "sucked out" from my side as if to touch him. Scary. A force-field.

When people love each other, the auras of their hands resting on a table overlap in a Kirlian photograph. When they argue, the auras retract. I photographed a tree on the cove today with this in mind— the sun and water sun-stripe directly behind the trunk so it looked as if the tree itself were radiating light.

Overheard, the two kids in the next room playing sweetly, then a squabble.

Tucker: "My daddy will get you. He's big and strong and will bang you on the floor wrestling."
Jordan: (silence) (*long* silence)

Tucker immediately turned conciliatory and the subject was changed. A few minutes later Jordan said, "Come on upstairs. I'll show you a real picture of him. *Real,* not pretend, *real real real.*"

I'm in Washington now with an older woman friend, for Jimmy Carter's inauguration. (She had extra tickets.) Today at the parade I saw a dreadful thing—an enormous float from Alaska, heavy, with lots of people riding on it, being pulled by a dog team. The dogs were straining against the pavement, their feet pads torn, bleeding, skin scraped off from repeated efforts to start the float. Some were bleeding at the hip joints too, and all panted desperately. It was hideous. I jumped the barrier, crossing the parade to a guard, and begged him to help. "I can't do anything, lady." Sought another. He said he'd make a call. Someone brought a dish of water. The hindmost dog was peeing blood.

Last night at the Kennedy Center we saw Tom Stoppard's *Travesties.* Afterward, while I was phoning for dinner reservations, a poster caught my eye—Hal Holbrook in *Mark Twain Tonight*—the role Harvey did his senior year in high school. But the dates were the thing: February 15–18. February 15 is his birthday, February 18 is his death day.

Amazing. Today at the Treasures of Tutankhamen exhibit I saw the prototype of the fly pendant I bought in Paris: "Fly Pendant of Queen Ahotpe, 18th Dynasty, 1567–1320 b.c.," the label said. The original was found in the queen's treasure. Mother of two Theban princes who fought a war of liberation against the Hyksos rulers of Lower Egypt, she herself rallied the Theban forces at a critical moment. For this the king awarded her the fly pendant, which thereafter became "a mark of rank given for valor in the face of death."

Home again, deflated, coming in from Kramer's. Finally, after six months of refusing to take a firm stand on the issue, he said he's decided not to see us under any circumstances after Jordan's therapy ceases—two more times.

Well, I pulled myself together laudably after Kramer's rejection but now I am undone again. Trigger to the plunge: his unexpected call to change Jordan's next appointment, hearing his voice, his query, "How are you?" Me bright, surprised, dripping from the tub, "Fine!" Why, when they do open suddenly—him, Philip— why can't I respond? I should have said how hurt and down he'd made me feel. How not only did I feel rejected but puzzled—how I couldn't comprehend why anyone would turn away from friend- ship offered. But all I said was "Fine!," responded to business, and hung up.

Startling dream last night—sent me shooting into the air bolt upright, ripping the covers from the bed as I awoke.

Genre: Harvey returns.
Theme: That's not entirely great.

He's been gone a year. I had thought him dead, but evidently he has only been angry with me, and now wants to come home and be cared for. He is dying, and bossy. I try to comprehend it while I respond to him, cheek against his tentatively, thoughts flashing as I struggle to understand. I remember seeing, touching him dead. Besides, I know all that I have been through. If he put me through the grief deliberately, it was unforgivable. I love him, though, and want to embrace him fully. But (this is the first dream with any "buts") no one can say how long he'll live, how many years of anxious waiting I'll be asked to endure again. I want him back but know this return will destroy my life, my mind. I don't want to go back to serving. All this is going through my mind as our cheeks touch. Then he sweeps into the house, assuming command, ordering me to clear my things out of his office. I protest, and the protest grows larger in me—"No, it's not fair. I earn as much as you now. I've made a life, struggled to do it, earned it." It is a gross disenfranchisement.

I awoke then, in alarm at the guilty thought that I would not welcome him back without regard for cost. But I felt good, too—knew it was a milestone. I remember clearly when I would have given my life's breath for five minutes with his spirit. Now, in this dream, I didn't want to give up my time (which would go to serving him), or even my office. I need him markedly less. It feels good, gives me confidence, and yet it, too, is a kind of loss. Will I keep losing him more and more, like this, until there isn't even a memory of love?

Driving home from Mystic at sunset, in a hurry to pick up my lecture notes and get to URI, I saw from the corner of my eye three swans in the cove. Something strange about one. A thread, from its mouth, taut, pulling something. Oh God! A fishhook. It had swallowed a fishhook! I pulled over quickly, ran to the rocks. Slowly, the bird floated toward me, dragging a large mass of seaweed. What could I cut the line with? Where was the hook lodged? Would the bird come to me? They're fierce, aren't they? I have to get to class. Who will help? Must leave, right *now*, but can't leave. What to do? Think. Conservationists.

I got into the car and drove home fast, called the Thames Science Center. Had a very hard time convincing anyone to try to find someone to help the bird. I wanted to do it myself, cared deeply, but had to get to work, was late already. No one there cared! Couldn't they see the horror of it? A smooth white swan with a hook in its flesh?

Finally one guy said, "All right. All right. I'll call the State Conservation Department for you." For me. For the *bird*, dammit!

I was already awake, uniquely awake—bolted up alert ten minutes before it rang.

"Mrs. Kantor, this is Cassie on B-1. I think you'd better come. Harvey's real bad." (Real l ba ad. Help, God.)

"Oh, Jayne." (OOo h h h, Jay ay ay ay ne.)

"He died." (ie aie ay ayd.)

"We just found him when we took his breakfast in. His roommate didn't even know."

Think. Do not feel. Ask hospital to arrange a ride.

"Dr. Austin will come for you."

Wake a sitter. Do not wake Jordan. Prevent Sharlene from leaving for work, get someone to her before I call.

"Steve? Harvey died."

"Don't tell me that."

"Get Mike to Sharlene's before she leaves."

Get dressed: earth shoes. Navy cardigan.

"Mother? It happened. Can you stand by? I'll call back when I can."

Catch sitter before she rings the doorbell. Philip arrives (I'm on the phone—Mike and Harriet), wearing his green parka, same as the last time I woke him, to stop Harvey's convulsions. Jordan is up. I take him into my lap on the rocker in his room.

"Daddy's very sick. I must go be with him."

Philip walks me to the car. Cold rain. We get in. He waits until I tell him to start the engine. Windshield wipers. Drive begins. Teeth clenched till jawbone cracks.

"This is un-sat-is-fac-to-ry. This is un-sat-is-fac-to-ry. This is un-sat-is-fac-to-ry."

Car stops. Philip waits.

"What will happen now?"

"He'll still be in his room."

"Will they let me stay with him?"

"As long as you need to."

"Then?"

"Then they will cover him and take him to the morgue downstairs."

Elevator doors open on his floor. Nurses look at me with blank faces, heaving eyes. Someone takes my arm. Philip is gone. The door opens slowly.

One eye is open. Yellow glaze. No gaze. Couldn't they have closed it? No, I need to know he's dead. The eye will teach it. Mute, shocked look: Doesn't look asleep. Black lips, blood blistered. I'm rocking sideways on my feet. I touch his forehead—cold as metal. I kiss the cold—must know it. Fear. The hair—the hair is still the same. I stroke and stroke, I try to comfort. Want his warmth, my feet between his thighs, curled close in bed. A nurse appears. "You should sit down." I draw a chair up close to him and softly cry. The sobs are silent. Fogle comes, as quiet, takes my hand. I lean my cheek against his arm. He curbs me.

"Get hold of yourself. Come into the conference room." Explains his shock.

"We never thought . . . the lab reports were not that bad . . . we have to do an autopsy . . . we must know why."

"I know why—it's that he had pain this time."

"We must."

"Oh, please . . ."

"We must."

Phone calls—urgent. Rabbi, gentle. Sharlene, accusing. The nurses: "Do you want to help us ready him?"

Deciding no, I ask to be alone. Remove distractions, collect awareness. Leaning on the table, head buried in my arms, I feel a whooshing up—a lifting wind as if some part of me—my youth?—were sucked up into the air beyond reclaim. I let it go, releasing this which I can give, to Harvey on his way. His room again. The roommate's gone. I press the windows open, needing air inside. Then sit beside him, blank with pain. They say the time has come. I watch them lift him to the stretcher, sheet his face, then grip the bar myself. I'll push him down. They look ahead, close others' doors, and one hand on his foot—dear, cold—and one hand on the bar, I wheel him to the morgue. A rubber-aproned man receives us, surprised that I am there. I won't let go of Harvey, frightened by the blood on rubber, until Eve comes down too. I beg her to stay with him.

"Please don't leave him alone."

In the emergency room they meet me, give me his clothes in a brown paper bag, which I hold to my chest. Philip has waited, drives me back. The rain still falls. At our door, his face is failure. Dumb despair.

I climb the stairs and find Jordan, take him up, and in the rocker where I nursed him, explain what cannot be.

Wild grief Sun-salutations. The dance of a slave before a blind and heartless universe. Bowed, broken, then defiant—alternating. To the rhythm of "this is un-sat-is-fac-to-ry" I sobbed and did Sun-salutations—two dozen, three—until I was covered with sweat and the emotions of writing it down were spent.

Casey Halston, a friend from chorus, just called from Boston where her husband is having brain surgery. She was worried about what she saw in the mirror.

"Deep lines from your nose down along on either side of your mouth?" I asked.

"Yes, yes!"

"They go away, I don't know how."

The lines in your face go away. The lines in your heart don't.

I hung up and went out into the garden, walked slowly around. I paused by the snapdragons—dry brown stalks—and pulled a seed pod off, rolled it absently in my palm. Then I looked at it more closely. It was bone-colored, skull-shaped, with openings for eyes, mouth and nose. Miniature—three-eighths of an inch long—like the skull of a fetus.

How rarely I think about the child I terminated, how dangerous such thoughts are to me. I write of them here as I did a year ago, in tiny script, wanting to hide them. A daughter . . . These last few weeks I've been swept by fantasies of one day having another child, convinced that I wouldn't again miss so much of its development by my preoccupations on the one hand with Harvey's illness and death and on the other with the conviction that I should be doing something more with my mind. I long for Mary to have her baby and wish she were the kind of woman who would understand my desire to put her child to my breast.

I came in out of the cold yard and went to the stereo, like an alcoholic to the bar, for a shot of Bach, groping at any order I could find. I should have put on piano music though. Casals's cello is only another voice, wringing.

Bad dreams, always it seems. Days of effort followed by nights of effort. Years, now, of anxious dreams. It is only when my waking life approaches the breaking point, when I feel I absolutely can take no more—only then, that night, does there come a dream of release, of love, of flight, of understanding. One night in a hundred I am freed. Last night was one of them.

Harvey visited me in a dream last night—February 18, 1977, the second anniversary of his death. A great gift was this dream.

He has come back. Come back healed, whole, himself emotionally and physically, full of love and yearning for me. He is well, not sick, not yet-to-die, but through it all and back. He has been gone three years. People are all around, good people—Mother and Daddy, Paul and Laura behind us, Maury on my right—but all I want is to get home with him, to be alone together, to cling to him. Feel utterly blessed to have him back. The fullness of our mutual love. He keeps giving me hugs and long kisses, which is embarrassing. I am ashamed of my embarrassment, but need privacy for the massive emotions sweeping through me. I have so much to tell him—think first of the awfulness with Spencer, the abortion.

It will have to wait. We are all sitting in a movie theater at the darkened seashore to watch an important film. Harvey and I hold hands, our hands fused by the indescribable flow of love passing through them. At one point I notice with surprise that his co-author is holding my other hand, the right one. I don't mind, but am unsettled to realize it has been without my knowledge, so exclusive has been my concentration on the left hand which Harvey holds. I am swept with a nameless joy in the presence of my husband, the love passing between us.

At intermission the sky lights up, a rheostat on command, and many get up to walk down the boardwalk for food. There are to be four "shorts" during intermission, though, and we stay to watch them. We all sit happily, like children, watching an artsy film running backward on a tiny screen. The titles are utterly ingenious—animals that crawl about, lively, then take positions as letters, race along acting just like animals but turning into exact words as they go along—not animation, not straight "reality" photographed, but some Reality I have never before witnessed. A new kind of reading— the words change into other words, moving, yes, but nonlinear.

Then Mother and Daddy get up to get food, and we go along, sociably. I ask Harvey if he would like to go home then (which is what I want) or wait until the end of the film. He says, "Let's watch a little while longer, then go." His right to choose—he just got back to life! He walks ahead of us and holds his hand out to me. Mother and Daddy urge me on, to take his hand. I try, but suddenly grow aware that he has been invisible for a few seconds, that I have been respond-

ing to the idea *of his physical presence, and that the hand he was holding out is really just a rose blowing on the ground ahead of us. I run as hard as I can to get to him, while it seems that both he and Mother and Daddy are merely strolling—but I can't catch up with the rose. It is odd: it isn't following natural laws. Then I realize the blowing rose is a wooden rose, a symbol he has left for me, and know in my heart that he is gone forever.*

I awoke with a wonderful warmth, not the anguish I usually meet when leaving him in the dreamworld for a consciousness of his absence. This is the first time this has happened. A simple feeling, unadulterated—love. This dream, a gift I carry into the third year.
   Now the tears do come.

The
THIRD YEAR
The Crack in the Teacup Opens
a Lane to the Land of the Dead

—Winter Yet Again—

A faculty meeting in Providence at noon. I was the first one asked to outline my course.

"Proseminar in General Studies: The Night Sky. The first half of this course will be called 'De-mystifying the Night Sky.' It will include naked-eye celestial observation, astronomy for absolute beginners (like myself), a sketchy history of science as it relates to astronomy, and pertinent mythology. The second half of the course will be called 'Re-mystifying the Night Sky,' and it will cover poetry and music and science fiction and painting—all works sharing the theme of awe in beholding the heavens at night."

I gave a list of the works I intended to use. Finished, whew. There was a pause, a long pause. Then everyone—exclamations, suggestions, "Can I sit in?"s. However, for the rest of the meeting people kept staring at me surreptitiously.

I showered early this morning, shampooed my hair twice with Scandinavian birch shampoo, scrubbed my ears, back, shoulders— everything, shaved my legs, clipped my toenails. Naked and clean, with a towel wrapped around my head, I stepped back into the bedroom. The bed was turned back neatly where I had slipped out. Across it lay the gauzy white nightgown Sonia gave me for Christmas. The two down pillows I bought on Harvey's birthday sat puffed up like fresh fat hens.

The telephone rang when I was halfway down the stairs. I hurtled myself down the last five steps, swerved past the table and grabbed it from the hook. It was a friend inviting me to a party for Philip and

Karen. They got *married*—three days ago—in England! I hung up and stood there with my hand on the receiver, eyes and mouth wide open. It wasn't surprising, and yet I was surprised. Jordan came swinging in from the living room, arms full of Lego blocks, but when he saw me, he stopped and asked warily, "Mommy, why are you looking so gloomy?"

I fixed breakfast automatically, stirring oats into boiling water, pouring juice. If Philip is married, then what I have clung to as decreed consolation will never be. And what is worse, it has been wrong all along. I cleared the table, zipped up Jordan's jacket, and we walked over to the Stonington Market. Josie lifted him up on the cashier's counter and gave him grapes to eat and I looked blankly at the array of fruits and vegetables. I had my list there in my hand, on a white paper plate, but all I could bring myself to buy was a bunch of pink hothouse rhubarb. When we got home Jordan pulled his Jordan-bench over to the counter so he would be tall enough and watched as I cut the stalks. Then he stirred flour and sugar into the bowl of sour fruit with a big wooden spoon. I showed him again how to weave a lattice-work crust and we put the pie in the oven. We each had some with supper. It was perfect—sugary crisp and tart. After I tucked him in bed, I came back downstairs and ate the rest of it—the whole rest of the pie—one piece at a time.

I am lying propped on an elbow, recovering in bed from all-night stomach cramps and diarrhea. I never want to see a piece of rhubarb pie again. Jordan just brought me in a get-well "card," punched out on red plastic Dymo tape—JAYNE LOVE HOPE LOVES AROUND YOU—and stuck it on the side of the chest near my pillow.

There is a sadness blooming in the boredom of this Sunday afternoon. I sit and gaze out over my desk into the empty gray street, trying to imagine what would cheer me. Seeing Claire and Michael, or Sonia; singing. I guess I should go up and work on the

"Stabat Mater," but it's not inspiring to practice without a piano. I could photograph, but I don't see anything worth preserving.

The Twenty-third Psalm stared out at me tonight from a book of poetry I was reading Jordan. It seemed out of place, sandwiched there between Wordsworth and Ben Jonson:

> *"The Lord is my shepherd;*
> *I shall not want.*
> *He maketh me to lie down in green pastures.*
> *He leadeth me beside the still waters.*
> *He restoreth my soul . . ."*

but I read the whole thing aloud to him. Then we exchanged a silent hug and I came downstairs and switched on the TV and immediately heard the entire psalm again on a program called "Bonzo." It's been what? two years since I heard or read that—it would have been at Harvey's memorial service. The children from chorus sang it, the force and purity of their tone made everyone gasp. My God, that was February 23rd, and today is February 23rd. And Harvey's bar mitzvah was February 23rd and his text was this psalm!

The air was cold but the light was orange and vibrant as I walked to the party for Philip and Karen this evening. The sun was setting over the harbor and everything white and wooden in the village glowed pale peach. I ran my leather-gloved fingers along the pickets of a fence I passed, expecting them to sing like a comb, but they didn't. Basically, though, I felt full of pleasure at my inclusion.

The warmth of Philip's cheek as I offered a congratulatory kiss caught me off guard for a moment, but I recovered quickly. Karen was beaming, and he seemed happy too, though a little embarrassed—pushing his glasses up on his nose and half hiding behind his hand. We had a long exclusive talk right in the middle of the party; he described his jogging route—he comes up our hill each night—and I got a little drunk, basking in his company. "It's Jupiter that has the moons, Jayne, Saturn has rings!" he corrected me, laughing. He quibbled with Karen over what day they had married—"February 16th, not 18th"—and I was surprised that they were not both certain about something like that. We sat for dinner in a gracious country kitchen—Windsor chairs, old silver, miniature geraniums—and during the meal he kept looking at me over the candles and smiling.

But on the way home, I thought of Harvey leaning back against his cranked-up hospital bed, stroking my head with an outstretched hand. "I know that you and Philip will be together after I die," he was saying, his face radiant with fever. "Oh, not forever, but for a while. He'll look after you, and that makes me happy." The memory coiled up around my insides and made me lean against a light pole for support.

I just got home from my final meeting with Kramer. Jordan already had his, on the 18th. My teeth chattered half the drive back, and now the house is freezing because I turned the thermostat down while I was gone. It was the first warm day of late winter—high 40s, low 50s maybe—and I was too optimistic about both the furnace and wearing just a sweater, and about child psychiatrists, too, I guess.

"Jordan will probably always feel jilted," he said. "There's really nothing more that we can do."

"But there must be some way to transform that fact, not to erase it but to turn it to good use. Some way to guide him right into his pain so he can put it behind him."

"Just let him get on with his life."

The conversation struggled along for a while and then I changed the subject and asked if he'd caught the TV special on childhood this week.

"I don't have time for television," he said impatiently, "I have grant requests to write," and got up from his chair.

As he reached to open the door, I said, "By the way, Philip Austin got married."

"So?" he replied. "Were you going to spend the rest of your life living out Harvey's fantasies or your own?"

I bit back the retort I wanted to fling, and didn't say any good-byes either—to have said anything would have been to misrepresent the fullness in me—but he did.

"I'll very much miss seeing Jordan *and* you," he said, and gazed at me in that way of his. I looked away and was silent. From the far side of the waiting room, I glanced back, and he was still gazing at me.

So. The future is now a total blank. No vague framework of fantasies to hold it up—no Philip, no Kramer. I look around this silent room and wonder. I reach out and pick up the yellow metal camel silhouette from the window sill. It is very cold. I look at the four-rams candlestick by the window seat, the wooden alligator treasure box, the standing elephants puzzle. The animals know how to live without a future. Something about them is complete in a way that I am not. I envy them, spared the rush of language. I wish I could know what it is they think about.

A dream:

I am with a group of people around a carnival stand. I see a pack of horses coming—five or six gorgeous, big animals, with white stripes down their brown noses. I appreciate their beauty but know how dangerous they are. For safety, I get into the car to photograph them. The others get in too, but keep rolling the windows down, trying to feed them. The horses try to force their muzzles in to bite me. One even says, "Which one is Jayne? Which one is Jayne?" and the people naively show him. I try to fend him off with a pillow. His jaws are breaking two of my fingers even through the pillow, crushing the bones. I scream at the others to roll up their windows. The horses bump against our car and rock it, and I am afraid it will overturn.

Heavy rain and dark clouds all day. The book plates came in the mail:

Ex libris
Harvey A. Kantor
presented to
the Kantor Memorial Reading Room
University of Rhode Island
by his wife and son

I spent the afternoon on the living room floor pasting them in and trying not to remember when he read each book—Dag Hammarskjöld's *Markings, Streets for People,* Henry Steele Commager. About 5:00 P.M. Karen called to say Philip feels too shy for me to photograph them for a wedding gift. Despairing at it all, I lay crumpled on the floor among the stacks of books, a pillow over my head to fend off Jordan's attempts to get me to react to him, for over an hour.

Someone rang our doorbell at 3:30 this morning, then left. I staggered to the door, opened it—no one there. I heard steps down the street—a voice for a second—maybe imagined. I yelled, "What do you want?" I was frightened and still half asleep. Thought of ghosts. Awful dreams blistered my sleep for the rest of the night.

I have kept Harvey's body beneath my feet in the room, or the ground, for too long—by choice at first and then the winter weather has made it necessary. Deep white-veined ice has formed on him, frozen in folds the way it seeps out of a cliff. In some places it is ten inches thick, in others, a foot or finger sticks out through it. I stand on him protectively. Then there is a thaw—is it ten days since the thaw? or since he died? I know the smell will start soon, but I don't want to let go of him for burial. I leave briefly and return to find out that while I was gone, the doctors have done a second autopsy without my permission. I am furious with a terrible sense of injustice and impotence. This autopsy has shown a broken neck; the doctors inti-

*mate murder, but remembering how ill he had been the night before
he died, I know it was a seizure so severe it snapped his neck. Another
finding—he had gone blind several hours before his death. A huge
pity wells up in me when I hear this. I want to bathe him, comb his
hair, but am afraid I'll be repelled by the smell seeping from the huge
incision roughly sewn up in his chest, his skull. A technician hands
me his brain in a clear plastic bag—heavy—with a crude remark,
and then apologizes, "Jargon, you know." It was the brain that
revealed the blindness. I look down at his chest incision, with the ten-
day rot of innards festering up through it—a gaping puncture where
they have forced in the sharp tool to suck out his organs and blood.
Maybe if I wear a surgical mask I can bathe him. I know his head
will flop around like a dead bird's, but I want my love to overcome
this, to go beyond.*

Ashamed of my own fear, I awaken. I handled my part in
Harvey's death badly—refusing to see he was dying, not being there
when he did die, not realizing his "spirit" was still close by afterward, allowing the autopsy, not staying with his body all that night
and while dirt was shoveled onto his coffin and well after. Of
course, it wouldn't have been right to subject Jordan to all of that—
or would it?—and I thought then that my greater obligation was to
him. But maybe that was the time Harvey needed my concentration
more than ever, in the immediate post-mortem pain and disintegra-
tion. I am sure now that it takes some time for a soul to shift into
whatever it may be metamorphosing into—that the process is gradual, not sudden, however traumatic the moment of death may be.
And I wish I had helped him, had at least tried to help him.

I ran into Poppy Mitchell twice this afternoon. We chatted a bit
on the sidewalk outside the news office, and she told me of a
coincidence with her son Nathan and Jeff Halston. They were born
on the same day, the same year, and both had surgery on the same
part of the brain on the same day, though a couple of years apart. I
didn't tell her, but I was thinking about my friend Jodie in Kansas

City whose friends Poppy and George lost a son. Here, too, are a
Poppy and George whose son died.

The main thing, though, was that she asked if Jordan and I would
like to go to St. Croix for spring break. Her brother, who lives there,
asked her to find someone to look after his house and dogs while he
comes here for Easter. I can think of nothing better: beaches and
sand and hot, hot sun. I told her yes at once.

It is Jordan's birthday—he is five years old. While he was at
nursery school this afternoon, I had the movers deliver a piano. It's
a big old family grand, a Chickering. I found it through our dentist
here and had it shipped from Boston. I stood in the yard, in the cold
sunlight, nervous and excited, clutching my sweater around me as
the men strained and pulleyed the mammoth instrument up a ramp
laid up the garden stairs. After long and tense maneuvering, they
got it inside and over onto legs I thought would never hold. The
heavy quilted covers were drawn off, and there it stood, brown wood
oiled and gleaming like the muscles of a wrestler.

Jordan was ecstatic. He sat down the minute he got home and
played "Funny Little Squirrel," which he had learned on his toy
organ, about fifteen times. It was hard to pull him away so the tuner
could work on voicing. He hung on the man, rapt, for an hour. I
am feeling much better.

My class arranged themselves up the steps of a wooden reviewing
stand at the edge of the darkest field on campus tonight and I took
their picture using only moonlight.

Last night I went to hear James Merrill read his poetry in a
crowded room in the basement of the library. One of the poems,
"Verse for Urania," was saturated with the astronomical imagery
that has been on my mind with the Night Sky class, and I spoke to
him about it afterward. He lent me some books to help with the rest

of the semester, and I have been grappling all day with an especially difficult and fascinating one, *Hamlet's Mill*, which maintains that ancient mythology was actually a preliterate form of science, the gods and places described really being codes for astronomical activity. In particular, the book relates the myth of Phaeton to a possible historical event when the earth was burned and jarred by some cataclysm that caused the Milky Way to seem to shift away from the path it once drew from celestial north to celestial south poles, requiring a new constellation or combination of them to fill that central myth-giving function.

The authors draw upon so many different cultures and eras that my brain hurts trying to keep up, but I am captivated by the consistency of their evidence and by the sheer boldness of the undertaking—the possibility that so many apparently disparate aspects of human experience could have this hidden connection, this meaning. It's an idea big enough to lift the whole town of Stonington on its shoulders and carry it off to Canada somewhere.

I usually avoid the first part of Interstate 95, taking old Route 1 up to the University because the trees are closer to the road, but tonight I was in a hurry, so I took the Interstate. I was late for class and driving way too fast. Just before the Westerly underpass I spotted a speed trap—four police cars on the other side. I hit the brakes and looked at the dash: 70. Odometer exact at 18600.0. I thought at once: Harvey. Why think of him? Get to 55. Harvey. The odometer. Why did that number make me think of him? 1860? Historical date? 186? What is in that number? 186,000! The speed of light! At the *speed* trap, my machine shows the speed of light! Speed of light . . . transition from matter to energy. A formula for death—that's what Einstein was talking about!

$E = mc^2$
Spirit $=$ body $\times$ speed of light^2
Harvey. Death. Light.
Hello, my love.

Einstein died on the 18th too—April 18, 1955.

This afternoon we're to do it again—walk fast the two miles out Napatree Point and back—Stella and Angie and I, to get in shape for running. Halfway out on Sunday Stella told us about a woman we know, who went out to Minnesota last week to help her sister have a baby. Husband, midwife, sister, a healthy baby—all in a cold cabin in rural Minnesota. But eight hours later the baby died. I shuddered, said "Christ!" or something—we all muttered our horrified mutterings—and then this howl came up out of me. I heard it out there about eight feet in front of me, kind of going toward the setting sun and kind of coming back toward me, as if it hadn't come out of me at all. And it flashed on me that the ocean was roaring and only those two would hear it and I didn't have to figure out how to stop it from happening. And with that thought, I couldn't stop it. So it went on and on and on—subhuman sound. I was astonished. I have heard that howl before—it came out of me when Harvey died—but still it shocks. Where does all the air come from? Angie and Stella flinched and drew back from me, appalled more, I think, by the moan than by the baby's death itself.

Coming back, they ran on far ahead, individually, working out. I walked with my head down, avoiding the horizon. I remembered the lesson with rocks and starfish the spring before last and knew I wasn't allowed to keep any of the subtle pebbles at my feet. A large black-veined one, though, reminded me of Harvey, and I took it in my hand. Turning to face the ocean, I coiled, then hurled it as high as I could until, I fantasized, it would pass the blue atmosphere of earth and melt into the black of space whence it came. Walking on, I realized I was humming "Come as close as the air" from the album *Changes* and really thought about that line for the first time. Then I sang it loud, my voice twisted by the grief in my throat. No one could hear how ugly it sounded. I paused to write "Harvey Kantor, 1944–1975" very big in the sand below the high-tide line, knowing another hour would wash it away. I stepped back toward the ocean and in my mind saw a light-colored wooden box about two feet long sitting heavily in the sand. Waves came up to it and lifted it a bit and drew it out to sea. Then the words themselves melted into the waves and nothing was left but glistening bubbles on the sand. Suddenly a wild exhilaration came up through me, and I started to leap, rising up and up to that charmed place in the air where, when your will is focused right, you can hang for a moment above gravity. Then, knowing I could run forever, I headed back, chilling happily in the high that comes, reliably, after four miles of hard walking.

I sat up straight in bed this morning when it was still dark, remembering something I can't recall having thought about before. It was in Storm Lake the winter I was four, the winter Bruce went off to school. The snow was so deep that winter that it covered telephone wires in places. Mother was working inside the house and I was alone outside. I had on my snowsuit and a muffler. I was moving out from the house down the hill toward the drifted sweep of the lake, into the sun. Miles of drifts—perfect white curves—lay before me, unmarked, sparkling. Flashing blue and pink and gold like diamonds. The wind moved across them, lifting transparent veils of whirling snow, which twinkled. Then it happened.

"This is why I was born," I thought.

I don't know how to describe it. It was as if what I then called "God" could see me, and I could see me too, from out in front as if I were the wind looking back down at me, swooping around through the air in the sunlight above the drifts. "This is why I was born." For that very moment, I meant. Only "moment" is wrong because I fitted into that little slot for all time. I didn't know the reason, I just knew that there was one, and that it was nothing I had known about before, and that whatever was happening then was it.

Goddamn—five weeks of silence and now Kramer calls and wants to see us again—as friends! The nerve. After he went over and over how he never sees his clients socially. I was shocked and told him so. He said, "I guess I *am* waffling on the issue. How about if I just see Jordan and not you?"

"What?!"

"Well, maybe you're right. . . . I probably shouldn't have called."

"Maybe *I'm* right?" (This artificial truncation wasn't my idea, Buster. I'm just asking you to be consistent.)

I don't know—there's more to it than I have a handle on. I'm both angry and smiling. I do like to talk to him and am pleased that Jordan and I were on his mind. I had felt that he doesn't appreciate us or care at all, had suspected his motives (financial gain) as well as his efficacy as a therapist. But this limbo of mixed signals is hard to take.

"I can see that I'm more comfortable sitting with ambiguity than you are," he concluded, and we both hung up.

March 30. I am torn today, scattered. The equinox was a week ago, but today is the first true no-coat day of spring and I want to be out basking in it. Instead, I sit here pressured by income tax forms, syllabus revisions and other indoors things with deadlines. It's our eighth anniversary and I need to plant something. I must make time, somehow, to be outside today.

There was no time for gardening, but I did make it to the tennis court this afternoon. When I was serving, I caught a sudden glimpse, in the place between the airborne ball and my moving racquet, of a rainbow corona arcing wide around the sun. It hadn't been there the last time I tossed the ball up. Stopping to gaze and point, I felt a surge of energy, and when we went back to playing, I smashed an ace across the net.

Spring

St. Croix, Virgin Islands: I am sitting on the edge of a yellow plastic chaise longue, digging both feet into the fine white sand and watching it sift through my lifted toes. Claire and Michael are swimming with the children. We didn't even unpack, just pulled out our suits, slathered each other with sunblock, and headed here to the beach. The wind is like a person's breath—warm and moist. Everything is warm in fact—the wind, the sand, the Coke bottle propped in the sand, the Coke inside the bottle, and the clear green sea itself—warm and bright. It's like a dream.

Claire brought jelly beans and Easter baskets for the kids, which she hid after they were tucked in bed. This morning they nearly took the house apart in the frenzy of the hunt, and the sofa cushions were on the floor and green plastic Easter grass was strewn all around when friends of our hosts stopped by to see how we were doing—embarrassing, but worth the children's squeals.

Five days already of house-sharing and beach play and photographs and children and intense conversation. Tonight is Claire and Michael's last, so we treated ourselves to a sitter and dinner out with a woman we met here. It felt wonderful to bathe slowly and see the white outlines of my bikini as I patted myself dry, to slip a delicate cotton dress over a new tan. We went together to a second-story restaurant whose balcony overhangs a swimming pool in a walled garden, and drank piña coladas and good white wine and ate vari-

eties of seafood and argued about life and laughed more than I have
in a very long time. While we were waiting for dessert I excused
myself to look for the ladies' room. Floating a bit from the wine, I
stopped to gaze down at the lighted pool, glowing blue in the dark
garden. It was all I could do to keep from pulling my dress over my
head and diving off the balcony down into it. I stifled the impulse,
though, and followed the back stairs down to where the waiter had
gestured. He said I had to go outside, which I did, but every door
was the wrong one. Finally I slipped between the tall hedge and the
wall leading back to the garden and peed right there in the bushes.
Perversely pleased, I returned for dessert—fresh lime mousse.

Claire, Michael and Elizabeth Jane left today, and tonight the
house seems dark and a little threatening. I heard a wild rattling in
the kitchen a minute ago and ran in from the bedroom expecting to
find a squirrel or some exotic Cruzan counterpart—lizards hang
from the walls in every room—but it was only two enormous cockroaches, three inches long. One rattled back up into the refrigerator
motor, and the other scrambled through some foil on the counter to
where I couldn't reach it.

We snorkled most of the day, Jordan and I, after buying used face
masks on our way back from the airport this morning. An unexpected apprehension tightened around me as I pushed slowly off
and forced myself to suck in breath for the first time underwater; but
then it eased, and I paddled over the shallow coral, entranced. The
water was crystalline and warm let us see everything it holds. The
light beneath its surface was soft, dappled, playing on the bottom's
perfectly rippled white sand. A school of silver minnows swam
toward my face, passing in quiet trust by either cheek. Black sea
urchins clung to the rocks like witches' pincushions; Jordan pointed
to slow worms the same color as the rock, beside them. I followed a
fish alone—vivid blue and orange—for many minutes, drunk with
the bright silence of its world.

Afterward, we went jogging on the beach; and whether it was a
result of the exercise, or perhaps a function of giving up my custom-

ary self-preoccupation, I don't know, but something in me opened to a single tall palm tree soaring above the others. I had been thinking about the wet sand beneath our feet, how the top half-inch gives softly and then is firm beneath, perfect for running. Warm, flesh-colored, endless, like a giant loving breast on the surface of the earth. That was when I saw the palm. One of its branches was moving in the wind, tracing a horizontal figure eight—an infinity sign—over and over in the air. No other palm was moving in that way, like an arm beckoning. I had the abrupt, distinct impression that the tree had been watching me, that it was calling me, or trying to show me something—a doorway in the air? A hidden entrance to another world? But what did it want me to do? Fly up there and try to pass through? Repeat its dancing on the beach? Change my thoughts, I know, but how? Then I felt a moment of complete relief, a kind of melting into that tree. I wished for my camera, knowing even so that any attempt to get the essence of the thing on film would fail, just as these words do. Something in the code of wind and frond was more piercing and precious than everything else I know.

After supper I tossed Jordan tennis balls at the neighborhood court, and then as it grew dark we walked the dogs. Red hibiscus flowers on shrubs around the houses we passed had already been sucked into the heavy dusk, but white blossoms glowed out strong, fluorescent almost. We could smell the limes and oleander. Later, we lay stretched out on benches on either side of the picnic table and Jordan picked Gemini out of the sky and wanted to hear the story of the twins again. I couldn't see them through the palm fronds above me—the familiar constellations are much higher in the sky this far south—but repeated the tale and then carried him in to bed and settled myself in front of the television.

Jordan couldn't fall asleep, so he came out to lie around with me on the couch, and we listened to Rostropovich play some Haydn cello pieces on PBS and talked a little, and I caressed him—both of us hot and me very sore from today's sunburn. (I feel as if too little skin has been stretched over too much body; had thought, wrongly, that I'd gotten enough tan to be safe.) He flopped on my legs, and we were casual, comfortable with each other's bodies as lovers are. Then he went back to bed, and I watched Ingmar Bergman's *Scenes from a Marriage*. By the end of it, I was coughing again, a combination of stress from the movie and cumulative allergy from lying on the dog-hair-covered couch for three hours. The coughing tensed up my body and destroyed the warm, rare lethargy our relaxed closeness had given. It was in bed, in the dark, propped on pillows to ease the wheezing, that I heard the cockroaches.

I was awakened this morning before dawn by a rooster crowing. Almost immediately, Jordan started to cry in his sleep. I reached over to the other bed and took his hand. In a minute or two he awoke, still whimpering, and said he had dreamed that the Good Humor truck came, and I wouldn't let him have any ice cream.

Then he went back to sleep and I got up and went into the kitchen and fixed a pot of herbal tea, which I carried in one hand, a cup and saucer balanced in the other, out onto the porch over the ravine to wait for the sunrise. How does the rooster know when it is coming? Slowly, the palm trees turned gray and I could make out the small orchids growing on pieces of driftwood hung around the porch. Today I must mist them. The sky along the horizon turned lavender and then flamingo orange, silhouetting the line of palms in the distance like a forest fire. By the time the sun itself burned through, the birds were making a terrible racket, and I didn't know Jordan had come up behind me until he slipped around the rocking chair into my lap.

I picked up the house and did laundry through the first part of the morning, and when I was hanging out wet sheets on the clothesline, I remembered how beautifully Mother used to whistle as she clipped towels to the long wires which ran parallel to the lake behind our house when I was small. There was a Baltimore oriole who always answered her—the words to the tune they warbled back and forth went, "In a pawn shop on a corner in Pittsburgh, Pennsylvania . . ."

About eleven o'clock Jordan and I drove around and up a small mountain to a tennis club built on its summit, to ask about lessons. One pro was available then, another in half an hour, so I went right out onto the court with an attractive blond fellow named Brian, who owns the club. I noticed his eyes at once—intensely blue, a parody, almost, of the Caribbean around us. I tried to concentrate on his instructions but kept seeing his thighs, the way he moved.

"Start low, finish high," he called out in a Southern accent. "Get your racquet back. Back! Get your racquet *back!*"

He was hitting the balls too hard for me to have time to prepare, and I was gasping from the heat. I hadn't brought a hat.

"You're going too fast. I can't keep up."

"You're just out of shape."

"No really, it's too hot. It's noon. I can't take the heat down here."

"Come on, move." He continued alternating backhands and forehands, making me run.

"I'm sweating. Please slow down!"

"Girls don't sweat. Move!"

"Maybe girls don't," I said through gritted teeth. "But women do."

"No, only men sweat, I've never seen a girl who sweated. Can't you remember to bring your racquet low to high?" He said it in a bored tone of voice, which made me want to slice into that hard body of his with it.

When the hour was up, I walked to the courtside table where I had left my purse and sank into a chair to watch Jordan's lesson finish. I was surprised when Brian sat down beside me, a gin and tonic in his hand.

"You never practice, I can see that. You just play. You have enough natural athletic ability to get the ball back, so you play, but you're never going to make it if you don't practice." What does he think I want to be, a professional?

Gesturing around me, I said, "This is an amazing spot—vistas, dominance. The cloud-line feels like it's pointing to right here. It's like an Indian burial ground or something. The air sort of jangles."

"What?" he asked, satirically, as if I were crazy. I could tell he didn't know what I was talking about. Jordan ran up to us followed by his teacher. I paid our bill at the counter and came back to the table to gather up our things. As I turned to leave, Brian raised a forefinger and said, "One morning when I got here early to open up, there was a rainbow—stretching from that court over there, the upper one, down to the others back there." He pointed glibly with his thumb over his shoulder and said nothing more, just smiled mockingly.

Tonight I keep hearing his voice, Southern, softly intense, authoritative.

This morning I had another lesson with Brian—or rather two—one in tennis, one in I-don't-know-yet-what. He worked on my serve for a while, touching me roughly, impersonally, to position my racquet. I was very aware of the contact.

"Toss it higher," he said.

I did.

"Watch the racquet face hit the ball."

I did. The serve was good.

"I said, 'Watch the racquet face hit the ball.' Aren't you listening?"

I turned to look at him—his eyes were toward the club.

"Finish with the racquet on your left. Don't look where the ball goes."

Again he sounded bored. I couldn't tell whether he was alienated from teaching or from me.

Then from the other side of the net he said, "Try to get these," and served three balls toward me that came like bullets. I couldn't possibly have returned them. Why was he doing this? Then he sent me backhands, relentlessly fast and unrelieved by forehands. I wanted to slam them back at him, but only felt weak, as if all my large muscles were going soft—stomach, arms, legs. I wanted to show him that I could play, and could have, if only I hadn't been playing against him. So what if he's a great tennis player? I thought a lesson was meant to give a person a chance to improve, not just to have balls rammed down her throat.

As we walked back to the table, he touched the middle of my back and said, "Your label's sticking out."

We sat around for a while with the other pro and they talked about building more clubs on other islands and going in together on a Lear jet. The men I know don't have money like that, and if they did they wouldn't spend it like that.

Then he turned to me and asked, "What does your husband do?"

"My husband! Don't you want to know what *I* do? My husband died two years ago."

They sort of raised their eyebrows and moved their chins back a little but offered no remarks and went right on with their macho banter about money. When Jordan and I got into the car, I paused and looked around, wondering again about the strange power of the site. Might it not be dangerous to have built something on that mountaintop, especially something secular?

I was nervous from my anger and the sexual vibes for several hours: how could I possibly be attracted to a man like that? Finally, around 4:00 P.M. I decided to call him, to puncture the tension with a rejection or else to get enough information so I could decide if I really detested this man or wanted to know him better. I didn't even know if he was single.

"Well, hello, 'Jayne-from-this-morning,'" he said. "I'm glad you called. How would you like to come to my place for dinner?"

There were potholes and ruts in the gravel road leading up the hill to his house, so I wasn't prepared for the ostentatious James Bond–style dome-structure which appeared at the top. Circular, with a tropical garden open to the rain in the center—full-grown trees and varieties of bushy palms right there in the living room— the place must have cost a million dollars. He doesn't own it, only rents with two roommates. I was disappointed to find them there, with dates, and wondered why anybody our age would want a roommate. He met me at the door in perfectly faded jeans and a chambray workshirt, both the exact blue of his eyes. Feeling a little foolish, I handed him the bottle of cheap champagne I had impulsively pulled from the refrigerator as I left, and he opened it, with a remark I couldn't hear. Music blared from the stereo—too loud for conversation—and I had to keep asking him to repeat what had been said. We sat on sofas in the living room then, where the others were passing joints around and talking casually about Newport and sex. I felt alienated from their decadent preppiness but didn't want to show it so I took a drag of the joint when it was handed to me and tried to adjust to what was going on.

"Let's put the steaks on," Brian said, taking my hand. He placed heavy slabs of beef on the kitchen grill and then drew me into his room and pushed me down on the unmade double bed.

"What *is* this?" I said, laughing and trying to pull away from him.

"I haven't been with anyone for a while," he whispered hoarsely, his weight on top of me.

"Oh," I said, matching his whisper mockingly, "would you like to compare 'whiles'?"

"Not really," he said, kissing me hard, then drawing his head back slightly. "It's been a month and a half."

"A month and a half—is that a fact? How would you feel about a *year* and a half?"

"I'd find that hard to believe."

"Well, it's true."

"Well then, let's do something about it." He rolled me over on top of him.

"Brian," I said, struggling to get away, "I just met you!"

"So?"

"So! So among other things, I have no protection."

"Ach!" he said, rolling away on his back, "I'm going to take a shower." He got up and went into the bathroom. What about the steaks? I could hear the shower running and lay there on the bed confused. Everything was happening too fast. The water stopped and there he was again, leaning against the doorway, a small towel wrapped around his hips, staring at me. I looked away—he was very beautiful—and started to sit up, but he kind of lunged down on me, pinning my arms to my chest and saying, "I intend to make love to you." I said, "No," and twisted my face away but he forced it back with a hand on my chin and kissed me, too hard. His shoulder muscles were hard as rock as I pressed up with my forearms, twisting.

"I mustn't do this. I might get pregnant. Let me go."

He let me sit up and we had a long confusing argument. Then there was more struggle—he tried to coerce me, both of us angry. Finally I was able to pull away, find my shoes, and run out into the night, buttoning my skirt.

The wind is blowing—whipping the palms and bougainvillea and roaring through the house and driving me crazy. I got no sleep at all last night.

On the Fredericksted road this afternoon, Jordan noticed the large body of a decapitated dog. Slowing, we could see that a front leg was missing too and crows were pecking at the neck. The stench was awful. Jordan got very upset and, trying not to cry, whined his questions and comments as we drove up into the rain forest. "It's not fair," he whimpered. I explained, unconvincingly, that animals don't understand about crossing streets, and he said, "Then people should give up cars and trucks." The engine hesitated, just as we passed an "evil eye" hanging on a tree, but I spoke knowingly to him about the "chain of nature"—how big animals often kill little animals—and worried in silence about the car. Something was definitely not right. It kept halting. Dark was coming on. What if we got stranded there in the jungle at night? "But nobody was gonna eat that dog!" he said.

We made it back down into town, barely, coasted most of the way. The car was out of oil.

Little sleep again last night—I tossed with frustration. Brian and I spent the evening together, though again with no privacy. About seven, I called him, ostensibly because I'd left my shampoo kit in the women's locker room but mainly because I wanted to say, "I'm sorry about last night. Do you think it would be worth it to try all that again?"

"Sure. I'll pick you up in an hour. We can get a pizza."

"OK. Eight o'clock. I'll get a sitter."

"Jayne?"

"Yes?"

"I'm glad you called."

We went to a little place he knew, but had only just sat down when a friend of his hailed him and pulled a chair up to our table. He was an impressive fellow—black, political science professor— who has just published a book on politics in the Caribbean; but both of them were condescending to me, surprised that I understood the word "pathology," for example, and because he was there I didn't get to know Brian any better at all. When we got back into his car— a big American car, I don't know when I last got into a big American car—I said, "Wait, Brian. I want to ask you something."

"What?"

"Did you bring any contraceptives?"

"No. I thought you were taking care of that."

I shook my head.

"I don't believe it!" he said, slamming the car into reverse. "It's too late now. The drugstores are closed."

He drove in silence, and I expected him to just drop me off, but when he pulled up in front of our house, he reached over and kissed me, gently . . . an apology? I said, "Well, thanks for the pizza," and reached for the door; but he pulled me back to him and said, "I'm coming in."

"You are?"

"We can still be close."

We talked a bit, not long, and then there was the same impassioned struggle as the night before, only my desire was now very strong. We fought and rolled and then were angry again from frustration. I wanted to hit him and I wanted him to hit me back, I wanted to bite and to be penetrated, to lose myself somewhere and not be able to remember any of it the next day. I didn't even care about getting to know him anymore. But reason held me back—it's twelve days past my period and couldn't be more risky. Before he left, he said, "You know, don't you, that if I'd wanted to be in you, there's nothing you could have done to stop me."

Everything's raging too fast, and now I'm on a plane back to Connecticut. Rule: if you want to have a casual affair, don't get hooked. But I wasn't! This just grew through our last hour together in the dawn and in the hours since then, a delayed reaction. It was hard again—the sexual frustration, the emotional frustration—and yet the miracle of simple hugging outweighs the others and I'm left wanting him, wanting to hear him disagree with me, wanting so much to have slept with him.

Last night, driving about the island, both of us were happy with long talking and anticipation. There was a growing closeness, despite the cryptic quality of his references to his past and plans. He talked freely about his sister who, it turns out, lost a child to leukemia; "It shattered the marriage," he said. Back home, unfortunately, there was a third misunderstanding. After our talk about it, each had again presumed the other was going to take care of contraception.

"I'm not going to put a piece of plastic on my body," he whispered angrily. "I never have and I'm never going to. Why didn't you get some foam or jelly?"

"They aren't safe," I moaned.

So our final night was again one of struggle, disappointment, and frustration. Humor, too, but mainly pain and anger.

Now why? Who the hell is this man and why was I drawn to him when he represents so much that I dislike? I'd like to know if I am in his thoughts at all. He seemed detached, but more frank and tender the longer we were together, especially in the kitchen this morning. We stood by the sink in the sunlight, whispering so as not to wake Jordan. He drank a glass of milk, then set it on the counter and pulled me to him in good-bye. He was dressed but I still had on my nightgown, and I felt small and vulnerable as he lifted me onto my toes with just a forearm behind my waist.

"I like you, Brian," I whispered in his ear.

"I like you too." And then he said, "I want you to write to me."

"What?"

"I want you to write to me."

I pulled back from him, surprised—incredulous, in fact. I'd figured he had more sense—and more defense—than to let himself get involved with someone who was going to fly away in five days.

What am I going to do? Is there any point in continuing the contact, in pursuing something that can bring only the most transitory fulfillments? Brian himself talked of the problems of being away from his New York "friend." I wonder who she is and marvel at my jealousy. I only met this person! Hell, my first tennis lesson with him was less than a week ago. I have to draw back enough to laugh.

Stonington again. I am feeling better—only a little nostalgic and, yes, happy that at least I met this man and was brave enough to get to know him a little. I was quite upset and weepy for a couple of days—I put the heating pad, on Low, beside me in the bed and fell asleep with both hands on it, substitute for his warmth. And more than once pulled out onto the left side of the road. But I knew the exact moment that my memory let go of him and said, "End of Phase I": it was while I was driving home from class last night. A distinct relief, as when, I'd guess, a sword has been withdrawn. Danger past, normal life loomed back up brightly familiar. And yet I feel bad, too. His voice, his smell, his expressions have already lost some of their immediacy for me. I wrote him yesterday, but wonder if it was worth the effort, if he will write me back.

Mother's Day.

I just finished cutting out the christening dress and coat I am making for Mary's baby. I had Sonia buy some Egyptian cotton in New York, guessing at how much I'd need. I put the extra leaf in the kitchen table just now and spread out the delicate white fabric and then pinned on a few pieces of the tissue-paper short-dress pattern I picked out yesterday. The fabric is so thin it responds to a breath—thinner than chiffon. Without measuring or looking ahead to see if there was enough length on the bolt or anything, I added about an arm's length to the skirts and cut in boldly with my orange shears. Then I unpinned the pieces, pulled up fresh fabric, pinned them on again and cut once more. There was nothing left over, not even an eighth of an inch. The blind random fit of paper to fabric, of dream to matter, worked out better than if I had measured it.

GreenEyes is back! Right now! I just saw her in the street out of the corner of my eye. I ran to the door, calling "Kitty." She started, called back, flew to me up the wall and through the hole in the screen, scrambling, wild for reunion. I petted and petted her. She cried and loved me back and then I offered her some ground beef, which I'd been inadvertently cooking all afternoon on Warm—just for her, it now seems. She didn't want to leave me to eat, leaping up again and again to rub her face against mine. Now she's eating. What a Mother's Day present! And on top of what happened with the fabric!

The only odd thing is . . . she's a "he." GreenEyes was female, had a scar from spaying and one on her nose. This cat looks just like her—gray Persian—obviously knows me, knows the way to the slit in the screen, and has the scarred nose, but is a tom.

I worked on the christening dress for Mary and Stephen's baby again this afternoon, explaining to Jordan that his great-grand-mother Blankenship had crocheted the lace I was using as inserts. I cut it off old pillowcases of Mother and Daddy's. I sat up in my sewing nook on the stairs balcony to do the hems and other hand-work and looked out over the roofs of the village periodically—small white houses with carefully tended spring gardens tucked away where you cannot see them from the street. GreenEyes slept curled up beside me, the back of his neck pressed against my thigh, purring. When we put him out for the night tonight, we tied a ribbon around his neck with our name and address Scotch-taped to it.

Another day of sewing. I made ten pillows from the red and orange flowered batik I bought in St. Croix and then upholstered the windowseat bed with orange canvas, matching the fabric I sent out for the wing chair slipcover. It came back today, which inspired this spurt. The living room looks great: cushions everywhere and everything bright orange and clear red and two big Boston ferns in carved clay pots hanging above it all. Vivid red and orange—these are the colors I want now, in my clothes too. I bought a red flowered blouse just like these cushions before our trip. It is almost an obsession. GreenEyes is batting at a buckle hanging down below the white director's chair, and I intend to sit down at the piano and treat myself to the right hand of Bach's First Partita.

A little girl from down the street has called and kept GreenEyes, claiming that she's had him since he was a kitten. I am feeling a petulant irritation at her and at Brian about the writing thing—in a dream last night he ignored me and I threw myself at him, literally, a body-block across the room—and at Harvey too, for dying, I suppose. I caught myself talking to him right out loud in the bathtub this afternoon, something defensive like, "Well, you should have come back." It startled me: I must have felt guilty about the attraction I felt for Brian and was trying to defend myself to Harvey. I spoke in a tone that said that if I hadn't felt hurt, I wouldn't have done it, as if I had gotten involved with Brian merely to punish Harvey, to hurt him back. Some pitiful child inside must think that he could have come back to me, to life, if he wanted to badly enough. It's ridiculous, but still I'm beginning to feel angry at him. I feel like I've paid my dues—the initiation should be over. I deserve someone to care about, to sleep with again. But something very fundamental in me says "No, you don't. Harvey's loving you, your happy years together, were a fluke. No one loved you before and no one will again. You've had it too easy in other areas. You've had yours and won't again be loved."

Trying to shake the thought out of my head, I went out into the garden with my teacup, to dry my hair. It's almost warm enough. The daffodils have given way to the tulips I planted—long row of sleek yellow blooms beneath the dark green arbor vitae—and the rhododendrons are heavy with white and light pink blossoms the way they were the week we bought this house. How excited and happy we were, hauling out shag carpeting and refinishing the wide-plank pine floors, carrying boxes of books. The row of tulips stops so awkwardly, right there where I ran out of time planting bulbs, three-quarters of the way to the end of the border. I remember that afternoon. Harvey was raking leaves. I was in a hurry to get the bulbs in before we left for the airport to pick up Mary and Stephen for Thanksgiving. The ground was cold and hard on the surface, cold and damp beneath. It resisted me and made my fingers ache. I resented taking time to dig the holes deep enough and to put the bone meal in before each bulb. When we had to leave, I said I'd finish in the morning; but in the morning Harvey was unconscious. Bone meal . . . I didn't know what bone meal was.

Am scrambling now to finish packing in the wake of an urgent call from Mary. She was in tears. The baby is almost due and her blood pressure is way too high. The doctors fear she might not survive a regular delivery. They want to operate but she's begged them for a week's delay and wants me there to care for her so she won't have to go into the hospital. We'll fly to Minnesota first thing in the morning.

White Bear Lake. Stephen met us at the airport and took us straight to the St. Paul hospital instead of home. The doctors say they cannot wait. He kept Jordan downstairs in the lobby while I rode the elevator up to Maternity. Here I am back in a hospital, I thought—familiar world of pain. Glass-walled rooms radiated like wedges of a pie, out and away from a central nurses' station. The curtains were pulled in Mary's room. When I opened the door, I saw her sitting there on her bed in the dark, cross-legged, in a sleeveless pink nylon nightgown, her belly huge and her face swollen from crying.

"They're going to do a Caesarean in the morning," she said, her face contorted with the effort not to cry. "We tried to call you, but you'd already left for the airport." And then she sobbed and said, "I'll never know what it's really like to give birth."

There were wadded-up Kleenexes all over the bed. I sat down beside her and put my arm around her warm strong shoulders.

"They won't even let Stephen be with me," she cried.

Stephen and I have been waiting outside the operating room trying to talk and read rumpled magazines for what seems like hours. He has gone for a Coke. Mary is giving birth, or rather, they are taking birth from Mary. A few minutes ago I went to the restroom and saw in the mirror the old strain lines, running from nose to mouth. Echoes of Jordan's birth and Daddy's death and many, many thoughts of Harvey: Harvey raging, unconscious, the lamb's wool restraints tearing skin away from his wrists and ankles; Harvey staring at me, motionless, doctors drilling into his sternum, a pool of blood bubbling up in the middle of his chest. A moment ago I caught myself referring to Jordan as "Mary" under the stress.

Jubilation! To hear "She's fine!," to hear "The baby is fine too," to see Stephen leaping down the hall to the telephones, jumping and hitting the air and making it ring like bells: "A daughter! We have a little daughter!" To see the baby—her beauty, her health and strength. I'm glad it's a girl. "Summer"—my niece. I want to hold her, smell her, claim her. I feel like a grandmother! Harvey, where are you? Daddy, can you see the granddaughter you wanted?

But how hard Mary held my hand coming out of anesthesia. She wanted to talk too soon; I told her, "Just hang on. Don't try to talk. Squeeze as hard as you need to." But she was wound tight with worry—worry that Stephen and Mother won't get along when Mother comes.

"But you have a beautiful little baby—the prettiest baby I've ever seen," I told her.

"That baby's sitting there in the nursery and I am here and I don't even care. None of this is right," she moaned. "I want you to impart to me the secrets of motherhood in thirty seconds and then I don't want to think about it anymore."

I waited at the nursery window while Stephen was with her. The baby, Summer, is utterly beautiful. Her flesh is pristine, petal-fresh, spared the stretch and pound of labor. She has our mother's perfect features. Other parents gathered to gaze at her through the glass, marveling.

Mary had a bad day: nausea, depression, pain. Her belly is so gas-bloated she still looks nine months pregnant. She's wiped out and doesn't want to see her baby and feels guilty about the lack of maternal feelings. I am frustrated at my impotence to help her. What can you do when someone you love suffers like that? The land of pain is so far away.

It is Monday night after a long Memorial Day. Stephen and Jordan are asleep, but I feel awake and excited. I was sluggish all morning—headachy and hung over from cat-hair asthma. I tried to nap with Jordan after lunch but couldn't fall asleep, so I got up and slipped quietly outside to weed Mary's vegetable garden.

The dirt is very black here, the way it was in Iowa when we were growing up. It was sun-warm and damp between my fingers as I pulled out clumps of grass to clear the space between the rows. When I finished the second aisle, I paused. I sat on my knees and scooped a warm pile of the earth into both hands, then lowered my face into its rich smell as into a hot wet washcloth. Bent over, I caught sight, out of the corner of my eye, of something there beside me. It was a small black bird, not four inches from my left knee. Holding my breath and moving very very slowly, I sat back up onto my knees, hands still full of earth. The bird watched me, magnified and clear, so near I fancied I could hear his heart beat. I knew that I could touch him if I chose. Smiling, and resting back on my knees,

I offered him the pile of earth. He cocked his head at it, then flew away.

The bird pulled me right up out of my fatigue and now I feel strong and energetic. After Jordan's nap—thank you God, for children's naps—I took him to McDonald's to celebrate his cousin's birth, then for a swim in White Bear Lake. A little "tennis," the balm of a bath, and then the relief of seeing Mary much improved—walking down the hospital corridor nearly upright tonight, talking freely, much less pain—completed the day.

When we got home, an hour ago, I went back out to the garden by myself. There was heat lightning all around the dark horizon, and thunder. I walked out onto the golf course and stood at the top of a hill, my white muslin gown whipped by a warm damp wind, feeling the storm charges billow out my spirit. Then I couldn't resist—I ran down the small valley and up the next hill, arms outstretched, inflating with power. Penned dogs barked behind me. I felt the electricity building in my body, then had a jolting thought: "I am running here on bare hills in an electrical storm, getting a charge out of my own energy?" I had to laugh at the high-flown romanticism of the previous moments and at the little figure suddenly scrambling, all practicality, in out of danger.

In the hospital corridor today, Mary seemed worse again—manic, artificial, affected. She paced and avoided eye contact, withdrawn from too much stress. I made the mistake of looking in at the nursery on my way out, right before feeding time. Summer was crying. All the babies were crying. I was swept with mother-anguish, wanting to hold and nurse each one of them, angry that Jordan had to be separated from me like that. I closed my eyes and turned away, then headed for the cafeteria for tea and a pastry to "transition" me out to rush-hour traffic. But I had to pass the emergency room on the way, and there I overheard a child screaming, a parent yelling angrily. Someone else, "Hold him down!" A sudden choking despair seized me as I thought, "All our worst fears—they come true."

Mary is still withdrawn. I am sitting in the car before heading home, eating Russell Stover chocolates from a box I bought in the gift shop. I wish, how much, that I could go back now not to a tired child, but to a man who would hold me, without talking, for an hour.

I went running on the golf course again last night. It was very dark and overcast. Four black shadows appeared over the hill, like the silhouettes of men, three in a line, one out to the side. Or were they shadows from another region, black and evil? They were obscure and hard to see; like the Pleiades, they seemed clearer when I looked off to the side rather than right at them. They seemed to move. Common sense said contrary things: "Bushes, keep going. Gang rape, run." Six months ago I'd have raced up into whatever they brought, swallowing my horror. But now it was only with effort that I mastered my flight instinct and continued toward them. Then I happened on an empirical test—ducking to see how their relationship to the horizon changed—and almost satisfied myself that they were bushes. I veered off and continued running, in other parts of the course. But I remember the fear: elemental, stifling. It rides close.

I bustled around all morning getting the house ready for Mother's arrival today and for Mary and the baby tomorrow. I picked out a little turquoise bunting to send to the hospital with Stephen and put fresh sheets on all the beds. When I was digging around in the linen closet, I came across the old copy of *The Better Homes and Gardens Story Book*, in which I learned to read. I lifted it out gently. The spine was broken and the yellow-green cover frayed. I turned the pages, a little hurt that Mother had given it to Mary. She had obviously forgotten that when I was a five-year-old, I knew the stories all by heart—before Mary was even born.

She arrived this afternoon smiling vivaciously through evenly clenched teeth. For the first couple of hours she spoke brightly without ever separating her jaws. But we had a good talk tonight, more open and honest than we've had in years. She was in the guest room, methodically unpacking her suitcase. I sat on the sofa bed as she transferred things to drawers.

"I want to ask you something, Jayne."

"Yes?"

"Do you remember last summer when you said to me, 'If I have had an enemy, it is you'?"

"Oh, Mother. That was because a protective parent is always a blocker, a thwarter. You didn't give me a chance to explain."

"Well, that is just what I want to talk about. I always saw you as a driven child and felt it was my duty as a mother to reduce stimulation and provide quiet, to keep education away from you."

"To keep education *away* from me!" Is this why they wouldn't let me accept the music scholarship at the University of Iowa when I was sixteen? Why they wouldn't let me study piano in addition to voice? Why they kept me from applying to Radcliffe or Wellesley? I felt betrayed. It wasn't because they didn't know better. It was all deliberate.

"All that any parents can do, Jayne, is what they feel is best at the time, and your father and I always did the very best that we knew how. I'm sure you will do the same with your son, too."

"But I would sell my house, sell everything I have, to see that Jordan goes to a good school!"

She sat down, a cushion away from me on the sofa bed, and almost letting tears break through, said, "I know I gave you nothing when Jordan was born. There was so much loving that could have been given." (At the time all she said was, "Your father had hoped it would be a girl.")

My anger disarmed—for the moment, at least—I reached for her hand and tried to reassure her.

"But, Mother, we understood. You had just lost Daddy. You needed help yourself!"

Pulling herself up very straight and running the fingers of both hands lightly through her hair to lift the curls, she said, "You know, I haven't that much time left to attract another man. When a woman reaches my age, her looks begin to go."

"Come on now, you're still lovely" (she is—fine-featured, blue-eyed, feminine). "But I hate to see you put your sense of self-worth in your appearance."

"Oh Jayne." She looked at me as if I were hopelessly naive. "The gentleman I'm seeing now likes to look at younger women. When we walk into a restaurant, his eyes go up and down the waitresses' bodies. You'd better believe that tells me something!"

"But Daddy appreciated women too. How many times did we hear him say 'luscious tidbit of femininity'? That's just healthy male!"

And then I realized something:

"Maybe you're only afraid because you have been beautiful. You've seen the effect of your looks on others. I've never had that chance, so I define myself through what I think and do. But you—you were Queen of the May! And now you fear a loss of value in other people's eyes. I wish you didn't feel that way. We're not our bodies, not our faces, not our hair."

"I think you ought to write that down. Write it down someplace men can see."

"Well, maybe having cared for someone who was ill, who degenerated physically, has something to do with my attitude. The loving doesn't diminish."

"*Your* loving didn't diminish."

"No one's would."

"I'd like to think you're right."

I hate to leave.

Mary and the baby just came home, Mary tense, the baby grave and dear. Mary went to bed, and I took Summer in the nook of my left arm, snuggling her against my red-flowered blouse. You forget how much a newborn weighs. I walked over to the window and held her out in front of me along my forearms, both my hands behind her head. She was breathtakingly beautiful, and asleep. What does your lifetime hold for you, my little one?

But Mother is here to take over, and if Jordan and I don't head north to the cabin today, we'll have no time there alone before she comes.

Summer

Cass Lake. Coming home. Relief. It can't have been a year since we were here. Familiarity, security, rightness. As if we hadn't left for Connecticut for a year—ever. This is my home—these trees, these stars, this sand and gentle air, *these* problems.

Tonight unloading our things from the boat onto the dock in the dark, I heard a splash. I looked down at my armload of books, purse, journal—journal! I threw everything back into the boat, kicked off my shoes, unbuckled my watch, set it on a dockpost, and jumped into the cold water, clothes and all. I took a deep breath and dived under the narrow strip between the dock and boatlift, ran my hands along the rippled sand bottom like Braille, came up for air, went down again. A clam, seaweed—up gasping, down again. Again. There was nothing within a six-foot radius of where I'd been standing. I just couldn't believe it. I stood in the water, panting, my hair dripping onto my soaked blouse. Then I went down again, re-checked everywhere I'd felt before, pushed myself. I could see a yellow-green blur of moon up through the water—then I surfaced again. It just couldn't be gone. But it was.

"Did you find it, Mommy?" Jordan asked.

I leaned my pounding head against the side of the dock and answered weakly, "No." Then I lifted my head. Twenty feet straight out into the lake something dark was floating in the moonlight. Something small and dark. Could it be . . . ? I walked slowly out, water weighing against my arms and shoulders, and then I swam cautiously, making no waves. Gliding slowly out on the still lake, like a silent canoe, was my journal. Carefully I reached, carefully, then grabbed. Red and white, three silver rings. I held it above my head and swam back side-stroke. How can a book float? The top cover wasn't even wet. My feet touched bottom, and I waded up onto the beach where Jordan was.

"Let me see. Did you get it?"

I held it out, dripping.

"I didn't think that a book could float," he commented.

I turned back toward the moon and answered, "Neither did I."

Inside the cabin, I reached up into the fireplace, opened the damper, and started a fire. I stood the notebook open on the hearth, its pages ruffled toward the flames to dry. The ink had been washed off only four or five pages. Then I took my wet things off and put on my old chenille bathrobe and settled back in front of the crackling fire.

Tonight I read Jordan "The Little Red Hen" from the *Better Homes and Gardens Story Book*. He burst into tears at an amazing spot—when the fox dumps the stones into the pot. The hen having escaped, the fox family goes hungry that night. He seemed to ignore the main plot and wept for the little foxes who didn't get any dinner, through no fault of their own.

The concrete of the front steps is warm against my palms. It's a special pleasure, sitting in an open doorway like this—back protected, face in the out-of-doors. The rose bushes at my right and left are loaded with fuschia-colored blossoms and furry yellow-and-black bees are buzzing softly at my elbows. Empty oatmeal bowls and juice glasses are beside my feet. I just finished disentangling Jordan's fishing line from the minnow bucket—"Leroy's Minnows: Guaranteed to catch fish or die trying." He is out at the end of the dock lying on his stomach in his overalls, patiently watching a red-and-white bobber which I cannot see but know is there. I just realized that I've been watching too. I'm waiting for the snakes—the garter snakes which live in these wild rose bushes on either side of the cabin door. They always startle me, and I was on guard through breakfast expecting their "sudden notice." But they didn't show. It's a strong image, though, a doorway guarded by two snakes. Make the snakes as large as the thorny bushes. Maybe I can work that into a multiple image with the Buddhist temple pictures from last year.

This afternoon I taught Jordan how to play Solitaire—seven piles across, aces go above. He watched closely as I demonstrated: "One, two, third card over. One, two, third card over. Put that there, and that there, and that there. Red-black-red. Numbers get smaller on these piles, get bigger up on those." And it just went on like that. It didn't stop at all. We played it through and won, our first game. Drat! Now he'll expect it to work out like that every time and feel cheated when it doesn't.

I was feeling lonely after Jordan went to bed but made some hot chocolate and took the steaming mug out on the dock with me and studied the stars. As I walked back up the dock, I gazed at Cygnus, the Swan. It seemed to be Harvey, huge and transfigured, flying with arms outstretched down the Milky Way. I wondered what ants think about the stars—stars *look* like ants. Now I'm here sitting close to the fire listening to Brahms String Quarters, perfectly happy, full of the soft summer night, knowing no companionship can better this kind of solitude. My huge shadow, flickering against the far wall, is as big as Ophiuchus in the southern sky. I am a healer too— I'm healing myself and am as big as that shadow, that sky.

Cooking pork chops on the grill out by the boathouse tonight, I thought I glimpsed a furry behind. It was clearly just my imagination. Within a minute, though, an enormous brown jack rabbit came running across the yard from behind the cabin, nearly touching my bare feet—then flashed off—the very sensation I had previewed. What is happening?

A kind of telepathy seems to run between Jordan and me, too. I nearly always waken just before he calls out to me from a bad dream. And time and time again I'll be thinking of something, then within a minute or so he says and does it. Yesterday inside the cabin I thought, I should suggest to the kids that they feed the chipmunk, and before I got to the door I saw them run from the beach, Jordan calling, "Let's give Quickie some peanuts." This morning lying in bed I thought, Today I'm going to whip bananas and orange juice together for breakfast, something I'd never done. On rising, Jordan said, "Will you make some banana juice for breakfast today?"

I remember the first time I noticed it, in a New York cab. Out of boredom I was silently reading the "extra charges" list, and when I came to "skis," Jordan abruptly remarked, "Mommy, when can I learn to ski?"

I was set off into a bad hour and a half (it's now 1:30 A.M.) by thinking about the inside of Harvey's arms—the muscles and veining, his forearms and curving biceps. Seeing them both strong and healthy and weirdly limp—the muscle tone altered by long hours of convulsions. Remembering them invaded—hooked into IVs for transfusions, sucked by syringes for blood tests. The festering sores after BCG injections—the beauty of his arms. A twisting grief—I feel all tensed and stiff now, nose plugged, head aching. But it is good to be in touch with the love.

The fire has burned down remarkably slowly. Earlier there was a whale with flames coming out of its mouth. I am afraid to go out and look at the stars tonight. Afraid to be cold. I am tired of trying to comprehend large things. Afraid of the dark night. I guess I can't be a hero every minute. Should accept it and let myself crawl, wounded, into bed.

My mind has slipped out of gear again. Just being awake wears me out. Fatigue, depression, reluctance to move at all. I sat slumped at the kitchen table most of the morning, leaning on an elbow. Jordan burst in with an empty peanut butter jar a while ago, exclaiming, "Quickie was inside this and licked every bit of the peanut butter off! Even his tail was inside!"

"Yeah," I said, and moved to the couch.

In a dream:

I am unable to find Kramer's office in an enormous shopping complex in Hartford. It is raining and we are late. Mother is with us and she will not hurry. People keep giving us directions that are wrong. It has been so long since we have been there that I cannot find the door. At one point I hit Mother in a total rage, slapping her cheeks sharply twice, as I have Jordan's when I could take his impudence no more. The shock of striking one's parent! She taunts me, "Why, you must be a widow!"—implying both that she understands the pain that had driven me to such an extreme and that she . . .

Jordan interrupted.

I can no longer remember slapping Mother in this dream, though I can still hear her remark. Not surprising that I have repressed it. When I was a child and dreamed of my anger at her or Daddy and wanted to hit them, my arms grew leaden, too heavy to lift.

You see—there was a full week of happiness—an almost radiant serenity and sense of rightness, especially with Jordan. Then, inexplicably, three days of fatigue, of listless daydreaming, unable to gear up for anything. Now just as mysteriously I am recharged. A completely satisfactory day—no energy lags. Relaxed, slow, open, strong. A black butterfly outlined in white suddenly before me on the path.

Why the low and why the returning high?

Incredible! Doing the lunch dishes just now, I was seized with the absolute certainty that the bird I've been trying to catch at the window was coming. I ran to the living room drying my hands on my jeans, grabbed my camera, squatted quickly into position—no

time even to focus—and she flew into the frame, then was gone.
I sat full of wonder at the premonition and my response. This
time I felt something and recognized it and acted on it. A first. I
have waited for her in the past and she's never come.

Sitting in front of the fire watching a sheet of flame lick up the
full length of the log, Jordan observed, "That's just like a backward
waterfall."

Jordan went down the beach this morning to play with a child
who arrived on the island and I went walking in the forest by myself.
I took the main trail back to Lake Windigo, past the stand of tall
virgin white pines. As a child I was afraid to walk beneath them,
thinking the mounds of dry brown needles would collapse under
me. Today I left the path and deliberately walked across them,
running my hands lightly over the rough trunks of the pines. Crows
cawed above me. Long shafts of sunlight revealed pollen floating
upward. Back on the path, I paused at the place where Harvey and I
lay down in a spreading stretch of ferns the summer after Jordan's
birth. Harvey was carrying him strapped to his chest in a blue sling.
We'd been walking off the colic, and it had worked—the baby's tiny
mouth gaped in sleep. We lay down with our heads under the ferns
so that when we looked up there were fans of lacy green against the
sky.

The main path ended at Lake Windigo and I turned left on a
narrower one which followed the shore, with trees on either side,
for maybe half a mile. They say there's nowhere else on earth like
this—an island with a second lake inside. I watched my feet, stepping over exposed roots, and wiped away from my cheeks the sticky
spider webs that crossed the path at face level. The crows flew on
above me cawing. A large animal snorted in the underbrush to my
left, then crashed up over a wooded bank, galloping heavily—
probably a buck. I strained to see him, talked softly, reassuring: "I'm
not going to hurt you. Come on back." But he was concealed by the

bushes and silent now, watching me. I turned and stepped down to
the edge of the lake. Water was seeping into surprisingly delicate
two-parted footprints—definitely deer. He'd been drinking from the
lake.

I turned back into the woods on a trail I didn't know; I walked for
a while and was surprised when the forest opened suddenly into a
small sunny swamp. Long grasses, brown cattails with their roots
hidden underwater, and on the far side of the marsh: four
shockingly blue wild irises. I didn't know irises grew on the island. I
picked my way toward them across some fallen logs but I couldn't
get close enough. The narrow sword-shaped leaves were still ten feet
away. I gazed at the blossoms, their blue burning itself into the
backs of my eyes—Japanese indigo. A frog jumped into the water at
my feet, propelling himself with sudden gliding kicks just under the
surface. The forest opened a little behind the flowers, so I balanced
back along the logs and circled around to where I could see it was an
overgrown path and walked into the woods again. After a while, I
came to a fork, bore right at random, walked on, another fork. The
sun was shining hard and I was walking blind—lost, I admitted—
but I didn't feel afraid. The island's not that big—you can walk
around it in a day. I was sure to come out somewhere. Something
small and red ahead of me caught my eye. I stooped and saw it was
strawberries, tiny, wild, and very sweet. I filled my palm and walked
on, eating. I was deep in the forest now, where the trails are kept
open only by animals. Another fork. The berries were gone, and I
stopped and crossed my arms, felt my T-shirt damp in the armpits,
long-sleeved, red. It was getting hot. I pulled the shirt off over my
head, tied it around my waist—there was no one to see—and
wandered on. But wait a minute. Hadn't I seen that leaning tree a
while ago? Was I walking in circles? I was supposed to get Jordan for
lunch. At this rate it could be nightfall before I got out of here. The
crows were beginning to get on my nerves. They'd been following
me for over an hour. "Knock it off, you guys." I whispered the chant
Spider Woman taught the Navajos:

> *"Put your feet down with pollen.*
> *Put your hands down with pollen.*

> *Put your head down with pollen. . . .*
> *The trail is beautiful,*
> *Be still."*

The path widened and the sun shone warm on my breasts. Three yellow butterflies danced in the air before me. I made my way around a place where deer had bent the grass into a large nest right in the middle of the path, stepped over glossy dark droppings, and realized—the thought uncurled up my back—that the crows had indeed fallen silent.

I stopped and quickly put my shirt back on, then squinted up at the empty blue sky. I blurred my eyes so I could look into the woods on either side of me, and broke into a jog. I ran until I hit a trail that looked like it might be the old lodge trail. It eventually fed me back onto the Windigo trail and when I came out again at the campground on Cass where I started, heart pounding, I went straight to the old red pump where a hotel burned down in the twenties, and pumped it up and down, up and down, until clear icy water gushed out over my cupped hands, and drank.

Today was my thirty-second birthday. Wild blue irises.

Mother has come, tired from helping with Mary's baby.

I told her about almost seeing the deer yesterday and she went into this cautionary tale about a friend of hers, an artist, who also went into the Minnesota woods alone. The woman had evidently just set up her easel and was starting to paint when a big buck charged out of the trees and attacked her. "It was rutting season," Mother said as if that explained it. Her friend was lucky to get out alive and spent a long time in the hospital, recovering. I can't imagine it happening like that, unprovoked. I wonder if he gored her—open wounds?—or broke her bones or what.

Then she said, "Besides, Jayne, there's quicksand in that swamp."

I dreamed early this morning that Jordan had had his friend Skip for an overnight and none of us had gotten any sleep. It was very,

very late. His mother would be angry. I couldn't get them to calm down. Already dawn was coming, but instead of "graying" after the night, the sky was "reddening." The thought, "Red sky at morning, sailors take warning," woke me.

Exhausted, I reached over and pulled the curtain aside to look into the woods. Startled, I saw the sky *was* red, ominous, just as in my dream. Fearing fire, I grabbed my robe and ran to the front door. The sky above the lake was weirdly green and apricot-yellow—bruised, yet marvelous, twisting somehow, colors changing quickly. Cautiously I stepped out. It was as if I had walked into a forbidden world, a world hurrying to transmute itself into daytime camouflage—Cinderella's coach becoming a pumpkin before my eyes. The air was strangely warm and still. Above, I saw clouds racing northeast, like a fast-motion movie. But around me on the beach everything was motionless and silent, the lake like glass. A great blue heron stood next to the dock staring at me accusingly for a long minute before it slowly lifted and circled up toward the coming storm. There, in the southwest where he had flown, a rainbow suddenly emerged, like a print coming up in the developer. It burned there—unreally—fueled by a sun I couldn't see, rising behind and below me, behind the forest, behind the island. A dawn rainbow—a rainbow in the wrong part of the sky. Everything seemed reversed, unpredictable, as if I had dived under water and come up in another world. I watched the entire life of that rainbow, afraid to look away. After a few minutes it faded, like the rest of the sky, into a uniform dark gray. Then the wind came up and it started to rain. I headed back in, grappling with the conviction that I had just witnessed a night-world not of darkness but of radiant color, a world which *darkened* into day, instead of brightening. I eased the door shut as much to preserve the awe as to keep from waking Jordan and Mother, and looked at the clock. It was 5:30 A.M.

The rain fell all day.

Astonishment—a letter from Brian. His apologies for handwriting, etc. brought some clarification. Maybe I intimidated *him*, as well. I was disappointed by the misspellings and shallowness—a highlight of the letter was a description of the tennis club's new "house drink," a "16-oz. Tangueray and tonic." That put me off. But the simple fact of hearing from him reawakened longings. He really had a double whammy for me. Not only was he an attractive man but also a terrific tennis player, and tennis has been a kind of sex-substitute the last two years, sort of a personal symbol, a surrogate activity. No wonder I fell. Brian, Kramer, Philip, Spencer—all were really only hopes for comfort. It won't work for me to find another man. I need to learn to stand alone. To stand alone, without yearning and without fear. Well, without unmanageable fear.

First Mother insisted on making Jordan a cardboard teepee, then scolded him for not playing in it—she had "gone to all that work." Then when he *did* play in it—happy wild Indians—she scolded him for playing too wild and locked all three doors of the cabin to keep him out. I came back from twenty minutes up the beach to find him in tears, alone in the yard. Mother angry. When he had said to her, "It's not fair; it's our cabin, too," she had yelled back, "It is *not* your cabin, not one inch of it! It is *my* cabin and *mine* alone and don't you ever forget it, not ever in your life."

Today Jordan and I left Mother and went with R.T., Martha Henderson, and a friend of hers by boat to Indian Bluff. An hour's ride upriver, then a steep climb. The minute I reached the top of the cliff, something eerie struck me. I smelled Harvey, literally smelled him—a distinctive odor he gave off when startled. It was as if he had been there just before we came, then was frightened off. I wasn't ready for this, struggled for control. I spread the cloth, then fell to my knees and started to unpack the food. I couldn't open myself to whatever might have happened next. Fought instead to appear normal, answering people's questions. Some extraordinary opportunity has now been lost. A power place, and I was not prepared.

We picnicked and I reconciled myself a bit—thought instead of our campfire's smoke signaling other look-outs through the centuries. The view there is rare for this flat country, magnificent even—miles of lakes and forests and the winding narrow Mississippi we had followed. As we packed to leave, Jordan stood at the summit looking out and said as only a solemn five-year-old can, "I'll remember this day all my life."

On the way home we dipped into the river picking yellow and white water lilies. Harvey, if I had been ready, could I have heard you, touched you?

It's time to go. Stonington sounds pressured to me, but the prospect of staying on in the strain here sounds even worse. In a way, I hate to leave Mother—she seems so helpless in her anger—but I'm just not big enough to stay.

It's painful watching Jordan flirt with strange men. Today at the airport he asked to carry the tennis racquet of a total stranger. I'd be embarrassed if it weren't for the lump in my chest which sees his need—cavernous—for a father.

We're in Kansas City now, at Harvey's mother's. She and Harriet refuse to speak of him. When I try to bring him up, they hurry to change the subject. I know they mean to spare us all pain, but it doesn't work. The closest we have come to acknowledgment was Harriet's horrified exclamation at how my hair has grayed since she saw me last. I don't want it this way. I want to be close to them. Maybe we all just need more time—years, I mean.

I'm here in town with Harvey's grave, but I haven't gone to see it. I don't like it—it doesn't speak of him. I hate it that they made me put a steel vault around him. How can the warm earth and rain ever get to him? How can he ever change—dissolve and die? How will I rest until he does? How can I possibly leave him to the rains? I want myself one day to become the blowing grass, fodder for a tree perhaps—to get up into the leaves with the sap, to move in the wind. Hard boxes prevent. Oh Harvey, forgive. If it weren't for that vault, then one distant spring our molecules might meet again, wind-borne.

In a dream:

Jordan is playing with a baby duck and a young duck. Far above us I glimpse an eagle soaring. Suddenly it drops, swooping for prey—the ducks! Fear for Jordan. It looms quickly—has the body of a man, a giant fifteen feet tall—with scaly muscular bird's legs and feathered wings. Before I can move, it has one talon on a duck, and one on Jordan's hair. It starts to lift him off the ground. I lunge for him, grab him around the waist. The monster tries to lift me off too. There is a powerful struggle. Danger, injury, but my will is fierce. I slash at him barehanded. He cannot match my mother-fury.

Stonington again. I almost wrote "home," but this can't compare with Star Island for "home." It is merely "back."

Tonight I said "Good evening" to the harsh old woman next door and she just sat there on her porch, stony, looking beyond me. Usually she goes inside when we walk by. How might I have offended her—by letting Spencer stay all night two years ago?

I've been thinking about moving to Cambridge. When I asked the admissions woman at a local private school about all-day kindergarten, she said, "Oh, we don't have 'that kind' of families at this school. Our mothers want their children home at noon."

The fellow I played tennis with yesterday—a single man staying with friends (the only single men in town are the ones passing through)—called to play again this afternoon. I told him I'd have to get a sitter and he yelled to a teenager in the background, not even covering the phone: "The widow has a five-year-old kid. Can you baby-sit? I *said*, the widow has a kid who needs watching while we play tennis." Not "Jayne" or "a friend" or "the person I'm playing tennis with," but "the widow"—as if my husband's death were the most striking feature of my personality. Is that what others think as well, or is he uniquely a jerk?

Grace invited Jordan and me for tea this afternoon. The first thing that struck me as we walked into her tended English garden was a wooden bowl of raspberries, almost two feet across, resting on the grass at the end of a hedge. "Have some," she said. I knelt and dug carefully into the mound of fruit, its warmth a surprise—as if the berries were small sleeping animals.

She was photographing watercolor paintings propped against the stone foundation of the house, making slides of her work. They were transparently lovely in the afternoon sun—floral still lifes. She gave Jordan a little bag and showed him how to pick the berries and we left him by the hedge and sat down. I told her I was thinking about moving to Cambridge, where the schools are better and where I might have a chance to date again.

"Stay here in the village, Jayne. Devote yourself to Jordan. There will be time enough for men when he is grown."

In a dream:

Rooey bounds up out of the basement of the hospital where a mean woman administrator has kept her for two and a half years. Another black Labrador, a male, comes first, then her. Daddy is back to life too, and Harvey is again with me—dying, ill, but not estranged. His body is shrunken to two feet long, skinny, aging. Grief that he is dying, but joy that we know it, accept it, and can tell and show each other everything we have meant to one another. In order to get near him in a little alley of the hospital basement, I have to squeeze in through a place about eight inches wide bordered with searing hot pipes to the ledge where he is lying. I feel the pipes burning my thighs but accept it—the drive to be near him, to minister to him, is so compelling.

Staying in Stonington vs. moving to Cambridge is a loaded decision because it involves choosing between the inner life here and a more active one there—stress, stimulation, accomplishment. I don't want to choose between these two aspects of myself, to give up either. Must remind myself that life is temporal, not spatial. There is room for both, in sequence.

I was up most of the night with Stella. I heard footsteps running up the hill toward our house and was on my feet in alarm and at the door before she got here. She was white and shaking. I led her up the stairs. In the living room, she turned to me and said four words: "My marriage is over!" Behind her by the windowseat the heavy old jade plant let go its roots and slowly keeled over to the floor. I sat her down and listened, made her take a bubble bath, tucked her into the sofabed under a down comforter, and wished I could do something that would really help. They're a volatile pair, but I think she'll be all right.

I have decided to move to Cambridge. Several decisive factors, one of which was Claire so certain on the phone just now—"Go, go!" Another was a nightmare last night about the school here. I had been waiting for a "sign" of some sort all week. But instead of a "go to Cambridge" sign, it was a "don't stay in Stonington" sign. In Cambridge Jordan will attend a truly fine school—Cambridge Friends—and will go all day. There will be movies, restaurants, other photographers, a whole variety of people. We can keep the house here for weekends until the oil bills start, then rent it out. So! I will look for an apartment right away.

I put forth a lot of effort yesterday and today, in Cambridge in the summer heat, house-hunting. We are very late, it turns out, to be finding something furnished.

Today I borrowed a friend's ID card and used the Harvard housing office. Still no luck.

In a restaurant called Autre Chose—full of café au lait, almond croissant, and sadness. A young man, handsome, yawning in a T-shirt, just stood up from the next table and stretched. Beauty like Jordan's. Overwhelming emotion at the thought of him grown.

I stayed over in Cambridge again last night and got up this morning in the fourth-floor walk-up apartment of the daughter of friends, feeling drugged from bad dreams and the week's frustration. It was still so hot, and I had worked under a lot of strain. I hung up the phone from my zillionth house-hunting call and cried. Funny—it was only a little, but it surprised me because I couldn't remember the last time I had cried—oh yes, the night we got back from Cass Lake a couple of weeks ago. Two weeks. That's a long time. But I am discouraged. I've worked hard to find a place to rent. This much effort ought to have yielded results. I had thought this was one of those categories of life-situations that *can* be shaped, brought round by quantitative effort. I've learned that there are things I can't control—no amount of determination and self-sacrifice will change the shape of a cancerous blood cell—but I had believed there were still other things I *could* control. I feel depleted, a failure. I want to go straight home to Stonington. Can't function in this heat. But I promised Stella coffee beans. . . .

Within three days of each other, two different people have spoken to me about a sea gull swallowing an eel. Different circumstances, but the exact image and description: the stomach bulges out, the eel won't all fit, the bird regurgitates it, and tries again. What do these coincidences mean? I am trying to listen.

I forgot until late tonight that Mother had called to tell me that, according to the horoscope page of her *Town and Country* magazine, the 16th was a perfect day for me to ask a favor. I didn't remember it until I was already home from Boston, exhausted from the heat and too tired to ponder a wise favor. All I could think about was having Harvey back; so, not to be too o'erweening, I asked the powers-that-be to grant me a dream of happy reunion. And the favor was bestowed. He came to me while I was singing, new music I didn't know. A hug long and longer and big as a room. Reassuring that my unconscious and/or the planets' alignment somehow gave me my wish. A little chastened by this demonstration, today part of me wishes I'd asked for something more substantial—for a house to materialize in Cambridge, for example. But another part of me is satisfied simply with the demonstration.

My gosh! Last night driving home from Boston in the dark, I felt a wave of longing to hear from Kramer—thought how it would feel to get word from him, imagined a letter, a card lying inside the door. Today, a postcard came from him for Jordan, a card from Canada. I found it lying under the mail slot inside the door! It said he'd been in Stonington a few weeks ago—while we were gone, evidently—and had thought hard about us. Didn't say he'd tried to be in touch. I wonder how his wife is doing. Hope they're not having a lot of trouble. The heat is what brought him back to mind—last summer all those long, boiling drives to New Haven, with him at journey's end.

I guess I shouldn't dismiss Mother's "planetary advice."

I read in yesterday's New York *Times* that the killer "Son of Sam" claims he got his commands to kill from a black Labrador named Harvey. And I, like all his victims, have shoulder-length brown hair. Is Harvey after me? Why do I think these superstitious thoughts?

Still no apartment in Cambridge. I am committed to the move—we'll stay with friends if we have to—but am getting concerned. I am tired and frustrated. I fade badly in the late afternoons these days. Maybe I should get some vitamins. I couldn't get my easel assembled today. Wanted to study prints on it but the hand screws were too hard to turn. Finally I just gave up and leaned against the door jamb and looked into the living room. I do love this house. That sweet old fireside chair . . . We never really had a fireside for it, just the woodstove. I can't seem to pick a fabric for it and finish this room. Like Harvey put off finishing his book—fearing he'd die when it was done.

Stella told me they're moving to California. House, Stonington, Stella . . . I sent off my orange-and-white-flowered going-away dress to the chorus yard sale this morning and now I want it back. I want it all back.

Should I go to the Center and get it? I want to—no one else should wear the dress that helped to consecrate the day Harvey and I joined our bodies and our lives—the day that led forcefully, severely, to this very one. I want to drive to Westerly and get it back; I could put it in the dress-up basket. I know though, that I shouldn't. I should every day thrust something that I love away. How will I ever find serenity if I keep this desire to have every-thing, to have Jordan, Harvey, my youth, this house? Each day, something that I love, something I think I need, I should cut away from my life. A finger, Bach Partitas, my jade plant, a friend like Stella, Jordan's blanket, the sense of hearing—how else will I learn how to die?

Coming to hate that which you must leave. The concept lets me begin to comprehend Harvey's cruelty toward me that last year. It wasn't that he hated me because I wasn't giving enough or under-standing enough when he was sick, as I've thought for a long time, but that he may have felt a need to deface that which he had loved, since it was being taken from him—much as Bruce and I defaced my treehouse the day before we had to move away from Storm Lake—the treehouse with a stairway, the treehouse on four trees that Daddy built for me. Paint and crayons and hateful words and ugly faces. Because we loved it, and our childhood there, and hated those who would inherit it. Maybe that was something Harvey felt about me.

Maybe he felt it, fleetingly, about Jordan too. How else to explain his refusal to come outside and watch him sledding down the front hill for the first time? Or yanking him—throwing him, practically—across the living room the week before he died. Jordan didn't get it, just laughed. Incomprehensible from a father previously tender—passionately so. If I had let myself see he was dying, if I had made myself try to feel what he was losing . . . I meant to, even taught my seminar section on "Death and Grief," but it came too soon. I kept thinking, "He'll get through this one. Later, when it's really bad, when it's obvious, we'll cry together."

Jordan has been fishing with a cane pole down at the town dock these last few days. He caught a small silver fish this morning and put it in a large white plastic wastebasket with some sea water. I took his picture smiling. Then he wanted to help cook blueberry pancakes. Right in front of me he grabbed the hot black iron skillet with both his hands. He was silent for a second and then a wail burst out. I grabbed his hands and put them under the cold faucet and called Philip, who said to bring him right over. At the office, Philip put the hands under cold running water again for about half an hour, then he salved and wrapped them.

When we got back home, Jordan found his fish had died. I took another picture of him holding the bucket, but this time the fish was floating stomach up, and there were big white bandages on both of Jordan's hands, and his eyes were asking "Why?"

Last night at bedtime Jordan pointed to the picture of him and Harvey that hangs by his bed and said, "Two Daddies." I looked at him quizzically, and he said, "Only one is not grown yet."

I am in one of those periods again—tired, rattled in some ways, above it all in others, making lots of spelling mistakes, leaving out syllables or replacing them oddly, running into the same people (strangers) several times each day. Every machine I got near fizzled today—the stereo, the vacuum, the television. And coincidences flash around me. Tonight, tired from practicing Bach's First Partita, I wandered over and picked up a magazine from the top of the stack—randomly, the first I've looked at in six months—the September *Harper's*. Turned by chance to an article by Joel Agee. As I read, my eyes opened wider and wider. First it mentioned the very Bach Partita I had just been playing. Then Emily Dickinson (my lecture), then dog-sitting (St. Croix), then Gould's humming on the recording of the First Partita (my private delight), then Ozu (whose film, *Venom & Eternity*, I taught this year). Just before the end, this message too: "Forget about time and meaning. Don't think about what you're saying; just speak the words automatically . . . understanding and emotion come later."

After his nap, Jordan took me down to the docks to show me something frightening: a huge sea turtle that had been spotted swimming into the harbor and was shot. Fishermen in a local bar had grabbed their rifles when the rumor hit, gunned their outboards, and made it sport. The animal lay there on the dock—three feet high and five feet long, decapitated. Enormous weight, like a young bull elephant. The stump of its neck was the size of a large tree trunk—feeding the nightmares of the children who gingerly touched its shell. I felt a great sympathy for it, a creature so old, it could have been alive during the Civil War. What an accomplishment, longevity like that. It swam in a world older than ours, more complete. Couldn't they have captured it and let it go, far out to sea, instead of butchering it?

Tonight at yoga, at the end of class, as we lay silent in Savasana, the Corpse Pose, Grace whispered:

> *Bless those you love,*
> *Bless those you do not love,*
> *And let them all go.*

My ears filled up with tears.

Fall

Still no house. School has begun, so we are staying with Julie and Richard on Beacon Hill while I continue the search. Their guest room is half underground, and the ankles of passersby above me on Myrtle Street are veiled by white dotted-Swiss curtains. It's disappointing to have lost this month as far as work is concerned, but I trust that nothing is ever lost completely. The real work must have progressed, simply as a function of effort.

Jordan has made a new friend at school; his name is Arthur. Tonight I pulled out one of the little books I bought a month ago to help us through the rough times moving and find it's about a child making a friend at his new school—name: Arthur.

I heard about an apartment on the second floor of a big gray house on Bowdoin Street in Cambridge, but the landlord is away. I meditated this morning, killing time. I fall rather quickly into a different state now. It's not what I have been led to understand meditation should be like—effortless serenity and all. For me it requires terrible effort—thoughts begin to form themselves into words and only a syllable or two or a single groping sound-shape gets past the gates of sub-vocalization before I wash it away, think void, think black on black, think about the place where the receding planes cross.

In a dream last night:

A big old boat, Viking-like, is drifting in toward us at Cass Lake. It has clearly been through a catastrophic battle—torn sails, people *wounded, starving, dead. A blond woman, with bleeding holes in her chest and head is holding on to the mast. The survivors are dazed. All in clothes of an earlier century. They fire off a cannon-torpedo which rushes through the water and up onto the beach. A child is riding it. On a worn green sled-board they have painted a message—*CAPTAIN JOHNSON FELL AT THE CROSSROADS, BLYTOWN.

Suddenly it dawns on me: they have somehow been picked up and thrust out into orbit in the middle of a war-battle—Civil War, maybe? Revolutionary? They have experienced it as a few days of horror and sleep; but on earth, centuries have passed. They have been moving so fast they haven't aged. They look at our ski boat, the lift, everyone dazed, as they wade, stumble ashore, begging for a doctor. It is incredibly fortunate that they landed here—a backwoods is-land—and not in a city where the future-shock would be deadly. I decide to hide them, teach them, care for them, help them adjust, before the authorities find out.

The blond woman leans on me. I hold both her hands and lead her ashore, saying gently, "The year is 1977." She is exhausted, con-fused, says, "Are you my grandmother?" I say, "No, you're mine— my great, great, great . . . thirteen generations-ago grandmother. Come, I will help you."

At last! The Bowdoin Street landlord returned, and we finally have an apartment. It's bigger than we need, too expensive, and embarrassingly furnished, but it is ours. The rooms are large and sunny with high ceilings and moldings, there's a fireplace and a bay window in the living room and an extra bathroom for printing. The furniture is '50s-modern castoffs, and someone put an awful chain-link fence around the yard, but there's a grape-arbor in the back, and tree branches touch the kitchen windows, so all in all, it's fine.

In Stonington for the weekend, to pack and clean the house. Jordan had his pal Halley over to play, and I heard him say to her, "I don't *want* to be the doctor. My daddy died, so I want to be something dangerous—fireman, or policeman—so I can be the one operated on."

I spent the day unpacking office things and setting up my darkroom in the extra bathroom here in Cambridge. The landlord's son helped me carry up the TV, and tonight Jordan fell asleep beside me watching *Music in Jerusalem.*

A long narrow word—"Clarion"—caught my eye through the window of an antique shop. A small bell rang as I opened the door. The owner told me the sign was taken from the stern of an old fishing boat. I paid for it and put it in the back of the car door.

Doing errands in Boston again today—I had planned to stop for lunch but was suddenly, inexplicably, seized with a compulsion to get home by two o'clock. It was just past quarter till. I ran to the car, pressed, hurried, drove very fast. Pulled to the curb in front of the house at precisely two. I sat for a moment, wondering, then pulled the key from the ignition and opened the car door. Out of the shadows across the street a cat ran toward me. A gray Persian cat with green eyes. A gray Persian cat exactly like GreenEyes. Astonished, I sat flat down on the sidewalk. The cat rubbed against me and mewed and purred and rolled and flirted—raised his right paw to touch me just like the other two, squirmed with "reunion." It couldn't be . . . I petted and fussed over him and finally he stepped away behind a tree and then, looking back several times, crossed the street and disappeared again into the shadows. I couldn't just sit there on the sidewalk, so I got up and opened the gate, climbed the porch steps and sat down there.

"I can't go inside," I thought. "I can't go on without dealing with this."

I looked up into the air to my left.

"What is it? What is out there?"

And then it seemed the cat had brought a message:

"It's OK. Cambridge is home now. Anywhere is home. Love is everywhere. You aren't alone, not really. See? Even I am here."

Tears welled up and I buried my face in my hands. For a minute I thought I might throw up. Gratitude unlike anything I've ever felt. And unworthiness. I hunched my shoulders and tried to hide.

After a long time, I was able to get up and go inside and fix a cup of tea. But still I kept my eyes toward the floor.

Back in Stonington working in the yard, I was startled by Jordan's basketball hoop overgrown by plants at the top of the wall—dying wild roses with large thorns, mysterious weedy vines with clumps of red grapey berries, climbing blue wildflowers—the backboard and hoop hanging with them. I thought at once to photograph it, then said "Why?" Stupid question for a photographer. I couldn't think of a reason. Besides, the good camera was in Cambridge, so I stood up on the park bench, tackled the mess with long-handled pruning shears, and soon it was all white and tidy again. Then it struck me: it was an image of a dead child. I nearly gagged. Now, five minutes later, I see it does suggest a loss, but of a milder kind. It's the basketball hoop of a kid who moved away.

A dream from several nights ago is still with me.

Harvey has returned from the dead to take me back with him. Someone else is with him. They move into the room fast. He looks well—the same really—but something intangible is different. His eyes do not focus and I guess that he does not hear, either. He seems to navigate by other senses. We speak through our thoughts. He heaves me up on his back to abduct me—I ride piggy-back, him standing, running strong through the room. No time to say good-byes. I go willingly, giving up everything, hoping though that we will pass nursery school on the way out, so I can give Jordan a look that will let him know my love for him is powerful (our love for him), even though I too have to leave him suddenly, forever.

Harvey and I run on (me riding), the other guy behind us on lookout, around a bend into a desert landscape—barren, a few shrubs, boulders. I expect we will take off for the stars, but he points to the rocky hill. Then I see what I have never seen: the boulders' slow tidal flow. We wait for them to flap up at the edge like a tent, soft, and slip under. Someone is pursuing us. We hide under the cloth of rock. I am afraid someone will sit on me or hit me and I won't be able to stand hard and still as a rock. They will feel me move or flinch, and discover us, and take me back. A woman is photographing a dark, hairy something (monkey?) on her bare foot, rotating her leg—she is about to kick me. Then Harvey shows me steps down into the earth. I am shocked, thought we'd go up into the next life. There is a momentary death-fear, then willingness, for him. Then we are making love, floating in the dark air under the rocks. Marvelous, but he is insubstantial. He is there—warm, embracing, inside me—but I can't feel him with my hands. I want to press his buttocks, to drive him deeper into me, but can't grasp anything. He is unquestionably there, and yet intangible, too. As I reach orgasm, I awaken.

I recognize a shift in my dreams of Harvey. Reunion used to lie in his coming back from the dead to our way of life. Now when he returns, reunion is conditional on my going with him back to the land of the dead. This seems more "realistic." I must be coming slowly to accept that he has in fact died and cannot return.

I was doing yoga this morning—a spinal twist—when suddenly a feeling came over me as if the top of my skull had quietly lifted and air were washing my brain with every breath. All discomfort in the strained position vanished; I wanted to hold it forever, hold the feeling. It was the same sensation I have touched in trying to meditate, only this time it came unsought. Perhaps this *is* what is meant by meditation—this floating relief. Perhaps I have been there already and didn't recognize it, expecting something more spectacular. Like my first orgasm—the question, "Could that have been it?" Now, as then, a learning lies ahead—an opening to its gifts.

In a dream:

I have decided at last to rearrange my Stonington bedroom. I notice all sorts of fascinating nooks and crannies—tiny closets, drawers, a padded windowseat—that I hadn't known were there before. I begin to strip the bed. It is dirty under the sheets—straw and sawdust tumble out of my blanket. Piles of earth fall to the floor. Suddenly I notice a branch on the dresser with a newborn monarch butterfly clinging to it. Another branch too, broken, with fruit on it, starting to wilt. I must get it into water. Outside the window are birds, coming near my eyes. One is a big blue starling. Another, a large black greedy young bird being fed by a tiny golden hummingbird. Suddenly it is swallowing her too, along with the food she offers. A friend bird helps to stuff her in. The young bird is so full its mouth remains agape, body like a blowfish, and I have to reach down in, down through awful stomach contents (worms, etc.) to rescue the still-faintly-moving golden bird. Am afraid she has already suffocated. I set her quickly on the open window ledge for her gossamer wings to dry. Can't handle her because she is wild and delicate. The next time I look, her wings are puffing up in the morning air, green and golden like spinnaker sails.

An unpleasant task today—rushing to get together a grant application. Cutting mats, mounting photographs. Multiple images of Harvey and Jordan, corpses and landscapes, animals afraid, birds, re-perception diptychs. I was nearing the end of the final stack when I realized I was also near the end of my supply of photomount corners. I counted the prints left, multiplied by four corners, counted stick-on corners. There were exactly the same number! I finished what I had to do with not a one left over.

A couple came into the Xerox place this afternoon while I was waiting for copies. She had on shoes like mine and he was wearing glasses like Harvey's. I wondered about them.

Boy, my pressure-capacity is certainly not what it used to be. The grant application deadline was October 15; I had only eight days to get the whole thing together because of my sudden late decision to apply. Sonia and Aaron came for a four-day weekend at the first, so I got nothing done on it then. They left Monday. Then Tuesday Virginia called, saying she wanted to fly in for Thursday–Friday. I told her about the stress-level here, but she insisted on coming, so I stayed up until 3 A.M. both Tuesday and Wednesday to get the proposal done before she came. When she left, I collapsed into total vegetation—did nothing but watch TV for two days. Am still feeling strained and depleted—have lost the rhythm of my life.

Jordan got a sucker caught in his throat! I grabbed him hard, at once, around the middle, threw him over my elbow, running, reaching for keys on the mantle. Hospital fast. Three seconds, four . . . halfway down the stairs, he coughed it up, vomited. Started to cry. Poor kid. Right away he had a diarrhea attack (like Sharlene when we told her about Harvey's leukemia) and his throat is still aching. What if it had been his windpipe? Could I have cut into his throat?

"Santa" had come by the Friends School riding on a firetruck. He showered the street with lollipops for the children to gather. The street. Real safe. It's not even Thanksgiving yet.

Work is going well again. I force myself to print in the mornings, then play around with Jordan in the afternoons. By evening I'm too tired to do much of anything. I have dozens of ideas but no energy, so I just watch TV or read.

In the morning I waken, still tired. Hard to get up—a forty-five–minute struggle—can't eat. I pull on my red warm-ups, feed Jordan, make him half a sandwich for lunch, wrap the other for myself, then walk him to school. I jog back. Straight to the darkroom. Work two hours. Energy flowing well by then. I eat the sandwich at break. Print another hour. Clean up. Unwind. Go get Jordan. I am sticking to it, making progress.

On my walk to school to pick up Jordan this afternoon, I passed a squirrel in the Y of a tree. The sun behind him was shining right through his ears, making the rims glow electric pink. For a second, a feeling passed through me as when Harvey was alive. It lasted only a second, but it was more important than all the work I did today. I never noticed squirrels' ears before.

This is our final weekend in Stonington. The house is rented as of Monday to a man who answered the ad in the *Times*.

I cleaned all day today and then raked the yard until it was so late that the scraping of the metal broom-rake on the bricks of the patio made sparks fly in the darkness. They must always be there, but we just never see them in the daylight. I wonder why they don't ignite the crisp brown leaves.

A day of rest. Everything I have to do is done—the house is ready. I played tennis this afternoon for probably the last time until spring. Afterward, I pulled up to the swaying white picket fence across the street from our door and just sat there in the car. That fence couldn't possibly save a car from rolling off the ten-foot drop into the backyards of Elm Street. A buff and yellow bird landed on a picket in front of me and sat perfectly motionless. His stare was riveting. I gave myself to looking at him. The details of his body began to stand out as if there were a magnifying glass between us: scaly yellow claws rolling into seams where they met muscular

furred thighs, white slanted stripes along each dark wing like high-
lights on the draping of a cape, a beak rounded at the root so that it
formed a perfect yellow dot between his eyes. He was so strong and
beautiful. I longed to have his colors on my body, in my house,
everywhere around me, longed to stretch out my arms like Saint
Francis and have him come to me in trust and let himself be held.

With that, the bird took off—a swift, sharp angle up across the
street to the slit in the screen of our porch and through it, onto the
porch itself! Was this really happening? I felt myself drawn out of
the car and up the inside stairs. The wish had been from deep
inside, filling my arms and legs. Could that be all it takes? I floated
out through the kitchen to where he would be. Slowly I raised my
hand, palm up. He hopped nonchalantly to my wrist—hardly any
weight at all, but a strong, prickly grip. His face was just a bird's
breath from my own. I stroked his back with a single finger. The
wings were stiff and crisp and cool. I touched his head and it was
warm. He looked at me and all around, blasé.

Then down beneath and to our right, Jordan came skipping
around the corner of the alley. When he caught sight of me with the
bird, he stopped, eyes and mouth widening. "We have a visitor," I
said softly, and he scampered up the stairs. The bird hopped onto
his open hands and he held him gently while I went for my camera.
The bird flew a couple times across the porch above us as I photographed him, then landed on the screen facing the sun, right leg
extended, tail fanned out like playing cards or like flower petals,
back-lit. I could see the grid of the screen through them, so it
seemed that half of him was on the far side, half on this.

We tried to put him outside through the slit then, but he wasn't
interested in leaving, so we carried him downstairs and outside and
tossed him carefully up into the air. He swooped a low and steady
circle back to us and landed on the picket fence again. We started to
sing then, to thank him for what he had given us—every song we
both could think to sing. After about half an hour, he flew up to a
pine branch, low, nearby, and stayed there while we repeated everything we sang before and danced around on the asphalt street between parked cars.

Finally we walked back across the street to take our baths. At the door, Jordan looked back over his shoulder and then up at me, satisfaction in his eyes. The questions in my mind were nowhere in his face. When we came out again to head back to Cambridge, the bird was gone.

Winter

The winter sun is small and weak these days, but it shines in on the kitchen table where I sit beside my white cyclamen plant and warms my arm like a friend's hand.

Clair and Michael have moved to New Hampshire, so we're only an hour's drive away from each other now. Before Thanksgiving dinner they solemnized their godparenthood with Jordan: candles and wine and the promise that they will care for him if I, too, should die.

After the children were in bed, we sat up late by the fireplace in the dining room and I told them about the bird. Claire nodded.

"One thing I especially regretted in moving away from Bucks County," she said, "was having to leave the white dove that lived in our barn. Did you ever see that dove?"

"No, but you mentioned it before."

"It just came one day and stayed. I hated like everything to leave that bird. But you know what?"

"What?"

"On the third morning after we moved in here, when I got up to go out and feed the horses, I looked up, and there on the rafters was a white dove."

It's cold out now. Yesterday at the baseball field, Jordan was standing at the pitcher's mound, and it was my turn at bat. The low winter sun hit a "V" in the roof of a house behind me, framing the whole baseball diamond in a perfectly aligned counter-diamond of light and shadow, with him at the center. Extraordinary. Exact.

The woman I see almost every day, the woman with the black wig, is standing down in the street again, arguing vehemently with someone invisible. She lives in the apartment building diagonally across from us. She wears a brown fur coat, that black, black wig and cotton gloves so white they should be performing surgery or handling uranium. She usually walks very slowly, right down the middle of the street.

The other morning when I took Jordan out to breakfast, there she was, sitting at the next table.

A whirlwind caught me just as I was getting out of the car to go in and get Jordan from school. I saw it coming across the empty lot, a vortex of dust and leaves. When it hit me, it threw grit in my eyes and sucked all the papers off the dashboard of the car up and out into the street. I chased them, grabbed and stepped on them, but one, a yellow sheet, just kept going up. I waited for it to drop, but it didn't. It rose and rose until it was just a little speck and then it passed through a hole in the clouds the shape of Harvey's glasses and disappeared.

I drove Jordan to school again this morning, mainly so I'd have to be taken back there to my car, and then went gingerly out for breakfast with the father of a child in his class. This man's wife died four years ago—killed herself or was murdered, it's still unclear. He thinks someone broke into the house. We had a good talk—much to share in what we've come through and much also that did not have to be said. He wants to see me again, but he seems unsteady and I warily covered myself by saying I was seeing somebody.

All day long then I had a hunger for fresh pineapple mousse. When Julie and Richard came for supper, they presented us with a fresh pineapple.

There is a controversy in the family about where to spend Christmas. I want everyone to come here to Cambridge this year. Boston is so festive and traditional during the holidays. And besides, here we are with an apartment big enough to hold everyone for the first and no doubt last year of our lives—will be back in our little Stonington house next year, totally broke. Besides, for the first time in ages I feel like cooking, decorating, entertaining, giving. What grounds for celebration this feeling is! I want too, for Jordan to have Christmas in his own house for once. Five years old—it's an important Christmas—and he wants Santa to come down his chimney. We both need a sense of being a family ourselves, of being able to produce a holiday feeling in our own home instead of camp-following, leeching onto other people's holidays, as if we were insufficient to make happiness on our own.

Basically, Mother wants everyone to come to Tallahassee where she can be The Mother, as usual; but she is flexible—will go wherever we decide. Bruce and Virginia want to have it at their house again—cheaper than flying. If they're going to fly somewhere, they want to go somewhere warm, definitely not here. They've had us all for Christmas, as has Mother. Now it's my turn, or Mary's. Bruce hurt my feelings by saying he didn't care if he ever came to my house for Christmas and why didn't just Mother and I have Christmas together since we were always so depressed—then they could have Christmas with Mary and Stephen and enjoy themselves. Mary and Stephen say they want Christmas at their place because they don't want to travel with the baby, but if it comes down to it, they'd go to Florida or Detroit, but not here.

Mary said, "So what if you have a big apartment this year? Don't you remember how much fun we had that Thanksgiving in Stonington when we slept on the living room floor in sleeping bags?" The Thanksgiving Harvey spent unconscious in the hospital, hovering near death, she had fun? Then she said, "Just because we don't want to come to your house doesn't mean we don't love you—you know we love you."

I scraped the skin off two knuckles tonight grating potatoes for Chanukah latkes. Blood dripped into the batter—not very kosher, but I can't imagine that it hasn't happened to thousands of women through the years. I just smiled and stirred it in.

Rabbi Friedman wrote us that he's taking an interdenominational group to Israel in six weeks.

I have been angry again the last week or so, angry at Harvey for getting sick, for supposedly choosing to die. But tonight I saw again his unconscious ragings, tied down in the hospital that November—all the insupportability of his condition at last roaring out of his being—and for a moment it flamed up in my gnarled mind that he didn't will it.

But that thought hurt so much I knew I couldn't hold on to it, knew I would come slinking back to the explanation that he felt defeated in the modesty of his position, the provincialism of that school, our town, and somehow in his choice of me—that he felt trapped in all of them and preferred to die rather than continue dealing with such mediocrity.

I clench these reasons in my fist and cannot remember being loved.

Tonight in the bathtub Jordan declared, softly but certainly, "Mommy, I need a daddy. To fool around with and tell me when I am wrong." I didn't know what to say to him.

Jordan is off swimming and shooting baskets with Tom, a Harvard medical student who shares a house with Jordan's teacher. His own father died when he was a baby. He is strong but easy-going and it's hard to think of a better model. That he should grow up like this, without a natural father, is exceedingly encouraging.

Claire and Michael offered us a Christmas tree from their land. We drove up there early, and when we arrived, they were sitting

around the breakfast table talking about New Year's resolutions—
they always pick a single word. Michael intends to back off a bit
next year from his business ambitions and "Diversify"—read, think,
do other things. Claire wants to move out of this exclusively domes-
tic period in her life and "Achieve." I didn't even have to think—a
word just bubbled up: "Listen."

"Not to other people," I said, "but to something I can't usually
hear. Intuition, maybe? Whatever it is that doesn't seem like it's a
part of you but must be. Those urges there's no reason for."

When we were putting on our coats, Michael told me that
Harvey was the first man he'd ever been able really to hug: "It was
just easy with him, natural, you know?"

Then we all walked out into the cold morning sunshine together.
Michael ploughed ahead into the snowy forest, carrying an ax, the
children floundered around on snowshoes, and Claire and I tried to
balance on the thin crust of the snow and not fall through. We
discovered we could walk across it as long as our will was focused
and our eyes were not. When concentration faltered, we'd crumble
through, stumble, laugh.

Someone spotted a perfect, rounded pine, and Michael chopped
a wedge from it and let the children finish it off. The sound of the ax
cracked through the silent morning. As we dragged the tree back, it
smoothed the tops off our footprints. Jordan and I drove back to
Cambridge with it strapped to the top of the car, happily, and
decorated it tonight while eating take-out Chinese food.

Carolers came to the door this evening and invited us to join
them. Wonderful. Jordan was excited. But when we all started to
sing on the steps of the apartment building across the street, he
hung back, clinging to the fire hydrant. He started to whine, then
cry. I took him home, and we talked; he felt left out because he
doesn't know the songs. I comforted him, saying the only way to
learn them is to hear them. He decided to try again. We followed
our ears to Linnaean Street and caught up with the group in the
middle of "God Rest Ye Merry, Gentlemen"—friendly, eyes meet-

ing. But Jordan cried again. They stopped and I explained. Kind, they said, "Then let's sing something he knows"—"Jingle Bells." But at that point he got hysterical—eyes closed, screaming. I had to carry him home struggling.

I felt very angry to be deprived of something as lovely and spontaneous as the spirit of that group and was harsh with him. Regrets cramped my heart afterward. The conflict between maternal love and self-preservation is deep.

It's not music per se that upsets him but my paying attention to it. When I sing, or even listen, he panics—equates losing my attention with losing my love. He must have my eyes himself, we must talk. The drain is tremendous.

Mother has come for Christmas, understanding my desire to celebrate joy's tentative return to my life, the need to mark it with visible ritual. On the telephone, she was shocked that I asked her not to stay the full ten days she suggested, but she came anyway, and I am grateful for her loyalty.

It has just been the three of us, but we've had a lovely time—the first Christmas I've enjoyed since the one when, home from college, I admitted to myself that Harvey and I were truly linked, and that to have his love I'd have to renounce my own religious heritage and accept the appurtenances of Judaism. I stood in church that week and wept my good-bye to the lifetime of winter happiness I had known—the full month each year when our family moved toward each other, smiling, wrapped in an atmosphere woven mainly by Mother, the mother I used to have—and may have again, but in a different way.

She is exhausted from the week at Mary's dealing with the baby and all and seems ready to relax, put her feet up, laugh. We had a very good time last night, talking late in the guest room, trying on each other's clothes like girls, trading stories, insights. She was pleasant, pliable almost, different than she's been in all the years since Daddy died. She was particularly excited when I had the harpsichord delivered—sat down and played "Butterflies," which sounded thin and plunky, but very sweet.

Christmas Eve was full of warm complicity as we stuffed Jordan's stocking and assembled toys—eggnog by the fire, tree lights flickering behind us. It was a relief to find her again, to see someone I knew in her face, to hear someone I recognized in her voice.

And this morning, Christmas morning, there was a special demonstration of our likemindedness. I was opening a gift from her to me and when I glimpsed what was inside, I looked up at her and pointed to a package near her feet. She unwrapped it, and together we raised red woolen shawls above our heads. Our eyes met, and something that had unraveled between us several years ago re-knit itself in the air between the soft cloth triangles.

This afternoon I put a special recording of the Twenty-third Psalm on the stereo for her—solo soprano with chorus behind— and went into the kitchen to start dinner.

> *"Yea, though I walk through the*
> *valley of the shadow of death,*
> *I will fear no evil . . . for thou art with me . . .*
> *Thou preparest a table before me in the presence of my enemies . . .*
> *Thou anointest my head with oil . . .*
> *My cup runneth over . . ."*

I popped my head around the door—her face was contorted in tears! I hurried to her side, took her hands, "What is it?"

The soprano went on,

> *"Surely goodness, goodness and mercy, shall follow me all the days of*
> *my life . . .*
> *And I shall dwell in the house of the Lord for ever . . ."*

"Only . . . a very . . . *young* . . . man," Mother sobbed, "could have written that," and then her upper body collapsed against me in convulsive heaves. I put my arms around her. The bones of her back and shoulders were delicate, like a bird's. We cried together.

I took her to lunch at the Harvest yesterday and found myself reaching out for her hand when we crossed the street, just as I do Jordan's. It was strange, compulsive. A reversal of some kind has taken place. I am the one who protects and suggests, who offers advice—instead of the other way around. Last night when I tried to get her to go to a movie with me, it was clear she wanted to, but she kept fabricating excuses. Finally, after much prodding, the truth poured out: she was afraid to go out in the city after dark without a man! Even though there were two of us and we'd drive right up to the theater door, she felt too frightened to face it. I was astounded, and forced her arms into her coat, saying, "How will you ever get on with your life if you won't confront these moderately stressful situations?"

The film we saw was *Close Encounters of the Third Kind*—absolutely wonderful. Something good exists in the sky, something that watches us and will one day reach down and take us up. I had suggested it because of her lifelong interest in UFOs. She didn't have much of a reaction, though—mainly seemed glad to get home alive.

Before she left today at noon, I showed her my photographs. It was the first time I have opened my work to her. It was hard for me because she didn't recognize at all what they are about. I had thought her own grief would show her the pain that lies behind them.

Well, she's lost to me again, but to have seen her ever so briefly—the long-ago-loved someone I remember from childhood—gives me hope for the next decade.

In order to get down into the basement where the laundry is here I have to go outside in back of the house by the woodpile. Tonight after Jordan was asleep I went out the back door with my basket, and the moment I got to the bottom of the stairs there was this sudden, enormous fluttering sound like . . . I don't know what . . . a big eagle, trapped and beating. I kind of squawked as I started, and that instinctive sound, the fact that it was so loud and involuntary, frightened me even more. I tried to assign a rational cause to it—squirrels scrambling in the woodpile? A man hiding behind the tree at the end? I called out, "Is someone there?" and had to smile at how reassured I was by the silence, as if, if the situation really were threatening, they'd have answered.

It was hard making myself go back out there two more times to switch and finish the loads, but I did it. I told myself that if it were a supernatural threat, which was my deepest fear—"bad spirit, winged"—I was just as vulnerable inside the house as out.

Jordan had a terrible nightmare last night—the first in many months. He dreamed there was a dead person on the stairs with glowing red eyes. He had to snuggle with it because he was cold and it was warm, but doing so made him turn into an old man, made his hair turn white, his skin wrinkle.

I cuddled him for a long time and let him sleep beside me for about fifteen minutes. I wanted to keep him here, close, all night, but worried about what the psychology books say.

His description of the dream was so vivid that it found its way into my sleep, as well. After he went back to his own room I dreamed about a villain with red eyes.

Another bad-guy dream.

I am being held at knife-point over a bed by a psychopath. Jordan stands helpless behind me, in danger. The knife blade is already pressed into my back between the ribs to the right of my spine and the man leans on it. The pain is severe, but the real fear is provoking him to jab—the blade will enter my heart. I have a knife, too—against his eyeball—but held up behind my back, awkwardly. I can't see. He pins my left arm behind me. Every time I press my knife ever so lightly against his eye, he jabs nearer my heart.

Suddenly, before I know what has happened, I have struck, quicker than a snake, and cut his head off. Something in me has sensed that he is about to glance away for a second, and I have whirled and attacked before either of us knew what was happening. Pure reflex— exactly like a snake's strike. I cut through his neck with one hand like an apple, thumb on the back of the neck.

Horror. Both at my violence and at the dark, dark red blood—black almost—pouring from the jagged flesh. My body has acted without knowing it. The whole thing has taken less than a second. Appalled but resolute—proud almost—I pick up Jordan in one hand and a child we knew who died, in the other, heavy as they are, and lift them over the gruesome corpse into the next room and safety.

I wakened, horrified. Stood up at once. Sat again, eyes wild, jaw open. Aghast. Reliving the cutting, the suddenness, the reflex. Nausea, but also a kind of awe. There was an animal in me in that dream, an animal quicker and abler than I, an animal that could strike, cut flesh, and save my life and my child's.

Formerly when I dreamed I was attacked, I could never fight back, even if armed. I could struggle but not pierce flesh. Weakness always flooded my arm, loosened my grip on the knife. Now, this revolting dream shows me that I really can fight back, so I feel safer, stronger. Yet it frightens me, too, because what saved us was not under my control. I committed a violent act before I even knew I had done it. Am I capable of this in real life? Do I want to be?

I have been playing our rented harpsichord as I did the piano in Stonington—to calm myself, to sort my thoughts. Hands busy, the whirling stops; patterns clear, insights emerge.

Jordan too. His musical sense is eerie at times. He sits there and plays away, discordantly but cautiously, as if he were trying to remember something he once knew, feel his way back to it. Often he'll end a series of chords that are nothing but noise with an accidental trill and a "real" chord.

Today in the car he said he wanted to learn to play "A Mighty Fortress Is Our God." Then startled me by saying, "I think I can already because the first notes are the same as in the start of 'Star Wars' only backward." He recognized the interval!

Playing early keyboard pieces today, I realized we're going to Israel in February. Odd, one of those nondecisions—a course you suddenly recognize you're on rather than choosing. Like that afternoon in Chapel Hill on the sofa when it came to me that I was going to marry Harvey. Not that I was going to decide it, but that something central in me had already changed without my knowing it, something which would alter the rest of my life.

This trip is hardly in that league, but that something beyond my rational control determined it is the same. The idea has been pulling me like the cut-off mountain in *Close Encounters*. It just feels right. We're almost out of money anyway, and I'd rather blow it on something significant than have it trickle away unnoticed.

As I was falling asleep some kind of feeling or thought or habit of being flashed through me and for the merest moment I was functioning under the assumption that Harvey was still with me. It dealt somehow with the togetherness of being about to file our income tax. Oh God. A relief so profound in that split second. Even in the context of a crabby situation, the sense of his companionship threw into palling relief the fact of my solitude in the next moment, the moment of "coming to"—it happened so fast—like the fleeting insight hearing the B Minor Mass again this week, when for a spirit's breath I remembered what it was like to fall asleep entwined together, not just *that* it was wonderful, but to *feel* the wonder of it once more. All our happiness must still exist in me somewhere.

New Year's Day. Still groggily abed.

I thought to myself driving home last night, musing as one unavoidably does on New Year's Eve, that it had been a long time since I had dreamed about Harvey. I was feeling sad again that I can't envision him well and wondered if he would come to me in the night, wondered if I could will him into my dreams as I did before. Then suddenly a real memory—concrete—crossed into consciousness. His fragrant hands. The warm sweet smell of his palm as I kissed it, fingers curling softly on my cheek. I remembered the fragrance of his hands, the exact loved smell, and something inside me tore slowly apart again. I could no longer drive, pulled over to the curb and sat in the silent car, rocking myself. Lost, sweet smell. Reminding me that there once existed someone who loved me, someone who flew in an airplane to see me, someone who drove me home to Long Island after late nights in the City, letting me sleep, exhausted, head in his lap.

Jordan has brought all his stuffed animals into my bed to do "math problems" and is lying snug and mussed under the new down comforter. (Both Harvey's and my old ones had worn thin and were leaking down, so I had them opened and their down joined into a large, soft new one with a fresh, pale blue cover.) I just read him *The Velveteen Rabbit*, trying not to cry from its sweet truthfulness, and ever since I finished he's been gazing out the window and holding the book tight to his cheek with both hands, snuggling it as if it too were one of his warm cuddly creatures.

Last glimpse of the outrageous Harvey I fell in love with. It was the January before he died—in the reprieve between Blast Crisis and his final round of chemotherapy. We were coming home from a movie. I was driving. Suddenly he told me to stop and slide over. Taking the wheel for the first time in a year and a half, since his seizures began, he zoomed us up on the sidewalk, full of glee—me shrieking, laughing, "Harvey, STOP it! WHAT are you doing?!" He drove all the way around Library Square on the sidewalk, genuinely light-hearted—young again.

Both of us used to trot along with that healthy brand of extroversion. Then his illness changed us—me first, I think. When we moved to Stonington, he'd walk down Water Street to get the newspaper, enjoying encounters with others, while I'd take Main so I wouldn't have to talk to anyone. Eventually, he turned inward too, at least at home, spending long hours alone in his study. A little of this turning in is good—it sharpens one's awareness of nonmaterial realities—but after a certain point it becomes subtly dangerous. I am near that line, I know, and don't know quite where to draw it.

I dreamed about Philip last night and Karen, about having grown beyond the prison of my expectation and acknowledging it.

We are in my parents' house in Ottumwa, gathered with other friends for a weekend vacation. Everyone has gone to bed early, but Philip and I aren't tired, so we stay in the upstairs den watching TV. Then the TV is off and I am explaining to him about all the feelings I have had, about Harvey's wanting us to be together and the subsequent localization of my yearning for comfort in thoughts of him. An after-the-fact unburdening, the feelings a thing of the past. He is understanding, compassionate, does not feel threatened or draw back. There is a tenderness between us and a kind of close humor—a willingness to accept the ridiculous in ourselves. We laugh and shake our heads. He reaches out to me for the first time, touches my cheek, my bare shoulder. Understanding, reassuring. Relief that the tension between us is gone.

We talk for three hours. Suddenly, when we have only a few words left to say, things start to happen around us. Jordan wanders into the room from a bad dream wearing green pj's, wanting extra loving; people call out to each other in the bedrooms; in the kitchen, someone is fixing French toast; the doorbell rings—it is Karen, a blanket around her shoulders, upset because Philip hasn't come to bed. I feel torn, have to comfort Jordan, want overwhelmingly to reassure Karen, and need just as much to conclude with Philip. Trying to do three things at once. I hug Karen, draw her in out of the night. I start to explain, willing her to know I covet none of Philip's love for her, that what I had wanted through those long early months was indefinable—a strange, crippling pocket of need that now is gone. Jordan whines and Philip waits. The noise around us becomes a din.

I awaken, frustrated at life's refusal to fall into clear patterns but relieved nevertheless to know my unconscious, too, is learning to let go.

I just realized: Philip never sent us a bill for taking care of Jordan's hands.

A new thought has just ripped through my mind about Harvey's raging when he was unconscious—that it was not the release of long-pent fury at having to die; but rather the screaming of a soul forced back, involuntarily, to this life. Maybe he was meant to die then and was denied it. Maybe I shouldn't have revived him when his heart and breathing stopped. Maybe it was my fault, my own, our suffering that last eighteen months—not because I was unlovable but because I resisted death. It makes sudden, clear, intuitive sense. My family was there for Thanksgiving. He hadn't deteriorated yet, hadn't had pain. We still loved each other directly. How much more like him to die suddenly, dramatically, than to linger and wither.

I turn in toward the sofa and start to cry. In my imagination, I feel someone stroking my head, soothingly. My cheek is resting on a woman's white-skirted lap. I am kneeling at her feet, long braids down my back like when I was six years old. The woman pets my hair while I cry, unbraiding it, combing her fingers through it, comforting. She whispers to someone I can't see. "It's Jayne. She's come." And they whisper too, "It's Jayne. It's Jayne." Through my tears I look at the white folds of her dress, unable to lift my head, and slowly realize who she is—she is Emily Dickinson. Sweet priestess, predecessor in the land of pain, there she is, inside me, helping.

Philip, Emily. Incredible that as soon as I gave up the one (hopes for a healer outside myself—Philip the doctor; God, Kramer was a doctor, too!), a vision of the second, an interior comforter, someone almost like a part of me, arose. Is it truly this simple? Just "Be brave, put down your crutches, I will help"? But who is "I"? Is it within me . . . or apart? It is certainly different from what I have known as "I." "I am that I am" of Moses' burning bush? Whatever it is, this Something responds to giving up, rewards it. I want to be worthy of its generosity, want the courage to continue.

This morning I drove to Hartford for an interview on my grant request. I tried to explain to the Arts Commission program officer about the coincidences—I even told him about the cat in Cambridge—and showed him how I'm attempting to deal with the question in my photographs. He scoffed and said, "I suppose the next thing you're going to tell me is that your birthday is June 30th."

What was he getting at? Had I put my birthday somewhere on the application?

"Yes, my birthday is June 30th."

"Oh, sure."

I pulled out my driver's license and handed it to him. He looked at it in disbelief. Reaching for his wallet, he pulled out his own. "Date of birth: June 30." The hairs stood up on the back of my neck and I blushed.

"See what I mean?"

Tonight Jordan asked me, "Mommy, do you ever get any spider bites?"

"Spider bites?"

"Yeah, *you* know, like big mosquito bites!"

"Well, at Cass Lake maybe, but not here. Why?"

"Look at this one." He pulled his pj bottom down a little from his waist and showed me the welt.

"They're all around my bed, they're white."

"They are? Show me."

He led me into his room and pointed to a couple of spiders, on the ceiling in between the stick-on glow-stars. They *were* white. I noticed a crack above the window, pointed to it and said, "That is where they're coming in. We can just caulk it there, and that will keep them out."

"No!" he said, alarmed. "They're *friendly* spiders!"

I have finished packing for Israel. Why Israel? It isn't simple. A kind of compulsion. February, month of Harvey's birth and death, the need to feel close to him now. A belief that I will find him again, somehow, in the landscape of his ancestors. And maybe also a final gift—to take his son to Israel.

The trip is for me too, though. There is a longing in me—a longing to find something for that self which is distinct from the self I share with Jordan, with Harvey. A pilgrimage, really. Like Chaucer's. Why did all those people go to Canterbury? God, there it is! Kantor-Bury. That's what I'm trying to do—bury Harvey. This whole trip an unconsciously designed way to say good-bye.

At odds with myself, I go to Israel both to draw close to Harvey and to lay him to rest. With both in mind, will I be able to do either?

The mail came just as we were heading to the airport: I got the grant! Just enough to frame a show.

"The gods send thread for the web begun."

Fourteen hours of delays by El Al. "Working on the brakes," they said. Brakes or bomb threats? Whatever, it gave me a chance to get better acquainted with Rabbi Friedman—Norm. We've never had any unstructured time together before. He has invited Jordan to sit beside him on the plane—a respite for me. Five-year-olds: if Israel really wanted to get the Arabs off its back, all it would have to do, truly, is marshal its five-year-olds and send them across the borders, in unrestrained conversation. The strongest soldier would lay down his arms and beg for mercy. Even Norm barked at him when jarred awake just now by his third "Can we play slap-jack yet?"—I didn't know that rabbis barked. A while ago, Jordan went down the aisle to talk to two little boys, and Norm asked about the sadness. I told him, "I'm no longer consumed with pain. It doesn't hum there in the background—a constant—the way it used to. Hours can pass without my thinking of it at all. I can now be 'reminded' of it, can be caught off-guard, forced to fight back sudden tears. Isn't that what most people think of when they think of grief? But isn't it what they expect during the first year after a loss, and not the third?"

His reply was very soft, almost a whisper, "It's a very personal thing, Jayne. There are no rules."

Still . . . three years is a demarcation line for me, I should be better than I am. Of course, there is improvement. To have hammered out a reasonably fulfilling life, Jordan and I together, one that embraces sunlight and music and friends; to have come to a kind of purpose—to know that my efforts point toward something, toward finding a clearer spiritual focus—these are gifts, achievements even.

But still I am troubled. I grow impatient with the pain. . . .

Jordan just brought back the two little boys from down the aisle. I met their mother and talked with her for a while—a sleek-haired young Israeli woman named Tamarra. She is moving back to Haifa with her sons after seven years in Brookline. She shared her fears for them—"From my high-school class of eighteen, six are dead"—and described her own time in the army. Then she told me about the husband she is leaving—trendy, American, into drugs—and her uncertainty about the life she'll find in Israel.

We landed in Tel Aviv in the pre-dawn hours. The airport was deserted and the air was exotically warm, like St. Croix. We drove directly to Jerusalem by taxi—Jordan falling asleep ten minutes before we reached the hotel, after not sleeping at all on the long trip over. We're supposed to be resting now, but I am too keyed up. Our hotel, the King David, is grandly European, turn-of-the-century: tall interior columns, potted palms, Oriental rugs. We have a balcony overlooking the garden. At four o'clock we're to meet the others and drive to Mea Shearim, the city's Orthodox section, for the beginning of the Sabbath.

A deluge of impressions—oranges so sweet and grapefruit and fresh dates and deep bins of almonds and cashews. Eight-inch bagels, fresh and surprisingly soft, coated with sesame seeds. Cheeses. Low sunshine glowing in an old man's white hair and great full beard as he whispered with others, black-robed, at the end of a dark cobbled square. Suspicious glances cast our way.

A sprawling model of Jerusalem in the time of the Second Temple—meandering, detailed, in a little park of its own, up very high—a doll's house for the past. Full Sabbath meal back here at the hotel, sumptuous, Kosher. All the food in public places will be Kosher, Norm has said.

The clear light here makes everything stand out in an exaggeration of three dimensions—almond trees in bloom, gulches, vistas—even all the guards with their machine guns. Young men of ravishing beauty, vitality, flashing eyes, alternating seriousness and deep warm laughter. Their joking is more like joy than frivolity. Life in Cambridge and Stonington seems aimless and dreamlike by comparison. The people are *awake*. Priorities aligned, no stupid grudges, empty pleasures. Genuine laughter, savoring of friends, of food, of sports. Jogging not so your jeans will fit or to avoid a heart attack at 50, but because next month you might be running to pull your kids out of machine-gun fire. A sense here, "Every act of mine has meaning, affects others in a real way, for better or worse." And yet a simultaneous sense of the insignificance of the individual. There are olive trees around Jerusalem which are 3,000 years old. To think that when Christ and his disciples rested beneath them, they had already pushed out their fruit every other year for more than a millennium. Ancient even in that long-ago time. They dwarf us. So many generations of people—soul after soul after soul.

We are driving north toward Tiberias on the Sea of Galilee. Wild anemones, the truest red—single blossoms six feet apart—cover the mountains. Startling against the spring green grass. The land through which we are passing, the Galilean Highlands, feels familiar to me—rounded mountains and small fertile valleys. Is it just my childhood's accumulation of Sunday School stories and watercolor Bible illustrations? Would Harvey have felt this too? Or could

I have been a shepherd in some long-forgotten lifetime? Solitude has grown natural, comfortable to me. I wonder if it weren't once my whole way of life. Could I have spent long hours alone on these hills, close to the animals and to an ineffable, powerful something?

A young Bedouin shepherdess just waved our van to the side of the road. Eyes averted, gold-toothed, she reached out her hand for chewing gum. "Juicy Fruit," she said, and again, "Juicy Fruit."

The Sea of Galilee is rougher than I'd imagined. Waves menacingly tall, not like any lake I've ever seen. As soon as we got off the van, before I could stop him, Jordan stripped off his shoes and socks and ran out onto the dock, yelling something. Waves were crashing over the boards, pulling on his ankles. The air was roaring. He couldn't hear me. I fumbled to remove my sandals and retrieve him, thinking of Christ in the fishing boat at night, commanding this lake's waves, "Be still."

We had St. Peter's fish for lunch and then drove up around the sea to a quiet mountain at the end, the mountain where Jesus taught the Beatitudes. I walked out away from the others onto the hill above the lake's changing blues. I could see that the wind was blowing hard down there, but up where we were it was quiet. "Blessed are the poor in spirit, for theirs is the kingdom of heaven." A comprehension spread through me. My knees grew weak, and I was afraid to look around—all those people there behind me. My legs wanted to kneel, but I wouldn't let them. I bowed almost imperceptibly—Harvey davening—looked out again over the sea, and returned to the group.

I have stepped out of the tour with Jordan for an overnight in Haifa, to rest and find Tamarra, our friend from the plane. Haifa is beautiful, like San Francisco—hilly, with pines and palms and the blue Mediterranean below—but exhaustion makes it hard to smile or eat.

I called Tamarra and she met us in a park where the boys could play. We sat on a bench like mothers in New York or Paris and talked while the boys kicked a soccer ball around. She was distracted, teary, explaining that she and her mother had fought. When she left with her children, I watched them walking down the street, her silky black pony tail swaying gracefully, and felt sad. I could not help her, would not even get to see her again, ever.

Afterward, Jordan and I spent an hour in the garden of the Baha'i Temple, photographing peacock statues and trees. A young blond man passed, nodded to me and said what sounded like "Hello, Jayne." My head whipped around after him. I wanted to follow, to catch up and ask, but was afraid I'd imagined it.

Looking up at me from the bus stop bench, Jordan aimed my camera and said, "That's it—look crabby."

We have rejoined the group and returned to Jerusalem via the West Bank of the Jordan River. Jordan stood in it, with jeans rolled up, up to his knees in translucent blue-green water, happy. It's a safe-looking stream, where we were, modest. His river. Reeds and big shady trees and a kind of Huck Finn feeling. The bus driver shook his head when he waded back in, though, and asked me, "How could you have named a Jewish child 'Jordan'?" Granted, the logic of Israel's defensive need of this strip is clear when one sees it—it is a narrow vulnerable place. What isn't clear is why they all can't live in peace, why they all can't drink from the same river.

Jericho. An oasis, but dusty, dry, and very hot. Deserted. I was thirsty. I asked if there were Cokes anywhere and was reproached by the driver again. "This isn't Cincinnati." I bought an orange from a black-gloved vendor. You could see so clearly where the one orange I had taken was missing from the hundreds of others. We walked then through the ruins of the Ommaya Palace. It was easy to imagine robed people moving through its arched halls, to see potted palms swaying, to hear fountains playing and the stamp and snort of dappled horses. Fifth Century Mosaics—a heron, lion, gazelle. Jordan jived around, snapping his fingers and singing, "Joshua fought the battle of Jericho, Jericho, Jericho. . . ." He only this week learned to snap his fingers.

Tonight Norm took us to dinner at a Chinese restaurant and insisted on paying the bill. We wrangled a bit—I'm used to people splitting these things—but he won out. Afterward, on the darkened sidewalk, Jordan begged to swing between us as we walked—a memory in his body of when he did that with Harvey and me? Like me, late in labor, mysteriously wanting my hand held up in the air—way up—not knowing why. Only later did I realize I had been reaching for Daddy, not yet a day dead. Helpless, in pain, a child somewhere in me remembered the reassurance of holding his hand and reached up for it.

Today we went to the battlefield at Yad Mordecai, the northernmost point of Egyptian advance in 1948. There are life-sized black silhouettes set up all over the hillside—armed soldiers—like shooting-gallery decoys. I wanted to go into a nearby memorial to the Holocaust as well, but was afraid for Jordan to see what might be inside. I asked one of our companions to keep an eye on him and then alone, carefully, walked down the stone stairway. The air was cool against my face. Underground there were photographs, thousands, perhaps—gripping not because the subjects were gaunt or gruesome but because they weren't. Photo-album shots: laughing fathers, children playing, mothers dressed up, smiling—faces on paper, voices that have been stilled.

Last night the adults went for dinner to a posh restaurant in the Jerusalem Theatre. Controversy broke out during the meal over "Who is a Jew?" Norm took the Reform position, "If a child is brought up as a Jew, he is a Jew," but his friend, a seminary professor here, was hard-line: "No, if the mother is not Jewish, the child is not Jewish." The color rose in Norm's face—I could see he was angry. I put more butter on the crisp roll in my hands, embarrassed by the implications for Jordan. Then, pretending it was any other intellectual discussion, I chimed in on Norm's side, only to have him back off. He was concerned, I think, to preserve the graciousness of the meal.

It has been a long day, full again of searing images. Jordan left Jerusalem early, invited by the others to Masada. I needed to rest and gather my thoughts. I'd hoped to sleep in, but couldn't relax, so I got up and set out to walk around the Old City. Right away I came upon a vast sunlit piazza—empty—with wide stairs leading to a mosque, golden in the morning sun. Magical Arab architecture. A single Moslem was there, alone in the sun, praying.

I walked on through the Arab quarter, picking my way through narrow lines of stalls—dark shops beneath the covered walks, with men on benches in front of them or sitting on blankets on the cobbled street. They fell silent as I passed. A baker coughed as he handled his dough, spit a yellow glob of phlegm the size of a hen's egg. A white enamel tray held goats' heads, fur boiled off. The eyes were blank and cold. Chickens' carcasses, nude, hung limp-headed from a stone stairway.

Later I stepped into an art gallery and was confronted by similar imagery—buff-colored sculptures of naked women, exhausted, bereft, their abdomens concave where the wombs should be, curved empty clear back to the spine—dozens of small grieving creatures draping themselves over wall edges and staircases. Some of them had no faces, only large gaping holes. "Expressions of a country's grief," the owner said. "Women's grief."

To Ashkelon today—a park of Philistine and Roman ruins near the sea—a relief from specifically Jewish history. I took pictures of Norm beneath a tree with interwinding trunks. When he pushed his glasses into place, adjusted himself, I objected, "No, that isn't how you look. Let them slide back down your nose." He sat there good-humored but stiff, an urban creature. I wanted him to drop his mask, to feel at ease like Harvey, to lounge and clown, but he didn't.

The hotel is on fire! Men are running back and forth in rubber jackets, shouting, pulling hoses. Jordan is stunned with excitement and fear. I am perched on a driveway wall, watching. Yesterday a city bus was bombed. Word is, now, it's been controlled: just something in the kitchen. A wall's been smoldering overnight. Smoke is everywhere, and water—the Oriental rugs are soaked. A fireman leans out a window, framed by heavy hand-hewn stones. His gestures seem Italian, hand upturned as if to be obscene, but thumb and middle finger meet. He's tense, dramatic, masculine. Jordan's standing near the truck by the front door, hunched up, hands in the pockets of his navy down jacket, like his father.

This was our last day in Israel. As Jordan awoke he said from his bed, "You know what I wish for more than anything? I wish I could play with a baby tiger outside its cage."

"Mmmm," I moaned, not wanting to wake up. "'Tyger, Tyger, burning bright, In the forests of the night.'"

"What?"

I rolled over.

> "*Tyger! Tyger! burning bright*
> *In the forests of the night,*
> *What immortal hand or eye*
> *Could frame thy fearful symmetry?*"

"It's a poem by William Blake."

"Oh. Tiger, Tiger, burning bright," he repeated.

"We're going to the Biblical Zoo today," I said, sitting up. "Maybe you'll get to see one there."

It was late afternoon by the time we got to the zoo. We walked together holding hands, Jordan in his white Christopher Robin hat with a plastic whistle on a striped ribbon around his neck. We looked at birds with golden-filament combs, and seals, and then there it was—an orphan tiger, romping freely in the shade! I couldn't believe it! He was big-eyed, baby-furred, playful. Utterly appealing, but not kittenish—weighed maybe thirty pounds—and when he stalked, freezing, his eyes grew cold and threatening. Then, as quickly, he was a babe again, adorable, confused. He kept trying to pounce on Jordan's sneakers—got a claw caught in his sock once and tripped him, frightening both of them. I looked into the dark straw-filled stall where he sleeps, an otherwise empty stable, and was swept with a desire to lift him in my arms, warm him against my chest, lick him as a mother-cat would, affirming the child in him. I needed to give him back some of the miracle he was giving us. But I was afraid—claws and teeth, sinews, growling. I touched him, felt his loins, struck by their warmth and muscular power and by the privilege of the act, but I didn't pick him up and now I regret that. Five years from now, ten, when we return to Jerusalem, that happy cub will be a mature male tiger. I will no longer be able to touch him. Even his keeper, beloved bottle-feeder and comforter since birth, will no longer be able to touch him. I was drawn to this man, dressed as he was, strangely enough, exactly like me—same khaki shirt, blue pants. He held the cub to his chest like an infant, calming him. Our eyes met. Could he calm me as well?

Right now Jordan is sitting at a low table across from me in our hotel room, swinging the oblong hook of a keychain back and forth in the sunlight above a pile of paper money. He is chanting, "Tiger, Tiger, Burning Bright. In the Center of the Night." Center, forest . . . it's all the same. In fairy tales, it always takes seven years to get out of the forest.

Our bags are open on my bed. I guess the trip is over.

February 15th. Harvey's 34th birthday.
Eleven hours into our flight home. The plane is nearly empty

and darkened for a film. Jordan and I lie sprawled on the luxury of three seats apiece. He is sleeping soundly.

My thoughts this morning in our pre-dawn taxi ride to Tel Aviv. Lying in the back of the cab, Jordan asleep beside me, I watched the stars in the southeast gradually fade—Antares in Scorpio the last to let go. I held on to that star, thinking, Could Harvey be there? He really wasn't any closer in Israel. There were special moments, of course, but the sense of culmination I wanted, of rounding off, of sealing my bereavement, wasn't present. No bush burst into flame. No great red bird larger than a man opened his flaming feathered wings for me. . . . Quiet tears. I watched the silhouette of my boots turn dark against the window as the sky grew toward blue behind them.

A woman was singing gently in Hebrew on the radio. The song I came to sing remains unsung. I patted Jordan's sleepy cheeks—fat little incarnations of our love—and wondered how many years more he will snuggle against me like that. Loss. A slow cleansing sense of loss. There is so much I don't care about anymore.

Odd, returning to Boston's deep snow after Israel's warm, earthy dust—blinking white after soft cinnamon: "the Blizzard of '78." School has been closed for the whole three weeks that we were gone. I find my Stonington tenant has disappeared, rent unpaid. And the boy I hired hasn't cleaned the apartment here or watered the plants—all are damaged, four favorites dead. Grief especially for the white cyclamen in the kitchen—its stems are draping limply down over the pot like dead worms—and the eight-foot palms in the living room, dry and brown like paper. It's true what Tagore says:

Everything good that comes to us—love, health, children, even potted plants—all are gifts. It seems outside our power to secure or protect them. But our sorrow—this is our own. This is the only thing we really have.

In pain, and in a desperate kind of hope, I have searched for Harvey. I have looked everywhere I could think of: in my dreams, in his son, in his doctor, in a man who looked like him, on the tennis court, in asthma, in Israel, in the night sky, in solitude. I haven't found him. My world is very small, and he is utterly gone from it. But my searching has brought me to the edge of something—a timeless place from which no happiness, no hope, no well-loved face can vanish. I stand on its brink, aware of something infinitely desirable—elusive and unforceable as a scent on the wind. The Wind. That is what I appeal to—the Wind that animates the universe. Offering it my sorrow, all I have, letting go even that—I beg it to enter me, to fill my lungs, my emptied life, and lift me forward.

A dream last night:

Strong firm green shoots coming up out of the cold earth between the rocks—proof of spring. I am the first to see them. Hope, after the long winter. But there in the yard, too, is a great stack of luggage— empty—having sat all winter. Superfluous that I bought a new backpack with all that to carry.

So much seems possible to me now, sitting at my table in the morning sunlight, watching a black-and-white cat outside step carefully into earlier small footprints in the snow. A crystal pot of oolong tea is before me, and a chocolate cake stirred up by Jordan is in the oven.

I am disappointed by my relapse into old habits of mind (triggered in December sometime, perhaps by the realization that we were running out of money). The return of bad dreams and fatigue. Worry about our house in Stonington and the tenant I trusted. Dreams about lost purses and Harvey and Daddy.

Yet despite this slipping back, I seem now to be able to pluck an hour out of a day's despair and declare it a sanctuary, an hour for yielding, opening, learning. What I just learned—"experienced" is a better word, because I wasn't able to repeat it—was a distancing from physical pain. I held my palm against the crystal teapot as I poured the boiling water in to see what would happen; and for a few

seconds, some flap lifted in my brain and let my inner self draw
back and away from the searing sensation. It felt a little like meditation. Then it burned again and though I tried, by Lamaze panting
and such, I couldn't quite defuse the hurting again. It had merely
happened. I wasn't responsible for it. Mysterious forces hint around
the edges of my thinking.

Sweet Tom. In the best tradition of self-appointed "big brothers,"
he made it over this afternoon, despite the snow, to spend time with
Jordan, to hear about his trip, to eat the cake he baked.
    After he and the cake were both gone, Jordan said to me,
"Mommy, do you have any problems?" And I said, "Oh just one.
It's about this tall"—I held my hand out from my waist—"and has
brown eyes and chocolate frosting all over its face." He laughed and
I swooped him up and whirled around. Still holding him, I said,
"What about you? Do you have any problems?" And he nodded and
said, "Just one. He's about this tall"—reaching above my head—
"and he has brown eyes and curly black hair." I looked in his eyes—
they seemed crestfallen after the delight of the moment before—
and said, "You mean Daddy?" He nodded quietly and I hugged
him.

I dreamed last night of finding and losing a new love.

*There is a casual group of friends, standing around talking in a big
old castle converted to modern usage. I am pushing through them, to
sign up for a tennis court. I am wearing tennis shorts, although the
others are dressed for a cocktail party. My thighs come very close to
brushing against those of a man I know, an old friend, who wears
tennis shorts too, and the air between our thighs crackles and snaps
with static electricity, making the hairs on our legs stand out toward
each other, like when you rub a balloon against your forearm or take
a slip off too quickly over your head. We both laugh, astonished and
amused. Our eyes meet and suddenly I realize we are in love. He has*

*realized it before me, maybe just before or maybe long ago, but it hits
me like a bolt of lightning—totally unexpected—this old platonic
friend. His name is "Art," and he is like Mark in Santa Fe to me, a
specially fond old friend. He looks like that actor who played Woody
Allen's friend in* Annie Hall.

*We both act casual since there are others around. He pats my bot-
tom, saying "Are you loosening up any?" I gesture to my shorts,
indicating I've at least been playing tennis. We agree to book a court
together. We work our way through the group to the counter to sign
up. Then he guides me toward some stairs to the basement with
double doors at the top. I ask, "Where are we going?," and he says,
still moving, "Oh, I just thought we'd go downstairs and kiss for a
while." I feel a rush of happiness. We run down a short flight of stairs
holding hands, to a landing. I glance out the window and turn back
against him, burying my face in his shoulder, full of horror. He holds
me, not comprehending. Then he too sees. It is nearly dark out. Ten
feet from the window, a small man is hanging by his neck, dead.
Drab clothes. Suicide.*

*We are dumbstruck, appalled. All desire, lightheartedness is gone.
We return to the group, tell the receptionist to call the police. I feel a
huge sense of loss. A human grief for the unknown little man, but an
even stronger one that I have almost known love again, but because
death intervened it might scare him away. And indeed that is what
happens. He is gone.*

*The castle has a most confusing floor plan. Certain parts are famil-
iar, but it is labyrinthine, and I can't really find my way around. I
have left Jordan at a day-care room somewhere and worry I won't be
able to find my way back. Then there is a lost child. The receptionist
asks me to take her to the day-care place, and I agree. Though I am
not confident of the way, I am confident that I can* find *the way. It is
difficult, many dead ends. I have doubts then, and am afraid.
Finally, we must stop. We wait out a long cold rainstorm huddled in
a tiny portico. It goes on and on, but I know that after the rain, hope
will come, and I tell the others who are also lost that there will be*

beauty in the weedy ruins when it's over. When the rain stops, it's right there in front of us—the place we've sought—where Jordan and the children are! I turn to the others and just by saying the words, cause them to see in the broken cement lush pink camellias, red amaryllis, pushing up and unfolding. Tropical palms and warm damp ferns. It's all there before us.

But then I'm back in the confusion of the adult party group in the main building. Lots of people there, like a college dorm with fin-de-siècle drawing room salons. I am with a woman friend. I want to see the man, my almost, but I can't recall his name. How can I not remember his name? Is it Mark? That's what I use—a risk. Then I see it written. Yes, it's Mark. He comes by, on his way out. He says good-bye to my friend—he has really been her love—and then to me. We are sitting on an S-shaped couch. He explains honestly and a little apologetically to her that he has a date with someone else. I feel angry and bereft for her, and for myself, but we both graciously let him go—say, "Good-bye. Enjoy." But as he moves around the couch my hands keep touching the softness of his coat, belying my ostensible willingness to let go. I am holding on so hard that his coat comes off in my hands as he moves away. I'm terribly embarrassed, but he doesn't even notice as he lopes off. It is Harvey's soft brown coat. Before I hand it to her I hold the furry collar-part to my cheek and think, "At least she will have his coat."

Wintry Sunday. I burned the sausage, but then slowed down and stood and watched a pancake I had poured into the skillet for Jordan—really looked at it, saw the suggestion of bubbles forming under its surface—you couldn't be sure, like right before the stars come out. Then faster and more certainly, exactly like the stars, those bubbles appeared. Then they began to pop, like stars twinkling. A whole night sky there before me in the circumference of a pancake, a skillet, a moment.

How to live so that this sort of thing—the mental connection—happens more often: that is a goal. To pick my way through life so that activities and friends are chosen for the way they contribute to this awareness or avoided for the way they destroy it, and then to try somehow to give it back again. It feels good to see this—to recognize, consciously, a value by which I want to live.

A dream last night.

I have been left with, by default have the responsibility for, a garage full of animals. A trusting lion cub who cuddles against me, though at first I am afraid of her teeth and claws. A tiger cub who hides behind a couch and mopes, grieved at its abandonment. A green parrot who perches above me, to whom I say, "Good morning," and who says in the softest, most understanding voice back to me, "Good morning." Then the parrot flies about my head and frightens me. It lands on my arm, hops to my shoulder and presses its warm feathered body over my mouth—sharp talons and beak near. I must conquer my fear. It will love me if I do not fear it. If it senses my fear, it will attack. Hard to catch my breath from panic and feathers—suffocating—afraid I will get lice from it so close. Then it falls. Like a rock. Dead at my feet. Starvation. None of the animals have been fed. I must get grain for the other birds, meat for the cats. Hurry, they will die. Who knows how long they have been neglected?

A special understanding, a love, opens in me to them—a feeling very like when Harvey was here. I fear the constant responsibility, both the toll of the strain on me and the fear that I will fail them, will not be able to care for them properly. But the central feeling is of love, a radiant, magical love that is the same whether it's for a husband or a child, a parent, tree, or bird.

This morning when Jordan and I went out to shovel away last night's foot of snow, he climbed to the top of the eight-foot mountain of old blizzard accumulation beside the drive and dove off into the soft new stuff, calling out into the silent morning as he fell, "Everlasting joy-y-y-y!"

Today is the third anniversary of Harvey's death.

School is still closed, but Jordan and I walked over there anyway to deliver his scholarship application. On the way, we cut through the playground. The snow was so deep only an inch of the park-bench backrests showed green above it. We felt ten feet tall—we *were* ten feet tall. Cars parked below us were reduced, ridiculed by the snow. Jordan told me he heard that people carved a life-sized *Tyrannosaurus rex* from it last week in Harvard Yard.

On the way back we stopped at the swings. Someone had wound them over the frame so they could hang above the snow. The delight of swinging, the relief of it. I let myself be slapped against the apex of each arc like the clapper of a bell. We faced toward the sun as we swung, the snow stretching out all yellow and blue spar-kles in front of us, as it did when I was a child. Dancing crystals— movement everywhere. And light, light . . . We sang swinging songs—loud, happy, pleased to be alone. Jordan taught me "Who Killed Cock Robin?" and "Zoom Golly Golly," and I taught him "Love Makes the World Go Round." Looking up, we sang,

> "High in some silent sky
> Love sings a silver song"

Jordan and I. Solitary park, winter morning. Singing in unison, swinging in unison, singing and swinging in unison.